man
at the
window

Robert Jeffreys has worked as an actor, teacher, builder, labourer, cleaner, real estate agent, personal security agent and playwright of the professionally produced stage plays *Cox Four*, *Covert*, *The Simple Truth*, and *The Messenger*. ABC Radio National featured his radio plays, *Covert*, which received an AWGIE award, and *Bodily Harm*. He has also published a poetry anthology, *Frame of Mind*. Robert's debut novel, *Man at the Window*, is the first in the Detective Cardilini series, set in 1960s Western Australia.

man
at the
window

ROBERT JEFFREYS

ZAFFRE

First published in Great Britain in 2019 by
ZAFFRE
80–81 Wimpole St, London W1G 9RE

A CIP catalogue record for this book is
available from the British Library.

ISBN: 978-1-78576-929-0

Also available as an ebook

1 3 5 7 9 10 8 6 4 2

Typeset by IDSUK (Data Connection) Ltd
Printed and bound in Great Britain by Clays Ltd, Elcograf S.p.A.

Zaffre is an imprint of Bonnier Books UK
www.bonnierbooks.co.uk

ONE

Day 1
St Nicholas College
10.30 p.m. Sunday, 25th October 1965

Before him sixteen ornate lampposts bordered the paths of the quadrangle. Their yellow light pooled on the grass and the paved walkways. During the day the quadrangle he now looked down on was filled with young boys. His boys. He drew in the warm night air, filling his lungs and expanding his chest, and dropped his shirt on the end of the bed. Proud of his bare chest with its curling tangle of coarse hair, he spread his arms wide on his second storey windowsill and turned to the windows of the boarding house on his right. In the lit dormitories he could see, in all states of dress and undress, figures of boys chatting and chasing one another. He knew that if he, Captain Edmund, was among them the noise would cease and they would hide their eyes in modesty from his gaze. A flash, a reflection of light, caught his eye. It was gone when he looked back to the quadrangle.

The quadrangle was bordered on three sides by double-storey red brick buildings fashioned in English public school tradition: austere, stately, with broad windows and wide limestone archways. He loved the tradition, the stability and the superiority. He filled his lungs again and slowly released the air into the night, his night. Shortly, when all lights were out, his door would open and close quietly. He smiled. The boy would arrive mute and trembling.

Directly ahead of Captain Edmund was the fourth side of the quadrangle, the riverside. An impenetrable blackness concealed a row of river gums and an embankment sloping down to a limestone wall – the school boundary. Beyond the wall reeds and paperbarks filled the hundred yards to the Swan River, now black and soundless as it slipped by. Across the river was farmland from which the rifle retorts of kangaroo shooters occasionally burst into the night.

The hum of voices emanating from the boarding house was fading. One by one windows blackened.

A sudden chatter broke the night and alerted Captain Edmund to four boys commencing a casual stroll across one of the quadrangle's diagonal paths.

'Is that you, Parkinson?' Captain Edmund called down to the boys.

The boys ceased their chatter, stood still and looked towards the window. 'Yes, sir, Captain Edmund.'

'Why aren't you in your dormitories?'

'Another ten minutes, sir.'

'It will take you more than ten minutes to get ready for bed.'

'Not if we hurry.'

'Let me see you hurry then,' Captain Edmund said.

'Yes, sir.' The boys continued to cross the quadrangle casually, now in silence.

'Run!' came the command. The boys jogged under an archway. The night settled and a few stars began to shine.

A crack like thunder echoed through the quadrangle. Captain Edmund disappeared from the window. A patchwork of lights turned on until the quadrangle glowed gold.

Dormitory windows crammed with eager, noisy boys, their excited voices chasing each other into the night.

TWO

Day 1
Kilkenny Road
11.30 p.m. Sunday, 25th October 1965

The glow from streetlights failed to penetrate the canopy of jacaranda trees that lined Kilkenny Road, Floreat. Only one house shimmered in light. Porch light, window lights and a passageway light poured through an open front door into the night. A Rachmaninoff piano piece surged and faded.

Eighteen-year-old Paul Cardilini walked quickly along the pavement towards the house. He pushed aside the front gate, took several hurried steps onto the verandah and went inside, closing the flyscreen door and the timber front door quietly behind him.

'Dad! Dad!' he called.

Stretched out on the lounge room sofa lay his father: a man in his forties, white singlet, business trousers, head hanging back over one armrest, socked feet resting on the other. Beer bottles lay like skittles on the floor.

'Dad, wake up.' The young man turned down the record player, Rachmaninoff fell to a whisper. He shook his father. The man's legs fell to the floor as he tried to sit up.

'Paul, hey. How are you?'

'You're drunk again, Dad,' Paul said tonelessly.

'No. No.'

'Drunk. I could hear Mum's music all the way down the street.'

'No. Why, what time is it?'

'It's after eleven.'

'Hell.' Rubbing at the confusion in his eyes, Paul's father asked, 'You eaten?'

'Yes. Did you?'

'I was waiting for you,' he replied, trying to focus.

'Rubbish. I told you yesterday I was eating at friends' tonight.'

'Oh. That's good then. I might go to bed.'

'Jesus, you were going to stop this.'

'Really. Yep. I will. But I'm going to bed now.'

Paul watched his father test the weight and balance of each step and reach for the doorframe as a support before turning down the passageway. Paul turned off the record player and delicately lifted the LP from the turntable. He slipped the record reverently into its dust jacket and album cover. He picked up the beer bottles and glass. Looking around the room, he sighed heavily before switching off the light.

Day 1
St Nicholas College
11.55 p.m. Sunday, 25th October 1965

The boy stood in his pyjamas outside Captain Edmund's door. He was barefoot as instructed and could feel the worn, coarse carpet on the soles of his feet. His right hand rested on the cool round door handle which he turned, easing the door open. Trying to smile he stepped through and drew the door shut behind him.

His foot pressed onto something sharp and hard, he felt it snag at his skin. Welcoming the pain, he pushed his foot harder to the floor. In the room the open curtains cast a rectangle of weak light. The light ended at the Captain's shoulders. The boy stood still. His foot throbbed.

'Captain Edmund,' the boy whispered.

A distant rifle shot sounded, unlike the shot that had sounded earlier that night, the one that had sent all the boys but him jumping from their beds and to the windows. He had lain in his bed, his stomach cramping so hard his eyes watered. He had heard the master come and shoo everyone from the windows after that shot, shoo them into bed. No one looked at him, still under his covers. He wasn't there; he wasn't there as he waited.

'Captain Edmund,' he whispered again to the figure.

A few stars shone through the window.

'Captain Edmund.'

He lifted his foot. The pain remained. He replaced his foot to the floor, the pain intensified.

'Captain Edmund.'

He lifted his foot again and put his fingers to his heel; it was sticky and a jagged shape clung to it. He pried at it and nearly called out in pain. He held the shape in his palm.

'Captain Edmund, I'm bleeding?'

'Captain Edmund, shall I go?'

A few more stars had gathered in the window.

The boy turned and placed his hand on the door handle. Trembling, alert for the voice, he turned the handle and waited. He pulled the door towards him, paused, then he stepped into the doorway. A light was on at the far end of the corridor to the right: a light that wasn't on before. He walked left to the fire-escape, smiling at the pain in his foot.

He felt the metal patterns of the fire-escape steps on his feet as the skin stuck and then pulled away from the tread. The bitumen of the path below pinched at his feet. When he reached the grass of the hockey field he rubbed his foot backwards and forwards to stop the bleeding. The hockey oval stretched to the edge of the school and a lone streetlight. Behind him, Captain Edmund's building blocked light from the quadrangle, so the boy was in darkness. Now he slid both feet along the grass. The pain had eased and he imagined the grass had sealed the cut; he was happy about that until he remembered he had hoped it might kill him.

THREE

Day 2
Kilkenny Road
6.30 a.m. Monday, 26th October 1965

During spring in Perth, early morning was the coolest time of day. At six thirty the sun shed light and gentle warmth. A persistent concert of bird calls emanated from the trees. Cardilini, wearing boxer shorts, singlet and thongs, slouched in the backyard of his home smoking his first cigarette for the day. He could see the sunlight, filtered by the trees, spread patches of fluid gold across the backyard: a backyard of overgrown plants, dead grass and cigarette butts. He didn't register the bird calls. He tried to remember what had happened last night, then gave up. One hand grabbed the fat of his ample paunch. He shook his head in disgust and ground out the cigarette butt with the heel of his thong.

'Time to get up, Paul,' Cardilini said and knocked on his son's bedroom door. In the kitchen he put a cereal box on the table. 'Breakfast is ready!' he called, as he walked past the door again to his own bedroom.

* * *

Cardilini pulled into the car park of the East Perth Police department. At 8 a.m. the air was warming, he was warming. He decided he would spend the day at his desk. The double brick, deep windows and high ceilings of the detectives' office provided protection from the day's heat. He would redo the paperwork on his only case, a robbery. He knew one of the culprits, or thought he did, and he felt it was quite reasonable to believe the man guilty. Anyway, he would make out a new report. The suspect wouldn't mind spending the day in a cell, hell, Cardilini wouldn't mind spending the day in a cell; at least he'd be cool. He'd spend the day pushing the papers around on his desk and get to the pub early. He figured he could do it again tomorrow before Detective Inspector Bishop, his senior, would complain. Not that Bishop wanted him for anything else. Bishop knew Cardilini was 'a waste of space'. Cardilini liked the idea of 'a waste of space'. Yeah, he would get two days out of it.

He pushed through the front doors of the building and stepped into the cool. A 12-foot wide corridor of apple-green linoleum ran to a central grand staircase of dark jarrah. On either side of the staircase the linoleum continued into offices and to the rear of the building, the uniformed officers' domain. Cardilini was a detective, a Detective Sergeant, so he hauled himself up the lino steps to the second floor and snuck past his boss's open door.

'Cardilini, is that you?' Bishop called.

Bugger.

'Cardilini, a teacher's been shot and I immediately thought of you.'

Cardilini paused in the corridor, stepped back and looked into Detective Inspector Bishop's office.

'That's nice of you,' he said. 'But I'm busy.'

'It's at St Nicholas College. You were looking for a new school for your boy, weren't you?'

'Very funny. That was six months ago, he's now left school.'

'Oh well, bad luck. I assigned you. They think it must be a stray bullet from someone shooting across the river.'

'What?' Cardilini asked, incredulous.

'Roo-shooters.'

Cardilini shook his head heavily. 'Bishop, that'll be a needle in a haystack job.'

'I know. So, you'll be able to put it to bed real quick and get back to your desk.'

'I see, it's like that is it?'

'No physical evidence came in. No bullet.'

'You're shitting me.'

'They think someone souvenired it.'

'Bullshit.'

'Yeah, I'm making it up. That's what I do all day, I sit here and make stuff up.'

'Always thought you did.' Cardilini turned from his boss's office, disappointed.

'Oh, Cardilini, you might want to know that the superintendent and the deputy commissioner attended St Nicholas College.'

Cardilini thrust his head back.

Bishop continued, 'They were contacted first. They can't have any involvement, of course, so they told me to go gently; don't want to damage the school's reputation, etcetera. Oh, and the body is already at the morgue.'

'What? That's bullshit, even they can't do that.'

'Do you want me to tell them you said that?'

Cardilini turned to walk to his desk.

'No need to tie up another detective,' Bishop called after him, 'take a constable.'

The constable available hadn't been a year in the job. Cardilini observed him expressionlessly for some time. He was Cardilini's height, six foot, with dark hair, dark eyes and even features. *He's too soft for the job*, Cardilini decided.

'Who are you?' Cardilini asked.

'They call me Salt, sir.'

'Okay, Salt. You don't speak unless I ask you to. If there's one thing I can't stand it's a loud-mouthed bore,' Cardilini said at a volume and manner as if intended for a particular loud-mouthed bore within earshot.

'Yes, sir.'

'Do you know where we're going?'

'Yes, sir.'

'Are you old enough to drive?'

'Yes, sir.'

'Get a car.'

'Yes, sir.'

Cardilini had started to sweat only minutes into their journey and couldn't settle on the seat. The metal of the dashboard, the vinyl seats, the glare from the windscreen, all annoyed him.

'There's a busted spring in this seat, Salt.'

'Yes, sir.'

'Next time you tell 'em who the car's for.'

'I did.'

'Bastards,' Cardilini said as he tried to crush the spring into submission with his backside.

FOUR

Day 2
Royal Perth Hospital
9.24 a.m. Monday, 26th October 1965

The body had been taken to the Royal Perth Hospital. Cardilini had Salt drop him at the front doors.

'Park the car and then come in and ask to be taken to the freezer.' Cardilini lit a cigarette as he walked through the double doors. He liked to stride along the corridor, he knew most of the nurses and he saw himself as a bluff, noisy uncle to them. He could make them laugh. He searched in vain for one he could tease.

'You wouldn't want to be sick in this place,' he announced at volume. A nurse with straight, shoulder-length black hair framing a square face stepped from a door.

'Detective Sergeant Cardilini, are you sick?'

'This is the last place I'd be if I was.'

'A number of people will be happy to hear that.'

Cardilini couldn't remember the nurse's name. He used to have a good memory for names, faces, and all sorts of facts about people.

'You'd be leading the pack, I bet.'

The nurse retreated through the door. *That shut her up,* Cardilini smiled.

* * *

In the basement, off the corridor to the 'freezer', the attendant, Colin McBride, had an office the size of two broom closets. He had compressed his body to suit: shoulders bent forward and a short sharp gait, but his big oval head, boasting thick black-framed round glasses, seemed outsized.

'Hey, McBride, you little ghoul, you got a body from St Nicholas College for me?' Cardilini called from the corridor.

'I wondered who would turn up. They sent you to bury it, did they?' McBride manoeuvred from his office.

'It's a shooting accident.'

'That's bullshit for a start.'

'What would you know?'

'More than you would,' McBride answered and Cardilini considered that was probably true.

'Well, no one's asking you. And I don't really care, I'm just following procedure.'

'Procedure, bullshit. If your mob were following procedure we wouldn't have a body until an investigation was done.' He pushed through a set of double doors ahead of Cardilini. On the autopsy table a grey sheet covered the form of a body, a black patch on one end hanging over a strangely truncated shape. Cardilini walked to the table and paused.

'Who brought the body in?' he asked.

'Ambulance.'

'Very funny. Which coppers?'

'No coppers.'

'What?'

'No coppers.'

'So, who authorised the bloody thing to come here?'

'The ambos were told to pick the body up. It was just a scheduled job for them.'

'What time?'

'Six thirty this morning. The teacher didn't arrive at rowing training.'

'Rowing? Who goes rowing?' Cardilini asked as Salt came through the door. 'Tell your story to Salt, he'll pretend he cares. Do you want to see this Salt?'

Cardilini watched Salt's features freeze and said, 'Nah, both of you nick off.'

When the doors swung closed, Cardilini reached to remove the sheet. It held fast. He began to pry from one side then tugged. Portions of brain tissue formed a neat arc through the air as the sheet fell to one side, revealing the body. A man in his forties dressed in trousers, socks and shoes, but no shirt. Not a lot of body fat, Cardilini noted. All quite normal apart from the fact that the top half of the man's skull was missing. The man's face seemed oblivious to this. His eyes open and clear, the mouth and chin angled suggesting he was exercising authority.

Cardilini had heard the fatal shot had come from a distance, possibly half a mile, from roo-shooters. The fact that the man's skull was missing suggested either a hollow-point or a soft-point bullet, designed to expand on impact. *Roo-shooters using hollow-point bullets?* Cardilini puzzled.

He picked up a probe and poked around in the brain cavity before laying it aside and re-examining the body from the soles of the victim's shoes to his gaping skull. *I don't like this,* Cardilini thought to himself.

He called finally, 'Salt. Come here.'

Salt and McBride entered. Salt stopped inside the door, his eyes widening as he stared at the gaping skull.

'Salt, examine the body. See if you can determine cause of death. McBride, come with me.' Cardilini left through the swinging doors, lighting a cigarette. McBride followed.

'Okay, smart arse. What do you think happened?' Cardilini asked.

'From the entry wound, a .303; from the exit, a hollow-point bullet. I'd say from a distance of two hundred yards max.'

'Who've you told?'

'You're the first one that's asked.'

'Get the body off that table, get it in an icebox. If anyone asks, say you haven't seen it. You got that?' Cardilini instructed.

'What's your conspiracy theory?'

'If you don't know, I'm not going to tell you.'

'Okay. I can tuck it away somewhere.'

'I'll get the photo boys down. I want the skull from every angle. Right. And no one touches the body. No one. I'm holding you responsible.'

'Are you okay to drive?' Cardilini asked Salt as they reached the car.

'Yes, sir.'

'Looked like he was teaching a class,' Cardilini said.

'Without a shirt?' Salt forced a smile.

Cardilini turned in his seat to take in Salt who was staring straight ahead.

'What about the top of his skull, notice anything?'

'Apart from it being missing?' Salt asked with a nervous laugh.

'Apart from that?' Cardilini questioned after a pause.

'No, sir.'

Cardilini watched Salt for a while then turned his attention back to the road. 'First corpse?'

'Yes, sir.'

Cardilini nodded. 'Now we're going to that school. You ever see a bull ant nest when you poke a stick at it?'

'No, sir.'

'Let's go. And make it quick, this car's cooking me alive.'

The city buildings slipped away quickly and now single-storey buildings lined the four-lane Great Eastern Highway. Cardilini had his window down, flanks of hot air pushing at his face.

'Wind your window down, Salt.'

'Yes, sir.'

'Are you going to say that every time I speak?'

Salt looked perplexed, 'Yes. Sir?'

Cardilini shook his head. *Soft.*

Suburban houses lined the street. Low buildings hunkered down against the heat like turtles. Gum trees gathered occasionally in parks trapped by low cyclone wire fences. Cardilini caught a glimpse of a swing, and an emptiness jumped to his throat.

'When did you finish training, Salt?' he barked.

'April.'

'So you're not a real copper, yet?'

Salt looked uncomfortable. Cardilini was satisfied with that answer. *Soft.*

'Forget everything they taught you if you want to become a real copper.'

'Sir?'

'That's right. They only give you the window-dressing there because you couldn't manage the real thing.'

'Yes, sir.'

'A teacher gets shot, no loss you might say, but we've got a job to do. You understand?'

'Yes, sir.'

'No, you don't. You've got no idea. Best to get that into your head from the start.'

Salt nodded slowly and focused on his driving.

FIVE

Day 2
St Nicholas College
12.03 a.m. Monday, 26th October 1965

The boy sat on the limestone steps descending to the hockey field. Darkness surrounded him. He began to feel invisible again; his body shivered, his shoulders and knees began bouncing uncontrollably and his jaw trembled, then he cried. He cried, staring at the lone streetlight at the bottom of the field. He held his eyes wide open, staring at the light as it blurred and ran. He held the scattering, staring vision as if to lose it would mean falling into a darkness from which he couldn't return. Eventually his eyes began to dry and his shoulders only occasionally shuddered. He was taking great gulps of air as if he'd forgotten how to breathe. This is how it had been every time he left Captain Edmund. Then his penis would stiffen, something that had never happened with Captain Edmund even though Captain Edmund had tried 'all his tricks'. But then that's not why the boy went; he knew that, he knew what was going to happen to him. Captain Edmund called him 'my little girl', 'my sweetie little girl'. A weight dropped through his body, leaving him wretched.

With the sharp object from Captain Edmund's room still in his palm, he walked to the corner of the administration building that contained the captain's room, to where a strip of light from the quadrangle came between the dormitory block and the administration block. Slowly, standing in shadow with only his forearm in the light, he opened his hand, palm up. He stared at the object. It reminded him of raindrops on a car window.

He'd sat in the car while waiting for his father when big fat raindrops started to fall. 'It's a good sign, son,' his father had said. When the rain struck the window it instantly spread, thin tendrils with droplets on the end. They held that shape for some time, or he imagined they held that shape. He couldn't decide if they were frightened or happy as they spread and hesitated before joining the other water streaming down the windscreen. And they kept coming, falling, hundreds of them, drumming like an army. His father had run to the car and burst in slamming the door behind him with a big grin on his face. 'That's a good sign, son.' They'd both been happy.

The object reminded him of that day, of his father. The boy's body convulsed and gusts of grief burst from his throat. He tried to hold them back but they sprung his mouth open and dropped him to his knees. He retched out the grief then slumped to his side on the path, still holding his palm and the object in the light. He opened his eyes on it and suddenly knew what it was. It was a bullet. He'd collected them from the rifle range, not spread like a droplet but flattened and misshapen.

He sat on his haunches and turned the bullet over, the base was intact, but the rest open, spread, searching. There was blood in his hand but his hand wasn't cut. He examined his heel, he saw puckered white skin but it wasn't broken. In his instep he saw dried blood, spider thin in the wrinkles of his feet and toes, he looked at his other foot, it also held the whispers of Captain

Edmund's room. He wet his finger and rubbed at the threads. Gradually, begrudgingly, they disappeared. Then he remembered the shot. That shot. The one that brought all the boys to the windows, the one the teachers, who had rooms on the other side of the building to the quad, said was just an echo from across the river. Captain Edmund had never lain on his back on the floor like that. He would lie on his back on the bed when he wanted things done to him, but not on the floor. And Captain Edmund hadn't answered. Had he answered? The boy became confused. Did he tell me to go? He'd never sent him away without first doing something to him. He opened his palm in the light and stared at the bullet again. Now it was a mallee eucalyptus flower, bright red, flung open to the sun.

He again imagined the car that was needed to kill him. He saw its light approaching, speeding at him. He would stand and step into its path, he felt the motion go through him. He imagined the headlight strike slowly buckling him. That's when it kills you, if it's fast enough. The kangaroos his father had hit had bounced and rolled and tried to stand. That was no good. They had to say his death was instantaneous. He swore to himself, it would be a speeding car. Busted would be worse, questions would shower on him. Dead he could smile, because no questions would get to him.

SIX

Day 2
St Nicholas College
11.30 a.m. Monday, 26th October 1965

On Cardilini's instructions Salt didn't park in the car park but on the lawn under some shade.

'Get your notebook out and look like you're taking notes.'

'Yes, sir.'

'And stay behind me,' Cardilini said as they walked towards the administration block. A tall, thin, elderly man exited the building and shuffled away from them in the shade of the cloisters. The lawns were immaculate, obviously. Obviously well-watered and growing like mad. *A nightmare for the gardener,* Cardilini thought.

The buildings on the raised riverbank stood marshalled like soldiers on parade, bastions against the ignorance of their urban setting.

The principal's offices were spacious and emanated scholarly endeavour. Paintings of past principals looked down disapprovingly at Cardilini. He bristled at the seeming opulence. *Sham,* he thought. Even the secretary's desk was twice the size of his own, and it was a solid dark wood, without the grey-steel drawers that screeched like a cat every time they opened.

'I'm Detective Sergeant Cardilini. Principal Braun's expecting me.'

The principal's secretary, Miss Reynolds, looked up, surprised for a moment, then gave herself a little nod as if just remembering. She viewed Cardilini from over the top of her spectacles, a sharp little bird.

'Dr Braun's busy, but I will let him know you're here.'

'That's very efficient of you,' Cardilini said with a wink to Salt that Cardilini was keen for her to see.

Miss Reynolds eyed Cardilini again, Cardilini bestowed a smile. Miss Reynolds departed.

'You'd think she was the bloody Queen of Sheba and Braun was the king. We'll see how long that stands up.' Cardilini craned over Miss Reynolds's desk, 'Thought she might be sitting on a nest of thistles.'

'Yes, sir.'

'They think they're better than the rest of us.'

'Yes, sir.'

'If you've got nothing useful to say, Salt, shut up.'

On her return Miss Reynolds said primly, 'Dr Braun is busy but understands you've a duty to perform and will see you straight away.'

'That's big of him. Take notes, Salt, "Miss Reynolds, secretary." You got that?'

'Yes, sir.'

'He's keen to get his first prosecution,' Cardilini told Miss Reynolds as he walked into the principal's office.

The principal sat at his desk, a pile of documents to his right. Braun took the top document, skimmed through it, and then placed it to his left. He completed several more while

Cardilini and Salt stood watching. Cardilini turned to Salt and mouthed 'wanker'. The principal raised his head midway through a document.

'You must be Cardilini?'

'Detective Sergeant Cardilini. This is Constable Salt. And you must be Joe Braun.'

'Dr Joseph Braun.'

'Okay, we all seem to be present. Shall we stop calling each other names and get to business?' Cardilini said as he sat in the chair opposite the principal.

The principal, taken aback, gestured Salt to the other chair.

'He likes standing,' Cardilini said. 'Now about this murdered teacher.'

'Murdered?' The principal reacted as if slapped.

'Take notes here, Salt,' Cardilini directed.

'No, no, no. It was a stray shot from across the river,' the principal stammered.

'No, no, no. It was a marksman's shot from less than two hundred yards,' Cardilini replied emphatically.

The principal's phone rang. He hurriedly picked it up and said he was busy.

'Detective Sergeant Cardilini, I am not sure where you're getting your information from, but this matter's been cleared away and I was told you were simply coming here to finalise the report.'

'Let me see the notes on the case, Salt.' Cardilini put out his hand while he stared fixedly at the principal. Salt placed his notebook in Cardilini's hand. Cardilini flipped pages of the notebook back and forth. The principal's phone rang again.

'No,' the principal shouted into the mouthpiece immediately on picking up the phone, 'Miss Reynolds, no.'

'Bull ants,' Cardilini mouthed to Salt.

'Now . . .' the principal started.

'Now, Dr Braun,' Cardilini handed the notebook back to Salt and gave the principal an exaggerated wink. 'I am sure you understand that if an ironclad report is to be made, correct procedure must be followed?'

The principal's brow furrowed and he turned his questioning gaze to Salt, who studied his notebook.

'Shall we?' Cardilini stood and gestured towards the door. 'I thought we should start in the room where the body was found.'

The principal after some hesitation stood, 'Are you sure this is the right thing to do?'

'Absolutely.'

'If . . .' the principal hesitated '. . . if you would wait in Miss Reynolds' office, my deputy, Dr Robson, shall attend to you. He discovered poor Captain Edmund. There are some important calls I must make, you understand.' Then he added with renewed confidence, 'Please see yourself out.'

Cardilini raised his eyebrows at Salt and they left the principal's office.

Miss Reynolds' cheeks were flushed as she sat rigidly at her desk. Cardilini leant against it, lit a cigarette and offered the packet to Salt who declined. Finally, the telephone on Miss Reynolds' desk rang. Picking it up, she listened a moment then uttered a sharp, 'Yes,' and hung up.

'Dr Robson, the deputy principal, will see you outside,' she said briskly and gestured towards the door.

'Charming,' Cardilini said with another wink as they left. 'You're taking real notes,' Cardilini stated to Salt while they stood outside.

'Yes, sir,' Salt replied as Cardilini shrugged his shoulders.

A middle-aged man wearing a threadbare grey suit hanging from bony, stooped shoulders approached reluctantly. His ashen face hung like his suit.

'Cardilini?'

'Yes. Robson?'

'Yes. I'm to show you Captain Edmund's room.'

'Show away,' Cardilini gestured. Robson stood for a moment darting his eyes between Cardilini and Salt, then turned resignedly and shambled back the way he had come. Cardilini and Salt followed.

'Why did you call him captain?' Cardilini asked.

'He was captain of the cadet corps.'

'You have a cadet corps?' Cardilini asked with a disdainful grimace to Salt.

'Of course.'

'Of course,' Cardilini mouthed to Salt.

Looking from the doorway, the Captain's second-level room was furnished with a single bed against the wall on the left, and on the right a roll-top desk and chair, two timber filing cabinets and a wardrobe. Cardilini tried the desk drawers, they held fast.

'Where are the keys for this?' He asked Robson. Robson pointed to a filing cabinet drawer.

Cardilini opened the top drawer and pulled out a bunch of keys, he tried several before one opened the roll-top. Cardilini examined the desk and drawers.

'A tidy gentleman.'

'He was,' Robson affirmed.

Cardilini turned to the filing cabinets and went through each one carefully before ordering Salt to take notes of the contents. 'Did you see the body?' he asked Robson.

'Yes.'

'Show me where it was.'

Robson hesitated before pointing to the floor.

'You lie down exactly where you saw Edmund lying,' Cardilini ordered.

Robson reluctantly sat on the floor. He shuffled for a moment and lay back with his arms and legs akimbo.

'Draw a picture, Salt,' Cardilini directed, as he walked to the sash window directly in front of where Robson lay. He pushed the window up and looked down into the quadrangle for some time.

'Finished, Salt?' Cardilini asked.

'Yes, sir.'

'Good. Go back to your notes on the filing cabinets. Please stand, Dr Robson.'

Robson stood. He made no attempt to dust his suit. Instead, he reached into his pocket and withdrew a small tin, from which he selected a partially smoked cigarette. Cardilini watched this and offered Robson a light before lighting a cigarette himself. He went back to the window and then turned to face the room. He looked towards the ceiling above the rear wall then shifted his gaze to above the doorframe.

Cardilini strolled forward and said over his shoulder. 'There would have been a lot of blood.'

'There was,' Robson said with a quick glance to Salt.

'You saw?'

'Yes.'

'Not a pretty sight,' Cardilini said unconcerned as he examined the floorboards. He then ran the point of a pencil along the gaps between the boards.

'You could say that,' Robson replied heatedly.

'When was the place cleaned?' Cardilini asked, examining his pencil.

'Once the body was removed, I understand.'

'Who did the cleaning?'

'Our cleaning staff. They have been given the rest of the day off. They found it quite traumatic.'

'Yep. There are specialist companies that do that sort of thing.'

'The staff felt they could be more respectful of Captain Edmund's passing.'

'Very loyal of them,' Cardilini conceded.

'A bullet wasn't found. If that's what you're seeking,' Robson said as he tipped the ash from his cigarette into the tin. Cardilini observed the action with distaste.

'That's right,' Cardilini replied.

'A very thorough search has been made already.'

'Oh yes, very thorough,' Cardilini said exaggeratedly. 'Friendly, were you, with Edmund?'

'Captain Edmund was a colleague. A man very loyal to the school.'

'A bit of a catch-cry, loyalty, is it?' Cardilini examined the wall above the doorway.

'It's very important to any institution. Just like the police, I suspect,' Robson replied archly.

Cardilini shrugged. 'How tall was Edmund?' he asked.

'Not a tall man.' Robson replied, eyeing Cardilini coolly.

'Shorter than you?'

'Yes.'

'How much shorter?'

Robson held out his hand at eye level.

'Finished, Salt?' Cardilini asked.

'Yes, sir.'

'Good. Make yourself that tall, Salt' Cardilini directed, 'and walk over to the window.'

Salt went to Robson's hand and bent at the knees until he reached the right height. Then he shuffled to the window and stood looking out. Cardilini stepped beside him and placed the index finger of his right hand on Salt's forehead and the index finger of his left hand on the rear of Salt's skull. He stood behind Salt and viewed down the angle his fingers created. Then he turned his attention into the room and returned to the spot above the door. He pulled the desk chair over and examined the same space with his eyes and fingertips. Satisfied, he replaced the chair and began inspecting the floor.

'Sir?' Salt asked; his knees had begun to shake.

'Yeah. Okay,' Cardilini replied. Salt straighten his legs as Cardilini opened the door and got down on his hands and knees. 'A lot of blood?'

'Yes.'

'You all walked in it?' Cardilini asked.

'No.' Robson replied emphatically.

'Someone did,' Cardilini said.

Robson looked at the floor curiously. 'No. The pool was intact.'

'You actually saw that when you first discovered the body?'

'I'm sorry to say, yes, I noted it.'

Cardilini stood and inched along the corridor to the left, 'Where were the skull fragments?' he asked without looking up from his examination of the carpet in the corridor.

'I didn't see any, thank goodness. And I didn't look. The body was gone when I returned with the cleaners.'

'What time did you first enter the room?'

'Just before six. Captain Edmund always rose punctually at five thirty.'

'Why did you come to the room?'

'The boys were mustered for rowing training and waiting in the quadrangle. I sent them ahead and came up here to fetch Edmund,' Robson answered.

'You at school that time every morning?' Cardilini asked, shifting his view of the carpet to catch more light on the spot he was inspecting.

'Dr Braun and I share the early starts.'

'Did the cleaners exit this way?' Cardilini indicated to the left of the passageway.

'Yes.'

'One of the cleaners had blood on them,' Cardilini said.

'I doubt that.'

'Who else was about at six o'clock?'

'Before six, just the rowers,' Robson answered

'Did one of the boys come up this way to rouse Edmund?' Cardilini asked.

'And discover the body and not say anything?' Robson queried mockingly.

'Perhaps, so they could souvenir the bullet.'

'No!' Robson stated firmly.

'You seem sure.'

'I'm very sure. There isn't a boy in the school who didn't respect Captain Edmund.'

'Were the rowers barefoot?' Cardilini asked.

'No. In shoes. It's quite a hike to the boat shed.'

At this point Cardilini had Salt hold the fire-escape door open while he examined the stairs.

'There's blood on these steps,' Cardilini said, and straightened his back. Robson and Salt craned forward to see.

'It could have been splatter from the cleaners' buckets,' Robson suggested.

'Did Superintendent Robinson or Deputy Commissioner Warren come out this way?'

'I believe the superintendent drew the deputy commissioner this way. I was at the other end of the corridor to stop entry.'

'Okay.' Cardilini said. He walked down the fire-escape. Glancing out to the oval, he recognised a familiar array of nets.

'Hockey?'

'Yes.' Robson said craning to see what Cardilini was doing.

At the bottom of the fire-escape Cardilini had got down on his haunches and was examining the bitumen. Robson and Salt started down the fire-escape. 'Don't step off,' Cardilini commanded, and the two stood one behind the other on the lower rungs.

'Which way did the cleaners go?' Cardilini asked.

Robson pointed to the left. Cardilini started to the right, walking slowly, surveying the bitumen. He then stopped and looked out onto the hockey field.

'Someone did pick up that bullet,' he finally said.

'Yes. I believe that was the previous consensus,' Robson glanced dismissively to Salt.

'Not very respectful, would you say?' Cardilini asked, starting down the limestone stairs.

'I think it's your officers or ambulance crew that missed it. It could still be . . .' Robson was reluctant to finish.

'In the body?' Cardilini asked.

'Yes,' Robson replied.

Cardilini shrugged.

'Finding it isn't worth traumatising the whole school,' Robson declared.

'Really? Who decides that?'

'A responsible adult,' Robson replied firmly.

'A crime scene has been disturbed and no one is worried. Is that what I'm hearing?' He started on the base of the wall at the other side of the stairs.

'You only lost a bullet, Detective Sergeant Cardilini. The whole school has lost a dedicated teacher and colleague.'

'Did you come across this in the academy, Salt?' Cardilini asked.

'No, sir.'

'Just starting out,' Cardilini said, indicating Salt to Robson.

'I'm aware,' Robson replied dryly.

'We might go for a stroll down to that row of gum trees on the other side of the quadrangle,' Cardilini said climbing the limestone stairs.

'I will need to check with the principal,' Robson said.

'No, you won't. This is a police investigation.'

Cardilini walked from the shade of the rear of the building around to the front, which faced the quadrangle. He stood in the shade of the cloister, reluctantly looking out onto the lawn and the row of gum trees on the opposite side. It was midday and the heat seemed to have a pulse and will of its own. The diagonal paths were paved with limestone, hard and hot. A few passing students, dressed in grey shorts and grey shirts with a gold and black school tie, stared openly at the three men.

'What time is lunch?' Cardilini asked.

'Twelve thirty.'

'Who sent the cleaners home?'

'The principal can answer your questions.'

'Bullshit. Everyone answers my questions,' Cardilini glared at Robson. Robson looked nonplussed.

'We don't swear at St Nicholas College. It's considered coarse.'

'And what do you consider a criminal record for withholding information?'

'You don't pay my salary, Detective Cardilini,' Robson replied coolly.

Cardilini regarded Robson for a moment, smiled, and then grimaced as he stepped out into the sun to cross the quadrangle. Robson and Salt quickly followed.

'We don't need you anymore, Robson,' Cardilini dismissed the deputy without turning.

'I've been instructed to stay with you,' Robson said. Cardilini didn't respond and headed directly across the lawn to the line of gum trees he'd viewed from Edmund's room.

'We are required to walk on the paths as an example to the boys,' Robson said as he stepped right to one of the diagonal paths. Cardilini ignored him. Salt stuck by Cardilini's side.

Robson quickened his pace getting ahead of Cardilini and picked up a sheet of paper by one of the gum trees. 'Litter,' he uttered sharply. Cardilini went to the tree where Robson had retrieved the paper. He stood beside the tree trunk and looked up at the window he had left open, then started to examine the tree and the surrounding grass before he began a slow descent of the embankment to the bordering limestone wall.

Clicking heels alerted Robson and Salt to Miss Reynolds's arrival. She called from the path. 'There is a telephone call for Detective Cardilini.' She paused for a moment and stared at Robson until he nodded his understanding.

'Detective Cardilini, there is a telephone call for you,' Robson said. Cardilini ignored him, his attention focused on the limestone wall.

'What's down behind this wall? Cardilini asked.

'There is a call for you,' Robson repeated.

'Tell them to call back. What's down here?'

Robson turned to Miss Reynolds who stood staring. 'It's his superior,' she called.

'It's your superior,' Robson relayed to Cardilini.

'Salt, jump up on the wall and draw a picture of what you see. Then, stand at that tree, where Robson picked up the paper, and let no one near it. You got that?'

'Yes, sir.'

'Let's go,' Cardilini said and started across the lawns. Robson and Miss Reynolds zigzagged at pace along the paths.

'Where's the telephone?'

'The principal's office,' a breathless Miss Reynolds called.

Cardilini ignored Principal Braun when he walked into his office. He sat in the chair he had previously occupied and pulled the phone towards him. 'Cardilini,' he stated. He sat and listened eyeing Braun who keenly moved documents from one side of his desk to the other.

'Yes. Yep. Yes, sir. Yep. Yep. No. No,' Cardilini said at intervals before he finished with, 'Would I do it any other way, sir?' and hung up. 'How about that?' he mused, 'Somehow, he knew exactly what I was doing?' and feigning amazement he asked, 'How could you account for that?'

'Detective Sergeant Cardilini,' Braun pushed a document aside patiently and leant back in his chair. 'I'm aware you've had a bad experience with your son's progress through education. However, that was not with our school.'

Cardilini sat back, eyebrows raised, a slight smile on his face. Braun continued.

'St Nicholas College has an impeccable reputation that is guarded rigorously by alumi, present students, parents and staff. A reputation hard won over decades, a reputation that will outlast all our current students and me. You could almost say it's an unwritten motto "Our school before all else". You can see it fiercely displayed when the boys play sport or when the teachers seek accolades for our boys.' Braun paused to determine if his oration was having the desired effect. Cardilini still sat with a slight smile on his face, so Braun continued with confidence. 'This is not your fault. I'm not blaming you. Your immediate superior, Inspector Bishop, simply failed to instruct you correctly. I believe you're aware that your superintendent and the deputy commissioner are old boys of St Nicholas, so you can see the serious attention this tragic accident has received.'

The sudden clamour of svoices as students broke for lunch caused the principal to stop his discourse, stand and close a window, before again seating himself comfortably and continuing his ovation.

Cardilini observed him and reflected on the similarity between this principal and the one that had eventually expelled Paul. He imagined them, along with several of his ambitious colleagues, running around with a high-stepping gait holding their hands firmly over their backsides.

'Cardilini,' Braun repeated.

Cardilini blinked several times. 'Yes?'

SEVEN

Day 2
St Nicholas College
12.30 p.m. Monday, 26th October 1965

As the students emerged for lunch, Salt had completed his drawing and was standing by the assigned tree. Boys, staring in open curiosity, slowly walked past. Salt tried to maintain a professional manner and pose but couldn't convince himself of the logic of Cardilini's instruction. The tree, obviously, wasn't going anywhere. Four younger boys, not content with a passing observation, stood directly facing Salt. Salt watched them. After a while they sat down so as to stare while eating their lunch.

Another, and then another, knot of young boys paused and started eating their lunch while staring at Salt. Soon, three older boys sauntered over and stood watching the gathering in disdain.

'Which one of you little durrs is eating pork? Because I can smell pig,' one of the older boys said. This received guffaws and laughter from his mates. The younger boys turned their heads passively to observe the older boys before looking back to Salt. Salt reddened with the insult but stood still.

'Oink. Oink,' one of the older boys said under his breath to the delight of his two colleagues. Salt reddened further.

The 'oinks' continued. Some of the smaller boys began fighting among themselves and rolling on the grass. Salt stood stricken.

'Get off that grass,' the command whipped at the group of boys. Salt jumped. Standing on the paving were two boys in grey suits, sixth form students. The younger boys jumped up and ran off along the path. The three older boys, also startled, stepped onto the path.

'Darnley,' called one of the sixth form boys sharply. Darnley, who'd mentioned 'pig', stopped and turned towards the caller.

'Yes.'

'Don't think your behaviour goes unobserved.' Darnley stood looking at him, unimpressed. 'Do you have something to say?' the older boy pressed.

Darnley smiled and nodded to his mates and the three of them casually walked away. The sixth form boys scrutinised Salt for awhile then turned their attention to glaring at passing students who hurried along, eyes averted. Soon, no students walked by. One of the sixth form boys walked closer and stood assessing Salt.

With deliberation the boy said, 'The shot came from across the river. They shoot kangaroos in the scrub by the river there.' He waited for Salt's reply.

Salt's eyes shifted to a young sandy-haired teacher in a wellworn suit walking towards them.

'Excuse me, Carmody,' the teacher called. The boy kept his eyes on Salt, ignoring the teacher.

'You're not wanted here,' Carmody said to Salt.

'Carmody, excuse me. Can I assist you?' The teacher spoke again.

'No. You can't,' Carmody said without turning. A look of helplessness filled the teacher's eyes.

'I will need to cite you for walking on the grass unless you come onto the path,' the teacher said to Carmody.

'That would be brave of you,' Carmody said and turned from Salt to join his friend on the path. They both walked off without further reference to the teacher or Salt.

'I hope they weren't annoying you. The sixth form boys like to exercise authority at times, particularly that one – Carmody. He's the unofficial leader of the boarders. There's a boarders' captain but everyone knows Carmody is in charge, even the principal. He should've been made head boy, that's why he's a little difficult.'

'Why wasn't he?'

The teacher seemed to consider this before ignoring the question and saying, 'The younger boys who were eating their lunch are day boys, even though they come from quite a distance.'

'Are you a teacher?'

'Yes. Though not on the permanent staff. Not an old boy, see. They'll keep me just until one of their own is available. That's a joke. God, don't repeat that, please.'

'I won't.'

'So, you're a policeman?'

Salt glanced down at his constable's uniform before replying, 'Yes'. The teacher nodded firmly in affirmation as if to reassure Salt that he was indeed a policeman.

'Well, I'm on duty. Can't linger. It's just strange seeing someone standing on the grass. Grass areas are out of bounds to all personnel. That's a school rule. The thinking is that the students roll about in an unhealthy manner when allowed on the grass. Even when watching sports, students aren't allowed to lie down together. It's unmanly. They're required to sit in a chair or stand. I'm sure that's half the reason the boys don't readily watch the sports. Well, I've got to go.' The teacher remained standing where he was, then asked, 'So, may I ask why you're standing there? It seems very curious.'

Salt hesitated until he saw Cardilini marching straight across the quadrangle grass towards him, creating a stir among the students. The teacher turned to where Salt was looking and took an involuntary step back.

'Clear off,' Cardilini barked at the teacher, who turned on his heel and smartly walked away. 'Salt. Watch and listen closely and take every detail down in your notebook.' Cardilini pushed Salt aside and stood examining the tree closely, 'Now, observe that branch. There, that one. What do you see?'

Salt studied it closely for some time then turned back to Cardilini. 'Sorry. I don't see anything,' he said.

Cardilini exhaled heavily. 'What should we be looking for?' he demanded.

Salt considered for a moment, but then shook his head in the negative.

'Okay. You're Edmund, right? Standing in the window. The open one with the curtains closed. Surveying your little kingdom, stuffed to the brim with how important you are, then bam half your head flies off and you get thrown back into the room to land flat on your back. Right?'

'Yes, sir.'

'Now. From where you were standing the bullet struck you, there,' Cardilini pushed his right index finger onto Salt's forehead, the force of it pushing Salt back, 'then the bullet spread but kept on the same trajectory until it blew off the top of your skull. And its exit was roughly there.' Cardilini pushed his other index finger on the rear of Salt's skull. His fingers now held

Salt's head as if in a vice. 'And you're looking out the window, right? So what are we looking for down here?' He took his fingers from Salt and stepped back. Salt turned to the window.

'The shot was made from down here somewhere?' Salt asked amazed.

'Go to the top of the class. Now impress me,' Cardilini said. Salt began to move around the area.

'There are a lot of foot marks around this tree.'

'Beside yours and mine?' Cardilini asked.

'Yes. And no one walks on the lawn.'

'Passable.'

'This tree could fit the angle of a bullet's flight,' Salt proposed, 'But that would also be possible if the bullet came from across the river.' They turned in that direction. From the top of the embankment they could see across the limestone wall to the river 200 yards away and beyond the river to low scrubland and open pasture. Cardilini dismissed the notion and turned his demanding gaze on Salt.

'Are we looking for signs of the shot being fired from here?' Salt asked.

'Clever boy. Yes.'

Salt began examining the tree.

Cardilini suggested, 'High possibility it was a .303 bullet that did the damage.' Then asked, 'Ever fire a .303 rifle, Salt?'

'No, sir.'

'Trust me then. The rebound pounds the stock of the rifle into your shoulder.'

'Yes, sir, I've heard that.'

'Right, it jumps back sharply. Now look at the branch.'

Salt stared closely at a branch chest high.

'Okay. Now look at me,' Cardilini said, 'We don't want to draw attention to that branch but a casual glance will show you where the bark's bruised and slightly lifted. It tells me someone used that branch to anchor the shaft of the rifle. And there are two more curious marks on branches further up. And on the trunk, someone's foot slipped when trying to climb the tree. You see these?'

'Now I do.'

'Okay. Commit this to memory and when you get a chance write it up in your notebook and draw pictures. I've got a feeling the photo boys are going to find themselves too busy to come out here. Did you get a good sketch of what was immediately over the wall?'

'Yes, sir.'

'That's good. How would you like some night-time investigation?'

'Um.'

'Good. Now can you remember what you've seen here?' Cardilini asked, gesturing to the tree.

'Yes, sir.'

'Let's get out of this heat. I know where we can get a good counter lunch.'

'Yes, sir. Are we returning to the school?' Salt asked, but Cardilini was already walking away.

EIGHT

Day 2
A pub
2.00 p.m. Monday, 26th October 1965

Cardilini finished his steak and eggs with chips on the side and was halfway through his second pint while Salt was still drinking his first glass of lemon squash.

'Do you go drinking with your colleagues, Salt?' Cardilini asked.

'Beer during the day makes me sleepy,' Salt replied.

'That's not what I asked.'

'Yes, sir.'

'What do they talk about?'

'The crimes and the characters, mainly. Or sport. Or girls,' Salt replied.

Cardilini nodded. 'So why did you join?' he asked.

'Just the usual,' Salt replied.

'What's that?'

'Justice,' Salt said shifting in his seat.

'That's the usual?' Cardilini asked before finishing his beer.

'Yes.'

'Sir,' Cardilini said.

'Sir.'

'Anything else happen while I was having a chat with my superior?' Cardilini tried to make the question sound casual.

'No, sir.'

'Okay. Tell me about it.'

'Nothing happened,' Salt said earnestly.

'Who were those people talking to you?' Cardilini asked impatiently.

'A teacher and a student.'

'Names?' Cardilini asked.

'The student was Carmody, in the sixth form and intent on defending the school's reputation.'

'What did he say?'

'That the shooting was an accident.'

'That's odd, isn't it?'

'I'm sorry, sir?' Salt was at a loss.

'Why would he come up and say that?'

'Being helpful?'

'Is that what it seemed?'

After some consideration, Salt replied, 'No.'

'What then?'

'Almost threatening,' Salt reluctantly revealed.

'Really. And you call that nothing?' Cardilini asked.

'I didn't think of it like that.'

'Like a policeman? You're at the scene of a crime, the first thing a criminal wants to know is, what do you know? They can't help themselves, particularly the stupid ones.'

'Carmody's not stupid.'

'How would you know that? He could be as thick as two short planks,' Cardilini persisted.

'The teacher said Carmody should have been head boy.'

'What happened?'

'I didn't get a chance to ask.'

'What was the teacher's name?'

'I didn't get a chance to ask.'

'Who are you, Mary Poppins? You're a copper, you make chances. No one leaves until you've got what you need,' Cardilini growled.

'Yes, sir.'

'Yes, sir. What about those scrawny ones?'

'They were probably fourth form boys. Carmody told them to move on.'

'Maybe that's what you should have done.'

'Yes, sir.'

'I might have a chat with Carmody. Here's a bit of police work for you, get me the name of the teacher.'

'How?'

Cardilini stood from the table and walked from the pub. Salt sighed and, leaving his drink unfinished on the table, followed Cardilini.

NINE

Day 2
East Perth Police Department
4.15 p.m. Monday, 26th October 1965

Cardilini sat slumped at his desk staring gloomily at his watch. Too early even for him to go for another drink. He pulled out a street directory.

He noticed a car could coast down the hill outside St Nicholas and park near the river. The houses were at least 100 yards from the marshy foreshore. It would be easy for a car to park down there, then for someone to walk to the wall, climb over it and crawl up the embankment. There, they could make the shot and retreat the same way. No one would be the wiser. Cardilini headed for the basement.

The stairs to the basement were cast concrete. In an attempt to soften the gloom, corded carpet pinned by steel rods travelled the length of the stairs but not their full width. Dust gathered on the raw concrete edges. In the basement the temperature dropped ten degrees. Every five yards caged lighting clung like limpets to the concrete ceiling. Here the corridor was completely covered in the official green linoleum as on the building's first floor. Timber doors lined the corridor, each embossed with gold lettering signifying the contents they concealed. Cardilini knew, despite the lettering, most rooms were given over to the masses of paperwork policing produced.

Halfway down the corridor he slouched against the doorframe of an office and tapped on the open door embossed ARMOURY. At the desk, ramrod straight, sat Senior Sergeant Acorn. Acorn reminded Cardilini more of a cuckoo clock than a copper. The Senior Sergeant was as fastidious as his moustache, which was always trimmed, as was his hair. Even his features, neat and understated, had a sheen and primness that also suggested daily trimming. Acorn raised his head in response to the tap. When he saw Cardilini he returned to his file without speaking.

'Thought I'd drop by and say hi,' Cardilini said.

'You said it. Goodbye,' Acorn replied without looking up.

'I wonder if you could help me out.'

'Out of where?' Acorn raised his head with a superior smirk.

'I'm chasing some information, if you've got a moment?'

'Is it work related?' Acorn lowered his head to the file in front of him.

'Yes, sir,' Cardilini said briskly.

'What's the case?' Acorn asked drawing his open diary towards him. He poised his pen above a line. 'Well?'

Cardilini smiled and sat in front of Acorn's desk. Acorn had a weakness and Cardilini knew it: a vanity about his meticulous record keeping.

'Just general information.'

'A case name or I will have to ask you to leave the office,' Acorn insisted.

'Hey, Acorn, it's me.'

'Yes. I know it's you, Cardilini. I seem to remember giving you confidential information once and ending up carpeted by the super.'

'Yes. He shouldn't have done that,' Cardilini said sagely.

'Yes, well, I don't remember you speaking up at the time.'

'It's something I regret,' Cardilini said with a fair approximation of a hangdog expression.

'What's the case?'

'St Nicholas College. A shooting accident.'

'A shooting? That I haven't heard about? I don't think so,' Acorn closed his file.

'The super dealt with it himself. The case is still a bit hush-hush,' Cardilini said with a wink.

Acorn shook his head in annoyance and made an entry in his diary. 'I can't help you if I don't have details of the case.'

'I'm currently writing the report. I just need some advice regarding the firearm in question.'

'What do you want to know?'

'The schools that go in for cadet training, do they hold .303 rifles?' Cardilini asked.

'That's not a firearm question.'

'A bit of leeway, please, Acorn.'

'It's Senior Sergeant.'

'Implied,' Cardilini assured.

'Army, Navy or Air Force Cadets?'

'I don't know. Any. All.'

'Typical Cardilini,' Acorn tutted, 'Yes, they'd have .303 rifles. Schools with a cadet program are required to have an armoury and secure all firearms.'

'Would St Nicholas College?'

'Yes. They would and do. The code of every rifle they have is recorded and stored.'

'Where?'

'Here. Where do you think?'

'Are they .303s, ex-service rifles?'

'That's correct.'

'Could you tell me how many rifles they hold?'

'Could I, or, will I?'

'Will you?'

'This is a legitimate enquiry? Right, Cardilini?'

'Yes. Absolutely.'

'And if I rang Bishop?' Acorn reached for the phone.

'Sure. Sure.'

'I shouldn't trust you, Cardilini,' Acorn said withdrawing his hand.

'No, this is one hundred per cent. Do you think I would risk doing that to you again?' Cardilini asked earnestly.

Acorn paused for a moment before he picked up his phone and dialled. 'Mrs Allenby, would you bring me the list of fire-arms and munitions held at St Nicholas College? Thank you.' Acorn hung up and indicated for Cardilini to note the time.

Cardilini did and smiled back encouragingly. Acorn maintained an expectant expression as he stared at Cardilini for the two minutes it took for Mrs Allenby to drop the file on his desk.

'Two minutes,' Acorn said pleased.

'Very impressive,' Cardilini replied and hoped his facial expression was saying the same.

'Forty-two,' Acorn read from the file.

'Can I borrow a bit of paper?' Cardilini asked as he patted his pockets for a pen.

Acorn shook his head in disgust and placed a clean sheet of paper and a pen on his desk. Cardilini scribbled as Acorn dictated, 'Forty-two Lee Enfield 4 Mk 1, two Owen Machine Guns. No live rounds.'

'That can't be right,' Cardilini blurted.

'What, can't be right?' Acorn scrutinised the file.

'No live rounds,' Cardilini replied.

'That's what the record says. And the record is correct. It's signed off by the Officer in Charge, C A P T A C Edmund.'

'Edmund?'

'Yes. I've actually spoken to him. Very military chap. Very thorough.'

'Where do they get the live rounds from?' Cardilini asked while writing.

'The live rounds are only issued at the rifle range,' Acorn answered.

'So a student could steal a live round from the rifle range if he wanted to?'

'Highly doubtful. These are army cadets, Cardilini, not the usual riffraff you're used to dealing with,' Acorn said, closing the file firmly to emphasise the point.

'What's the C A P T A C, stand for?'

'Captain. That's his rank as Instructor of Cadets. It's not a real service rank.'

'In the Cooke case you matched markings on bullets for a number of rifles, right?' Cardilini asked.

'Yes, 60,000 .22 calibre rifles. It wasn't me personally,' Acorn replied.

'No. Okay.'

'Do you have a bullet?' Acorn asked.

'Not quite.'

'Why aren't I surprised? Anything else?'

'Could I take that list?'

'No!' Acorn drew the file to himself protectively.

'Can I get a copy?'

'You have a sheet of paper and a pen. Copy it now.'

'Could you get Mrs Allenby?'

'No.'

'Are the numbers sequential?'

'No.'

Cardilini sighed and leant on Acorn's desk to copy the numbers. When he finally finished he grunted, 'Thank you,' and started to walk away until Acorn called for his pen. Cardilini reluctantly placed it back on Acorn's desk and left.

TEN

'The super wants to see you,' Bishop yelled as Cardilini passed his office.

'Why?'

'Go and ask him. Now.'

Cardilini turned and headed back to the stairs. The 'brass' were on the third level. The third level, to distinguish it from the lower levels, had red linoleum streaked with white. Suggesting royal blood was one theory, but Cardilini sub-scribed to another: the red linoleum was due to the amount of backstabbing that went on.

Cardilini had joined the police force a few years after Superintendent Robinson and they'd been good friends as constables together in a small country town. He knocked on Robinson's door, and entered.

'Where the hell have you been?' Robinson demanded.

'Taking a dump.'

'Bloody long dump.' Cardilini sat. 'Did you know Dr Braun called today?'

'Yep?'

'A murder? How the hell did it turn into a murder? There was shooting across the river. A stray bullet. What's the matter with you?'

Cardilini asked, 'What if the rifle was fired from the grounds? Maybe a 180-yard shot. A marksman,' Cardilini said.

'A marksman! That's all we need. You got any proof of this? It's over, Cardilini. I've just had my balls kicked for five minutes by the deputy commissioner. It was a shooting accident, for Christ's sake.'

'I might be a lazy bastard, but I'm not stupid, Robinson.'

'Did Salt see it like that?' Robinson asked pointedly.

Cardilini paused, perplexed. 'No,' he replied.

Robinson stood and strode to the door. Halfway across the room, he stopped, turned and said, 'Sit on your fat arse, Cardilini. That's what you're good at.' He walked out.

Cardilini was left staring out the window with a new furrow in his brow.

Eventually Robinson returned and sat comfortably before flicking Salt's notebook towards Cardilini.

'Have a look at these,' he said.

The notes were precise and objective with no assumptions and no conclusions, just facts: date, times, places, names and diagrams. Just like they taught at the academy.

'He's good. Isn't he?' Robinson asked after a few minutes. Cardilini stopped his study of the notebook and gently placed it on Robinson's desk and sat back.

'Well?' Robinson encouraged.

'Is he your man?'

'What's that supposed to mean?'

'He's written his notes to suit your story of a stray shot from across the river.'

'My story? Careful, Cardilini. The deputy commissioner and I investigated and drew that conclusion. Well, where are your notes?'

'Yeah, my notes . . . um . . .' Cardilini cast his eye about as if looking for them.

'Yeah. I forgot what a great detective you are,' Robinson said sharply.

'What about the angle of trajectory of the bullet?' Cardilini asked.

'We thought of that and decided it was impossible to determine,' Robinson replied.

'Oh. Right. I see.'

'What do you see, Cardilini?'

'I see there was never going to be an investigation. So you got the lazy, fat copper to sign the report.'

'Have you got hard evidence?' Robinson insisted.

Cardilini shifted in his chair. All he had was what McBride at the morgue had told him, that it was a shot from around 200 yards with a .303 calibre rifle. But McBride wasn't a forensic expert.

'There was bruising on a tree . . .' Cardilini started.

'I read it. A schoolyard full of boys. Half of them would've climbed that tree.'

'It's out of bounds,' Cardilini said.

'Oh, well. There you go. Rock solid evidence.'

Cardilini sat staring at Robinson, 'So what do you expect me to do now?'

'Make up a report. A stray bullet from the kangaroo shooters across the river. Accidental shooting. Tragic event. The whole northern bank of the river will be banned for recreational or professional shooters. Job done.'

'And if I don't?'

Robinson gave Cardilini a hard stare, then said, 'I'm not even going to answer that. You're pissed off because of what happened to your boy and want to get some of your own back. We know you went in with an agenda. You've annoyed a number of people.'

Cardilini seemed stunned, 'How do you know I went in with an agenda?'

'And I thought I could rely on you.'

'Hang on. If you know so much, why do you need me? You do the report. Leave me out of it,' Cardilini demanded.

Robinson looked to the side as if reluctant to reply then said, 'You're starting to look like dead weight around the department. And I thought it was something you could handle quickly. Keep everyone happy. Not like that robbery you've been sitting on for a week.'

Cardilini sat up straighter. 'That's an exaggeration.'

'How long do you think you can stretch that case out for?' Robinson asked.

'I have a suspect,' Cardilini evaded Robinson's question.

Robinson sat back with a sigh and pushed a bit of paper around with his finger for a moment before asking, 'What did you think of Salt?'

'I'll reserve my judgment,' Cardilini replied.

'That would be a first. Is he a good copper?'

'What do you mean?'

'Will he make a good copper?'

'Why're you asking me?'

'Come on, Cardilini I'm not asking as your super, it's just you and me talking here. The department is going to invest in this kid, send him to university; it's the commissioner's idea. He wants to know what a *real* copper thinks of him.'

'Oh, I'm a *real* copper now, am I?'

'See, obstructive. You know what I mean. Before Betty's death there wasn't any better . . .'

Cardilini stood, angry, 'I'm not listening to any of this bullshit.'

'Sit down, Cardilini,' Robinson growled. Cardilini stood defiant. Robinson relaxed, 'Okay. I know who you were and you know who you were. Let's leave it at that.'

'Okay,' Cardilini sat and asked, 'What about forensics?'

'They're down there now. Bloody McBride misplaced the body,' Robinson answered.

'Why didn't you get forensics on the scene this morning?'

'We were going to, of course, but basically talked ourselves out of it. The range from across the river fitted perfectly with the angle of the shot. And the boys would have been arriving shortly. The sixth form had exams. It just seemed a bit bloody minded to put everyone through the ringer when both the deputy commissioner and I were certain what happened.'

'How did you know about the range of the shot?'

'I rang Acorn.'

'I was just talking to Acorn and he hadn't heard of a shooting at St Nicholas,' Cardilini replied.

Robinson raised his eyebrows, 'Checking up on me, now?'

'No.'

'I didn't mention St Nicholas to Acorn. A .303 is deadly at a mile. The opposite riverbank is maybe eight hundred yards. According to Salt's notes you figured that out anyway.'

'It never occurred to you that he could have been shot from the school grounds?'

'No, it didn't occur to us. What did occur to us was that those crazy bastards across the river, that the local coppers can't seem to catch, were shooting roos at the time Edmund was shot,' Robinson said.

'Yeah. But it would make perfect cover.'

'A marksman? A .303? Hundreds of boys, twenty teachers, don't you think it would have been reported?'

'Yeah, maybe.'

'Maybe? Are you kidding me?' Robinson asked in disbelief.

'How do you know the body had been there seven hours?' Cardilini asked.

'The doctor, but anyway, forensics have it now.'

'You had a doctor there?' Cardilini looked surprised.

'Of course, you idiot. We do know a little about due process.'

'I didn't get a doctor's certificate stating death.'

'You didn't need a degree to figure cause of death on this one. However, there's a certificate in the tubes somewhere. Ask at secretarial.'

'Was your doctor an old boy of St Nicholas?'

'Yep. Seemed the best thing.'

'Yeah, yeah. Sure. And the bullet?' Cardilini asked.

Robinson looked thoughtful and said, 'A student, exiting via the fire-escape, is a possibility.'

'What was a student doing there? What time did he exit? What time was the blood left on the steps?' Cardilini asked.

'All right. Okay. I get it. Yes. In an ideal world we wait for forensics. Point taken. But the living are worth protecting, too, Cardilini.' Robinson adjusted a pen on his desk before asking, 'How's your boy doing?'

'What? Oh. Pain in the arse,' Cardilini replied.

'Working?'

'No.'

'Would he still be keen on going to the academy?'

'He would, why?'

'Just interest,' Robinson replied.

'I didn't think they would consider him now,' Cardilini said, puzzled.

'Of course . . . the right word . . .' Robinson nodded his head slightly to indicate it could happen.

'Really?'

'Yeah. He would be starting next year.'

'Are you bloody kidding me?' Cardilini sat forward eagerly.

'No. It was always on the cards.'

'But he stuffed up?'

'The right word, Cardilini, can change a lot of things. You know that.'

'Yeah, but I just thought . . .'

'Anyway. I'll leave that to you and Paul to discuss. It's a great chance. Try not to blow it, Cardilini.'

'So, what does that mean?'

'Nothing. You've got a job to do. Get on with it.' Robinson pulled a file towards him, 'And don't forget Salt, we want him to get a real sense of how things work. Mentor him.'

'I'm the last person to mentor anyone.'

Robinson replied dismissively, 'Do your job, Cardilini. I want a report, Thursday. Forty-eight hours. Now, I'll catch you later. And take Salt's notes.'

Cardilini left the super's office confused.

'Did he chew your balls, Cardilini?' Bishop yelled as Cardilini walked past.

'Paul could get into the academy,' a troubled Cardilini replied.

'I'll be buggered,' Bishop declared.

At his desk Cardilini drew a diagram of his own from Salt's notes and stuffed it into his pocket.

ELEVEN

Day 2
Kilkenny Road
9.15 p.m. Monday, 26th October 1965

When Cardilini arrived home from the pub his sister, Roslyn, and Paul were sitting in the lounge watching television.

'Robert.' Roslyn stood, smoothing her apron. 'We've already eaten. We rang the office but they didn't know where you were.'

Paul stood to face his father, 'Yes, they did. But they didn't say. You bloody know Aunty Roslyn cooks tonight.'

'Hey. Paul. Hey, mate.'

'You've been to the pub,' Paul said bitterly, 'You're a bloody drunk.'

'Paul,' Roslyn chastised.

'What, Aunty? He's not a drunk?'

Cardilini put his hand up as though to ward off an attack, 'I did. I had a drink. I need to sit down and think.'

'You . . .' Paul clamped his mouth shut and left the room.

'Paul, please. Please come back.' Roslyn called.

'Forget him. Ungrateful little . . .' Cardilini stopped, disappointed with himself, and called, 'Hey, Paul, I got something to tell you.' A door slammed. Cardilini stood awkwardly.

Roslyn observed him for a moment before turning to the kitchen, 'I'll heat your dinner.'

'Will you stay for a bit? It's much better between Paul and me if you're here.'

'No. I can't stay. It's late,' she said disappearing into the kitchen.

'You going out?' Cardilini called after a pause.

'No,' came the answer.

Cardilini sat fighting the impulse to get a bottle of beer from the fridge. 'Would you like a beer?' He called.

After a moment Roslyn stood in the doorway carrying a basket.

'Five minutes, t'll be ready. Make sure you turn the oven off.'

'I'll walk you home.'

'Don't be silly. It's a two-minute walk.'

'There might be a chance for Paul to get into the academy,' Cardilini said.

'How?' Roslyn looked searchingly at Cardilini.

'It's just a chance. I'm not sure myself yet,' Cardilini said turning aside.

'Oh, dear God, please. He needs something,' she said gripping Cardilini's arm.

'I know.'

'Robert, if you can do this, it would mean so much.'

'Yeah well . . . it's not yet . . . you know.'

'Don't say anything to him unless you're sure,' Roslyn said, 'He doesn't need another disappointment.'

'Okay.'

'And don't say anything now. You look awful. Don't you have to shave for work?' She reprimanded.

'I was in a hurry.'

'Goodbye,' Roslyn said with a sigh and left.

'Thanks. I'll turn the oven off,' he called reassuringly, and then looked back into the house. *I should have stayed at the pub*, he thought.

When he was sure she had gone he went to the kitchen, took a bottle of beer from the fridge and sat at the kitchen table. Paul stood in the doorway.

'Son, do you want a drink?'

'No.'

Cardilini attempted a friendly smile, 'You didn't mind a drink with the old man before.'

'Before, you weren't a drunk.'

'Son, you don't understand.'

'No. I understand. Everyone understands. You're a pathetic, selfish bastard.'

Cardilini pushed his chair away from the table.

'You want to hit me?' Paul braced himself.

Cardilini reacted as if punched, 'What? I've never hit you. I'd never hit you.'

'It would be easier than watching this. I told Aunty Roslyn not to bring any more meals around,' Paul left the doorway, 'And don't leave the bloody oven on again,' he yelled from the passageway before a door slammed.

Cardilini stared at the unopened beer bottle for some time. The oven timer sounded, he placed the unopened bottle back in the fridge. He drank several glasses of water then, with knife and fork in hand, sat down to eat. It wasn't long before he checked his watch, put the knife and fork on the table, covered the untouched meal with a tea towel, and walked into the passage.

'I'm going out, son. For work. I'm taking the car. Did you hear me? I'll see you in the morning. Okay?'

TWELVE

Day 2
St Nicholas College
11.15 p.m. Monday, 26th October 1965

Cardilini pulled his car up on the tree lined sand verge adjoining the riverbank 200 yards from St Nicholas College. A thin crescent moon to the north provided no illumination. Cardilini waited for his eyes to adjust. The only light came from a few college windows 500 yards away. It silhouetted the trees Cardilini had stood under during the day. He moved twenty paces away from his car. It was invisible under the canopy of paperbarks. A fleet of cars could be hidden here. The closest house was 100 yards away and completely surrounded by a yard full of tall trees. It looked abandoned. A car with its lights off could coast down the hill or come via the deserted river road, as he had done, then leave. No one would be the wiser.

He started up the road verge until he came to the stone wall on the riverside boundary. He picked his way along the wall which at this point was well over head height. One hundred yards in, and about a yard from the wall, grew a river gum. He slipped by it and continued further, the ground rising and causing the wall to fall in height comparatively. Soon he was able to pull himself up and look over. He was 15 yards past the quadrangle. The inside of the wall was inky blackness. He went a little further, pulled himself over the wall and dropped to its base, then moved back along the bottom of the embankment to where he'd been that afternoon. He sat and listened. The occasional chatter of boys reached him. He began crawling up the embankment and stopped. He was three yards from the tree he had identified as being used by the marksman when two boys came running along the top of the embankment to that exact tree. He froze. The boys squatted by the tree in silence. Cardilini was convinced they would see him and was about to stand.

One boy said, 'Look, there's some more.'

'Leave them,' the other boy instructed.

Cardilini watched as they arranged something at the base of the tree before leaving in a crouched run. He waited five minutes. No other figures appeared. Lampposts at each corner of the quadrangle were now the only illumination. Cardilini crept forward until he was at the base of the tree. Several sheets of paper were sticky taped to the trunk and others were pinned to the ground by rocks. He took a sheet from the tree and two from the ground and slipped back down the embankment. After waiting several minutes he went back the way he'd come. Shortly he was in his car and driving home.

Morning found Cardilini seated at his kitchen table. He had shaved and made himself a cup of tea. A breakfast cereal box was on the table with an unused bowl and spoon. Cardilini turned towards the kitchen door as Paul entered.

'I thought you'd gone.' Paul said.

'Do you want a cup of tea? Fresh pot.'

Paul shrugged and sat at the table looking at the cereal box and bowl. Cardilini put a cup of tea in front of him.

'Why're you doing this?' Paul asked.

'I was wondering if you had plans?'

'Oh, shit. What? You want me to shift out?'

'No. No.'

'What then?'

'A career? Work?'

'You want me to pay board? Want some drinking money?'

'No.'

'I can't drink this,' Paul pushed the tea away from him, 'You always make me feel like crap. Why do you think I wait until you leave before getting up?'

'No. Paul. Let's not do this. Please. I'm serious.'

'Are you sick?'

'No.'

'What then? What do you want out of me?'

'I just want you to be happy,' Cardilini said. A stricken expression fixed on Paul's face and he left the kitchen. His bedroom door slammed and Cardilini winced.

THIRTEEN

Day 3
East Perth Police Department
8.45 a.m. Tuesday, 27th October 1965

The three images were spread out on the desk before him. They were drawings of a figure either lying or standing akimbo. The figure's arms were raised above its head holding what appeared to be a rifle, the narrow barrel in one hand and the stock in the other. In the two drawings taken from the tree, the legs of each figure were separated but the ankles and feet were covered as if by a concrete cast. The drawing the boys had placed under a stone was cruder and the figure's feet were visible.

'Hey, Cardilini, someone to see you,' another detective called from his desk. Cardilini remembered hearing a knock and turned around to see Salt standing at the door.

'What are you doing up here?' Cardilini called.

'I was told to report to you.'

'That means you wait downstairs in the uniformed area until I want to see you.'

'I do know that. I wasn't going to come up but it was strongly suggested I should. I'm sorry.'

'Don't be sorry, don't do it. There are rules. You follow rules, don't you?'

'Yes, sir.'

'Well, go.'

Salt turned and left.

'Why are you busting his balls?' a detective called, 'It's the high-ranking uniform mob who think we should mingle.'

'Yeah, well. Life's hard,' Cardilini replied, as his attention was drawn back to the images. No facial features were even suggested, but it was the concealed ankles and feet that confused him. He stood from his desk and struck the pose in the images. He stood for some time until his arms tired.

Someone called, 'Shit, Cardilini, maybe go and get a drink.'

'Very funny,' he said and sat.

He examined each piece of paper in detail. Two of them were torn from exercise books, one was a piece of A4 file paper with hole reinforcers. Also, the diagram from the ground had half a dozen practice signatures on its reverse side. It was either intentional or the boy wasn't very bright. Cardilini determined that the name was Mossop.

He stood and marched upstairs to the top brass, tapped on Superintendent Robinson's door and entered.

'I didn't ask to see you,' Robinson said as Cardilini sat.

Cardilini dropped two sheets of paper on Robinson's desk. Robinson pulled them towards him, annoyed. He studied the sketches then asked, 'Where did these come from?'

Cardilini told the full story of his previous night's excursion. Robinson didn't say anything but stood and went to look out of the window behind his desk.

'What does it mean?' Cardilini asked.

'You don't know?' Robinson asked as he turned.

'No. I don't get it. Is it some kind of freedom symbol?'

'That's what I thought,' Robinson agreed then added, 'Have you spoken about these to anyone else? Salt?'

'No. I think there might have been another one yesterday when I was walking across the quadrangle but Deputy Principal Robson snapped it up.'

Robinson sighed. 'Prowling around the school at night. What if you'd been seen?'

'I knew I wouldn't be seen.'

'You just said you nearly were,' Robinson replied annoyed.

Cardilini matched him, 'Well, I wasn't.'

The two men stared at each other.

Cardilini sighed, 'Okay. So what are these?'

Robinson sat, his manner relaxing, 'Some kind of silly kid's thing.' He pondered Cardilini for a moment.

'What?'

'Your behaviour is starting to go off the radar, Cardilini. We've all noticed it but it seems to be getting more erratic.'

'Me?'

'You're bringing me kids' drawings,' Robinson replied frustrated, 'And where was your partner? Rule number one.'

'Salt?'

'Yes, Salt.'

'I was going to but at the time I . . .'

'Wasn't thinking clearly, I'd say.'

Cardilini tried sitting shame-faced for a moment while Robinson stared at him. Then he asked, 'Have you seen this before?'

Robinson stared at Cardilini as if making up his mind and said solemnly, 'It's just disgruntled kids, nothing to do with Edmund's death. Cardilini, think about taking compassionate leave. You've got ghosts and they're stopping you from seeing clearly.'

Cardilini looked back, dumbfounded. He knew he wasn't the copper he used to be but had never considered he wasn't capable of the job. He enquired cautiously, 'What about Paul?'

'You get yourself together and I'm sure there'll be a place for him.'

'When?' Cardilini asked anxiously.

'When the placement notices go out he'll receive one in the mail. Don't muck that up, Cardilini. Are these all the sketches?'

'Yes,' Cardilini lied, hanging his head.

'Sure?'

'Yes.'

'Now go. I'll ring tonight. Go. And if you have any desire to stay in the force, don't mention these. It's too ridiculous. You were such a good cop. But I've just about had enough.'

Cardilini walked to the door slowly, turning a few times seemingly to convince himself that this was happening. Robinson pointed to the door and mouthed, 'Out.'

Cardilini hovered at the top of the stairs. He took the remaining sketch from his pocket and studied it. Robinson had said 'just disgruntled kids'. Disgruntled, about what? Cardilini started back, then decided against it and continued towards his office.

'Where have you been?' Bishop called.

'Robinson.'

'What now?'

'He thinks I'm losing it.'

Bishop tried to remain expressionless and dropped his eyes to the paperwork on his desk.

'What? No pep talk? Not going to say, I'm a great copper?' Cardilini asked.

Bishop's expression was blank when he raised his head.

'Thanks for nothing,' Cardilini said and walked off.

He stood looking at his desk, opened a drawer and pulled out a framed photo of himself, his wife Betty, and a young Paul. He put it on his desk before returning it to the drawer.

Speaking to no one in particular he called, 'Got work to do.'

'Too early for the pub, Cardilini,' came a reply.

'That's what you think,' Cardilini said and left.

Crossing the car park, Cardilini heard running footsteps behind him.

'Should I get a car?' Salt asked.

'Not for me,' Cardilini kept walking.

'Where are we going, sir?'

Cardilini stopped and turned to Salt, 'What does your instinct tell you about Edmund's death?'

'Instinct?'

'Yes, you've heard of it?'

'Yes, sir. In the academy it's pointed out that investigating officers following their instincts not only led to a low conviction rate, but also to some dubious convictions.'

'Bullshit.'

'The information came from the Public Prosecutor's Office.'

'There you go then. They wouldn't know if their arses were on fire,' Cardilini said, hearing the belligerence in his voice. He knew he had thought the same thing. Several cases had gone through their department that he knew were suspect. But he hadn't hesitated to go drinking with the detectives when they got a conviction. He held his gaze on Salt's open, innocent expression. He imagined what Salt was seeing. He turned and started towards his car.

'Sir?' Salt called after him. But it was Betty's eyes he was seeing.

Day 3
Kilkenny Road
11.15 a.m. Tuesday, 27th October 1965

Cardilini walked into his house. Paul was lying on the couch with a book. Cardilini went to the kitchen and put a glass, a bottle of beer and an opener on the kitchen table. He took his coat off and placed it on the back of a chair and sat looking at the beer bottle. Paul walked to the door.

'Why are you home?' he asked.

Cardilini didn't answer.

'Go to the bloody pub, that's what you usually do. Don't do this here.'

Cardilini kept staring at the beer.

'Just go. Get out of here,' Paul yelled.

Cardilini placed both hands palm down on the table.

'Don't bring this home, Dad. Not to Mum's house. Just go. Go.'

Cardilini rubbed his chin and moved his palm across his mouth several times before closing his eyes and standing. He opened his eyes and grabbed the beer bottle as if it was a great weight and placed it back in the fridge. He sat back at the table again with his hands palms down as if he would violently launch himself at any moment. Paul moved to him cautiously and took the opener and glass from the table and put them away. He filled the kettle, lit a flame under it and put fresh tea-leaves in the pot, all the while looking at his father. Then he sat at the table to wait for the kettle to boil.

'What is it, Dad? What's happened?' Paul asked. Cardilini did a slow turn of his head until he faced Paul. Paul was taken aback with the intensity of his father's stare.

'Would you still like to go to the academy?' Cardilini asked.

'What? The Police Training Academy?'

'Yes.'

'But I can't now, I have a criminal record.'

'Would you still like to go?'

'But, Dad. You know I can't. Don't do this,' Paul said, wincing.

'If the conviction was voided and you were accepted would you want to go?'

'How could that happen?'

'Would you want to go?' Cardilini asked, reigning in his emotions.

'Yes. Yes. Yes. But how?'

'You making a pot of tea?'

'Yes.'

'I won't stay. I have to do some thinking. I won't take the car. I'll walk.'

'Can I take the car?'

Cardilini gazed at Paul for some time before answering, 'Yes. The academy is a long shot. Don't mention it yet.'

'But is it even a possibility?'

Cardilini ignored the question and said, 'I should be home for dinner. Maybe. But you go ahead and eat.'

'I'm going to Aunty Roslyn's. But I'm not telling her you'll be coming.'

'No. Good idea,' Cardilini said and walked out of the kitchen.

FOURTEEN

Day 3
Reabold Hill
7.00 p.m. Tuesday, 27th October 1965

Cardilini stood in a spot he and Betty had found on Reabold Hill. They would stand hand in hand and watch the sunset across the top of the scrubby banksia and wattle trees. It was here, standing beside Betty, away from the tangle of human misery that was his working life, where he had glimpsed wonderment.

Now, a defiant sun resisted its fall to the horizon. It was the first sunset he'd witnessed here since Betty's passing. After her death he'd wanted to swear denouncements to God and now figured he was close enough to be heard, even though he questioned His existence. But if there were such a character listening, Cardilini silently informed Him of what he thought of His grand plan in general, and in particular, what he thought of Him taking Betty. To ensure his message gained attention, if there was any attention to be gained, he liberally peppered it with expletives. Cardilini wondered when anyone had last spoken to the great man in such a way. But doing so gave him a sense of relief, and he smiled at the passion with which he delivered the reprimand to someone who probably wasn't even there. Even so, he couldn't help adding, *Betty was an angel on Earth and you'd better take good care of her until I get there.* He wiped away tears from his eyes as he watched the sun blinking through the gum trees.

Gum leaves, a dirty dark-green during the day, became brighter and then, as the sun sank, glowed gold. The trees became dark-waving silhouettes before disappearing altogether. The moon was yet to rise so Cardilini stumbled his way back along the path.

Kilkenny Road
8.10 p.m. Wednesday, 28th October 1965

As he walked along his street he recognised one of the brass's unmarked police cars outside his house. A knot formed in his stomach. It had been an unmarked police car that brought Paul home that time. Every fibre in his body told him to walk away and go to the pub, drink a calming pint before returning home. But, as if wading through waist-high mud, he continued along the footpath to his house. He noticed, with some relief, that his car was in the garage.

Robinson got out of the unmarked police car and stood in front of Cardilini.

'What's happened?' Cardilini asked urgently.

'Nothing.'

'Paul?'

'No. I've come to see you.'

'Is Paul home?'

'No one answered the door.'

'Come in.' Cardilini led the way into the house and called for Paul, until he saw the note on the kitchen table. *'I'm at Aunty Roslyn's. If you're not too late come over. I'm sure it would be okay. Thanks for the lend of the car.'*

'Come and sit down. Do you want a cup of tea?' Cardilini asked Robinson.

'Okay.' Robinson sat. 'Where've you been?'

'I was at the park.'

'Not drinking, I hope.'

'No.'

'You haven't had a drink?' Robinson asked surprised.

'No.'

After pausing a moment Robinson said, 'I might have been jumping the gun this afternoon. Pressure from above, you know.' When Cardilini turned his head to take in Robinson's attempt at an apology, he added, 'Jesus man. You look awful. Have a drink.'

Cardilini opened the fridge door, 'Will you join me?'

'No.'

Cardilini closed the fridge door slowly and sat.

'So,' Robinson joined him at the table, 'tell me what's troubling you about the shooting?'

Cardilini paused and asked himself the same question. His instinct told him it wasn't an accident. His instinct also told him the principal, staff and students were all liars and that there was a conspiracy at the highest level of the police force to cover up a murder. He sighed heavily. What concrete, irrefutable evidence did he base this instinct on? He looked blankly back at Robinson: Robinson, his mate. Robinson, a smart copper; a copper who only got convictions on evidence; a smart copper like Cardilini had once been.

'You're scaring me, Cardilini.'

'What if I have lost it?' Cardilini asked.

'Then I'd say, yes, go on leave, as of this moment. I know the copper you can be, Cardilini, but I'm the last one batting for you. If I'm gone, you're out.'

Cardilini realised he may have been getting chances for awhile.

'What's it going to be, Cardilini?' Robinson asked.

Cardilini turned to the fridge and studied the handle. He remembered picking it out with Betty. Their first new refrigerator.

'Yeah. Well. I better do my job,' Cardilini suggested as he turned back. He wasn't really sure what he meant by that.

'Yeah. You better do your job. Do some real policing. Evidence. Facts.'

'And what if it turns out to be other than an accident?' Cardilini asked. 'Not that I'll be looking for it,' he added quickly.

'If it's not an accident . . .' Robinson started then paused, appearing reluctant to finish. 'I hope to Christ you're wrong and so far, you've got no evidence to indicate it wasn't an accident.'

Cardilini nodded and tried to ask casually, 'The missing bullet?'

'Unbelievable I know, but we can be confident it wasn't your shooter.'

Cardilini wasn't going to argue with that.

'Do your job. Be smart. Use Salt. In five years he could be your boss if you don't get off your arse.'

Cardilini didn't like the sound of that. 'Still want that tea?'

'No. You have a couple of days to complete the report. And don't go throwing your weight around. You know it's a pathetic trick.'

'Who said –' Cardilini started aggressively but stopped, partly because he knew it to be true, partly because of Robinson's expression.

'Facts. Leave speculation to the coroner,' Robinson encouraged.

Cardilini nodded. Again he asked himself why he wasn't doing that anyway.

'Salt will pick you up the next few mornings, just like he would the top brass. Try not to spend all your time in the pub.'

'I don't need Salt, or picking up . . .' Cardilini stopped when he heard the front door close.

From the kitchen doorway came a surprised, 'Mr Robinson?'

'Paul, great to see you,' Robinson was quick to smile. 'How do you feel about the news?'

'News?' Paul asked and turned to his father.

'Dad didn't tell you? Well, I'm going to be the first to congratulate you. Tell him, Cardilini.' Robinson took Paul's hand and held it expectantly, 'Cardilini!'

'Paul, Mr Robinson has dropped by to . . .' Cardilini addressed Paul then turned to Robinson, 'Don't you think we should wait?'

'What's to wait for?'

'Paul might've changed his mind,' Cardilini replied.

'Paul, do you still want to go to the academy?' Robinson asked, still holding Paul's hand.

'Yes. I told Dad that, didn't I, Dad?'

'Yes, son.'

'There. Congratulations, you've been accepted into the '66 intake.' Robinson shook Paul's hand vigorously.

'Really?' Paul stared back wide-eyed as his grin spread. He turned his head from one to the other, 'I didn't think it possible anymore.'

'It's true, your dad and I have been working on it for a while.'
'Dad?'

'Your father had trouble keeping it secret. But we wanted to be sure. And now we're sure. Right, Cardilini?' Robinson held Cardilini firmly by the shoulder. Cardilini nodded in the affirmative.

'Is that why you came home early?'

'That's why,' Robinson filled the gap.

Paul exhaled heavily, 'This is, this is . . . fantastic. I'll go and tell Aunty Roslyn.'

'How's your aunty? Still single?' Robinson asked.

'Yes. Dad, are you happy for me?' Paul enquired, 'You look miserable.'

'He's worried about you. He's beyond happy. Aren't you Cardilini?'

Paul walked to his father and hugged him tightly. 'Thanks, Dad,' he mumbled, before turning to Robinson and shaking his hand firmly. 'I won't let you down. I won't let you down. It wasn't my fault, you know. Honestly, it wasn't my fault.'

'We know, Paul. Just needed to get a bit of water under the bridge before the record could be voided.' Robinson put his arm around Paul's shoulders and gave him a squeeze, 'Now go and tell your aunty while your dad and I finish up.'

With a last glance at his father, Paul ran out.

'He looks like he's matured bloody well. He'll make a good copper.' Robinson eyed Cardilini shrewdly, 'You'll need to set a good example.'

'If he gets disappointed now, I don't know what I'll do,' Cardilini said evenly.

'Disappointed!' Robinson checked the passageway. Content that Paul had gone he turned on Cardilini and said reasonably, 'He's disappointed he's got a drunken, fat-gut slob for a father.

But he's man enough to still give you credit, still stick by you. Any other son would have walked out months ago. Wake up. You've been a bloody drunk the last year. I sat with the boy at the East Perth lockup because you were too drunk to get off your arse. You've been given space because of Betty. Now is the time to do some police work and stop feeling sorry for yourself. And I've changed my mind, you're not to spend any time in the pub while on duty because you can't handle it. You muck this up and you can say goodbye to your career and Paul can forget about the intake. Have you got that into your bloody head?' Robinson was finished and, not waiting for an answer, strode out the door.

Cardilini threw open the fridge, grabbed a bottle of beer and then fumbled so violently for an opener he emptied the contents of the cutlery drawer onto the floor. He slammed the bottle on the table unopened and stormed out of the house.

•

FIFTEEN

Day 4
Kilkenny Road
6.12 a.m. Wednesday, 28th October 1965

Cardilini smoked several cigarettes sitting on the back step. An overcast morning sky hung above him like a sentence. The day hadn't warmed up, yet beads of perspiration spotted his face and arms. While smoking, Cardilini kept running his free hand through his hair unconsciously. He flicked his cigarette butt towards a withered garden bed then walked over and pushed it and a number of other discarded butts into the soil.

He turned and observed Paul standing on the back verandah watching him. They stood looking at one other until Paul turned and entered the house.

'Do you want breakfast?' Cardilini called, following him in.

'Yeah. Show me how you prepare it.'

Cardilini put a box of cereal on the table. They both looked at it.

'Do you eat cereal?' Cardilini asked.

'No.'

'I thought that box lasted a long time,' Cardilini pondered as he put the box away. 'What do you eat?'

'I make bacon and eggs. Just like Mum.'

'Oh, yeah.'

'Shall I make some?'

'Sure.'

'For you, too?'

'No. I couldn't. Not this morning,' Cardilini replied. 'I'll make some tea.'

Cardilini climbed into the Chief Inspector-grade car without speaking to Salt. He immediately felt confined.

'Where to, sir?' Salt asked after a pause.

'What've you been told?'

'The superintendent said to tell you that the principal, Dr Braun, would be expecting us this morning.'

'Oh, great,' Cardilini said and tapped out a cigarette.

'And to act as your driver and take notes.'

'And if I ask you not to take notes?'

'It would be better if you sent me away at those times,' Salt proposed.

'Who's instructing you?'

'Superintendent Robinson.'

'Why do they want you in on this?'

'I believe I was the only constable available.'

'And I suppose you believe in Father Christmas?'

'Pardon?'

'So, you report to Robinson?'

There was a moment of silence before Salt answered, 'If he asks, sir.'

'Yeah,' Cardilini replied, unconvinced, lighting his cigarette.

St Nicholas College
8.30 a.m. Wednesday, 28th October 1965

The cloud cover had burnt off and Cardilini was sweating profusely by the time they arrived at the school. Salt parked the car under the shade of a eucalyptus and waited for Cardilini's instruction. Arriving students stared at the car and its occupants. Cardilini seemed reluctant to move. Finally he opened the door and pushed his weight through. He stood and stretched, looking down onto the hockey field. His moist shirt clung to his back. He pulled it away while he watched the students pass. Few made eye contact and those who did only furtively. He shook his head and sighed before walking towards the administration block. Salt locked the car and followed him.

Cardilini paused as they reached the quadrangle, 'Do you notice anything, Salt?' Salt took in the students, the quadrangle and the view to the river but didn't reply.

'The trees,' Cardilini prompted, and continued walking.

Miss Reynolds greeted Cardilini, 'He's expecting you.' And giving the slightest nod to Salt, she opened Principal Braun's door.

The principal stood and came around his desk to greet Cardilini with an outstretched hand, ignoring Salt. Cardilini took the hand and shook it, guardedly.

'I'm sorry about yesterday. We got off on the wrong foot. I was out of my depth. Captain Edmund's death shook all of us more than I realised, me included. I think I just wanted it not to be true,' the principal said as he retreated behind his desk. 'The boys and their parents had to be informed, we've done that, and thankfully shooting is now banned from the north shore of the river.'

'Why do you think such a shot hadn't happen before?' Cardilini asked.

'Good question,' the principal conceded. 'It's never been a problem. The wall along the riverside was always considered high enough to completely protect the school. Obviously not for those four upper rooms, however. Besides, the farmers were considered responsible. They always have been in the past.'

'Right.'

'Keeping the parents uninformed creates rumours. So, naturally, you have our full cooperation to curtail any speculation. Please take a seat.' Braun indicated a chair.

Cardilini sat, his stomach knotting and perspiration running down his face. He mopped at it with his handkerchief.

'I'm sorry I had to go over your head, but your manner . . . it's difficult for an outsider to understand how fundamental, to all of us, the school's reputation and exemplary name is.'

'I'm beginning to understand,' Cardilini answered.

'I know. So where would you like to start?'

'The armoury.'

Braun shot Salt a startled glance but Salt had his head down. 'Why? That doesn't seem reasonable.'

Cardilini pulled a crumpled and now damp sheet of paper from his inside pocket and read, 'Forty-two .303 *Lee Enfield number 4 Mk 1 rifles. Two Owen Machine Guns.*'

The principal stared back blankly. 'That was Edmund's area. It might take a while to organise that.'

'That's all right, I can wait,' Cardilini said calmly, feeling a slight panic internally. Why was he doing this?

'I'm not sure how to go about it.'

'Do you have a key?' Cardilini asked.

'Well,' he picked up the phone, 'Miss Reynolds, come in here, please?' He replaced the receiver looking at Cardilini.

Miss Reynolds entered. 'Do we have keys to the armoury, Miss Reynolds?'

'We might have, but they would be among Captain Edmund's possessions.'

'Right. That's what I thought. While I think of it, that break-in we had a while back, did that get reported?'

'Yes.'

'Was the armoury also entered?' Braun asked.

'It hasn't been mentioned, sir,' Miss Reynolds answered.

'The armoury?' Cardilini asked.

Braun replied, 'Yes, some of the local louts pried open the canteen door which is near the armoury. When was that, Miss Reynolds?'

'Nearly two weeks ago, it's in your diary,' she replied.

Cardilini glanced at Miss Reynolds who stood looking stony-faced at the principal.

'So. We don't know how long it will take to find those keys but I will inform your office once we do. So, that's underway.' The principal gave a slight shooing motion and Miss Reynolds left. He turned brightly to Cardilini, 'What's next?'

Cardilini slowly folded the sheet of paper and returned it to his pocket, 'I see the trees adjoining the quadrangle have had the lower branches lopped.'

'Yes. It was reported by a teacher that boys were seen climbing the trees.'

'Okay. Could I speak to that teacher?'

'I don't know who it was,' Braun answered.

Cardilini looked back stubbornly.

Braun dialled his phone, 'Miss Reynolds, who reported the boys climbing trees? I see.' He hung up.

'It wasn't recorded. The pruning was a simpler solution than constantly patrolling the area.'

'Could you ask the staff?'

'No. Boys are always climbing the trees.'

'Where was the report of the theft made?'

'We deal with East Perth.' The principal consulted an open page of his diary. 'That was on the 14th of October.'

'Fine. What's next on the list, Salt?' Cardilini asked, wiping his forehead.

'You wanted to finalise a report on the room, sir.'

'That makes sense. Thank you, Salt. Well, we'll leave you now. Don't mind us. There's a teacher and some students we will have a chat with later.'

'Who are they? As you know the body wasn't discovered until the next morning. And the sound of distant rifle fire wasn't unusual. Sometimes, it sounds quite close but that's to do with the inversion layer, I've been told. As I'm sure you know. So no one witnessed the shot.'

'I have to confirm that for the report. So, perhaps, if I could speak to the boarding master who was on duty that night and a random selection of say, two boarders?'

'Fine, I'll arrange that.'

'No. I mean randomly selected by me. So, a list of boarders, please?'

'Is that really necessary?'

'Yes,' Cardilini tried to sound reasonable but at the same time asked himself why he was acting so bloody minded. *Why risk my and Paul's future?*

* * *

A troubled Cardilini and Salt entered Edmund's room unescorted. Cardilini took off his coat and moved a chair to the window and sat.

'Take off your jacket if you want, Salt.'

'Yes, sir,' Salt replied and remained standing, unmoving.

'So, what do you make of all that?' Cardilini asked.

'I'm not sure.'

'Let me know when you are,' Cardilini said, taking out a cigarette.

'Everything he said is perfectly plausible.'

'Perfectly. So how would you proceed from here, Salt?' Cardilini shifted his chair so he could look out the window.

'I'm not sure what we're investigating, sir.'

'Neither am I. Wasn't that in your lessons, Salt?'

'Not that I recall. Are we still doubtful the shot came from across the river, sir?'

'Who's asking?' Cardilini asked turning to Salt. Salt averted his eyes. 'Difficult, isn't it, playing both sides, Salt?'

'Yes, sir,' Salt answered non-committedly.

'They've thought of everything.'

'Or, they are simply stating the truth,' Salt replied.

'Or that. But it would be nice to find that out for ourselves. Don't you think?'

Salt contemplated before asking. 'Don't you believe what they've told us, sir?'

'No. Do you?'

Salt looked out the window then back to Cardilini before replying, 'Yes.'

'How handy. Please, tell me what's so convincing.'

'The alternative is that someone intentionally shot Captain Edmund,' Salt said flatly.

'That's right, exactly.'

'What would be the motive?' Salt asked.

'Were you in the cadets, Salt?' Cardilini asked ignoring Salt's question.

'No, sir.'

'Neither was I. Mind you, they didn't have cadets at the school I attended. And I couldn't swear they had teachers either.'

'Yes, sir.'

'The boarding master on duty the night of the shooting and the students, Carmody and Mossop, that's who we're going to talk to.' Cardilini instructed.

Salt made an entry in his notebook.

'And we'll have a look for the keys while we're here,' Cardilini gestured Salt towards the desk.

'Yes, sir.' Salt started going through the drawers. 'Would it be worth going to the armoury?' he asked.

'Yes. And why would we do that, Salt?'

'To examine any signs of a forced entry.'

'Yes, that should be interesting. We'll get that deputy to show us, I think. But keys first.' After a while Cardilini stood and stretched, 'Any luck?'

'No, sir.'

Oppressive heat greeted them as they crossed the quadrangle with Deputy Principal Robson.

'In for a storm,' Robson said.

On the other side of the quadrangle they walked down to the basement level of the buildings behind the dining block. A series of roller doors were raised to reveal a manual arts workshop. Further along was a canteen with similar roller doors also raised.

'That's the woodwork room and that's the canteen. One of the roller doors on the canteen had been pried open,' Robson said before turning right and going to a timber door boarded with iron strips. He pointed to the door, 'The armoury.'

Cardilini inspected the door. It didn't appear to have been tampered with. 'What made Braun think there might have been a break in at the armoury?' Cardilini asked.

'I didn't know he thought that,' Robson replied.

'Surely he would have told you.'

'I'm on the academic staff,' Robson shrugged and opened his tin box to push some cigarette butts around before selecting one. Cardilini watched this for a spell then offered one of his own, which Robson accepted. Cardilini lit both their cigarettes.

'What did you do immediately after discovering Edmund?' Cardilini asked.

'I rang the principal.'

'Not the police?'

'No.'

'Not an ambulance?'

'What would've been the point of that?' Robson asked.

'What happened when the principal arrived?'

'I followed the boys to the rowing shed. They went about their business. Then I took them back to the dining hall. They all had bacon and eggs. A special treat for the rowers. Captain Edmund usually joined them.'

'And then?'

'The principal asked me to stand guard at the top of the stairs. Your colleagues had arrived by then.'

'When did the school find out?'

'Morning tea, the teachers were told.'

'Told what?'

'A stray bullet struck Captain Edmund.'

'How did you feel about that?'

'I'm not sure what you're asking,' Robson replied.

Cardilini moved on, 'Then what happened during the morning?'

'You arrived and tried to push us around with your swearing and belligerent manner,' Robson replied evenly, looking at Cardilini.

'That didn't get me far,' Cardilini said with a glance to Salt. Salt was taking notes. 'Got that, Salt?'

'Yes, sir.'

Robson butted a half-smoked cigarette out and placed it in his tin box, 'The principal has that list of boarding staff and students you wanted. If we may go back?'

'Sure,' Cardilini answered.

'No one knows where Captain Edmund kept the keys,' the principal informed them, 'which is a concern. However, here are the lists you asked for. I feel I must guide you so you don't waste your time or that of the staff and students.'

Cardilini scanned the lists, 'Fine. Let's see. I'll speak to Mr Abbott. Jot that down, Salt. And students? A sixth former, Carmody. Jot that down, and second former, Mossop.'

'I wouldn't waste your time with Mossop. I know the boy. Not very bright. Can be troublesome.'

'I'll try and manage.'

'Pick another,' the principal suggested.

'No need.'

'Make sure you take notes, please, just in case the parents should inquire,' Braun said.

'I've my own personal dictaphone.' Cardilini gestured to Salt.

'Very well. Miss Reynolds will show you the room to use.'

SIXTEEN

Day 4
St Nicholas College
11.35 a.m. Wednesday, 28th October 1965

The room had an adjoining wall to the principal's offices and windows that opened out onto the cloister beside Miss Reynolds's office. Cardilini noted someone could, if they so desired, sit below the windows and eavesdrop on any conversation taking place.

Cardilini turned and said, 'Keep an eye on those windows, Salt, we don't want anyone listening in.' Salt and Mrs Reynolds shared a brief glance.

Cardilini entered the classroom followed by Miss Reynolds. A shudder went through him. Hardwood chairs sat behind desks with inkwells arranged with military precision. He imagined himself sitting halfway up the room, the fat kid. He walked to the front of the room and read the tightly scripted writing covering the blackboard.

'History,' he said over his shoulder.

'Shall I send for Mr Abbott, Detective Sergeant?' Miss Reynolds asked.

'Did you enjoy your time when a student at school, Miss Reynolds?' Cardilini asked as he turned.

'Very much. I was at an all-girls' school. I cried bitterly when it was over.'

'Have you been tempted to return to an all-girls' school?'

'Yes. But this was my first position after secretarial college. I've been here thirty-five years.'

'Surely there must have been positions available?'

'There were opportunities but by then I felt loyal to St Nicholas. I still do.'

'And I'm the one trying to tarnish the school,' Cardilini said.

'It would appear so.'

'Yes. Send for Mr Abbott. And thank you, Miss Reynolds.' Cardilini watched her turn and leave. When she had walked past the windows he said to Salt, 'What do you think?'

'They are very loyal to the school, which is commendable . . .' Salt paused.

'Go on.'

'It's possible their loyalty is hampering their responses to the investigation.'

'Starting to feel played are you, Salt? Never mind. It's a big world,' Cardilini said and started pacing the front of the class. Shortly Mr Abbott tapped on the door. He was a slight man in his thirties, with closely cropped thinning brown hair, rimless round spectacles, grey trousers, white shirt, and an unusually colourful tie. He stood as if at attention.

'Come in.'

Abbott walked past Salt with a brief nod. Salt took a seat at the side of the class.

'Please, take the teacher's chair,' Cardilini said.

'Not necessary,' Abbott replied.

'Okay, I'll take it. Pull up a chair.'

Abbott stared briefly at the students' chairs then chose one, brought it to the aisle and sat.

'Tell me how the evening of the twenty-fifth proceeded from, say, seven p.m.?' Cardilini asked with a nod to Salt.

'All the boys are in their prep classes at seven p.m.'

'Prep?' Cardilini asked.

'Preparatory. Time for the boys to complete homework and do general study in their form classrooms.'

'So there is no one about the grounds?'

'There shouldn't be. A roll is taken, the boys sit in their forms and teachers are present.'

'Which form were you responsible for?'

'I was the duty-boarding master. I was in the staffroom.'

'That's the room next along from the principal's offices. Windows facing the quadrangle?'

'That's right. I was doing some marking. No students were sent down for discipline.'

'What happens when they're disciplined?'

'Depends on the teacher.'

'Just give me a range then?'

Abbott took a quick glance at Salt who was busy with his notebook. 'They can be caned. Some teachers give them a sharp smack on the head, others give them detention.'

'What do you do?'

'What I feel is justified,' Abbott said, straightening his shoulders.

'Continue with the evening.'

'It was quiet. At eight the second form finished prep and went to the boarding house. I went over and to make sure they had gone to the bathroom and were ready for bed. At eight-thirty I spoke to them to make sure they were all in bed and then I turned the lights out.'

'What did you say to them?'

'I'm not sure. What I say depends on what's been happening. It could have been about an upcoming sporting or academic event. It could've been anything. I'm just trying to settle them down.'

'Then what?'

'I stayed in the boarding house for the rest of the night, mostly in my duty teacher's room. It's on the second level of the building to the left from here.'

'Are all the boarders housed there?'

'Yes.'

'Go on.'

Abbott continued recounting how the third through to the fifth form went to bed. He added, 'The sixth form are given more leeway in organising their own study timetable due to their exams. But it's lights out for them at eleven.'

'Did you see Captain Edmund that evening?'

'No, he wasn't on duty that night.'

'Did you hear or see anything unusual?' Cardilini asked.

'Yes. There was shooting across the river. It wasn't particularly loud but my room faces the street. At one point the boys whose dormitories faced the quadrangle were creating a ruckus.'

'At what time was that?'

'Just before eleven. I went to quieten the fourth formers on the second level.'

'What was it about?'

'Sometimes the retort of the shooting can sound very close. Sound can travel in funny ways. They settled. I went to several other dorms on the second level and I could hear senior boys downstairs doing the same thing. I was back in my room by eleven forty-five. I don't have to get up for sports in the morning but the boys were abuzz when they were showering. I had to quieten them. Then I heard about poor Captain Edmund. I hope this will be sufficient to cease the roo-shooting.'

'It was. Was Captain Edmund liked by the boys?' Cardilini asked.

'Being liked isn't a wise aspiration for a teacher in a boarding school.'

'How did the boys regard him?'

'They respected him. He was very thorough, very fair I think, but would not tolerate any nonsense or . . .' Abbott sought for words.

'Or?'

'The boys had to behave like young men, not children. He didn't like boys who weren't loyal or didn't fit in.'

'Could you give me an example?'

'Captain Edmund expected the boys should all muck in and not think themselves special.'

'How did he go about this?'

Abbott gave a quick look at Salt before speaking, 'Just normal punishment. He is – was – a tougher teacher than me.'

'Are you an old boy?'

'No.'

'Do you have any doubt in your mind that this was an accidental shooting?'

'No.'

'If Captain Edmund discovered the armoury broken into and a rifle missing, the same night the canteen was broken into, how do you think he would proceed?'

'The canteen break-in was weeks ago. It was local louts. And it's not the first time. He would have reported it straightaway. He would take that sort of thing personally. But it wasn't broken into so there wasn't a rifle missing.'

'How do you know that?'

'They have cadets just about every day of the week, they march with their rifles.'

'Each boy has a rifle?'

'I don't know, but it would be obvious if one was missing.'

'Would it?'

'Yes, with the competitions, the shooting competitions. A number of years running our boys won the Schoolboys' State Marksman Awards.'

'How about that?' Cardilini mused observing Abbott, 'Any other questions we had for Mr Abbott, Salt?'

'The keys to the armoury,' Salt said.

'I've told Dr Braun this already. Captain Edmund didn't keep the keys to the armoury in his room. It's possible some of the senior cadets might know where they are.'

'Got that, Salt?'

'Yes, sir.'

'Great. Thank you, Mr Abbott,' Cardilini said, standing.

'I've been instructed to get Carmody when I leave. May I ask why you chose Carmody?'

'Random selection.'

Abbott stood and glanced again at Salt. Cardilini walked with Abbott to the door, shook his hand and returned to his chair.

'Can I ask what you are thinking, sir?' Salt asked.

'I'm thinking speculation is not necessarily good police work. No more speculation, Salt. Let's just follow facts.'

'Yes, sir.'

'You haven't changed your style of note taking, I hope.'

'No, sir.'

* * *

Carmody entered the room and stood for a moment, scrutinising Salt with expressionless brown eyes. He then walked to the front and sat on a desk.

'Carmody,' he announced.

Cardilini smiled broadly, taking in the handsome, even features and dark hair. 'Thank you. I chose names at random just so I could get a sense of what boarders recalled of the evening.'

'I would have thought I was randomly selected because I had a falling out with Captain Edmund,' Carmody replied coolly.

'Really?' Cardilini said with a look to Salt, 'That sounds like a good reason, too.'

Carmody gave a brief glance to Salt before saying, 'Let me save you some time. It was an accidental shooting, from across the river.'

'You heard the shooting?'

'We all heard it.'

'One shot in particular?'

'One shot in particular at about eleven p.m. sounded close, but then they do at times,' Carmody said.

'The inversion layer?'

'That's right, sound bounces off a heavy layer of moist air.'

'So. No doubt?' Cardilini asked.

'No doubt.'

'Do you think it's possible that if someone knew this, they could disguise their own rifle fire?' Cardilini asked.

'No. We're all farmers' sons, a shot this side of the river, if you're suggesting that, would be too obvious,' Carmody replied with steady eyes on Cardilini.

'And the falling out with Captain Edmund, what was that about?'

'He wasn't strictly a captain,' Carmody corrected.

'Okay. The falling out?'

'A dispute over the use of the term, "loyalty".'

'Go on,' Cardilini said and affected an interested expression.

'He considered loyalty to be strictly defined according to his parameters. I saw it differently. It was unresolvable. He spoke against my nomination for head boy because of it.'

'Were you bitter about that?' Cardilini asked tilting his head.

'Annoyed, rather, that the other staff were bullied by him.'

'Bullied?'

'He was loud. Overbearing. Machiavellian. He didn't like to be crossed,' Carmody replied.

'Why did you speak to my constable?'

'Your presence here isn't doing anything for the boys' stability, it's leading to misunderstanding and speculation.'

'Are you in the cadets?'

'I was.'

'Until?'

'The disagreement at the end of last year.'

'Do you know where the keys to the armoury are kept?' Cardilini asked.

Carmody didn't answer.

Cardilini continued. 'How would a team of men breaking the armoury door down suit the stability of the boys?'

'I can show you where the keys are. It won't do you any good,' Carmody replied.

'Did you know a rifle was stolen?' Cardilini asked.

'Was it reported?'

'I don't think it was.'

'Then it wasn't stolen. I think you will find all rifles accounted for,' Carmody said.

'How would you know?'

'I know – knew – Mr Edmund.'

'Did you know that from a study of a bullet we could reveal the specific gun that fired it?' Cardilini asked.

'But you would need the bullet,' Carmody replied and then added, 'I'll show you where the keys are if you like.'

'First get Mossop, then show the constable their location,' Cardilini instructed.

'Mossop will be worse than useless,' Carmody said, 'unless you want to talk to the stupidest boy in the school.'

'It might be a pleasant change.'

Carmody looked steadily at Cardilini then turned and left.

'Arrogant prick,' Cardilini said.

'Yes, sir. Do you think all the rifles will be there?'

'Don't know. But I bet they've all been cleaned recently.'

'Are you developing a theory, sir?'

'Can't help it,' Cardilini replied.

'How did he know there isn't a bullet?'

'One of the boys overheard a conversation. They could've even overheard the super. I've done it myself. For some reason I thought children didn't listen or aren't interested. Big mistake.'

'I thought he might have it,' Salt said.

'That means he would have been the first to the room.'

'Yes, sir. I wouldn't put anything past him,' Salt said looking towards the door sharply.

'Speculating, Salt? Tut, tut,' Cardilini said.

'Mossop,' Carmody announced.

'Thanks, now go with Constable Salt,' Cardilini said.

Mossop had a face like a dinner plate. His eyes were wide apart, his close-cropped hair highlighting ears growing like mushrooms from his large head. A broad mouth was forced permanently open by wayward teeth clasped in large steel braces. He stood in the doorway, legs spread like a sailor.

'Mossop, let's go for a walk.' Cardilini walked past Mossop out to the quadrangle and stood on the lawn.

Mossop stared at him wide-eyed before joining him, 'We're not allowed on the lawn,' he said spinning his head around to see if anyone was watching.

'You don't have a choice.'

Cardilini walked to the centre of the quadrangle with Mossop following and sat on a low wall encircling a large lemon-scented gum tree. 'Take a seat.'

Mossop sat a little distance from Cardilini, still looking around to see who was watching.

'I want you to see something,' Cardilini said, pulling the sketch from his pocket, 'The other night you placed this at the base of that tree. Why?'

'No I didn't,' Mossop answered sharply.

'Your name's on it,' Cardilini said.

'No it's not.' Cardilini turned the sheet over. 'Oh. That side. Yeah, well,' Mossop said.

'You were seen.'

'No we weren't.'

'Placing a rock on it.'

'Who saw us?' Mossop asked.

'Does it matter?'

'I want to know who dobbed.'

'It wasn't a student,' Cardilini replied.

'Oh. Will I get into trouble?'

'What does it mean?'

Mossop looked around before indicating the lemon-scented gum tree under which they sat, 'These trees drop their branches.'

Cardilini turned and looked up at the tree, 'When?'

'Anytime they haven't enough water.'

'Stupid place for it then,' Cardilini said.

'That's what my dad said,' Mossop said smiling.

'So what does this sketch mean?' Cardilini persisted.

'What?' Mossop asked, looking to the tree.

'The sketch.'

Mossop pondered for a moment, 'I don't know.'

'Why do it then?'

'We saw another one and thought it meant something, so we did one too.'

'But yours is different.'

'No it's not,' Mossop replied affronted.

'What do you think it means?'

'No idea. Aren't you going to ask me about Captain Edmund?' Mossop asked enthusiastically.

'What would I ask?'

'If it was a shooting accident?'

'Was it?'

'Yes,' Mossop replied sharply very pleased with himself.

Cardilini looked at Mossop for a moment before asking, 'What did Carmody say to you?'

'He said not to disgrace myself.'

'He didn't tell you anything else?'

'No.'

Cardilini looked across to the boarders' dormitory block, the broad tall windows with limestone surrounds and a giant portico. He wondered what brief the architects were given and wondered the effect these grand traditional surrounds would have on a growing child.

'How do you know it was a shooting accident?' He asked.

'Everyone says so.'

'Carmody?' Cardilini asked.

'Yes.'

'You respect Carmody?'

'Yes. Everyone does. He won't even let the teachers hurt you, like Mr Willet, who would always slap me on the side of my head. One time when Willet hit me, Carmody said to him, "Mr Willet, I think that's enough, don't you?" Then he told me not to use Mr Willet's nickname anymore.'

'Did Mr Willet stop hitting you?'

'Yes.'

'What's his nickname?'

Mossop, surprised, said, 'I'm not allowed to say it.'

Cardilini nodded and smiled. He turned his eye around the quadrangle again. Did these grounds, buildings, uniforms and traditions tell the students they were special, superior, destined to lead those that attended the crumbling, asbestos-ridden public schools? The buildings were certainly telling Cardilini that he hadn't taken his education seriously. In fact, apart from a few students and fewer teachers, no one had taken education seriously at his school. Did anyone ever mention going on to university? He couldn't remember. He smiled, acknowledging he was feeling envious of Carmody. No wonder he didn't like him.

'Good lad,' Cardilini said.

'I'm thinking of being a policeman. Why don't you wear a uniform?' Mossop asked Cardilini.

'I'm a detective.'

'I'd wear a uniform, like Salt.'

'You should talk to the constable then. Did the rifle shot startle you?'

'No. I was asleep. We're on the other side of the boarding house, but plenty heard it. They had to be sent back to bed.'

'So, no ideas about what you drew? What if you were a policeman, what would you say?' Cardilini asked.

'I think it's something to do with Lockheed. He was expelled,' Mossop said a little sheepishly.

'When was Lockheed expelled?'

'Last year. Carmody stuck up for him.'

'Was Lockheed a cadet?' Cardilini asked.

'Yes, sir.'

Cardilini had sent Mossop back to class and was still seated when Salt approached him.

'You got the keys?'

'Yes, sir,' he replied, handing the keys to Cardilini.

'Where were they?'

'In a recess near the armoury door.'

'That seems very lax.'

'"Loyalty is stronger than locks." Captain Edmund's saying, sir.'

'Where's Carmody?'

'Gone back to class.'

'Did he speak to you?'

'He's quite serious about our presence causing speculation that's unsettling to the school.'

'Right. You didn't go into the armoury, did you?'

'No, sir.'

'You go to the car. I'm going to stop by Edmund's room.'

When Cardilini returned to the car he had an armful of files, 'Off we go. I've some "prep" to do.'

Salt gave him a sideways glance, 'Where to, sir?'

'Home for me. You'd better go back to East Perth.'

SEVENTEEN

Day 2
St Nicholas College
12.55 a.m. Monday, 26th October 1965

The boy heard voices coming from the boarding house. He with-drew behind the administration block. He wanted to run for the hockey field, but he stayed still and shrunk into the shadows. The voices stopped, his breathing stopped. He ran to the other end of the building and near the fire-escape steps he looked out into the quadrangle. He saw two figures, one creeping, the other walking slowly along the path near the gum trees. He recognised the walking figure. Both soon disappeared into the dark beneath the gums. He watched, breathless, with the shape sharp in his palm. He searched the shadows, and saw movement again, both figures walking briskly towards the canteen. One carried some-thing long, narrow at one end and fat at the other: a rifle. He felt the bullet firm in his hand. If he ran behind the dining block that made the fourth side of the quadrangle he could watch them come down. He dashed into the shadow of the hockey field to avoid the light from the cloister. His feet felt like they weren't touching the ground. He sprinted along the rear of the dining block to the far side of the science building which had the canteen, the woodwork department and the cadets' armoury in its basement. Captain Edmund's armoury.

Perched near the canteen 30 yards from the armoury, he felt the cold cement flattening the soles of his feet as if trying to push him from the earth. The sky, the endless night, calling him to fly like a skyrocket, to burst into a million sparks of light then drop black, invisible as ash. He waited, eyes straining. Nothing. Silence. Until his eyes found a thin sliver of light below the armoury door, a scalpel cut of yellow in the darkness. He sat still, hugging his knees and staring, a fist thumping in his chest telling him he had hope.

EIGHTEEN

Day 4
Kilkenny Road
1.15 p.m. Wednesday, 28th October 1965

'Dad, I got a job,' Paul announced on his father's arrival.

'How?' Cardilini put the files on the kitchen table and turned to Paul.

'I applied, and I didn't need to mention the charge,' Paul wasn't able to suppress a smile.

'Okay. Where?'

'Lakeway Drive-in.'

'Oh.' Images of the drive-in, summer nights, Paul as a child in the front between him and Betty. He pushed them from his mind.

'It's a job that I could keep doing once I go to the academy.'

'You get paid at the academy,' Cardilini reminded him.

'Dad, I know what the pay is. What if I want a car?'

'We've got a car,' Cardilini said too gruffly as he felt a shift in the earth.

'My own car.'

Cardilini paused for a moment, then shook his son's hand.

'That's wonderful. So when do you start?'

'Friday and Saturday nights. Then they'll see how I go.'

'I'm sure your bosses will be pleased.'

'Yep. I'll make sure they are.'

'You tell 'em your old man's a copper,' Cardilini said and then felt stupid.

'Dad, don't be dumb.'

'A job, fantastic,' Cardilini replied but felt the opposite. He hadn't realised how much Paul being at home or being angry at him was a grounding for him. He knew if he didn't have Paul around he would happily drink himself to oblivion. He started towards the fridge and froze before turning back to Paul.

'Yes. You wanted me out of the house and working,' Paul said with a look of concern.

'Did I?'

'Dad?'

'Maybe.'

'They're going to give me a uniform and a hat. Remember when we went with Mum, the people behind the counter?' Paul asked.

'Yep. Sharp uniform.'

'Yeah. So what are you doing home?'

'Just some homework,' he pointed to the files.

'Do you want some lunch?'

'Lunch? What do you do for lunch?'

'I make a sandwich. I'll make you one.'

'My stomach's a little upset. I might miss today. You go ahead, I'll take this into the lounge.' Cardilini gave his son a pat on the back and took the files. He had an overwhelming desire to flail, to fly off the handle and storm to the pub. They could all go to hell.

'I'll make a cup of tea,' Paul called down the passage.

Such a surge of emotion hit Cardilini that he thought he was going to cry. Taking a gulp of air he pushed at the feeling. He hadn't been sober for this long in nearly a year. He sat and looked at the files as if reading them, but the words were blurring. *I'm falling apart*, he thought.

Captain Edmund was thorough. Every cadet had a file. Every file had the complete details of the cadet, even blood type. Edmund had written reports on each student every term. Both Lockheed and Carmody had a termination date on their file with the comment, 'Failure to accept authority'.

Lockheed was expelled from the school a week after that date. Cardilini checked for Lockheed's address.

'I'm going out and taking the car,' Cardilini called.

'It would be good if you could come to Aunty Roslyn's for dinner tonight.'

'We'll see,' Cardilini said and started for the door.

Claremont
2.45 p.m. Wednesday, 28th October 1965

Lockheed lived in Claremont. Cardilini pulled up at a single level red brick house with a 'For Sale' sign in the front yard. He knocked. A woman in a blue blouse and slacks opened the door. A dark blue band held her blonde hair back. Thin wrinkles gathered under her eyes giving her attractive face a harried expression.

'Yes?'

'Mrs Lockheed?' Cardilini asked watching her wary eyes.

'Yes.'

'Detective Sergeant Cardilini.'

'Yes?' Mrs Lockheed asked without a hint of interest.

'Is your son home?'

'Yes. Why?'

'You heard about the death of Captain Edmund?'

'Yes.'

'We're following up on any student who had a falling-out with him,' Cardilini tried to capture an official tone.

'Why?'

'Just procedure.'

'I heard it was an accident,' Mrs Lockheed shifted her weight and looked past Cardilini uninterestedly.

'That's right, Mrs Lockheed, that's what we're thinking. Nothing to worry about. He was a strict teacher.'

'That's not all he was.' Flint cracked in her eyes.

'Meaning?'

'Nothing. It would just be perfect for them if I was to say anything to you now.' Mrs Lockheed started to turn aside.

'Them?'

'The school principal and my husband for starters. Anyway, let's get this over with,' she gestured him into the house, 'we have a lot to do.'

'The school principal and your husband?' Cardilini asked.

Mrs Lockheed turned a stony gaze to Cardilini and walked down the passage into the kitchen. As he followed, Cardilini noted boxes in various stages of being packed in the side rooms. In the kitchen a slender teenager wrapped glasses in newspaper.

'Detective Sergeant Cardilini, John. The detective is following up with students who had a . . . falling-out with Edmund,' Mrs Lockheed said acidly as John looked questioningly to her.

'If you have any information that might assist,' Cardilini said to Mrs Lockheed. She narrowed her lips and shook her head in the negative. Cardilini looked to John. He watched his mother.

'John,' Cardilini said.

'Yes?'

'Why were you excluded from the cadets?'

'This is ridiculous, you know why,' Mrs Lockheed jumped in, 'I'm sure the whole school population knows why. And if you don't know, ask them, it's their story.'

'No one has told me anything,' Cardilini said. He was trying to understand the situation but nothing was making sense.

'Did you ask them?'

'Failure to accept authority, is what's written in John's file,' Cardilini replied.

'Really? And is that why he was expelled? Is that why we've both been publicly humiliated and his father . . . oh. Do whatever you have to do, but we're not going through that again.'

'What? What happened?'

'The principal will give you the answers. That's how it works, isn't it? You'll all get together and make up what you want. I know. My husband's a St Nicholas' old boy. So are the deputy police commissioner and the superintendent. I know exactly how this will end. Experts have taught me. You're an amateur, Detective,' She spoke with such venom that Cardilini took a half step back. John sunk into a kitchen chair.

'John. John. Don't. You have nothing to be ashamed about. It's them. They should be ashamed. Don't, John. Stand up,' Mrs Lockheed urged her son while her eyes filled with animosity. 'Get on, and get out,' she snapped at Cardilini.

'Mrs Lockheed, John, I'm completely at a loss. Was John's expulsion something to do with the cadets?'

'I don't believe it. Who sent you?' Mrs Lockheed demanded.

'No one sent me.'

'Then why are you here?'

'I need to discount an intentional shooting.'

'And we're prime suspects?' Mrs Lockheed laughed maniacally, 'Of course. But that would make our complaint true, wouldn't it? If I went to the trouble of shooting the bastard? But then if I could shoot someone I wouldn't have stopped with him,' Mrs Lockheed threw the words at Cardilini, her eyes cutting him so sharply he looked away.

'Mum. Please.'

'No, John, I would have shot him. And I'd like to believe someone did shoot him intentionally. Then I might be able to believe in justice again.'

'Mum. Mum, please.'

'Why would you want that?' Cardilini asked, confused.

Mrs Lockheed looked at Cardilini as if seeing him for the first time. Then slowly, as if a new idea was occupying her thoughts, she asked 'Why do you need to discount an intentional shooting? It was an accident. Wasn't it?'

'An accident is the current official conclusion.'

'But you don't think that? Why?' Mrs Lockheed put her arm around her son's shoulder.

Cardilini looked at the two similar faces challenging him and thought of Betty and Paul. He shook his head, 'I haven't said that.'

Mrs Lockheed stroked her son's shoulder, 'Sit down,' she said, 'ask your questions.'

Cardilini took his time pulling out a chair opposite the pair. Mrs Lockheed sat beside her son.

'A boy, Carmody, insists the shooting was an accident,' Cardilini finally said.

'That's interesting. He's the only person I would trust at that school. What's your question?' Mrs Lockheed asked.

Cardilini searched in his pocket and withdrew the sketch, which he smoothed with his hands while saying, 'A number of sketches have been secretly placed at the base of a tree in the quadrangle.' He pushed the smoothed sketch across the table. The boy involuntarily jerked his head and shoulders back.

'There, there, John,' she patted him on the shoulders and raised her eyes to Cardilini, 'You're either a complete and utter bastard or you're completely stupid,' Mrs Lockheed said flatly.

Cardilini didn't discount either one.

'You have a question?' she asked.

'I don't know what it means,' John said.

He stood and walked out of the room shaking his head. Mrs Lockheed watched him leave then turned stark eyes to Cardilini, 'I will, never, never forgive those who did this to John. And that includes Edmund. I despised the man.'

Cardilini sat back in his chair no closer to understanding the situation. Mrs Lockheed turned from observing Cardilini and called, 'John, please come back. We're not going to be beaten by these people. Come back.' John entered the kitchen and stood rigid. 'None of this is your fault. It's these people who are despicable, John. Remember that.'

'Yes, Mum.'

'Do you have a question?' she demanded of Cardilini.

Cardilini struggled to ask his question, 'Can you tell me what this represents?'

Mrs Lockheed turned to her son who shook his head.

She turned back to Cardilini, 'It's a discipline. A tradition, apparently. As punishment the cadets are required to stand with their rifles above their heads. It becomes very painful eventually, I'm told.'

'I see,' Cardilini retrieved the sketch and put it in his pocket.

'You came for that? No. They want to know if I still believe my son,' Mrs Lockheed accused Cardilini.

'Mum. No. Please.'

'John. It was that man.'

'Can I go then? I can't . . . I can't . . . please.'

'Will you stay in your bedroom, please, John, until I come?'

'Yes.'

'I won't be a moment. Don't worry.' Mrs Lockheed watched through the kitchen doorway until she heard a door close. When she turned back to Cardilini, she had a tear running down her cheek. She made no attempt to conceal or wipe it away. Cardilini found it difficult to look at her.

'Do you have children?' she asked.

'A son, Paul, he's eighteen.'

'I have three children. John was our shining light, forging the way ahead for his brother and sister. Now he won't leave his room. The other children think their father left because of him. None of this has been of our own making.'

Cardilini looked at her, wanting to help but completely at a loss.

'John has lied to me on occasions. On this occasion he isn't lying. He hasn't the cunning to make the story up. If his father weren't such a weak man he would know that, too. Captain Edmund followed a school tradition in using this punishment. I believe records were kept as to how long a boy could stand like that. But Captain Edmund decided to add –' Mrs Lockheed stopped as if her words were caught in her throat. Then with laboured breath she continued, 'to challenge the boys further Captain Edmund would unbutton the boys' trousers and push their trousers and underwear down to their ankles.' She swallowed heavily several times as more tears tracked her cheeks. 'He explained that this was how it happened in the army and if any of them had any aspirations to one day defend their country and their mothers and sisters –' she stopped again and steeled herself for what was to come. Cardilini wanted to reach out, to comfort her but he sat spellbound, almost breathless.

Mrs Lockheed continued. 'Then to ensure they were made of the right stuff, he proceeded to flick their penis. A boy at this time might "fail to accept authority." To the poor children who did continue, Edmund would push the end of his baton between the boys' buttocks . . . and that is all I can say. I believe he continued in other ways; very, very evil ways.' She closed her eyes, her face tense, and pushed at the tears running down her cheeks. 'We have attended three young men's funerals over the years. One recently. A very high number I would think. The St Nicholas men won't tell you this. You would need to talk to the mothers and they mightn't tell you either. Now please, see yourself out.'

She stood and left the kitchen. Cardilini heard her whispering, 'John,' and the opening and closing of a door. He sat staring at the chair Mrs Lockheed had vacated.

NINETEEN

Day 4
East Perth Police Department
3.30 p.m. Wednesday, 28th October 1965

'What happened to you?' Robinson asked as Cardilini dumped himself in a chair in the superintendent's office.

Looking at Robinson, Cardilini knew he was possibly jeopardising Paul's placement at the academy. But the eyes of Betty and Mrs Lockheed haunted him, forcing him on, Betty demanding he be the policeman she loved and trusted and his belief that the truth would ease the anguish and fear in Mrs Lockheed's eyes. For his own redemption too, he could not give up; to accept defeat or accede to pressure was to guarantee he drink to his demise.

'You look awful,' Robinson said.

Cardilini watched Robinson's expression turn to alarm and felt a small, encouraging voice say this was the only way to his and Paul's renewal.

'The Lockheed boy was expelled for accusing Edmund of abuse,' Cardilini said evenly.

Robinson stared uncertainly at Cardilini.

'You knew?' Cardilini asked.

'Of course.'

'And . . .?'

'It was dismissed as malicious rubbish.'

Cardilini was trying to dismiss the image of Mrs Lockheed's anguished eyes, 'Was it?'

'Yes,' Robinson said firmly, 'Braun spoke to Edmund.'

'How do you know all this?'

'I happen to be on the school board,' Robinson said, daring Cardilini to say anything.

Cardilini considered Robinson for a moment before asking, 'When will the autopsy report come in?'

'Probably already completed, check your pigeonhole occasionally. And a copy will go to the Coroner. What're you expecting?'

'Calibre of the bullet,' Cardilini replied.

'Either .308 or.303 I heard,' Robinson replied.

'They have a bunch of .303s at the school.'

'So?'

'McBride was convinced it was the type of entry .303s make,' Cardilini said.

Robinson shrugged, 'How would McBride know?

'The war. I guess. I didn't ask.'

Robinson shook his head and sighed.

Cardilini said, 'Acorn could test the school rifles for recent firing.'

'Do you think the roo-shooters are borrowing the school's rifles?' Robinson asked dumfounded.

'Yeah, that's what I think. What do you reckon? Am I onto something?' Cardilini shot back.

'I reckon I need a good reason to pull Acorn in on this.'

'Could Acorn detect if a rifle had been fired?' Cardilini asked.

'Has anyone checked the rifles since the shooting?' Robinson asked.

'I don't know. The principal and teachers didn't know where the keys to the armoury were. Only a senior boy did.'

Robinson paused before snapping out, 'You can't give it up, can you?'

Cardilini glared at Robinson. 'I didn't know we had a choice.'

Robinson sighed, 'And when this proves pointless will I get my report?'

'Yes,' and Cardilini nodded his assurance.

'If I make this call I will also have to call and calm a lot of nervous people,' Robinson warned, 'Are you sure you aren't just being bloody minded?'

'I'm sure I'm not being bloody minded,' Cardilini replied, hoping that to be the case.

'If it proves you are . . .' Robinson left the words hanging as a threat over Cardilini before picking up his phone and dialling. 'Hi Acorn. Robinson. Cardilini wants you to . . . how many rifles, Cardilini?'

'A bunch,' Cardilini said.

Robinson directed, '"A bunch" of rifles need to be examined for recent firing at St Nicholas College.' Then, shaking his head said to Cardilini, 'Forty-two. He told you.'

Cardilini shrugged.

'Acorn, what's it going to take to find out if any have been fired in the last four days?' He looked at Cardilini and shook his head as he listened. 'No. No. This isn't *Ben-Hur*. Can someone get out there and if there's any suggestion one has been fired we'll proceed from there.' He listened for a moment, then to Cardilini asked, 'Have there been any cadets using them since the shooting?'

Cardilini shook his head.

'No,' Robinson said into the receiver. He listened for a while longer.

'Good. Cardilini will be in touch,' he said and hung up, 'Okay?'

'Thanks.' Cardilini stood.

'And don't upset him. You know what he's like.'

'I'm a new man,' Cardilini assured Robinson, and left the office.

St Nicholas College.
4.30 p.m. Wednesday, 28th October 1965

'How come you have this grade of car?' Acorn asked, sitting in the passenger seat as Salt drove him and Cardilini to St Nicholas College.

'No idea,' Cardilini said from the back seat, 'Do you know, Salt?'

'I put your complaint about the other car on the record, sir,' Salt said.

Acorn turned and raised his eyebrows at Cardilini.

'Good boy, Salt,' Cardilini said flatly.

They pulled up in the St Nicholas car park.

Robson, in his shapeless grey suit, stood smoking and waiting for them. He pinched his cigarette out and returned it to his tin.

'Robson,' Cardilini said and nodded.

'Cardilini, I've been sent to escort you.'

'Very decent of you,' Cardilini answered.

'Are you ill?' he asked Cardilini.

'No. Senior Sergeant Acorn this is Dr Robson, Deputy Principal.' They shook hands as Cardilini started towards the armoury.

'You look awful,' Robson said to Cardilini.

Can't be as bad as I feel, thought Cardilini.

When they arrived at the armoury Robson asked if they would be powdering for fingerprints.

'Any point, you think?' Cardilini asked.

'No, half a dozen staff I know tried the door since we realised the keys were missing,' Robson said with a smile, 'but it seemed the sort of thing you might do to create a little more drama.'

Cardilini threw the bunch of keys to Salt, 'There you go, Salt. Earn your wages.'

'Are they our keys?' Robson asked.

Cardilini nodded, 'What are the chances of St Nicholas retaining their permit for rifles if there's no system of security?' Cardilini asked Acorn.

'That's viewed very seriously,' Acorn said with such an expression of meticulous determination that Robson stepped away.

'I'll be over here if you need me,' he said.

'No need to stay.'

'I'll be here, anyway.'

'Open, sir,' Salt called from the armoury door.

'Okay. Senior Sergeant Acorn will do his magic,' Cardilini said.

Acorn, wearing soft gloves, entered the armoury and flicked on the lights followed by his torch. He then unlocked a steel rod that passed through the trigger guard of the first half dozen rifles. Withdrawing the first rifle from its rack, he opened the breech, placed the butt on the floor and shone his torch into the breech while looking down the barrel. Cardilini walked to Robson and offered him a cigarette.

'No, thanks.'

'Do you have a son? Cardilini asked.

'Yes. I've a sixteen-year-old,' Robson replied.

'My boy's eighteen. Does yours attend St Nicholas?' Cardilini asked.

'Yes.'

'Do you get a discount?'

'No. I pay full fees due to the exorbitant salary they're paying me,' Robson said dryly.

'Tough.'

After a pause, Robson said, 'I don't think my boy's impressed with me. How about yours?'

'I know my boy isn't impressed with me. For good reason though. But I'm working on it.'

'How do you do that?'

'Well. Just started. I'll let you know how I go,' Cardilini said and offered his packet again. Robson took a cigarette with a shrug.

'Filthy habit,' Robson said.

'Tell me about it.'

They both inhaled and exhaled in satisfaction.

'What do you hope to find?' Robson asked, indicating the open doorway.

'Now? Honestly? Nothing.'

'Is it just because, "we think we're better than the rest"?'

'What's that?'

'That's what you said isn't it?' Robson asked and exhaled.

Cardilini laughed and wandered back to the armoury doorway.

He stood and pondered how Robson would know he said that. He tried to remember when he had said it and to whom. He must have been overheard. Then he remembered he'd said it to Salt after Miss Reynolds had left the room. But how would Robson know? Had he said it loudly? It occurred to him he hadn't. Maybe Salt told someone? It's a small city, particularly if a St Nicholas boy heard it. Maybe there were more than two of them in the police force. Good chance.

Forty minutes later Acorn switched off his torch and stood in the doorway looking at Cardilini.

'Can I speak freely?' Acorn asked.

'Salt, stay by the doorway. We'll wander over there,' Cardilini said and walked some 30 yards away before turning to Acorn, 'What is it?'

'Nothing.'

'What?'

'Nothing. Apart from the fact that all rifles, bar one, had been cleaned a few weeks ago. Dust gathers in the barrels. Not sediment from the shell, but dust. Even though I'd give the armoury a nine out of ten, as it's quite airtight, dust still gets in. Also after time the oil used to clean the barrel has a tinge, some say a sheen, it's more of a tinge for me. But fresh oil is quite discernible.'

'Fascinating.'

'Yes. All bar one.' Acorn took out a piece of paper and read, 'one, one, three, one, seven, two,' looking expectantly at Cardilini.

'What?'

'The serial number of the very recently cleaned rifle. Now, I would say it's very unusual, in a cadet situation, for one rifle to be cleaned separate from the rest. Uncalled for, even. If at inspection the cadet was required to re-clean his rifle, it would be done on the spot. All rifles are locked together: no exceptions. Captain Edmund, by his records, you can tell a lot about a man by his records, by his note taking,' Acorn, raised an eyebrow here, not wasted on Cardilini, 'was a meticulous man. If you were such a man, you'd have at your fingertips, or close by, the records, so that you'd know whom rifle one, one, three, one, seven, two belonged to, the date the rifle arrived at school, and when it was last fired.'

'Really? Why?'

'So you could identify the student who is currently responsible for it.'

'Good point,' Cardilini conceded.

'Shall I give this information to your constable?' Acorn asked.

'I'll take it,' Cardilini replied quickly.

'You'll lose it and I will have to tell you again. I know Salt, he is a meticulous record keeper and note taker. It's rather obvious why he's with you.'

'Why?' Cardilini asked as his stomach tore at itself.

'His record keeping, Cardilini. You're going to waste this information, aren't you? And that fellow is right – you look dreadful, see a doctor.'

'Acorn, walk with me for a minute.'

'If necessary.'

Cardilini stretched out, trying to ease his stomach, but the knot started to crawl up his throat until he thought for a moment he might pass out. He all but staggered to the tree he wanted and leant against it.

'What?' Acorn demanded.

'Second level, building across the quadrangle, window third from left.'

'Yes?'

'That's where your friend lost the top of his head.'

'I didn't say he was my friend.'

'Okay. He must have been standing at the window. And the shot came from across there?' They both turned and looked at the opposite bank of the river.

'Eight hundred yards,' Acorn said.

'Yes.'

Acorn wandered beyond the tree in both directions and stood with his hand to his mouth looking up at the window.

'What do you think?' Cardilini asked.

'What do you mean? Be specific, for heaven's sake, Cardilini.'

'Is it possible?'

After a considerable show of investigation Acorn said, 'A .303 is lethal at a mile. A stray shot, missing a kangaroo is possible. But the kangaroo, if that's what they were shooting, would have needed to be about ten to fifteen feet high. As that's an unlikely scenario, the shooter must have fallen backwards as he was firing. No wonder he hasn't come forward.'

'If you wanted to shoot Edmund how would you go about it?' Cardilini asked.

'Is this what you call policing?' Acorn frowned.

'Humour me.'

'No.'

'Okay. If someone knew their rifle well, knew their skill level well, knew where the keys to the armoury were, and wanted to shoot Edmund, how would they go about it? Your scenario? Please.'

'A cadet couldn't get his hands on the keys to the armoury,' Acorn stated as an undeniable fact.

Cardilini knew different. 'Please, Acorn. I'm dying here.'

'Will you see a doctor?'

'I'll see a doctor.'

'An experienced rifleman, or a cadet for that matter, would know exactly what he was capable of at two hundred yards. It's a length they train at. So he would pick a spot that distance, he would take into account prevailing wind, air density and perhaps light. He'd need an anchor point, like a tree.'

'This tree?' Cardilini pointed to the tree he hung off.

'That would only be a shot of about a hundred and eighty yards.'

'Does it make a difference?'

'Everything makes a difference.'

'Go on.'

'But, yes, this would be a convenient tree. A branch where that cut is would be okay, if he was tall enough.'

'How tall?'

'He'd need to be over five foot. But, he would have to be a serious marksman. A very serious marksman. One in hundreds. Highly sought after in the services. But it's impossible to disguise the sound. A .303 has a crack that could wake the dead. So back to a fifteen-foot kangaroo. Can I go now?'

'Yeah. Thanks.'

'Any point in taking the rifle?' Cardilini asked.

'Not until you have the bullet. Anyway the scenario is ludicrous,' Acorn stated and started back towards the armoury and Salt.

Cardilini slowly followed.

TWENTY

Day 4
Kilkenny Road
9.00 p.m. Wednesday, 28th October 1965

Cardilini sat at his kitchen table. Having been through Edmund's records he'd identified the four most successful marksmen. He rang Acorn.

'Cardilini, it's nine p.m.'

'Acorn, I identified four cadets who achieved tight clusters of three around the bullseye.'

'Impressive.'

'Is it?'

'The fact you're still working, yes. The clusters are great for a cadet. But they aren't the ones you're looking for. How far did you go back?'

'These are current students.'

'Any assigned the rifle identified?'

'No, the three boys that use it can't hit a barn door at two paces.'

'But you must ask what could possibly provoke that sort of reaction towards a teacher? Where's the motive?' Acorn quizzed. Cardilini didn't answer, so Acorn continued, 'I suppose probability would suggest at some point St Nicholas produced a marksman of the skill required.'

'Okay. Thanks, Acorn.'

'Good luck.'

Cardilini replaced the receiver and started to gather the files, mentally noting he would make a list of all past students who had been assigned the rifle. Unlike Acorn, Cardilini he knew teenagers who were capable of every variety of adult crime.

Paul came into the kitchen. 'Dad, there are some boys to see you. I put them in the lounge.' Cardilini stared back curiously but Paul only shrugged. Cardilini walked past him into the lounge. Two St Nicholas boys stood as he entered. One was Carmody.

'Hello, boys. This is a surprise.'

'Hello, sir.'

'A bit late to be out and about isn't it?' Cardilini asked.

'Just on our way back to school. Burnside is a day boy and I had leave to be with his family tonight,' Carmody replied.

'What can I do for you? Sit down.' The boys sat back on the couch, Cardilini sat in an armchair and Paul leant against the doorframe.

'Detective Sergeant Cardilini, this is Burnside, he's head boy at St Nicholas,' Carmody said.

'How do you do?' Cardilini reached out his hand; Burnside got up and shook it. 'This is my son, Paul.' Burnside and Carmody shook hands with Paul then resumed their seats. Paul sat in the other armchair.

'Sir,' Carmody began, 'I hope you don't find it too unacceptable that we've come in this manner.'

'I do find it unacceptable, but, now you're here, you better tell me why.'

'We had dinner with John and Mrs Lockheed this evening.'

'Go on.'

'Mrs Lockheed said she recounted to you what John had told her regarding Captain Edmund.'

Cardilini, with a glance to his son, nodded. Carmody and Burnside exchanged expressions.

'John was ultimately expelled for refusing to retract his accusations,' Carmody said.

'So I heard.'

Carmody and Burnside appeared hesitant.

'We were wondering if you believed John's story?' Carmody asked.

'What story, Dad?' Paul asked.

'It's a case I can't discuss yet. Sorry, son. Carmody, Burnside, do you believe him?'

Again they hesitated. Carmody took a deep breath and exhaled.

'No, sir.'

Cardilini leant back in his armchair and studied the boys. *Why was it so important they came here to tell me this? Their faces, so intent, so filled with purpose.* He knew he did believe Mrs Lockheed, because she believed it, but he also knew that what she believed could be wrong, and very likely it was.

'So why would John make up such a story?'

Carmody and Burnside looked at each other and, turning back in unison, shook their heads. Cardilini was now convinced they were lying. *But why? What do they know? Who are they protecting?*

'Why are you so keen for me to disbelieve him?' Neither replied. 'Well?'

'Your interference is unnecessary, we know Superintendent Robinson completed a thorough investigation,' Burnside said.

Cardilini shrugged noncommittally.

'Were you on the Eric Edgar Cooke case? Hanged last year?' Carmody asked.

Burnside looked sharply at Carmody.

'Yes,' Cardilini answered taking in Burnside's reaction.

'What were your feelings about his execution?' Carmody asked and received another sharp look from Burnside. Cardilini sat looking at Carmody, Carmody met his gaze.

'Time to go boys. Don't come here again,' Cardilini stood. 'That's official.'

Paul turned in surprise to his father.

Cardilini continued, 'I'm not sure what you think you're playing at but this isn't a game. A man's death isn't a game.'

'We agree with you, sir,' Carmody stated as he and Burnside stood.

Cardilini shook his head and walked to the front door, which he opened. Carmody and Burnside shook Paul's hand again and left with nods to Cardilini.

Carmody stopped abruptly on the porch and turned, 'I'd appreciate it if you didn't trouble Mrs Lockheed any further.'

Anger rose in Cardilini's chest. He shut the door firmly on the boys.

'What was that?' Paul asked.

'Arrogant little pricks.'

'What? Dad?'

'The bloody gall. The bloody gall. That boy just invited a shit storm.'

'What? They seemed fine.'

'Stay out of this, son. You wouldn't understand.'

'I wouldn't, but two schoolboys would?'

'That's enough. I've got to think,' Cardilini left Paul and went to the kitchen. Before he realised it, he'd poured himself a beer.

'I thought you weren't drinking.'

'I'm not. I don't need you telling me what to do. I get enough of that everywhere else.' To prove his point he drunk the glass down and poured another.

'Don't do that here. Go to the bloody pub.'

'I'll do what I bloody like,' Cardilini thundered.

'Drunk,' Paul spat out and turned away.

When the front door slammed, Cardilini bellowed, 'Good riddance.'

Day 5
Kilkenny Road
2.00 a.m. Thursday, 29th October 1965

A marked police car pulled up outside the front of Cardilini's house. Light was in every window and spilled through the open front door. Two constables climbed from the car and stood conferring before walking up the driveway. They called out at the front door several times without response. One constable left the porch to walk around the side of the house while the other entered. They both arrived at the backyard at the same time.

There Cardilini, still in his work clothes, mumbling and cursing to himself, was turning the earth with a spade in what might've once been garden beds. Covered in dirt and sweat, he wiped his eyes with his forearm and plunged the spade into the dirt, pushing the spade deep before turning the sod and moving to the next spot.

'Detective Sergeant Cardilini. Sir. Detective Cardilini.'

Cardilini looked up. 'Fuck off.'

'Sir. You must stop. Complaints have been made.'

'Fuck 'em. Fuck 'em.'

'Please, sir. Please. Detective Sergeant Cardilini.'

'Who the fuck are you? I don't know you.'

'We're from East Perth. Can we go inside?'

'No, you can fuck off.'

'Would you come with us, please, sir?'

'No. I left off doing this for twelve months. I'm not going to stop now. I'm not going to stop. I've got to get it done.' Cardilini continued his digging.

The constables conferred quietly then asked, 'Can we help?'

Cardilini stopped digging and turned to view what he had completed. He started laughing to himself and staggered backwards, 'You idiot. Done the wrong bit.' He collapsed onto his backside holding the spade to stop himself from toppling further. 'Look,' he pointed to the constables, 'that's supposed to be lawn. Betty's going to . . .' Cardilini paused and squeezed his eyes closed.

'Sir. Would you come inside, please?'

Cardilini tried to focus on their faces, 'Oh yeah, you're at East Perth. You're Salt's mates, eh?'

'Yes, sir, Fowler and Riley.'

'Yeah. So what do you want?'

'It's after two in the morning.'

'Oh, yeah. Okay. Well. A bit noisy, eh?'

'Yes, sir.'

'Someone rang up?'

'Yes, sir.'

'Good boys. Good boys. Yeah. I might go and lie down.'

Cardilini had trouble rising so the constables assisted him to stand then they walked together up the back verandah stairs. At the back door Cardilini stopped and indicated he was fine to walk. The constables stood back.

'I might have a shower. Make yourself a cup of tea, boys.'

'Shall we sit in the kitchen while you shower, sir? We'll put the kettle on.'

'Yeah,' Cardilini stood still at the back door, 'No. I might lie down for a bit.' He turned to a large timber-framed couch that sat on the verandah facing the backyard and settled himself full length, his head on one armrest and his feet on the other.

The constables stood watching for a few minutes.

'What do you think?' one asked.

'He's asleep.'

'Might as well have a cup of tea.'

The other nodded and they entered the house.

TWENTY-ONE

Day 5
Kilkenny Road
6.00 a.m. Thursday, 29th October 1965

At sunrise Cardilini blinked his eyes open, staggered to the laundry on the back verandah, drank from the tap and stripped off his filthy clothes. He stared at them on the floor then, shaking his head, put them in a tub for soaking and headed to the bathroom.

Showered and shaved, he tidied and swept the kitchen, put the rubbish out and forced some cornflakes down, accompanied by four cups of tea. Only slightly recovered he returned to the kitchen table with Captain Edmund's files before him.

Paul interrupted him at 9 a.m. 'There's an unmarked car and driver out the front.'

'Last night . . .' Cardilini started.

'No. I'm moving to Aunty Roslyn's. You're a disgrace. The neighbours told me what happened last night. The academy won't want me now. Anyway, I don't think I could go.'

'I'm sorry.'

'That hasn't meant anything since . . .' Paul shook his head and went to his bedroom.

Cardilini sat with his eyes shut, his stomach knotting and his head roaring. When composed he picked up the files and stood at Paul's door.

'I know I'm a disgrace, I know what your mother would think, but I want you to know . . . I am trying to turn things around.' Cardilini stood a while longer then headed for the front door and the car at the verge.

'Salt,' He said as he sat.

'Sir.'

Cardilini closed the car door.

'Where to, sir?'

'Did you hear about my performance last night?'

'Yes, sir.'

'How bad was I?'

'Calls started at the local branch at midnight. I think you were out in the backyard then. A senior constable at East Perth sent the car around.'

'How bad?'

'No damage. The constables stayed about an hour or so. It was a slow night.'

'Was a report made out?'

'No, sir.'

'You thank those boys for me.'

'No disrespect, sir, but I'd rather not.'

'I beg your pardon?'

Salt sat silently staring forward.

'Can you explain yourself?'

'I'd rather not, sir.'

'You think I should be on report?'

'I'd rather not say, sir.'

Cardilini turned and looked at his house. The front lawn, once immaculate, was now dying in patches. The rosebushes along the fence, without their winter prune, were wild and snarled and reaching out across the footpath. 'It's a bloody mess, and I forgot about the roses. Okay. East Perth, Salt.'

'Yes, sir.'

'And Salt, get that old, beat-up, shit-box of a car back again.'

'Yes, sir.'

* * *

Acorn watched with pen poised as Cardilini spoke. 'Two years ago, St Nicholas had a cadet who won state marksman awards two years running. Captain Edmund had recorded every score the boy achieved over a three-year period. The boy, Williamson, had been assigned rifle number one, one, three, one, seven, two.'

'What were the boy's scores?' Acorn asked.

'He regularly produced groups of five at two-hundred yards.'

'How regularly?'

'Jesus, Acorn.'

'You want me to make a judgment? How regularly?'

Cardilini pulled a sheet of paper from his pocket and counted, 'Seven from twelve his first year, nine from ten his second year, plus winning the state school boy titles.'

'A farmer's son, familiar with shooting a .303, no doubt.'

'No. Lives in the city.'

'A natural, perhaps. But I don't think it was a marksman that made that shot, I think it was a stray shot. Target shooting is usually at the chest. That's how cadets train. Never a head shot. In your scenario the shot would be intended for the chest, and .303 is a kill-shot in the chest, so the shooter missed his target. Either way Edmund's death was the result of a miss-shot, which supports strongly a miss-shot from across the river.'

Cardilini didn't need to hear that, but he should have known. He was missing too much. What else was he missing? And why was he pursuing this line on the shooting? What hard evidence did he have? Scuff marks on a tree, a tree in a school playground full of boys, boys happy to sneak around at night wouldn't be too afraid to climb a tree. And yet, he was trusting McBride or wanting to trust him.

'It would be the height of arrogance to attempt a head shot from that distance. And you said the boy left school two years ago. It would take training to achieve that shot, or lucky arrogance.'

'I have a candidate for the arrogance,' Cardilini said, thinking of Carmody.

'Can he shoot?'

'Fair to middling.'

'Was it his rifle?'

'No, but could he practise with it? Knowing the results it produced for Williamson?'

'I'm sure that's the sort of thing school cadets could do. Captain Edmund might have even encouraged it among his better marksmen.'

'Would it make a difference to their accuracy?'

'Possible.'

Cardilini looked at his notes.

'I think your assassin scenario is shot full of holes,' Acorn said smugly.

'It would seem so.'

'The defence could come up with any number of army instructors that would see it my way. Wouldn't look good in court.'

Cardilini nodded, sighed, thanked Acorn and left.

Back at his desk a spade lay across his chair. He stood looking at it for some time, gradually the heads of his colleagues turned to watch him.

'Actually, that's pretty funny.'

A general round of applause and laughter greeted this. 'So, how are you brushing up, Cardilini?'

'Getting there,' he said with a sheepish smile and shifted the spade to the side of his desk before sitting.

'You can keep the spade. It was bought out of your share of the Christmas fund.'

'Great,' he said and patted the spade, 'I might just leave it here.'

'Cardilini,' Bishop called from the open doorway, 'you're wanted upstairs. Superintendent Robinson.'

Cardilini knocked on Robinson's door.

'Yeah. In you come. Sit down. You aren't making this very easy, Cardilini.'

'No, sir.'

'"No, sir?" Since when have you called me, sir?'

'Since now.'

'Sucking-up is not going to do you any good.'

'It's not sucking-up.'

'Fine. I should put you on report.'

Cardilini nodded in agreement, 'Do it, put me on report.'

'What?'

'I need a kick up the arse for last night.'

'Still don't mind telling me my job it seems,' Robinson said.

Cardilini shrugged.

Robinson looked quizzically at Cardilini, 'on report, means you can't afford to muck up.'

Cardilini replied dismissively, 'I know what it means.'

'Right. You're on report, three months. That's going to make a few people happy. And get a few of the new wave off my back,' Robinson said perfunctorily and sat looking at him, 'Now, you got something for me?'

Cardilini shifted to one side of the seat then the other before replying, 'I was just about to type it up.'

'Accidental?'

Cardilini ran his fingers through his hair and squeaked out, 'Yes?'

'Is that what you think?'

Doubt gripped Cardilini as he stared at Robinson. He wanted to say yes, he wanted to get back on track, see Paul happy again. He knew that after last night, if he had any super other than Robinson, he could easily be on suspension.

'Yes . . .' he croaked out and despite everything couldn't help adding, '. . . and no.'

Robinson looked towards the ceiling and ran his hand across his brow. 'You got evidence the prosecutor would accept?' Robinson asked, pulling a diary towards him.

Cardilini shook his head then said, 'Students going out of their way to insist it was an accident. Students protecting someone.'

'Your opinion.'

'The sketches?'

'A protest? A celebration? Who knows what goes through the head of a schoolboy?'

Cardilini's eyes narrowed as he looked at Robinson, 'You do. You were there. What did you think?'

'You don't dob on your mates, you don't break ranks, you take it like a man and get on. That's what the boys are taught and that's what they're doing,' Robinson said.

'Right,' Cardilini couldn't argue with that.

Robinson fingered the pages of his diary as Cardilini looked on anxiously. Robinson slowly closed his diary and casually asked, 'Do you want someone else to look at it?'

A wave of relief went through Cardilini and he tried to reply equally casually, 'Might be good.'

'Really?' Robinson asked shocked.

'Yeah. Acorn's convinced the shot came from across the river and I've really got nothing. I'll type up the facts we've got.' Cardilini sat up and breathed fully for what seemed like the first time in ages.

'Thank God for that.' Robinson gave a rare smile.

'I'll get to it,' Cardilini said standing.

Robinson cautioned, 'Going on the facts the next copper will see it the way myself, the deputy commissioner and now Acorn see it.'

'Yeah. I know,' Cardilini nodded and left.

Cardilini set the report in triplicate in his typewriter. Despite his fingers poised over the keys, he sat looking at the spade leaning against the side of his desk. Then, as if waking, he pulled a dog-eared Teledex from his desk drawer. He flicked its pages until he found the one he wanted then pulled the phone towards him.

'Goodman, it's Cardilini. A favour. Can you check if a Bradley Williamson, born August 1947, was either conscripted or enlisted? St Nicholas, that's him. The second. What's basic training? What's he doing now? Rifleman, what does that mean? How intense? Where? Swanbourne? Sydney? Vietnam?

When? Really? Okay. No, you're not missing anything here, same old, same old. Yeah. Cheers. I owe you.'

Cardilini hung up and studied the notes he'd made. He dialled again.

'Acorn. How would a second-year army recruit, who's been doing specialist training in the rifle corps for eighteen months, suit my scenario?' Cardilini listened then replied. 'The one I told you about who won the state schoolboy titles two years running. Yes, but could he make that shot?' Cardilini held his patience. 'Could he, if he wanted to, make it? Could he? Good. Could a defence attorney find a specialist to argue against that possibility, probability? Thanks.'

Bentley
11.10 a.m. Thursday, 29th October 1965

Fifteen minutes later, with Salt driving, Cardilini travelled to a home in Bentley.

Salt pulled up beside the verge.

'Wait here. I might only be minutes,' Cardilini said as he got out of the car.

Cardilini opened the low, white-picket front gate. Yellow roses were blossoming the length of the front fence. Red brick paving separated two expanses of tidy green lawn and led to the front timber verandah. Cardilini knocked on the flyscreen door while he looked at the nearby potted plants and a couch and armchairs placed to face the street. He shook off images of Betty's neglected garden.

The front door opened and Cardilini focused his eyes to see through the flyscreen into the gloom of the house.

'Yes?' A woman's voice asked.

'I'm Detective Sergeant Cardilini from the East Perth Station. I wanted to have a chat to Bradley.'

'Bradley's in the army.'

'Yes. I know, but isn't he home from training before going back to Vietnam?'

'He goes to the Swanbourne barracks every day.'

Cardilini stepped back as the flyscreen door opened. A woman of forty or so stepped onto the verandah wiping her hands on a tea towel. Her brunette hair with thin lines of grey was swept back from her forehead and tied with a ribbon. She's been baking, Cardilini figured, a fine dusting of flour was on her apron.

She looked out to the police car with Salt at the wheel. 'My husband's at work.' Unsure, pretty, hazel eyes looked up at Cardilini, 'Do you want to come in? I can make you a cup of tea.'

'No, thank you. Do you know when Bradley will be home?' Cardilini asked.

'I don't know. Do you know when he goes back to Vietnam, Detective Cardilini?'

'No. Sorry. Haven't you been told?'

'No. They won't say. It's very nerve-racking. Please come in, you've come all this way.' Mrs Williamson stepped aside.

Cardilini looked past her down the hallway. No, he didn't want to know these people; he wanted their son to be a murderer. He shuddered inwardly at the thought.

'No. Really,' he said shaking his head.

'Why do you want to talk to Bradley?'

Cardilini didn't have the stomach for another Mrs Lockheed episode.

'It's nothing. Just finalising a report. Bradley might be able to fill in some blank spaces.'

'Is it about Captain Edmund's death?'

'In a way. Yes.'

'It was a shock to us all. When Bradley arrived home, he hadn't heard because he was travelling, he couldn't believe it. Bradley was a favourite of Captain Edmund's.'

'Travelling?'

'Home from his base in Sydney. He'll fly back there when we get a date,' she sighed deeply, 'We're proud of Bradley, but people are starting to say hurtful things about Vietnam. It's not the boys' fault. Do people expect them to go to prison for not going? I'd like to ask those protesters if they would do Bradley's prison term.'

'Was Bradley a conscientious objector?'

'No. What do you think, should our boys be going over there?'

Cardilini remembered the nervousness he had about the possibility of Paul being conscripted. He hadn't thought about the right or wrong of it. He just knew he didn't want Paul to go to Vietnam.

'How does Bradley feel about going?'

'He just said his mates were going and he had to be with them.'

'Did he enjoy his time at St Nicholas College?'

'Yes. Very much. He was a prefect. He was captain of the first eleven. He won two state schoolboys marksman trophies.'

'What did he want to do before being conscripted?' Cardilini asked, as he formed a picture of the boy arriving home in his school uniform, telling his parents he had been elected prefect, bright shiny faces greeting him, loving him. Could he pull a trigger and kill a man?

'He wanted to do law but didn't get the grades. He might have been a policeman. Standing up for his mates was very important to him,' Mrs Williamson said with a tinge of regret in her voice.

'It seems a St Nicholas trait.'

'The last principal was a wonderful man, the boys adored him.'

'When did Braun arrive?'

'Bradley was in the fourth form, so four years ago. Sure you don't want that cup of tea?'

'And Captain Edmund?'

'Same time. Both Victorians. A lot of us couldn't understand why we were getting a Victorian principal. It didn't seem right.' She looked up to Cardilini with a quizzical expression, 'He wasn't a St Nicholas old boy.'

Cardilini looked into her eyes and saw Betty's. He often tried to fight the compulsion, mainly with alcohol, but sober, something in his chest wanted to reach out to total strangers. Mrs Williamson waited on his reply while viewing him curiously.

'I must go,' Cardilini said.

'Please,' Mrs Williamson grabbed his arm, 'You're not telling me something. Can you keep him from going back to Vietnam?'

Cardilini saw the desperation in her eyes and felt the firm grip on his forearm.

'How does your husband feel about Bradley going to Vietnam?'

'He's a man. What can he say? He supports Bradley. I used to, but I can't anymore. He's our only child. My only child. My son. Can you understand?'

'I have a son, Paul. He's eighteen.'

'Bradley's nineteen.'

'Paul missed the call up. He's our only child.'

'Ask your wife how she feels and listen to her. She'll know better than any man that it's madness that sends them.'

Cardilini turned and looked to the car. He wanted to be in it and driving away.

'I can't, she died.'

'Oh. I'm so sorry.' She let her hand fall helplessly from Cardilini's arm. 'I know Bradley and his mates play up a lot. Is that why you want to see him?'

'No, it's nothing really. I'll go to the Swanbourne Barracks.'

'Yes. Very well. He's a very good boy. He'd never do anything wrong.'

'I'm sure,' Cardilini said and walked to the car.

'Did you get a call-up, Salt?'

'No, sir.'

'What do you think about our boys going to fight in Vietnam?'

'I haven't thought about it,' Salt replied.

'I bet you have. Would you have gone?'

'Yes, sir.'

'Happily?'

'Yes, sir.'

'How did your parents feel about it?'

'I don't think they said,' Salt said looking ahead.

'What does your father do?'

'A farmer.'

'What does he think about you being a plodder?' Cardilini asked.

'He's not happy.'

'Why's that?'
'He thinks it's too dangerous.'

Salt slowed the car at the boom gate of the Swanbourne
Barracks. A corporal walked to Salt's window.

'Detective Sergeant Cardilini to see the Duty Officer.'

The corporal walked back to his booth, made a phone call,
then stepped out and put his weight on the boom gate to raise
it. Salt drove through.

TWENTY-TWO

Day 5
Swanbourne Barracks
12.15 p.m. Thursday, 29th October 1965

A sergeant stood lean and upright on the verandah of a bungalow watching Salt park the car. The sergeant's green uniform was ironed to shininess, his boots were mirror-black, and the brass on his buckle and gaiters shone like gold. His face was clamped as if hiding the distaste of a recent acidic meal. He watched Cardilini lumber from the vehicle and approach him, followed by Salt.

'Detective Sergeant Cardilini,' Cardilini announced.

'Yes.'

'Constable Salt,' Cardilini added.

'Yes.'

'And you are?' Cardilini widened his eyes, 'Notes, Salt, notes,' he snapped his fingers at Salt.

'Sergeant Fowler.'

'Sergeant Fowler, I was wanting to speak to Bradley Williamson,' Cardilini asked over-politely.

'Private Williamson? That won't be possible.'

'Why's that?'

'Private Williamson is not available.'

'When will he be available?'

'There's no way of determining that.' The sergeant and Cardilini faced each other until Cardilini stepped into the shade of the verandah.

'And you expect me to turn around and go at this point?' Cardilini asked.

'That's correct.'

'I'm not. Pass that up your chain of command.'

'It won't make any difference.'

'Let's try it, shall we?'

The sergeant stood, the distaste in his mouth clamping his face further.

'If you would like to follow me.' He turned and walked through the front door of the bungalow.

Bare timber floorboards and walls covered in lime-green paint greeted them. A desk was strategically placed in front of the only adjoining door. Facing the desk were six rattan chairs with their backs to the wall.

'Take a seat, gentlemen,' the sergeant said and he walked to the chair behind the desk and sat.

Cardilini looked at the chairs' uniformly small bases with torturous arched-cane backing.

'Will we be waiting long?' he asked.

'Difficult to say.'

'Try.'

'It's not up to me to say.'

'What's not up to you to say?'

'How long you'll be waiting.'

'Who's it up to?'

'The captain.'

'Where's he?'

The sergeant looked back mutely.

'In there?' Cardilini headed towards the door behind the desk. The sergeant stood and stepped in front of him.

'Back off. Go to your chair,' he ordered.

'Or what?'

'Back off.' The sergeant braced himself.

Cardilini tried to sidestep but the sergeant matched him, swiftly blocking Cardilini's way.

'Very well, tell your boss I'm here,' Cardilini said, stepping back.

'He's already aware of that.'

'Why are we waiting then?' Cardilini barked.

'This is the army, sir. We don't schedule time for impromptu visits from civilians. Surprising as that may seem.'

'All right. Let's stop crapping around,' Cardilini threatened.

The sergeant looked back firmly.

Cardilini called to the door behind the sergeant, 'Captain, I know you're in there this is a police investigation. You have a minute to comply with an official request or I'll leave and you can talk to your superiors about it.'

The sergeant took a step forward.

'Salt, if this man tries to interfere cuff him immediately.'

The sergeant turned a hostile gaze to Salt.

'With pleasure, sir,' Salt replied.

Cardilini turned to Salt in surprise.

'Still waters, Sergeant, be careful,' he said, indicating Salt.

The adjoining door opened.

'What's going on here, Sergeant?' demanded a red face thrusting from a tight-fitting uniform.

'Detective Sergeant Cardilini and Constable Salt, sir,' the sergeant snapped out.

'Not prepared to wait your turn, Detective Sergeant Cardilini?'

'Not prepared to be stuffed around, Captain.'

'Sergeant. Why are they here?'

'To interview a Private Williamson.'

'Did the sergeant tell you that won't be possible?'

'Yes, he did.'

'So. Explain why you're still here.'

'What's to explain? I want to see him,' Cardilini insisted.

'What part of, "It's not possible", are you having trouble with?'

'I know he's here.'

'Yes. He's here.'

'Let me see him,' Cardilini demanded.

'Private Williamson is currently involved in a specific training program involving thirty other troops. This program will be in place until they are shipped to Vietnam. Where, I'm sure even you know, we are fighting a war. How does your enquiry match up to that?'

'While he's in Australia you know we have the authority to speak to him on legitimate police business.'

'You're a Western Australian policeman, correct?'

'Yes.'

'We've been polite to this point. This base is under Commonwealth jurisdiction. You're not a federal policeman. No one is compelled to answer your questions. Take your complaint to the federal police where I'm sure they will put all their resources at your disposal to solve, what, a urinating in public charge? Try to get some perspective, Detective Sergeant Cardilini.'

'Fine, I'll wait until he leaves the base,' Cardilini said.

The captain shook his head in disgust, 'You have a minute to get off the base or I'll have you escorted off. And, just for my pleasure, please try to resist the men I send to help you on your way.' He disappeared through the door.

The sergeant smiled broadly as he picked up the phone, 'Send Smith and Jolly to the captain's office,' and as he hung up, 'hand-to-hand combat trainers,' he said, smiling at Cardilini and Salt.

Cardilini turned to Salt and nodded for them to go.

'It would be a pleasure to have a drink with you off the base sometime, Sergeant. Pass that on to your captain too.'

'Yes, sir. I'm sure he'll be interested.' The sergeant looked at his watch.

The corporal leant on the gate without lifting it, smiling at Cardilini and Salt waiting in the car. Two thickset men jogged towards them. One went to Salt's side, the other to Cardilini's and pushed their pulpy faces close to the windows. The corporal held the gate a little longer and then pushed it open. Salt drove through.

'That went well,' Cardilini said to an unresponsive Salt. 'Were you aware it was Commonwealth property?'

'No, sir.'

'Williamson will have to go and see his family at some point. We'll catch him then.'

'You haven't told me why you are wanting to speak to Private Williamson, sir'

'He's an exceptional marksman that was at St Nicholas a few years back.'

Salt sighed and increased his concentration on his driving.

'Wild-goose chase. You think?'

Salt added another level of concentration to his meticulous driving.

'It's a question. I expect your answer,' Cardilini said.

'I don't even believe there are wild geese, sir. I think you're inventing them.'

Cardilini watched the passing houses.

'Drop me at home,' he said.

Claremont
3.50 p.m. Thursday, 29th October 1965

Mrs Lockheed answered the door. 'I thought I'd see you again.'

Cardilini followed her down the passageway to the kitchen. Boxes still cluttered every space.

'You want to know why I changed my story?' She said as she sat and gestured Cardilini to take a chair.

Cardilini watched her. She had a faint smile about her mouth as she slowly moved a strand of hair from her eyes.

'No. I want to know why you sent Carmody to tell me that.' Cardilini sat.

'I didn't send him. He's a law unto himself.'

'Why's he so keen to convince me it was an accidental shooting?'

'Ask him. But since you're asking me, perhaps he's thinking the same as you, that it mightn't be an accident.'

'So it's all to save the school's reputation?' Cardilini asked.

'Yes,' she replied quickly.

'You weren't thinking of the school's reputation when you fought for your boy.'

Mrs Lockheed struggled for control. 'What lengths would you go to protect your boy, Detective Cardilini?'

Cardilini reflected on his behaviour through Paul's troubles. 'I'm not a good father. If that's what you want to know.'

'It's not what I asked. I assume you wouldn't do a lot to protect him.'

'Let's go with that.'

'Just like my husband. Did your wife say anything to you?'

Cardilini turned his head to the side as if avoiding a glancing blow then asked, 'Do you still believe John?'

'What did Carmody say to you?'

'That John was lying and you knew he was.'

'Carmody stood by John at every stage of this tragedy. He was a better man than John's father.'

Cardilini understood, *and a better father than you*, was implied.

'Did you try to find out about the boys who died?' She asked.

'No.'

'Of course not.' Mrs Lockheed shook her head ever so slightly. 'The establishment wouldn't approve.'

'It's not always like that,' Cardilini said but wondered when it wasn't.

'Not even the Masters' boy?' she asked.

'Why do you ask that?'

'That was suicide. His parents found him. He'd hanged himself from the back verandah,' she said, nervously brushing her throat with her fingertips.

'Do you think there's a connection between Edmund, the cadets, and these deaths?' Cardilini asked.

'I pray there isn't.'

'John?' Cardilini questioned gently.

She stood up and took a deep breath. 'Suicide isn't the "done thing", didn't you know?' She looked back nervously. She held her face firm but her eyes seemed to shudder.

'Carmody asked what I thought about the execution of multi-murderer, Eric Cooke,' Cardilini said.

Mrs Lockheed steadily met his gaze.

'Was Captain Edmund's death an execution?' Cardilini thought he saw Mrs Lockheed fight a smile. His eyes moved rapidly between her mouth and eyes. He sat back and ran a hand unconsciously through his thinning hair.

'Now you're being ridiculously fanciful,' Mrs Lockheed finally said and started walking to the front door.

Cardilini followed.

TWENTY-THREE

Day 2
St Nicholas College
1.21 a.m. Monday, 26th October 1965

The boy crouched in his spot looking across to the armoury door when the sliver of light disappeared. He strained his eyes, willed himself to see in the darkness; a darker hole appeared, a doorway, blacker against the black. He stopped breathing, he imagined his heart thumping his ribs apart and throwing itself at the mercy of who he might see. Nothing. Then movement, the blacker black disappeared, a dark shape, a head, appeared at the corner of the armoury, then a body, then another; the light before them, tall dark shapes moving away. He ran across the space and crouched at the corner of the armoury looking out at the figures not ten yards away. They stopped, one turned and he saw the features. It was him. The boy lifted his head in the light as if to say, 'See me'.

'I see you. Go back to your dorm the way you came. After breakfast report to me in the sixth form common room. Tell no one.' The figure turned and started walking away.

'Who was that?' his companion asked.

'I'll tell you later.'

'What do you think he saw?'

'Later.'

They stayed in the shadows of the gum trees as they walked to the dorms.

He knows me. He knows me. How? *The boy sat in a trance.* Does he know what Captain Edmund did to me? *Fear seized the boy; he trembled wildly against the bricks, pushing his body at them, harder and harder, feeling the building trembling with him. He saw the shadow of the building shaking, he saw the roof shaking. He ran to the grass and vomited. He was helpless in the grip of the clenching fist encircling his stomach, squeezing him again and again, like his father's fist on a cow teat.*

TWENTY-FOUR

Day 6
St Georges Terrace
1.54 p.m. Friday, 30th October 1965

Cardilini hitched a lift with a patrol car to an office at Council House, St Georges Terrace. He'd skipped lunch. He'd learnt that suicides in the state were monitored at the coroner's office and was now knocking on a door on the sixth floor identical to the fifteen doors he'd just passed.

A plastic tag slipped into a purpose-built slide on the door read, 'Dr Loretta Young'. Cardilini considered the temporary nature of these name tags compared to the gold-embossed names of the police hierarchy.

'Come in.'

He opened the door. Dr Young sat with her back to a view of Langley Park and the Swan River. She stood from behind her desk and walked forward, her black hair gently curling to her shoulders, eyes dark and skin fair. Her handshake was soft and warm. She had a trim figure and dressed smartly. Cardilini guessed she was in her early forties. He automatically checked his fly and poked some straying shirt back into his trousers as she returned to her desk.

'What can I do for you, Detective Cardilini?'

'Suicide.'

'Yes?'

'Deaths by suicide at St Nicholas College in the last six years.'

'Are you serious?' She asked aghast.

Funny response he thought and answered with a firm, 'Yes.'

'It's not that simple,' Dr Young vacillated. 'For a death to be classified as suicide there has to be a coroner's finding stating such.'

'Okay. You're the person to see, though?'

'I suppose. It's only a temporary position. I'm a lecturer at the University of Western Australia.'

'So what do you do?'

'We do have a record of all coroner's findings here.' She gestured to a series of filing cabinets lining the wall on her right.

'How many?'

Still staring at the filing cabinets, 'I'm not sure.'

'Can I go through them?'

'I'm not sure.' Dr Young hadn't moved.

'You have a reason?' Cardilini asked, trying to appear patient.

'I don't think it's for public release.' She walked to a cabinet and pulled at a drawer, it was locked.

'I'm not *public*.'

'No, of course not.'

'You do have a key?' Cardilini asked. Dr Young looked lost.

'Who filed them?'

'I've just shifted in here.'

'Who filed them?'

'I don't know. Perhaps Mrs Pass.'

'Where's she?'

'She's . . .' she waved her index finger towards her right.

'That way?'

'Yes. I'd better show you. You're a detective?'

'That's right. Detective Sergeant Cardilini.' Cardilini heard the impatience in his voice.

'So this is an official request?'

'That's right,' Cardilini measured out.

Dr Young walked past Cardilini, opened the door and walked to the right.

The clacking of her heels as she walked down the corridor told Cardilini that at least she knows how to look the part.

To the right an open area appeared where six women sat, each at a desk with a typewriter. Dr Young walked to the desk of a woman in her fifties with dark, grey-streaked hair held neatly back by an ornate hairpin. She had a full figure, rounded features and clear brown eyes.

'Mrs Pass, excuse me, please.'

Mrs Pass shifted her steady eyes to Cardilini.

'This is Detective Sergeant Cardilini. He's from the East Perth Central Police station. And he has an inquiry about the records kept in my office.'

'Yes?' Mrs Pass asked without shifting her eyes from Cardilini.

'I want to track down any suicides of students at a particular Perth college.'

'Mmmm. That could be possible.'

'Really?' Dr Young asked in some surprise.

'It will take some time,' Mrs Pass said.

'I've got time,' Cardilini said looking at his watch knowing he had no time.

'My time. I've maintained those records for fifteen years. I'm the only one who will go through them,' Mrs Pass said leaving no room for doubt.

Cardilini turned quizzically to Dr Young who appeared a little upset and gave a slight shrug. 'That would be the case, then,' she said coolly.

'Okay. When would you have time?' Cardilini addressed Mrs Pass.

'Why do you want them?'

'Why? I want them. That should be sufficient,' Cardilini insisted.

'Perhaps for you.'

'Those records could help me identify a murderer. And, actually, I *don't* have time. So are we going to do something or are we going to sit on our bums playing pat-a-cake?' Cardilini clenched his teeth and swore under his breath before saying, 'That mightn't have come out as I'd intended.'

'Seemed clear to me,' Mrs Pass said as she stood and led Dr Young and Cardilini back down the corridor.

Two hours later Cardilini sat in an empty office opposite the typing pool with three files in front of him. Three St Nicholas boys' deaths. Boys around Paul's age. Three families, three mothers, three fathers, three sets of brothers and sisters, three extended families of grandmothers, grandfathers, aunts, uncles, cousins and friends affected.

A car crash, on a straight country road.

A farm boy who had used firearms since he was eleven 'accidentally' shot himself.

Six months ago a boy hung himself on a back verandah. His parents discovered him when they came home from a concert. The Masters' boy.

Cardilini leant back in his chair and swore violently at the ceiling.

He calmed down and completed a neat summary of his findings.

St Georges Terrace
5.45 p.m. Friday, 30th October 1965

'Sorry for what I said earlier,' Cardilini said to Mrs Pass as he stood at her desk with the files. Only one other typist was at her desk. Cardilini checked his watch.

'Detective Sergeant Cardilini, honestly, your attitude was refreshing.'

'Yeah, well. I appreciate your help. I might need access to them again.'

'Fine. Come straight to me.'

'Dr Young?'

'Still finding her feet. Not so easy to step into the public service at that level without upsetting a number of people.'

'She upset you?'

'No, she's smarter than that.'

Cardilini nodded, smiling, 'I might see you again.'

'You might,' Mrs Pass said turning her eyes to her typewriter, 'By the way, these walls, they're like paper, we all heard you swearing.'

'Sorry.'

'No, as I said, refreshing. Not a lot of passion around here.'

Day 7
East Perth Police Department
9.45 a.m. Saturday, 31st October 1965

Cardilini arrived at East Perth station with the intention of laying out to Robinson what he'd discovered and what he was now becoming convinced of. He went straight to Robinson's office, ignoring the two officers loitering sheepishly outside.

'Robinson,' he started.

'Where the hell have you been?'

'I was following up another line and I'm certain I'm onto something.'

'Yeah. You can forget that. Something's come up.'

'Wait until you hear what I've got.'

'Shut up. There's been a complaint made against you.'

'Oh, shit.' Cardilini recalled the cold look Dr Young had given him at the Coroner's offices.

'It was nothing,' Cardilini reassured Robinson.

'I don't think so, Cardilini.' Robinson held up a sheet of typed paper with the police insignia and headed, 'Internal Charge Sheet'.

'What's the complaint?' Cardilini asked, not liking the expression on Robinson's face nor the charge sheet.

'Have you had any dealings with a student named Mossop?'

'Yes. He was a boy I interviewed.'

'Who was with you when you interviewed him?'

'Umm. We were out on the school quadrangle.'

'Before you went out onto the school quadrangle?'

'What's this about?'

'The boy went to the principal and said you exposed yourself to him.'

'What?'

'You heard,' Robinson said distastefully.

'Bullshit. Absolute bullshit.'

'You'd have to say that wouldn't you?'

'What?' Cardilini swung his head like a stunned boxer.

'He also alleges that you showed him a picture of a boy with his pants down and you wanted him to do the same.'

'What?'

'Did you show him one of those sketches?'

'It was his sketch. The idiot's name was on it. And the pants weren't down,' Cardilini thundered.

'You told me you'd given all the sketches to me.'

'It was different to the others,' Cardilini offered as an excuse.

'So now you're lying to me?' Robinson thundered back.

'Yeah, but . . .'

'And, do you have a completed report on the shooting?'

'No, but . . .'

'You're off the case. There will be a hearing as to what the boy has said.'

'You know it's bullshit.'

'So I ring up Braun and say, "Cardilini said it's bullshit?" Is that how we'll deal with it?

'That's how they deal with it,' Cardilini threw back.

'Were you alone with the boy?' Robinson demanded.

'Salt . . .'

'You sent Salt off to get some keys. I've already checked his notebook.'

'I'm being set up,' Cardilini said.

'You've made a mess of this. I've put Spry and Archer on to finish the report.' He pointed outside the office. 'Give them the file. Salt will assist them from now on.'

'Salt has no idea what's going on.'

'And you do, do you? What? What's going on?' Robinson's frustration was evident.

Cardilini considered his options. Just shut up and let the establishment boys have their pound of flesh to save his job . . . or go for broke.

'There have been three deaths in the last three years, one suicide, high possibility two others were also. Edmund has been there four years. I think his death was a planned execution. Carried out by an executioner. This is an attempt to shut me up.'

Robinson looked back in amazement. 'If we're talking about the same deaths, I know some of those families. I went to school with two of the fathers. Only one death was a suicide: the boy hanged himself. The others were tragic accidents. Christ, Cardilini. You're self-destructing. The internal investigation will go through this on Friday. Don't try to lie to them, it would cost you your job. Now get out.'

Cardilini stood and stared at Robinson.

'I've given you every bloody chance Cardilini,' Robinson said staring back. Cardilini dropped his eyes and slowly nodded before turning and leaving.

TWENTY-FIVE

Day 7
East Perth Police Department
9.56 a.m. Saturday, 31st October 1965

'Hey Cardilini, I'm checking your notes. Now which foreign country invaded to execute Edmund?' Spry, the office comedian, asked as he thumbed pages in a file. Archer and a few other detectives laughed.

'Very funny. So what are you going to do?'

'We've done it already. "Accidental shooting." Acorn confirmed the probability of an accidental shot from the other side of the river.'

'What about the bullet disappearing?'

'What about it? Some kid pinched it and is now too frightened to return it.'

'Did Acorn tell you one of the rifles had been fired recently?'

'He told us one had been "cleaned" recently, not "fired".'

'Did you speak to the principal?'

'Yep. A deputy. A boarder. A house master.'

'And?'

'And? What?' Spry asked palms up.

'There's no fooling you guys?' Cardilini said.

'We didn't go in and accuse everyone of murder either.'

'Yeah, Okay.'

'Anyway, how's the bullshit complaint going?' Spry asked.

'Internal hearing, Friday.'

'You really pissed someone off at that school, didn't you?' Spry commiserated with a smile. Cardilini nodded mutely. 'They'll go through you like a bad case of the trots. Take a clean change of underwear.'

'Thanks. Did you get an autopsy report?'

'Not yet, but what difference would it make?'

Cardilini considered this, considered the faces that had led him to be convinced Edmund had been murdered: Carmody, Burnside, Mrs Lockheed. 'Did you speak to a Bradley Williamson? I marked him in one of the files.'

All the other detectives had walked away by now. Spry pulled up a chair and lit a cigarette.

'I saw the other boys' files you marked, we read your notes on the deaths of the three old boys.'

'Go on.'

'I heard you had stopped drinking?'

'Yeah. So what?'

'Nothing. Just, maybe you're not at your sharpest here while coping with that too.'

With a shake of his head Cardilini considered Spry and Archer. They were thorough, he'd worked with them both on occasion, and they were the types who always followed the dots. But if a dot was missing they weren't opposed to slipping one in if it led to the right conclusion.

'Come on Cardilini, give yourself a break. The word is, the kid who's accusing you doesn't know if he's coming or going. Apparently the principal warned you.'

'Yeah. He did.'

'You should go home. Bishop wouldn't care.'

'Yeah, thanks, Spry.'

'No worries. When you've got your act together, come out with Archer and me.'

'I don't need my act together to go out with you two,' Cardilini said.

Spry smiled, giving Cardilini a thumbs up as he walked away.

* * *

'I might call it a day,' Cardilini said to Bishop five minutes later.

'I wondered what you were doing here. When is . . .?'

'Friday morning.'

'Good luck with that. It sounds like you pissed off the wrong kid.'

'Yeah.'

'They're just going through the motions, Cardilini. A kid's word against a cop's word. It's not going to fly.'

'Yeah. I know,' Cardilini said. And he did know, the whole thing would be dismissed, there was nothing to back the boy up.

'It will turn out like the other one,' Bishop said.

'Which one?'

'Didn't you have some kid dobbing on a teacher, and even his mates said he was lying?' Bishop said, returning to his work.

'Where did you hear that?' Cardilini asked.

'Weren't you talking about it?' Bishop looked up.

'No. No. I didn't tell anyone.'

'It was your case. Maybe Salt was telling someone. Salt and Robinson? I don't know, it was after work when we were having a drink.'

'Salt and Robinson? Doesn't make sense.' Cardilini knew he hadn't told Salt; only Carmody, Burnside, Mrs Lockheed and Paul knew of it.

'St Nicholas old boys,' Bishop said as explanation.

'Who?' Cardilini asked sharply.

'Robinson and Salt.'

'Salt?' Cardilini said shocked.

'Yeah. Thick as thieves. But I thought you knew that.'

'No. I've been . . .' Cardilini didn't finish, he didn't know what or where he had been; asleep, in a fog, stupid?

'We thought you did and that's why you were keeping Salt at a distance.'

'No. So when was Salt at St Nicholas?'

'He went back to the farm at the end of form four. Salt's old man and Robinson were at school together.'

'How long ago was Salt at St Nicholas?' Cardilini asked.

'Would have left, what, four years ago.'

'Bloody hell, Bishop, you didn't think to tell me?'

'Not really. You'd have given the kid a hard time if I did.'

'Of course I bloody wouldn't,' Cardilini said but thought, *of course I bloody would have.*

'So how would Salt know about Lockheed unless Carmody or Burnside told him?' Cardilini asked himself more than Bishop.

'You've lost me. Anyway, all done and dusted. When the hearing is over and if you're still sober I'll give you something decent. I'll give you a real murder.'

'Thanks,' Cardilini said and wandered the corridor trying to figure out what the ramifications of Salt being a St Nicholas old boy were.

Kilkenny Rd
11.30 a.m. Saturday, 31st October 1965

Paul was on the verandah reading when his father drove in. Cardilini sat in his car and ran back over the images of Salt and himself in the principal's office, of Salt with Miss Reynolds, with Robson, with Carmody. What a fool they must have thought me. He had the urge to confront Salt, blow his top at him and then do the same to Robinson. *Yeah, that would work.* Carmody or Burnside must have told Salt about coming to see me.

Eventually Paul called out, 'Dad, what are you doing?'

A distracted Cardilini got out, 'Just have a phone call to make then I might go out for a spell. When I come back I thought I'd do some gardening.'

'Gardening?'

'Yeah. Remember? You used to mow the lawn.'

Paul, then Cardilini looked out at the matted and dead grass covering the front yard.

'It's not too bad. It'll come back. You'll see come January we could have a lovely, tidy lawn here,' Cardilini mused as he wandered out and stood in the middle of the dead patch on the right of the path. Runners of grass had sought refuge among the roses and in what used to be flowerbeds bordering the path. Cardilini pulled one from among the rosebushes. The roots popped naked from the dry soil as he pulled. He stood with it in his hand.

'I never saw Mum doing that,' Paul said.

'But, what do you think? Would she be pleased if we smarten the front yard up?'

'Yeah. I think she would. But there's nothing to mow.'

'Okay. You water where the lawn should be and I'll get the shovel and cut the dead runners from the garden beds.'

'Dad, I said I was going to move into Aunty Roslyn's,' Paul said flatly.

Cardilini tried to look at his son but couldn't, instead he said, 'Think I'll prune the roses.'

'Did you hear me?'

Cardilini imagined Betty's eyes on him.

'Son . . .' Cardilini started but still couldn't look at him.

'They won't let me in the academy. Will they?'

'Son . . .'

'Jesus, Dad. You . . .' Paul had the words but shook his head and turned into the house. Cardilini expelled a breath and silently finished Paul's sentence with a series of expletives. He wandered to the roses at the front fence. Long, woody, thorned branches reached for him. Betty's eyes told him he had to set things right. He turned and walked to the house, picked up the phone and began dialling as he shook his head.

'Deputy Principal, Dr Robson,' Robson answered.

'Hi Robson. It's Cardilini.'

'Yes. Should we be talking?'

'Don't see why not.'

'What do you want?' Robson asked.

'A chat.'

'Chat away.'

'You're at the school?'

'I picked up the phone, didn't I?' Robson answered after a pause.

'Can I come by?'

There was another pause, then, 'I'm going down to watch the cricket. I'll be sitting on a bench, by myself, no doubt.'

'I'll see you there.' Cardilini hung up. 'I'm going out, Paul. I'll make it all good. Just, can you wait?' Cardilini called and stood breathless in the hallway. When no answer came he walked to Paul's door. 'I've been put on report. It's a good kick up the bum. Really, your old man's trying to . . .' his words stopped and his lips hung loosely as he breathed heavily at the door. 'Just, please . . . wait . . . just don't go.' Cardilini finished and walked down the corridor. He knew he couldn't return to the house if Paul wasn't there. He paused at the front door, called 'I'm going,' and listened intently to silence before leaving.

TWENTY-SIX

Day 7
St Nicholas College
12.50 p.m. Saturday, 31st October 1965

The day settled warm and lazy into the afternoon. A faint sea breeze teased the tops of trees but failed to find its way into Cardilini's car. At a set of streetlights he leant over and wound down the passenger window.

Cars were parked along all the school's internal roads and clustered on one of the ovals. He nudged his EH Holden into the shade beside a Mercedes and a Pontiac before walking up the road in the shade of pine trees. Boys dressed in casual clothes were wandering around in groups of two to five. The visiting team's spectators were in their school uniforms and stood around the cricket oval. A raked pavilion of red brick was perched on the side gaping out at the players. Adults occupied most of the seats. Cardilini envied their calm expressions.

He watched the figures in white running, and smiled at the sound of an oak bat striking the leather ball. He had never played the game. He was about to express his opinion on the stupidity of the sport but instead shook his head, admonishing himself. He looked around for Robson.

Robson was sitting by himself a third of the way around the oval on a shaded bench. As Cardilini made his way around the boundary, there was another crack of the ball and bat, some lively calling and Robson and others clapping. Cardilini turned to the pitch and players: nothing seemed to be happening. Reaching Robson's bench he sat and took out a cigarette.

Offering the packet to Robson he asked, 'How are your boys going?'

Robson declined a cigarette. 'All out for one seventy-two.'

'Is that good?' Cardilini lit his and inhaled.

'Depends. The opposition are three for seventy-nine.'

'Oh. Could be close?' Cardilini suggested but had no real idea.

'Yes.' Robson took a butt from his tin. 'There's no point asking me about Mossop. The principal's handling it.'

'Do accusations such as the one made against me often find their way to the police?'

Robson scrutinised Cardilini. 'Who said there were other such accusations?'

'Mrs Lockheed.'

Robson took a deep inhalation on his cigarette and butted it out on his tin cover. 'They're going to find out smoking is bad for you.' He tapped his tin on the wooden bench and replaced it into his coat pocket.

'How do you know?'

'I'm a scientist. I do know that in the right dosage fifty per cent of what you inhale could kill you within hours.'

'Tough.' Cardilini inhaled and, sated, expelled the smoke.

'I never believed John Lockheed or his mother,' Robson said.

'Why?'

'I've worked with Edmund for four years.'

'Which told you?'

'It was abhorrent what the boy said. Ridiculously fanciful. Malicious.'

'What part?'

Robson turned to Cardilini's expressionless face.

'Standing with a rifle above their heads was practised before Edmund came to the school. I've seen them do it. Edmund stood them in front of the window facing the quad. He was a military man.'

'Was he? As an instructor of school cadets his rank was honorary.'

'When I say military man, I meant he affected all things military. He was rejected by the services.'

'How do you know?'

'He told me. Some medical reason, I didn't enquire. He always had the boys' best interests at heart.'

'And he's not capable of the things John Lockheed said?'

'No. Talk to other people who knew him.'

'The parents of the boys who've since passed away, do you mean?' Cardilini cocked his head quizzically.

Robson turned his attention to the cricket. 'Carmody's bowling. He's the first eleven captain. He made fifty-eight runs.'

'Was he in the first eleven when Bradley Williamson was captain?'

'What's that intended to prove?'

'Carmody would have been a fourth form student?' Cardilini pushed.

'Then, yes, Carmody is one of a handful to make the first eleven while in form four.'

'Were the boys close?'

'Williamson was a mentor to Carmody. Williamson was a real leader and a very loyal student,' Robson said.

They both sat watching the cricket. Cardilini remembered boys at his school playing cricket, the posh boys.

'Bad luck,' Robson called. 'Carmody was hit for a four,' he informed Cardilini.

Cardilini clapped and said, 'Bradley Williamson won the state school boys' shooting titles two years running.'

'I know, quite a marksman. Why the interest in Williamson?'

'No interest. Just, he was a cricket captain, like Carmody.'

Robson shrugged.

Cardilini asked, 'The boys who passed away: 1963, 1964, and tragically the boy who took his own life this year were all cadets, some discharged for disciplinary reasons. We know the discipline. What part couldn't they manage?'

'I've no idea. I said I know what Edmund did. We all did. It wasn't a secret. It was considered appropriate in the traditions of the school. The rest is too disgusting. I believe the disgruntled boys all decided on the same or similar complaints to discredit Edmund. Like Mossop's complaint about you.'

'That's a lie.'

'Of course. As were the accusations made about Edmund.'

'So all accusations against Edmund are untrue?'

'Yes, it's beyond belief. When on duty in the evenings I spent a lot of time with the man. I knew him.'

'I hope you're right.'

'I am right.'

'Otherwise there could be more tragic consequences for young men and their families.'

Robson clapped as Carmody got a wicket. Cardilini looked at the scoreboard, a timber structure with numbers hanging from it, attended by schoolboys in St Nicholas uniform. The visitors were 4 for 92.

'If, hypothetically, the boys' accusations were considered plausible – I still can't believe it – but say *if* the boys' claims were plausible, what difference would it make now?' Robson asked.

'To the boys?'

'Yes.'

'You could save a boy's life. Lockheed's for a start. The mother is too frightened to let him out of her sight.'

They watched as the new batsman struggled through the first few balls of a new over.

'The sketch you picked up from the bottom of the tree the first day I was here, did it show trousers around the boy's ankles?' Cardilini asked.

'I didn't look.' Robson was staring at the field.

'How many have you picked up since?'

'It became an epidemic until Carmody spoke to the boarders.'

'Were you there when he spoke?' Cardilini asked.

'No. It was part of Carmody's conditions.'

'Conditions?'

'We foster leadership. The principal thought it appropriate.'

'And you?'

'Carmody doesn't require anyone's endorsement to influence the boys.'

'You don't like him?' Cardilini asked.

When Robson didn't answer Cardilini rephrased, 'You don't trust him?'

'No, I trust him and respect him. "Like" is too subjective. I "liked" Edmund.'

'What was the reaction at the school as these boys' deaths started?'

Robson turned a serious face to Cardilini, 'What do you think? You've a son. It's gutting, like the solid earth under your feet has turned to slime. I taught those boys, they had everything to live for. And their deaths, apart from poor Masters', were accidents. And I do not *like* or respect what you're trying to do,' Robson said, standing in an attempt to calm himself.

The boys began moving from the oval.

'The boys are breaking for tea. Do you want a cup?' Robson asked politely.

'Sure. Thanks.'

They walked from the shade into the sunlight. Cardilini felt the give in the grass under his shoes and recalled lazy, innocent summer days he'd spent kicking a football, before becoming a policeman.

'Did any of those boys who passed away play cricket, Robson?' Cardilini asked as they walked side by side across the oval.

'You ever been afraid, Cardilini?' Robson asked.

'Yes.'

'I'm afraid. I'm afraid because you're trying to plunge us into a nightmare beyond comprehension.' Robson stopped short of the grandstand. 'I'm not even sure you should be at the school, so if you would wait here, I'll get you a cup of tea,' he said and walked off.

Cardilini looked for Carmody. He was standing separate from the others next to a tall, gaunt, elderly man who appeared familiar. At one point they both turned to look at him then continued their conversation. Parents were mingling with the boys. Cardilini could see stern words of advice being issued. Carmody eventually joined the group and received a number of pats on the back. *You'd think he was winning a war,* Cardilini thought.

Robson returned to Cardilini with a cup of tea. They both stood silently looking across to the players. Carmody separated himself from the team and walked across to them.

'What do you think our chances are, sir?' Carmody asked Robson.

'I wouldn't bowl yourself again. But, well done.'

'I agree, sir.'

'Clarke has three for sixteen. Does he have any overs left?' Robson asked.

'Yes, sir.'

'Bowl him, and who would you bowl with him?' Robson asked.

'Morrell.'

'Good choice, they haven't been able to hit him.'

'Are you enjoying the game, Detective Sergeant Cardilini?' Carmody asked.

'Parts of it.'

'What parts would they be?'

'Where you were hit for a four.'

Carmody smiled, 'Yes. It doesn't happen often.'

'It doesn't,' Robson confirmed.

'And it won't happen again,' Carmody said and nodded respectfully before walking away.

'I do respect the boy, Detective Cardilini. Despite everything, I believe he is of good character,' Robson said.

'Who's the skinny old chap in the tea line?' Cardilini asked pointing.

Robson turned to Cardilini surprised, then returning his gaze towards the gathering said, 'An interested spectator.'

Cardilini accepted this with a nod.

Robson took Cardilini's empty teacup and saucer and they parted company.

Cardilini started towards his car before becoming aware of a group of young students staring at him. He stopped, 'Any questions, boys?'

'No, sir,' one eventually replied. Cardilini continued to his car.

Kilkenny Rd
4.15 p.m. Saturday, 31st October 1965

Paul was standing on the front verandah when the car pulled into the driveway, he watched his father walk towards the house. Cardilini looked up at him and stood still.

Paul spoke defiantly, 'I'm going to help with the garden because it's what Mum would want.'

Cardilini nodded. 'The academy's still all good,' he said and swore to himself he would make it 'good' no matter what it cost him.

Paul looked back, defeated and disbelieving. He took a breath before saying, 'But I'm working at the drive-in tonight.'

'Great, son, great,' Cardilini enthused.

Paul looked at him for a moment then said briskly, 'Mum never pruned the roses in summer because they had flowers on them.'

Day 8
Kilkenny Road
12.10 a.m. Sunday, 1st November 1965

Six files sat in front of Cardilini on the kitchen table. They were Captain Edmund's files on the boys: Carmody, Lockheed, Williamson, Sheppard, Doney and Masters.

Cardilini had drawn up neat lists in an exercise book.

- 1963. A sixth form boarder, Colin Sheppard, died by an accidental shooting
- 1964. A sixth form boarder, Peter Doney, died in a car accident while on holidays at the family farm
- 1965. An old boy, Geoff Masters, died by hanging
  - Bradley Williamson and Geoff Masters graduated in 1963
  - All had been in the Cadets together and played sport together
  - Carmody and Lockheed, plus the boy killed in a car accident, Doney, had been discharged from the cadets for disciplinary reasons
  - These boys all knew each other well. The total boarders numbered 132
  - The following discounted intentional shooting as fanciful, or considered it plausible and worth concealing, or knew it to be a fact and decided to cover it up:
    - Deputy Commissioner Warren
    - Superintendent Robinson
    - Dr Braun
    - Dr Robson
    - Mrs Lockheed
    - Carmody

A cover-up in case it leads to revelations of Captain Edmund's abuse and their failure to act? Cardilini asked himself.
- Salt left St Nicholas in 1962, the year before Edmund arrived

Blankly, he studied the list. He checked his watch: 12.20 a.m. Paul was due home soon. He packed up the files nervously and stood on the front porch to wait. The night was empty of noise, disconcertingly so. He walked to the front gate. Two porch lights across the street did little other than light themselves, likewise two streetlights. He checked his watch again. His stomach hollowed. *Paul's gone to his aunt's,* he thought. He took several nervous breaths.

He turned to the house. The hall light was on. The front door open. The house empty.

A thin yellow light brushing the front porches of the houses opposite caught his attention. A car had turned into the street. He heard the rubber on bitumen and the familiar roar of his car. He released a breath thankfully. The light pool in front of the house intensified as the car slowed and turned into the driveway. He watched Paul pull up, dowse the lights, switch off the engine and get out of the car.

'Dad. What are you doing?'

'Nothing, just . . . nothing.'

Paul, still standing with the car door open, watched him. Finally he asked, 'Have you been drinking?'

'No. Absolutely not.'

'You sure?'

'Of course I'm bloody sure . . .' then softening, 'Son.'

'Why are you outside then?'

'It was late, I just thought I'd wait for you.'

'Jesus, don't start that Dad.'

'I was working. I wasn't just waiting for you,' Cardilini finished gruffly but held Paul with his eyes. Paul in turn watched his father suspiciously.

'You didn't crash the car?' Cardilini demanded.

'Of course bloody not,' Paul shot back.

'Good. I'm going to bed,' Cardilini said and turned to the house, anxious to hear the car door close and Paul follow him.

TWENTY-SEVEN

Day 8
Kilkenny Road
5.45 p.m. Sunday, 1st November 1965

Cardilini was weeding along the rear fence when Paul called him from the house.

'What is it?'

'A Mrs Masters on the phone.'

Cardilini walked into the house.

'Thanks, Paul. How's the garden out the front looking?'

'I'm sure you'll find something wrong with it.'

Cardilini grimaced and picked up the phone.

'Cardilini,' He said.

Cardilini stood on the front verandah watching Paul watering the buffalo grass runners he'd planted. Runners he'd retrieved from around the tank stand.

'They'll cover by the end of summer,' Cardilini said.

'Maybe.'

Softening light and lengthening shadows had drawn several of Cardilini's neighbours outside to water their front gardens too. Cardilini waved and stood on the verandah steps.

'Hungry, Paul?'

'I'm working tonight. I told you I'll eat there.'

'That's right,' Cardilini hovered a moment, then said, 'I'm going to finish up the back.'

'Who was that lady?' Paul asked.

'It's the mother of a boy who hanged himself this year.'

'Jesus, Dad. Not so matter-of-fact,' Paul rebuked looking towards the neighbour's house.

'Sorry.' Cardilini stood waiting.

'How old?'

'Nineteen.'

'Jesus Christ. Nineteen! Why?'

Cardilini wandered over to Paul and stood by him watching the water fall on the soil. The water wasn't penetrating the earth but beading and running off into little pools. 'I think he might have been abused by a teacher,' Cardilini said.

'How?'

'Sexually.'

'Jesus, and you're going to catch the teacher?' Paul turned to look at his father.

'Someone caught him.'

'Good.'

'They shot him.'

'Jesus. So what're you doing?'

'Trying to find out who shot him.' They both watched the water. 'That water isn't going in,' Cardilini said. Paul looked at his dad for a moment and then went back to his watering. 'What?' Cardilini asked.

'Nothing.'

'You think he shouldn't be caught?' Cardilini asked.

'I didn't say that.' Paul put his finger on the nozzle to spray the water.

'But do you think that?'

'No, but, what if the teacher did it again?'

'He did, a number of times, causing two other possible suicides.'

'Oh my god. Possible? Can you find out for sure?'

'I was thinking I should. Just wasn't looking forward to it,' Cardilini replied.

'But, if it's your job?'

'Yep.'

Cardilini was conscious of his son looking at him, conscious that the alcohol had given him a haggard look. He knew there were times Paul would turn away rather than look into his eyes. And he knew why, as he too had seen the beaten, lost look in them.

Paul said, 'The water pooling like that used to happen for Mum too, but she used to do something about it.'

'Do you remember what she did?' Cardilini asked.

'No.'

They stood watching the water pool.

'I still might go to Aunty Roslyn's,' Paul said curtly without turning.

'I know. I hope you don't. But I know I've been worse than useless,' Cardilini said and walked towards the house.

A church
6.30 p.m. Sunday, 1st November 1965

The place Mrs Masters had chosen for her meeting with Cardilini was a church. A bell tower soared square and solid beside its gabled roof. Cardilini walked around the side to the rectory as instructed. It was built in the same cream stone as the church yet still looked as though it clung to its side incongruously. Cardilini knocked on the door. A priest in his clerical clothing and collar opened it.

'Detective Sergeant Cardilini?'

'Yes.'

'Father O'Reilly. Come in.'

The front door led into a parlour furnished with five mismatched armchairs, a small writing desk and an excessive number of standard lamps shedding pools of yellow light. Mrs Masters sat in one of the armchairs. The flesh on her face hung from her eyebrows as if too heavy or too beaten to stand firm. Thin shoulders arched forward, timid fingers moved continuously on a cup and saucer. Cardilini's stomach sank.

'Mrs Masters, Detective Sergeant Cardilini,' Father O'Reilly said.

Cardilini nodded, as did Mrs Masters.

'We're having tea. Would you like a cup?' Father O'Reilly broke the silence.

'Yes, please,' Cardilini said despite his stomach making every indication it would be unwise to drink anything. He sat beside Mrs Masters.

'How do you do.' He held out his hand. Mrs Masters left her cup alone for an instant to put her hand limply in his. He held it while he said, 'I'm sorry for what you have suffered.' She withdrew her hand and looked to Father O'Reilly.

'Mr Masters isn't aware of this meeting.' Father O'Reilly said. Cardilini nodded.

'He lost his faith,' he said smiling at Mrs Masters then continued to Cardilini, 'Mrs Lockheed spoke about your visit to her house and about your questions.'

Cardilini nodded, Mrs Masters kept her eyes on O'Reilly.

'We're hoping you might be able to help us understand why Geoffrey took his own life.' O'Reilly finished.

Mrs Masters turned her attention to Cardilini.

'What reasons did Geoffrey give for leaving the cadets?' Cardilini asked her.

'He was asked to leave,' Mrs Masters said.

'Why?'

'Is this to do with Geoffrey taking his life?' O'Reilly asked.

'It could be.'

'I don't see how,' O'Reilly said.

'Mrs Masters, what did Geoffrey say to you?'

Mrs Masters turned to O'Reilly who answered for her, 'We're not sure that it is relevant. We believe some boys made up accusations.'

'Did you believe your son, Mrs Masters?' Cardilini asked ignoring O'Reilly.

O'Reilly persisted, 'Detective Cardilini, Mrs Lockheed said you might have information to help us understand . . .'

'In a moment. Did you believe your son, Mrs Masters?'

'The school is in my parish. Captain Edmund was a member of this parish.' O'Reilly inserted.

'Mrs Masters.'

'Yes.' She looked at her cup.

'Did your husband believe your son?' Cardilini asked Mrs Masters.

'I don't know. He was angry with Geoffrey. I think he believed the principal,' Mrs Masters said.

'Had your husband attended the school as a student?'

'Yes.'

'Has Mrs Lockheed told you what her son, John, said,' Cardilini asked slowly, 'about the discipline inflicted by Edmund?'

'Yes.'

'Was it similar to your boy's account?'

'Yes.'

'No. No. No. Impossible!' O'Reilly exclaimed.

'Could it be true?' Mrs Masters whispered.

'No,' O'Reilly insisted.

'Prior to your son, two other boys died,' Cardilini said.

'From our school? The country boys?' Mrs Masters asked.

'Yes.'

'Tragic accidents,' O'Reilly asserted.

Looking directly at O'Reilly, Cardilini spelt it out. 'The boys who spoke up are either lying or they're telling the truth. As abhorrent as it maybe to you, Father O'Reilly, it can't be ignored.'

'No, it can't be ignored. But can any good come of it now?'

'There could be other boys. Revealing the truth could help them,' Cardilini said turning his eyes to Mrs Masters. She looked up hopelessly.

O'Reilly walked away then turned and addressed Mrs Masters. 'Geoffrey had left the school two years ago. Had he ever said anything else about his allegations?'

'No, but he was never the same. He was never the same.' She brought a handkerchief up to her eyes.

O'Reilly looked accusingly at Cardilini.

'I will try to find out as much as I can, Mrs Masters, and I will keep you informed.' Cardilini said. She accepted this with an upward look. Cardilini could see the woman was half-dead. He knew the instant she had died was the moment she saw her son hanging; it was still in her eyes. Cardilini felt he was looking at the image himself. Two half-people looking at each other. He swallowed the sorrow in his throat.

'I'm so sorry you lost your wife,' Mrs Masters said. Cardilini thanked her and turned the hollowness of his eyes towards the door. Mrs Masters grabbed at his hand, holding it for a moment. When released, Cardilini walked to the front door and O'Reilly followed.

Outside, Cardilini put a cigarette into his mouth, lit it and inhaled deeply. O'Reilly did the same. They could hear Mrs Masters weeping. O'Reilly gently closed the front door.

'It's very fresh for her. I was sorry to hear about your wife, also,' O'Reilly said. Cardilini exhaled. O'Reilly continued. 'You've been a topic of conversation since your arrival at the school. The community around the school is very tight, very protective.'

'So, who are you protecting?' Cardilini asked without turning.

'No one.'

'You mightn't think so but you're possibly protecting a predator whose victims are only revealing their injuries in death. Have a think about that,' Cardilini said and walked to his car.

'What if you're wrong?' O'Reilly called after him. 'A good man's reputation.'

'What if I'm right?' Cardilini said and climbed into his car.

TWENTY-EIGHT

Day 9
Kilkenny Road
5.50 a.m. Monday, 2nd November 1965

On his front porch with a cup of tea in his hand, Cardilini appraised the work he and Paul had done. The front yard was beginning to reflect the hand of authority again. The rosebush branches peeked courteously above the fence palings, the dirt of the lawn area was now firmly contained and sodden. Every edge of footpath paving was weed-free and he had weeded and watered every garden bed. He wasn't sure why he watered the bare soil but felt the better for it.

All the while the image of Mrs Master's face inserted itself between him and what he was working on. Her sorrow was so raw, so all-consuming and so familiar. He sighed heavily. Was it possible the Masters' boy committed suicide for reasons independent of Edmund? He didn't know if he was chasing a killer or the truth, and he wasn't sure if he wanted to catch either.

At 8.45 Cardilini made a call. 'Mrs Pass, this is Detective Sergeant Cardilini.'

'Yes?'

'Hi. I was just wondering if you had a look at those files you gave me?'

'No,' she replied crisply.

'The coroner only confirmed suicide in one case.'

'The boy who hanged himself?' she enquired, all business.

'Yes. In your experience of dealing with the records, are the others suicide?'

'I would have to re-read them. If the coroner isn't one hundred per cent convinced he'll always say "Death by Misadventure", "Accidental". However, he's careful in his wording. He'll indicate the probability of suicide without stating such. He's hopeful that someday the number of our young men dying will be investigated.'

'Could you have a look at those files?'

'Those three?'

'Yes.'

'Possibly. Why?'

'I've lost objectivity,' Cardilini confessed.

'Easy to do.'

'Could you?' Cardilini asked and waited.

'There's a teashop half-way up London Court called The Bell. I'll be there at ten-thirty.' Mrs Pass said.

'Thanks. So will I.' Cardilini hung up and stood looking at the phone. Mrs Pass puzzled him.

London Court
10.30 a.m. Monday, 2nd November 1965

City workers and shoppers walked the pavement. So many faces in thought. Cardilini imagined what each one's expressions concealed: loved ones, sunny days, beaches, work, movies, family gatherings, or a nesting evil that could erupt at any moment. He tried to hunt it out in a face, a gesture, a tone, a posture. It was an occupational addiction. He saw Mrs Pass walking up from St Georges Terrace. She moved like the others, independent but inexplicably joined to everyone around her. Cardilini envied the innocence.

'Detective Sergeant Cardilini.' Mrs Pass stood in front of him. Her face and her tone held the office composure. She had applied lipstick and brushed her hair making Cardilini wonder about how his own hair looked. He ran a casual hand over his chin to check if he had shaved: he had.

'Mrs Pass. Lead the way.'

She turned without speaking and marched to a doorway. Tables suitable for four crammed the space in front of a curved glass display cabinet. Occupants of several tables sat close together conversing over their cups and saucers.

'Tea or coffee?' Mrs Pass asked Cardilini when she reached the counter.

'Tea.'

'Two teas, thanks.'

'I'll pay,' Cardilini said.

'No, you won't.' The firmness of her reply surprised Cardilini. He turned to see if anyone else had witnessed Mrs Pass's strong response. A couple in their thirties glanced from Cardilini to Mrs Pass.

'I expected to pay for any drinks,' Cardilini couldn't resist when they were seated.

'That's usually the case. I understand that,' she replied.

'Then?'

'I'm a widow.'

Cardilini took a moment to assess her face.

'I'm sorry to hear.'

'It's been years.' She turned straight to business. 'I read the files. This is not my opinion, this is the intended reading by the coroner.' Mrs Pass clearly stated, 'A fatal single car crash with a young male at the wheel often means the coroner investigates further. If the road is an isolated country road but well known to the driver, and the car for no apparent reason swerves into a tree, he will make observations that won't state suicide directly and also won't result in an open verdict. But a cautious reader will understand there's a possibility the person took their life. The shooting accident verdict read the same.'

Cardilini exhaled heavily.

'Is that what you wanted to hear?' Mrs Pass asked.

'No, but it's what I thought.' Cardilini turned his attention to his tea.

'Did the families think it suicide?' Mrs Pass asked with some gravity.

'I don't know.'

'Does anyone else think this besides yourself?'

'Not as far as I know.' Cardilini looked for her reaction.

Mrs Pass stirred her sugarless tea and said, 'We decided to wait before having children. I regret that now.'

Cardilini leant forward, toying with his cup before taking a sip.

'What's your opinion of the coroner's findings?' He asked.

'My opinion is quite worthless, Detective Cardilini.'

'You're the most informed person in the state, besides the coroner,' Cardilini corrected.

'The coroner's secretary?' She said archly.

'Okay, the coroner's secretary then you. What do you think?'

'The suicide rate of our young is alarming. Particularly in the country,' she said looking directly at Cardilini.

'Yes?'

'There are three ways to view these files. One, the St Nicholas College community suffered two tragic accidents and one suicide in four years. Two, the St Nicholas College community is experiencing an exceptional cluster of suicides. Three, somewhere between one and two. However, all three are frightening and must be investigated. That's my opinion.'

'Thank you.' Cardilini took a sip of his tea. 'I'm a widower,' he said and immediately wondered why he did.

'I'm sorry.'

'Twelve months.'

'Oh, dear. I'm so sorry. Children?'

'Paul, eighteen.'

'Eighteen?'

'Yes,' Cardilini replied, suddenly feeling guilty about the person he had been for twelve months.

'My name's Colleen.'

'Robert. But call me Cardilini.'

'So what're you going to do now? You said previously the information would help you catch a murderer?'

'Yes, I did. If you identified the person responsible for these boys taking their own lives, what would you do?' Cardilini asked.

Colleen avoided his gaze and asked, 'Do you believe one person is responsible?'

'Yes.'

'So you're calling the person responsible a murderer?' Colleen reasoned.

'No.'

'So what will you do about him?'

'He's dead, recently shot.' Cardilini replied.

'The death of the teacher at St Nicholas was accidental. I know.' She leant forward and said in hushed tones. 'It's shortly to go to the coroner.'

'That's what everyone thinks,' Cardilini said.

'But not you?'

'No.'

'Is a parent responsible?' She asked, frowning.

Cardilini shrugged. Colleen held him with questioning eyes.

'What?' He asked.

'If a parent was guilty what would you do?'

Cardilini fingered his teacup without answering then rose from his chair as Colleen stood.

'I'm sorry,' she said, 'I shouldn't have asked that. I hope I've been of some help though. Goodbye, Detective Sergeant Cardilini.' She started to walk away but paused, her eyes softening. 'I don't envy your task.'

Cardilini mumbled a goodbye. He sat and sipped his cold, milky tea. His gaze fell to the lipstick on Colleen's cup. *I miss that*, he thought.

TWENTY-NINE

Day 10
Williams
6.50 a.m. Tuesday, 3rd November 1965

A fragile blue sky prepared for the hard heat of day.

Cardilini allowed two and a half hours to drive a distance of 100 miles to the south-west town of Williams. His plan was to stop at the Halfway House for breakfast, although food had lost its appeal since he had stopped drinking.

The police report that the state coroner received in 1963 stated that Colin Sheppard had died of accidental gunfire while carrying a rifle. The coroner, according to Colleen, had left an open finding. Senior Constable Saunders who completed the report was still stationed at Williams and expected Cardilini early morning. Mid-morning he would drive 15 miles to the Sheppard wheat and sheep farm to meet Mr and Mrs Sheppard.

Cardilini drove through the corridor of pine trees in the hills above Armadale. On a Christmas holiday to Albany, four years ago, he'd driven the same road. A bustling, busy, talkative trip. Every fibre in him ached for that moment, ached for Betty laughing beside him. Tears blurred the road ahead. He wiped them away harshly with the sleeve of his shirt. It was hard to believe he was once that man.

The town of Williams gathered its buildings on the left of the South Western Highway, mainly stock agents and farm machinery suppliers. An occasional residential bungalow with a broad corrugated iron roof sat behind the commercial strip. At 9.35 a.m. Cardilini pulled his car into a parking space directly outside the police station. His shirt stuck to his back and two hours with the windows down had left him feeling windblown.

The flyscreen door squeaked, announcing his entrance, and a uniformed officer looked up from his desk.

'Cardilini. Can't understand why you bothered to come. I rang East Perth this morning, spoke to Bishop, he doesn't know what the hell you're doing.'

'Did you speak to Superintendent Robinson?'

'No.'

'He could tell you what I'm doing.' *Being a bloody nuisance*, thought Cardilini. The officer relented at this and stuck out his hand.

'Saunders.'

'Good to meet you, Senior Constable.'

'So, what do you want? You read my report?'

'I just want to ask a few questions.'

'No harm, I guess. Cup of tea?'

Cardilini and Saunders sat on the back verandah amid the sharp, pungent smell of gum trees. Stick-like trees with dry, peeling bark flourished in the yard.

'Even though the scheme water is through, few people water their yards,' Saunders said looking out at a dead patch of lawn.

'I've been tidying my front yard,' Cardilini said. 'I hadn't done anything for twelve months.'

'I remember the funeral being posted. Sorry about your loss.'

'Thanks.'

They sat in silence. Past the yard, taller gums could be seen tracking the meandering Williams River.

'Much water in the river?' Cardilini asked.

'No.'

'Didn't think so.'

'So?' Saunders asked rolling a cigarette. 'Your questions?'

'In the report you said the Sheppard boy probably tripped while carrying a loaded rifle.'

'That's right.'

'Is that what you think?' Cardilini turned to check Saunders's response.

'There wasn't any other possible reason.' Saunders exhaled a stream of smoke into the oppressive air.

Cardilini watched Saunders for a moment before asking, 'How did you imagine it happened?'

'I don't know. It happened.' Saunders turned glass-eyed to Cardilini.

'You didn't say exactly how the rifle and body were found,' Cardilini said quietly.

'Didn't I?'

Looking away from Saunders Cardilini said quietly, 'No.'

'So, what's the point of this?' Saunders snapped.

'Just questions.'

'What will the super say the point is?' Saunders asked as if prepared to rise and make the call.

Cardilini took a deep breath. 'He'll say, "Tell that fat copper to get in his car and get back to Perth."'

'Good thing I didn't ring him.'

'I appreciate that.'

'Still. What's your point?'

'Earlier this year a boy from the same school hung himself.'

'Shit,' Saunders said and shook his head. 'Country boy?' he asked.

'City boy.'

'Bloody hell. How old?'

'Nineteen. His parents found him. He'd hung himself from the back verandah.' Cardilini said slowly. Shaking his head, Saunders spat some tobacco from his lips. Cardilini continued. 'Last year another boy, same school, died in a single-car accident on a straight country road he knew well. A country boy. There were no signs of braking before the car hit a large tree.'

'You think there's a connection?'

'All three were cadets at the school where complaints and rumours existed about an abusive teacher,' Cardilini said.

'What sort of abusive?' Saunders asked lightly.

'Sexual abuse.'

'Shit. You bullshitting me?'

'No,' Cardilini replied.

'So, what? Are you building a case?' Saunders asked

Cardilini watched as Saunders stubbed out his cigarette vigorously on the verandah. 'The teacher was shot,' he said.

'Dead?' Saunders looked up sharply.

'Yes. Accidental shooting the report reads.'

'Sounds like a good outcome to me.'

'I believe other boys could be at risk if the denial by the school continues.'

'Cardilini, I won't be changing the report.'

'I'm not even thinking that.'

'Good,' Saunders acknowledged, then volunteered, 'I think the Sheppard boy shot himself.'

'Bloody hell, Saunders, why didn't you say that?' Cardilini stormed.

'Get stuffed, Cardilini. It's a report, not a speculation. That's the coroner's job,' Saunders returned, equally strong.

'Was the body found beside the firearm?' Cardilini calmed and asked.

'Yes. But I knew Colin. I played footy on the town team with him. He was too sensible. The body was found on a rise that looked out on the southern paddocks. It was beside a tree stump, a tree stump that makes a good seat. He wasn't a clumsy, or a careless boy. He was a good kid.'

'Did you tell the coroner?' Cardilini asked.

'I answered his questions. He didn't ask me what I thought.'

Cardilini stubbed his cigarette out and flicked the butt towards the dead lawn as Saunders had done. 'What do the parents think?' he asked.

'You're going there, aren't you?'

'Yes. In about an hour,' Cardilini answered.

'Ask them. I didn't have the heart to,' Saunders said.

'They read your report?'

'Yes. The dad, Mo Sheppard.'

'Did he say anything?'

'No, and I didn't ask him what he was thinking. But he shook my hand and nodded as if thanking me.'

Cardilini nodded his understanding while Saunders rubbed his hand across his forehead. Their eyes drifted back to the bush. Cicadas suddenly seemed to spring to life.

Cardilini saw the homestead half a mile from the road in acres of flat, stubble-strewn paddocks. It was tucked amid clusters of trees that sheltered sheds and water tanks. To the right of the house in a broad, flat-roofed shed, Cardilini saw the distinctive winged tail-lights of a Chevrolet Impala. As he pulled up under the extended branches of a gum tree, he saw green lawn bordering a red cement path leading to the verandah. Standing there with her hands on her hips was a woman in her forties. Cardilini, conscious of her gaze, walked steadily from the car to the path. He stopped at the bottom of the steps to the verandah.

'Coming all the way from Perth I suppose I'll have to invite you in,' came the greeting.

'Thanks,' Cardilini replied.

'My husband will be in from the shed shortly. Better follow me.' She turned to the dark shadows of the passageway, letting Cardilini deal with the flyscreen door as it swung shut. 'No point talking to me until he's here. Have a seat. I've a bun in the oven.' She put the kettle on the woodstove, opened the fire grate and poked inside for a moment.

'Thank you for seeing me,' Cardilini said

'I wouldn't be too quick with your "thank you". This is his idea, not mine. I can't see the point of it.'

The rear flyscreen door banged closed and a heavy-set farmer took a step into the kitchen and stood solidly to allow his eyes to adjust.

'Detective Sergeant Cardilini?' the man asked.

Cardilini stood and extended his hand.

'I'm Murray, and you've met Dot.'

'I'm not here,' Dot said and clattered some crockery.

'Dot can't see the point of you coming all the way from Perth,' Murray Sheppard said.

'That's the only reason I let him in,' Dot said over her shoulder.

'I spoke to Senior Constable Saunders . . .' Cardilini started.

'Stop right there. Mo, you take the tray onto the verandah, you follow him, Mister. I'll decide what sort of talk goes on in my kitchen. You carry this,' she said pushing the tray into Sheppard's big hands, 'don't drop it.' A jug of milk and a bowl of sugar were given to Cardilini. 'Go. Scoot.' Dot returned to her oven.

Cardilini sat on one of two wrought iron chairs at a small, round, wrought iron table. Sheppard set the tea things down, gave a shrug and a smile and re-entered the house. A dog walked over and sniffed Cardilini's leg then returned to a collection of hessian bags where it circled twice before sitting. Cardilini's eyes wandered to the sheds, the trees and the parched and bristling paddocks.

Sheppard returned with a steaming sliced cake, fresh from the oven.

'It's been difficult, and now our youngest is away at St Nicholas . . .' Sheppard said as he sat. 'Mrs Lockheed said you were investigating a possible link between our boy and two others.'

'I'm sorry. She shouldn't have said . . .' Cardilini started to protest.

'Let's not worry about that. You tell me what you're doing?'

Cardilini inhaled the dry air and said, 'I'm investigating the circumstance of the deaths.'

'Is this something to do with Edmund?'

'It's possible.'

'I'm not sorry the man is dead. I'm beginning to think he hurt my boy, the gist of which I believe you got from Mrs Lockheed,' Sheppard said.

'Yes.'

'Dot will have none of it. She doesn't understand there are deadset bastards in the world. But I don't need to tell you that, I suppose.'

'No.'

Sheppard sighed heavily. 'So, what do you want to know?'

Realising the implications his questions could have for the Sheppards, Cardilini asked slowly and quietly, 'Do you think it possible your boy's death wasn't an accident?'

To Cardilini's relief Sheppard replied promptly and without hesitation. 'Yes, and, no.' Cardilini waited. 'I won't be disputing Saunders's report,' Sheppard emphasised.

'I won't be asking you to,' Cardilini replied quickly.

'And I won't be helping you catch the fellow who shot Edmund.'

'It was an accidental shot from across the river,' Cardilini stated.

'Did you go across the river?'

'No.'

Sheppard continued angrily, 'I did. You think we're all idiots? I wasn't going to send my boy to a school where some moron could shoot him. I met the farmer, made it my business. He doesn't allow a .303 to be fired on his property. Neither does any other farmer out there. I believe them. They run cattle, expensive cattle. No one shoots for sport. They do roo culls. And professional shooters use .243s. Go and speak to him.'

'I will. So you don't think it was an accident?' Cardilini asked.

'Which, my boy or Edmund?' Cardilini turned his eyes from the challenge in Sheppard's. 'Come a long way for nothing it would seem. Eat some cake. If you don't eat her cake, she'll be real cranky.'

Cardilini took a piece. It was dry in his mouth.

'Don't worry, I'll say you liked it,' Sheppard said as he rolled a cigarette. 'You better understand, someone has done the world a favour by shooting Edmund.'

'It's to no one's advantage if we start shooting each other. Edmund should have been investigated and brought to justice,' Cardilini said.

'He was investigated, wasn't he? No one could believe he did it. I didn't until Mrs Lockheed contacted me. What an idiot I've been. I think he got justice. What do you think?' Sheppard's eyes fixed on Cardilini.

'Mr Sheppard, I'm not going to argue with you.'

'Good. Haven't much time for arguments.' Sheppard lit his cigarette. 'And, if you're not a bloody fool get on with your career. And let your boy get on with his.'

Cardilini stood confused. 'What do you know about my son?' Sheppard stood too and squared up to Cardilini. The dog crossed between them and barked, its eyes rolling towards Cardilini. Neither man flinched. The dog kept barking.

'Shut that dog up,' came from inside the house.

Sheppard turned his eyes from Cardilini. 'Sit down, Paddy. We aren't going to do anything. Just facing off like a couple of old man roos.'

'I don't know what your game is, I feel for your loss but you don't scare me, Sheppard,' Cardilini said.

'That's funny, I scare myself, and I don't scare easily. Still it's good to know you have some backbone.'

'I didn't know everything I was doing was such common knowledge.'

'Now you know. Maybe I've been a bit too direct. Kind of lost balance. Maybe said too much. Wouldn't surprise me.'

'Do you know who shot Edmund?' Cardilini asked surprised at his own question.

'Yes . . . is what I want to say. But if I did, I wouldn't be telling you.'

'But you know who did?'

'Accident, wasn't it?' Sheppard said with a half-smile. 'Someone took a .303 to a roo cull, I think you'll find.'

On Sheppard's instruction Cardilini didn't say goodbye to Dot.

Kilkenny Road
3.30 p.m. Tuesday, 3rd November 1965

Cardilini arrived back in Perth mid-afternoon. He rang Spry at East Perth to ask him to find out which Melbourne school Edmund had been at before taking up his position at St Nicholas. Also, the current posting of the constable who wrote the Wongan Hills car crash report. Spry complained but Cardilini knew he'd do it. Then he started to clean the house. He started with the sleep-out where he now slept. He hadn't spent a night in the main bedroom since Betty's death. It was Betty's room.

When the phone rang it was Spry. Cardilini noted the details and decided he would make the calls in the morning.

Paul arrived home to find Cardilini standing in the doorway of Betty's room.

'What're you doing?'

'I was thinking of vacuuming.'

Paul stood beside him. 'Smells like Mum,' he said.

'Might just leave it.' Cardilini suggested.

'Yeah. I think that's best.'

Cardilini slowly closed the door and turned to Paul. 'I can cook tonight.'

'What?'

'Sausages.'

'You have to have something with them.'

'Potatoes.'

Paul stood in the hallway seemingly undecided then he said, 'Aunty Roslyn asked me to dinner.'

'Good, good. You two catch up. Say hello from me,' Cardilini said and turned into the kitchen. Paul stood watching him for a moment then walked to his bedroom.

Day 11
Kilkenny Road
8.00 a.m. Wednesday, 4th November 1965

Cardilini sat by the phone with his notes spread out before him. The first call was to the Marlborough School for Boys. He waited for the principal to come on line.

'Marks.'

'Principal Marks?' Cardilini asked.

'You're the detective from Perth?'

'Detective Sergeant Cardilini. Ringing about Captain Edmund.'

'We heard. Tragic. What do you want to know?'

'Why did he leave your school?'

'Chasing greater opportunity, I believe.'

'Was there any reason for you to mistrust him around the students?'

'I gave him an excellent reference.'

'Yes. But was there?'

'The man has passed on. Is there any point to this?'

'Some students have made complaints about unwanted sexual behaviour towards them.'

'Over there?'

'Yes.'

'I can't help you. I gave the man an excellent reference.'

'So you say. I take it you had similar complaints.' Cardilini waited for a response.

'I can't help you, Detective Sergeant Cardilini. I know what you're chasing. I won't be damaging the man's reputation at this point.'

'Or your school's reputation?'

After a pause, 'Anything else I can help you with, Detective Sergeant Cardilini?'

'Not right now.'

The phone went dead and Cardilini dialled the Fremantle Police Station.

THIRTY

Day 2
12.45 p.m. Monday, 26th October 1965

With his back to the wall, the boy stood in the corridor near the sixth form common room door. Head down, he watched the black, polished shoes and swishing grey-trousered legs of students walk past. Voices filled the corridor and his ears: deep voices, talking, calling to one another; they seemed older than his father's or other men's voices; wiser, terrifying voices; voices that could look in his eyes and see his shame. The bell for period three sounded. There were too many shoes to count now, too many to see correctly, black blurs against the bare floorboards, too many voices, none speaking discernible words, instead making a hum and clatter like an engine. The engine followed the shoes down the corridor and out the door. He knew he wouldn't move until . . . he wondered how long.

A pair of black brogues stopped in front of him, the punched-leather holes winking at him. Settling on the shoes were grey-cuffed suit trousers. When all was perfectly still and silent, his name was spoken. He wondered if he would ever be a boy who

could wear brogues. Would he ever be old enough? He doubted
he would, he doubted he would be allowed to get older. Somehow, he knew that if he could ever wear brogues, he'd be safe.
His name again and this time he was told to look up. He slowly
moved his head. It had to be slow because the gears in his neck
wanted to go the other way. It was a three-buttoned suit, the
bottom button undone. His eyes froze on the second button, his
head wouldn't go any further, the gears locked, his eyes blinked
rapidly but they too were locked.

'Did you pick something up from Captain Edmund's
room?'

His eyes shut and the gears moved his head up and down.

'I want you to hide it. You must never mention it to anyone.
Do you understand?'

The gears moved, his eyes shut.

'No one is going to hurt you again. You're a good boy, never
think any different. Do you understand?' The gears worked
quickly, thankfully. 'Now run to class. If anyone says anything
tell them you were speaking to me.'

The boy ran, his face aching with a wide smile, eyes streaming. He couldn't wipe them quickly enough. The sleeve of his
jacket was sodden but his eyes were clear when he entered the
classroom. He was told he was late. He apologised and said the
boy's name, and that he was speaking to him. The teacher told
him to run faster next time and hoped that Carmody was able
to talk some sense into him. When the boy replied that he had
done, the teacher said in that case then he didn't mind the boy
being late. This was met with a murmur of approval from the
class. The boy sat, feeling inquisitive eyes on him. Carmody
was a king and he'd said he would never be hurt again. This
caused rapid breathing that pushed the smile back to his face.

He fought it. He was a good boy. Thank you, dear God. He knew Carmody would speak to him again one day, and he'd spend every second up to that meeting proving that Carmody was correct. He was a good boy.

The jumping of his heart told him: you can start again.

THIRTY-ONE

Day 11
Fremantle Train Station
8.50 a.m. Wednesday, 4th November 1965

Mr and Mrs Doney's son, their only child, died in a single-car accident the previous year at Wongon Hills. Now they lived in an apartment in Forrest Street, Cottesloe, waiting for the settlement of the sale of their farm. Senior Constable Young, who'd compiled the initial report for the traffic branch, had, earlier in the year, transferred to the Fremantle branch. Cardilini organised an appointment with him for 9 a.m. at the Fremantle train station.

This suburban train station appeared a poor cousin to Perth Central. The government architect had included design characteristics of the period in the stone portico and red brick buildings, however, its size suggested little future growth for Fremantle Port.

Cardilini waited for Senior Constable Young to come from the platform. When the timber carriages rattled away, Young, a tall, angular man with short, greying hair, walked towards him.

'We had some idiot steal a conductor's bag and machine,' the constable said by way of excuse for the location of the meeting. Then, 'Aren't you suspended?'

Cardilini had crossed paths with Young on a number of occasions, usually at crime scenes, and he knew him to be a tough but honest copper.

'No, on leave, just tying up a few loose ends.'

'Funny thing to be doing on leave.'

'Yeah. Hilarious. You remember the accident?'

'Of course.'

'You knew the boy?'

'I knew of the boy.'

'You've seen a few accidents. Was it suicide?'

Young shook his head and said sarcastically, 'Why don't you get straight to the point, Cardilini?'

'Well, was it suicide?' Cardilini persisted.

'Who'll ever know?' Young was evasive. 'He could have fallen asleep.'

'Do you think he did?'

Young looked to the sky and pursed his lips. 'Highly unlikely.'

'Did he accelerate into the tree?' Cardilini asked.

Young looked to Cardilini as if assessing him and asked, 'You read the report?'

'It wasn't mentioned.'

'That's right, and you know why?' Young asked.

'I'm not going to ask you to change your report,' Cardilini reassured.

'I've heard that before.'

'No one will know of this conversation,' Cardilini said.

'Don't shit me, Cardilini. If this didn't matter, you wouldn't be asking and you'd be glued to a cold beer somewhere.'

'Stop being a hard bastard. What did you see?'

Young scratched his cheek then said, 'I think he lined the tree up from five hundred yards away and powered into it as fast as that jalopy would go. The bloody thing disintegrated around him. I don't know how the traffic boys handle it.'

'Me neither.'

'I'll say you're lying if you try to use that,' Young warned, staring straight at Cardilini.

'Fair enough. Thanks, Young.'

'What for?'

Cottesloe
3.30 p.m. Wednesday, 4th November 1965

Norfolk pine trees grew high on both sides of Forrest Street between Broome Street and Marine Parade. The Doney apartment was halfway down on the right. A double-storey, red brick block of four apartments, two up, two down. The Doneys lived on the second storey.

Cardilini knocked on the door. Mr Doney let him in. Doney, not a tall man, had dark hair and a round boulder head on broad, heavy shoulders. Large pieces of furniture left little space to manoeuvre between them. Lounge suites, sideboards, occasional chairs, clustered side tables, standard lamps and pouffes filled the room. A hollowed elephant's foot that held umbrellas and walking sticks stood by the front door. Framed photos covered every flat surface and hanging pictures stared down from every wall. Only an army badge, crossed rifles supporting a crown in a laurel wreath, inscribed 'Royal Corps Australian Infantry' secured a space of its own on the sideboard. Beside it, a small vase of freshly cut yellow roses. Cardilini had noticed similar roses blooming along the driveway.

'Take a seat,' Mr Doney said.

Cardilini sat in an armchair.

Mrs Doney, a small woman who seemed to have folded in on herself, gave Cardilini a brief glance of her dark, bird-like eyes. Mr and Mrs Doney sat opposite on the lounge.

'I'm sorry for your loss,' Cardilini said.

'Thank you.'

'And I'm sorry to trouble you.'

'No trouble,' replied Mr Doney.

Mrs Doney left to make a pot of tea and Cardilini and Mr Doney talked of the weather, of farming, and eventually, when Mrs Doney had returned and poured the tea, settled on the subject of St Nicholas College.

'Did Peter talk about why he was discharged from the cadets?' Cardilini asked.

'No.'

'Were you surprised?'

'No.'

'Why?'

'Why should we be? He didn't like it,' Doney said flatly.

'Did he say what he didn't like about it?'

'Peter wasn't one to complain.'

'He was dismissed for not accepting authority,' Cardilini said.

'That's what we heard. Anything else?' Mr Doney asked.

Mrs Doney now stared, unmoving, at Cardilini.

'Was Peter an experienced driver?'

'An excellent driver. The steering went. Could happen to anyone.'

'Did you tell Senior Constable Young about the steering?'

'What else could it have been?'

Cardilini turned his gaze from Mr Doney to Mrs Doney, who dropped her eyes.

'Any other questions?' Mr Doney prompted.

'How was Peter's state of mind before the accident?'

'Terrific.'

'Where was he going?'

'When?'

'When he took the car?'

'He was . . . that road goes down to the highway.'

'He was too young to have a license. Why would he be going that way?'

'He was going to check a fence,' Doney said with a quick glance to his wife.

'I see,' Cardilini said.

Returning his cup and saucer to the tray Cardilini casually said, 'Tragic about Captain Edmund.'

Doney's eyes turned murderous.

Cardilini didn't exhale until he was in his car, where he fought a feeling of wretchedness.

Bentley
6.30 p.m. Wednesday, 4th November 1965

Evening gathered methodically on the verandahs, among the trees and towards the end of Williamson's street. From his car Cardilini watched its slow encroachment. *I'll wait until the streetlights come on*, he told himself. The streetlights came on and the gloom darkened but he continued sitting. Casual glances came his way from a man watering his front garden. He sat stubbornly. The man went inside his house. A car turned into the street. Cardilini watched it slow down and pull up at Williamson's house. Cardilini opened his car door and walked towards the car. Bradley Williamson stood by the vehicle waiting for Cardilini to approach.

'Bradley Williamson?'

'Who's asking?'

'Detective Sergeant Cardilini, East Perth branch.'

'I've heard about you.'

Cardilini paused. Williamson was six foot, square, trim and compact. He held Cardilini in an unblinking gaze.

'From who?' Cardilini asked.

'Ask your questions, I might answer or I might not.'

'Did you shoot Captain Edmund?'

Williamson tilted his head back and laughed.

'Did you?' Cardilini asked again when Williamson had settled.

'They said you had a one-track mind.'

'Who?'

'Difficult is it, living with that?' Williamson asked.

'No. Getting away with murder is difficult.'

'Experienced that, have you?'

A *man in complete possession of himself,* Cardilini thought, *a strong, honest, straightforward man; a man other men would follow without a second thought.* Cardilini fought an instinct to like Williamson.

'Do you know who shot Captain Edmund?' he persisted.

'You're getting boring, Cardilini.'

'Answer me and I'll suddenly get interesting.'

'I was on a train from Sydney when it happened, but you've been told that.'

'What?'

'My mother told you I was travelling at the time of Edmund's death.'

Cardilini remembered Mrs Williamson telling him. The booze had rotted his brain, he thought.

'I know why he was shot,' Cardilini said.

'Tell me?'

'For the deaths of Geoffrey Masters, Colin Sheppard and Peter Doney.'

Williamson didn't respond.

'Maybe you didn't pull the trigger but you and others decided it was time to stop Edmund's abuse.'

'You've lost me, Cardilini, but how's Salt going?' Williamson asked.

'Who was it, Mo Sheppard, Doney? They're farmers, they'd have access to .303s.' Cardilini continued.

'Constable Salt will make a good cop. He also sees everything in black and white,' Williamson ruminated, ignoring Cardilini.

'But you don't see everything in black and white?' Cardilini asked.

'Oh yeah, I do. There's right and there's wrong. You've got to choose where you stand.'

'And you think you have chosen, right?'

'But I guess, Cardilini, you don't get to choose. You get told what's right and wrong.'

'What Edmund did was inexcusable.'

'Not everyone agreed with that. But the shooting was accidental, don't you read your own department reports?'

'Did *you* read it?'

'Have a good life, Detective Cardilini,' Williamson said in parting. When almost at the door he turned, 'I hope your boy does well at the academy.' He walked into the house with Cardilini watching him until the door closed.

Without Williamson as his prime suspect, who? And what threads needed to be in place for Williamson to read the report of the shooting? Cardilini shook his head as he returned to his car.

THIRTY-TWO

Day 12
Kilkenny Road
8.15 a.m. Thursday, 5th November 1965

Cardilini and Paul cleaned up after breakfast.

'So what's your plan today, Paul?' Cardilini asked.

'Going to the library again. I might finish my leaving certificate through a technical college.'

'Don't jeopardise the academy,' Cardilini said absently.

'You're telling *me* not to jeopardise the academy?'

'No just . . .' he caught a glimpse of Paul's eyes '. . . I have a few calls to make then I'm heading out.'

'I'd be going in the evenings.'

'That's good. That's very good son.'

'Yeah, very good. You're not doing anything to muck it up are you?'

'No. No.' Cardilini said, all but tiptoeing from the kitchen. He stood with his hand poised over the phone, *I'm doing the right thing,* he told himself, *I'm doing what's needed for Paul and me.*

His first call to Great Southern Rail confirmed the dates of Williamson's train arrival in Perth. From the Sydney train the passengers changed to the Perth train in Adelaide. The clerk thought a train manifest might be available at Sydney or Adelaide but not in Perth. He couldn't say if the passengers were checked at Adelaide.

The Adelaide Trans Australian Airways office provided a list of flights accessible to the Sydney train's arrival into Adelaide. Williamson could disembark the train in Adelaide, take a taxi to the airport, catch a flight and be in Perth two days before the train's arrival. A copy of their flight manifests would be sent to the East Perth station.

Cardilini dumped the bulk of his chest on the counter of the typists' pool. On seeing him, Mrs Andreoli, an attractive blonde woman in her fifties, continued her typing.

'Hi, darling, I'm expecting a radio facsimile,' Cardilini said.

'I'm expecting a new car, *darling*, but I don't think I'll get it.'

'Very funny. Can you check?'

'Don't need to. I can hear the bloody thing when something comes through. I'll put it in your pigeonhole.'

'It's important.'

'You should see the bucket of bolts I'm driving.'

'Don't forget.'

'I've already forgotten.' And she waved him away.

Cardilini stood staring at Mrs Andreoli. They had once been very friendly. He walked away wondering how much of a pain in the arse he must have been the past year.

Cardilini rang Constable Saunders in Williams. 'Hi Saunders, it's Cardilini.'

'How did you go with Sheppard?' There was a little smile in the question.

'Interesting fellow. Does he have a .303?'

'Yep.'

'Do you think he could shoot someone?'

'Why not? If he had reason.'

'He has reason.'

'Then,' a firm response, 'yep.'

'Could you check around to see if he's capable of hitting a target at two hundred yards?'

'I'm capable of hitting a target at two hundred yards,' Saunders laughed.

'All right, a bullseye? A cluster of five out of five?'

'These guys shoot roos. I've been with them. There are half-a-dozen who constantly hit their target,' Saunders concluded.

'Was he home on the night of the twenty-sixth?' Cardilini asked.

'Is this an official investigation?'

'No, but . . .'

'Can't help you. It's difficult enough in a small community without nosing around for no reason.' Saunders hung up.

It made sense that Doney could also make the shot. And he was in Perth at the time. In fact, there were a hundred farmers with sons at St Nicholas who could have reason, access, and the ability to shoot Edmund.

Cardilini went downstairs to the secretaries' pool and the detectives' pigeonholes. A sheet of paper sat neatly in his pigeon-hole. *Yes. Yes.* Cardilini pulled it out and scanned it. He scanned it again. Then, slowly, went from name to name. He crossed to Mrs Andreoli's desk.

'Anything else come with this?' he asked.

'Yeah, but I'm hiding it from you.'

Cardilini grunted and, returning to the second storey, pondered the manifest. Williamson's name wasn't on it. He could have used a false name. Awkward but not impossible. The manifest listed surname, first initial and booking agent.

Eventually, back at his desk, Cardilini obtained the phone numbers of the four booking agents used. He rang them and verified the identity of twenty-seven individuals; five fitted Williamson's description, three he had contact details for, two he didn't. He started to ring. The first three provided employment details. Cardilini checked the employer's number given with the phone-book number of the employer and rang them. The employers verified the individuals were indeed as identified in the manifest. He started on the phone book to find the remaining two. Twenty-one calls later he had verified their existence.

Disappointed, he tidied his desk thinking about his hearing tomorrow when his phone rang. It was Constable Saunders from Williams.

'It so happens Sheppard was away for three days. He left town on the twenty-fourth and arrived back on the twenty-seventh. He and a friend from Wongan Hills drove to Lake Grace for an Elder's sale. I checked. They were legitimate auctions of farming equipment. Two hundred visitors went to the town. Farmers going to the wall in Lake Grace means good value purchases for everyone else.'

'The Wongan Hills friend, was he a farmer?'

'I'd say so.'

'How did you find out?'

'I'd just forgotten. A number of farmers went. They don't take the wives. So bit of a piss up, too.'

'What was the Wongan Hills farmer's name?'

'Jesus, Cardilini.'

'Doney,' Cardilini said under his breath as the phone clicked.

Sheppard and Doney could show their faces at Lake Grace before heading to Perth. Sheppard could possibly contact the farmer to find out when the roo cull was taking place. Then he takes the shot while Doney waits in the car. They had a powerful motive, they knew how to accomplish it and they had the skills and rifle to do it. Now to prove it.

Day 5
St Nicholas College
4.35 p.m. Thursday, November 1965

The boy sat with his back against the gym wall watching boys play handball. He used to be a star handball player, he was quick, he had been one of the best in his form.

'What are you looking at, creep?' a third form boy from the courts called to him. He stood and walked away. 'Creep.'

There was a radio shack near the science department where all the brainy kids hung out. He wandered down and sat opposite its doorway on a low brick wall, looking in.

'Harper, do you want to come in?' Mr Copus, his science teacher, asked. The boy shook his head and stayed seated, looking in.

Brain-Box Boxel, from his form, poked his head from the door and called, 'Hey, Harper, come in! We're making crystal sets.' The boy shook his head. He had the feeling he was protecting them from what had happened to him, but Captain Edmund's dead and no one will ever find out, *he reminded himself. He pushed himself from his seat and wandered to the* doorway and stood there. Boys were sitting on high stools at a long table.

'Do you know how to solder?' Mr Copus called.

'No, sir.'

'Better get over here then. Hurry up, you can watch.'

The boy wandered to the free stool Mr Copus had pointed to.

'Harper, is it?' an older boy beside him asked, the boy nodded. 'You can watch me.' The boy climbed onto the stool.

He walked alongside Brain-Box to dinner. Brain-Box talked and talked, he had two crystal sets and he was going to lend one to the boy. Brain Box listened to his crystal set in bed at night, when the cricket was on. The boy would listen to the cricket too. Brain-Box didn't mention Captain Edmund or Carmody. Harper thought that even though they were at the same school, Brain-Box must live in a different world to him. The boy prayed as they walked to dinner that his world, now that Captain Edmund was gone, would go wispy and blow away like smoke.

'Well . . . well?' Brain-Box was demanding of him but the boy hadn't been listening, dark shadows of fear had caught him.

'What?'

'Come to the dorm and pick up the crystal set straight after dinner, dozy.'

The boy nodded.

At the dining hall he forced himself to stand where Brain-Box stood and not go and stand alone at the back. Brain-Box talked and talked until another boy told him to 'shut his fat gob'. After that, Brain-Box continued in a whisper. The boy looked at the boy who said that and felt a stirring of anger and wondered why he had no anger when he was called a creep. 'You have *nothing to fear anymore, you're a good boy,' Carmody had said. He looked for Carmody. He was standing on the steps waiting for all the kids to arrive and stand quietly.* I've nothing to fear anymore, *the boy repeated to himself as Brain-Box whispered into his ear.*

THIRTY-THREE

Day 13
East Perth Police Department
7.50 a.m. Friday, 6th November 1965

The breakfast Cardilini swallowed wanted to return to his mouth. He'd arrived early at East Perth and sat smoking at his desk. He recalled some of the nervous characters he had grilled in the interview rooms. With ten minutes to go he went up to the third level where the internal investigation interview was to take place.

'You okay, Detective Sergeant Cardilini?' his union representative, Mrs Burns, asked as they sat in the corridor. She was a dowdily dressed, middle-aged woman with poorly-bleached hair clutching a large cloth bag to her lap like a security cushion. Her arrival surprised Cardilini, not just because of her appearance but because union reps weren't a usual addition to the East Perth station. Any station for that matter. Most employees saw their allegiance to their colleagues and the department before the union. Even being seen with a union rep could be considered an act of betrayal.

'Fine,' Cardilini replied.

Two uniformed police walked past with curious glances to Cardilini and Mrs Burns.

'You won't be able to smoke inside,' Mrs Burns informed Cardilini.

'Since when?'

'You need to appear a little concerned,' she cautioned.

'I'm concerned. Why do you think I'm smoking?'

'I think you should put it out before we go in,' she instructed warmly.

Cardilini shrugged.

'Did you know Mossop is coming to the station?' Mrs Burns asked.

'No. Why?'

'They might want to verify your comments.'

'How can he verify my comments? He's made the whole thing up.'

'I'm just saying.'

'So why are you here?'

'We were asked to come. Maybe they're taking it seriously this time,' Mrs Burns said with a tinge of moral indignation.

'Great.'

'It's part of a new look.'

'Wonderful. So what're you going to do?'

'As I said, we aren't usually invited.' Mrs Burns smiled comfortingly. 'Hopefully, you'll be believed.'

'Hopefully?' Cardilini burst. He wasn't comforted and lit a second cigarette from the first.

'If I was a detective,' Mrs Burns smiled again, 'I would think you're looking nervous.'

'If you were a detective, you'd be right.'

* * *

'You have the charges, Cardilini?' asked Winfield, the internal investigating officer. Chapman, his offsider, took notes. Cardilini knew them both well. Detectives rotated through the internal investigation branch. Cardilini had done a stint too. The thinking was, only those who knew how things worked would know when a policeman overstepped the boundaries.

'Charges?' Cardilini corrected, '*Complaint*, surely?'

'Complaint. Sorry.'

'Thank you,' Cardilini said.

'Thank you,' Mrs Burns echoed. The two investigating officers looked at her then at each other.

'No need for you to do that,' Chapman said. Mrs Burns nodded.

Winfield queried the presence of Mrs Burns with a glance to Cardilini. Cardilini shrugged.

'Okay. So did you expose yourself?' Winfield asked.

'No, I didn't.'

'An older boy, Carmody, brought the boy, Mossop, to you and you told Constable Salt to go with Carmody, and leave you alone with Mossop.'

Cardilini shook his head frustrated. 'Not to leave me alone with Mossop, but for Salt to further the investigation, you idiot.'

Winfield and Chapman exchanged annoyed glances.

'Mossop is alone with you when you expose yourself,' Chapman said.

'I didn't expose myself,' Cardilini shouted.

'That is in dispute,' Winfield said.

What?' Cardilini asked.

'In dispute,' Winfield said. 'We don't know the truth of the matter.'

'Winfield, I'm telling you the truth. There isn't a dispute,' Cardilini insisted, ignoring Chapman.

Winfield turned uncomfortably towards Mrs Burns.

'Winfield?' Cardilini called.

'Cardilini, hang on,' Winfield replied.

'Did you ask the boy exactly what he claims he saw?' Cardilini asked.

Winfield drew back in disgust. 'No.'

'Not that, you moron. He said I showed him a picture, yes?'

'Right, he said you showed him a picture of a boy with his pants down.'

'Good. Did he say it was his picture? With his name on it?'

'Was it?' Winfield asked.

'Ask him. He's here, isn't he?'

'Cardilini, you're not in charge of this. Get that straight,' Chapman remonstrated with a look to Mrs Burns.

'Yes. Fine. I understand that. I'm only trying to help. Right, Mrs Burns?'

Mrs Burns looked to Winfield and Chapman before she replied, 'Yes.'

'Chapman, check that with the boy,' Winfield instructed.

'Get him to explain how he knew the figure didn't have his pants on,' Cardilini said. Winfield nodded his confirmation and Chapman begrudgingly left.

Winfield and Cardilini exchanged a number of communicative glances; Winfield indicated Mrs Burns' presence was a surprise to them, Cardilini indicated similar while Mrs Burns inspected the architraves. Chapman returned and nodded in the affirmative. Cardilini waited before asking, 'What did he say?'

'The figure had his pants around his ankles,' Chapman replied.

'Thank you.' Cardilini reached into his inside coat pocket and put Mossop's sketch in front of them, 'That's his sketch. There's his name. The figure has trousers on.'

'Hard to determine. Not much of an artist.' Winfield pushed the sketch to Chapman.

'There's nothing around his ankles,' Chapman said.

'No.' Cardilini reached for the sketch. 'Evidence in an investigation,' he said to Chapman and pushed the sketch for Mrs Burns to view.

'He lied about that. Why? Surely that makes everything else he said suspect?' Cardilini demanded.

Winfield and Chapman conferred.

Winfield unwillingly looked towards Cardilini. 'Another boy saw you doing up your fly.'

'Oh. Great. Who?'

'We don't have a name,' Winfield said, avoiding Cardilini's gaze.

'You're kidding me?' Cardilini burst.

'We were told just before we came in.'

'Who told you?'

'The deputy commissioner.'

Cardilini sat stunned as he stared at Chapman and Winfield. They stared back mutely.

'What?' Mrs Burns asked.

'Anonymous comments aren't normally considered evidence in complaint cases,' Cardilini said. 'Are they?' he confirmed with Winfield.

'No,' Winfield replied.

'Oh. It could still be good then?' Mrs Burns smiled at Cardilini.

'No,' he retorted, then asked, 'Where do we go from here, Winfield?'

'We'll have to get back to you.'

Winfield and Chapman left the room exchanging confused glances with Cardilini.

'So, is that it?' Mrs Burns asked.

'Yep. That's it for now.'

'Oh, well. Nice meeting you, Cardilini.'

'Likewise.'

Cardilini watched Mrs Burns walk away with a casual air of achievement and wished he could feel the same way.

He was standing at the urinal considering why the interview had been hijacked with the arrival of Mrs Burns and the presence of Mossop at the station, when Mossop walked in and stood at an adjoining urinal.

'Good afternoon, sir.'

'Mossop?' Cardilini blinked several times to reassure himself that it was, in fact, Mossop.

'Yes, sir.'

'How are you enjoying your trip to the police station?' Cardilini asked looking towards the door.

'Not my first time. We pinched some bamboo from the Memorial Park in Narrogin for our high jump. The gardener hauled us in. That was the first time.'.

'Okay. So why did you make up your story?' Cardilini asked, trying to assume an air of 'all this is quite natural'.

'I can't explain it exactly. But it's the right thing to do.'

'Oh, is it? How do you work that out?' Cardilini demanded.

'You were setting out to damage the school.'

'Oh yeah. Who's the other witness?'

'Don't know.'

'Carmody put you up to this?' Cardilini said finishing up.

'What happens is up to you,' Mossop articulated care-fully.

'I see. You can tell Carmody,' Cardilini said sharply, 'it's another loose ball.'

'It's another loose ball?' Mossop repeated.

'Yes, it won't work. That's it. Did you come in here on purpose?'

'Yes, sir, to say, "What happens is up to you."' Mossop exaggerated his shake and adjustment.

Cardilini nearly laughed, before asking, 'And if I satisfied Carmody, would you say you made it all up?'

'Yes, sir.'

'Wouldn't the school see that as very bad of you?'

'It's complicated, sir,' Mossop said and left, leaving Cardilini shaking his head in disbelief. He anticipated a squad outside the door poised to arrest him, but when he left there was no one in sight.

He walked to the detective's office. Half his colleagues were at their desks. No one called a greeting.

'What don't I know?' Cardilini called out.

'Deputy Commissioner was down here. Wanted to know if anyone had knowledge of you abusing suspects. No one said anything,' Spry said with a glance to the office entrance.

'Thanks.'

'Stop looking for skeletons,' Spry said.

Cardilini nodded his understanding. Skeletons at St Nicholas were the last things the old boys would want. And Deputy Commissioner Warren wasn't going to let it happen on his watch, was he?

The accidental shooting report had been completed. So why is that fat copper still sniffing around? Cardilini figured that question had been asked a few times. A good question, too. Cardilini wished he knew the answer.

'Not wanted here. Going home,' Cardilini said into Bishop's office.

'Sounds good to me,' Bishop replied without looking up.

*　*　*

'Detective Cardilini.'

Cardilini turned. Salt walked down the corridor towards him.

'Salt.'

'Sir, would I be able to talk to you?'

'About you being a past St Nicholas boy?' Cardilini asked.

'I wanted to tell you.'

Cardilini shook his head. He didn't want to talk to Salt. He saw him as part of the whole machine that was corralling him.

'I heard the deputy commissioner has come up with another eyewitness,' Salt said.

'Now how do you think that came about?'

'It's not the school. I know that for a fact. I thought you should know.'

'Who then?'

'Carmody.'

Cardilini nodded. 'But why for heaven's sake?'

'I think some boys would follow Carmody into the trenches,' Salt replied. Cardilini sighed in disbelief. Salt continued. 'I remember, even in second form Carmody was a leader. He would stand up to all the third form boys who would traditionally bash second formers. He just wasn't intimidated by them. Even when he was flattened in a fight, he was defiant and he never dobbed.'

'Sounds like a thug,' Cardilini said but didn't believe it.

'He was good enough for the first eleven when he was in fourth form.'

'So he can play cricket. Big deal.'

'He stood by Lockheed even though he knew it would cost him head boy,' Salt said.

Cardilini nodded and pushed open the front door to the station. Salt followed.

'So why am I getting a lecture on Carmody?'

'Sir, I think you need to take him seriously.'

'You take him seriously; I think he's an arrogant prick.'

Salt stayed step for step with Cardilini as he walked towards his car.

'What is it, Salt?'

'Do you still think Edmund was intentionally killed, sir?'

Cardilini had been waiting for the question, he smiled at the tremors in Salt's voice and wondered how far his answer would be reported that night.

'Not anymore. See you, Salt.'

THIRTY-FOUR

Day 6
St Nicholas College
12.35 p.m. Friday, 30th October 1965

The boy stood in line at the servery window. He'd been given the duty of supplying his table with their meals.

Voices, crockery, cutlery, and chairs scraping on the timber floor filled the space. Mossop pushed in behind the boy. This action usually caused raucous complaints from the second formers behind but Mossop had reached the status of an untouchable. The school population knew what he claimed about the policeman. They knew he was taken from class for special meetings. The boy and Mossop shared an accounting class, the class the boy had returned to after speaking to Carmody.

'Why were you speaking to Carmody?' Mossop demanded and grabbed the boy's shoulder. The boy looked to others around him to push Mossop to the back of the line, but they just looked back. The boy looked to one of the 'good kids' of second form, a boy not averse to telling the other boys when they were wrong, a boy willing to accept abuse from some of the 'tough kids'. He

showed no emotion; his eyes were glacial as he looked back at the boy.

'What's it to you, Mossop?' The boy said, avoiding the eyes of the boys in front who had stopped their own conversations and turned to watch and listen.

'We have a right to know,' Mossop said, some of the boys around them nodding.

'Go and ask Carmody, you're his little pet,' the boy said and this brought a range of derisive noises and grins.

'Shut your faces,' Mossop snapped.

'Get to the back of the line, Mossop,' came a voice from the rear.

'Shut your gob.'

'Yeah, get to the back of the line,' another voice.

'Shut up.'

'Run crying to Carmody,' yet another voice.

'I'll smash the next one to say anything. He should tell us!' Mossop said, pushing the boy who fell into another boy in front of him. That boy turned and pushed back. Soon all the boys were pushing and laughing. A voice bellowed. It was a sixth former at a table close to the servery. The boys' noise stopped but they kept pushing each other until they neared the servery window where they became consumed with balancing their plates on steel trays before rushing back to their tables where two students from each form sat waiting for their meals.

'What was that about?' a fifth former at their table asked the boy.

'Someone pushed in.'

'Who?'

'I couldn't see.'

'Rubbish.'

Someone at the table whispered, 'Creep.'

'That's enough of that,' the sixth former said without looking up.

'He knows who pushed in, but he won't say,' the fifth former said to the older boy, who in turn looked up as if to say, 'who cares?' then continued eating.

'He should say if I ask him,' the fifth former complained.

'Do you know, Harper?' the sixth former asked.

'Yes.'

'Why didn't you tell?'

'It's disloyal, sir.'

Laughter broke out at the table.

'You don't call me sir,' the sixth former said. Then turning to the fifth form boy asked, 'Are you happy with that?'

'He shouldn't have answered me like that.'

'He's right, Harper, you got that?' the sixth former said.

'Yeah, creep,' someone whispered.

'That you, Dillon?' the sixth former asked and continued eating.

'Yes.'

'Yard duty after lunch. You make sure he does it,' he said to the fifth former who nodded his approval. The third former, Dillon, gave the boy a threatening grimace.

The sixth former wrapped it up with, 'Harper, straight after lunch you get your brother and wait for me on the steps.'

'Yes.'

As soon as the students were dismissed, the boy scurried between chairs to where his brother sat. He rapidly said what was required. His brother looked back miserably and nodded bleakly. They stood several yards apart on the steps outside the dining hall. The sixth former eventually approached them and signalled them to stand together so he could talk to them.

'I want the name-calling of your brother to stop.'

The boy's brother looked back hopelessly, 'What can I do?'

'Don't you think it offensive?' the sixth former asked.

His brother tried to avoid the question with movements of his body and head. He eventually said he didn't think he could stop the name-calling. The sixth former looked out into the quadrangle where a few boys wandered the paths while others were in the shade of the cloisters. The two brothers stood in a wretched state before him.

'Do you want it to stop, Harper?'

With a shy look to his brother the boy replied, 'I don't care.'

'Still, it shouldn't happen. I'll see what I can do,' the sixth former said.

'Sometimes that makes it worse,' the boy piped up.

The sixth former nodded his head, 'I've seen. You try and ignore them then. But I can't have it said in my presence, understand?'

'Yes.'

'Yes,' his brother echoed.

'Right, off you go.'

The brothers walked down the steps, separating to walk opposite ways. His brother turned.

'Who's the worst?' he called.

'Third formers.'

'Who?'

The boy shrugged his shoulders.

'Give me one name,' his brother demanded. The boy knew it meant his brother would have to fight the boy, which was demeaning, as his brother was in fourth form.

'I don't know their names.'

His brother looked back with understanding then asked, 'What are you going to do?'

'I think it'll stop,' the boy replied.

'How? Carmody? You be careful. You don't want to get on the wrong side of Carmody.'

'I'm okay.'

'I'm sorry,' His brother whispered and walked away.

Left alone on the stairs, the boy looked around for somewhere out of the way to spend the fifteen minutes before next period.

THIRTY-FIVE

Day 14
Kilkenny Road
5.30 a.m. Saturday, 7th November 1965

Late afternoon Cardilini had weeded the backyard, planted runners and was now pruning one of the bottlebrush trees. Betty had previously instructed him in the task but he wasn't sure if this was the right time to prune them. Even so, he had a mental picture of how it used to be and a strong urge to make it right again. Climbing down from the ladder, he stood back to assess his work. The tree looked like it was leaning to one side.

'Dad, Phone!' Paul called from the back verandah.

'Take a message.'

'It's Superintendent Robinson, he said it was important.'

Cardilini smiled. 'Good.' Salt would have passed on his response and now, seeing as he was finally playing their game, he hoped it would be Robinson calling to say Mossop had withdrawn his accusations. 'Paul, how does that look?' he asked pointing to the tree.

'You've cut it all lopsided,' Paul said and returned to the house.

Oh well, next year, Cardilini thought and followed him in. 'Robinson.'

'Three other boys have stepped forward as witnesses.'

Cardilini's jaw hung slackly as he took that in. 'Impossible.'

'What on earth is going on, Cardilini?' Robinson asked, 'What did you do at that school?'

'I don't understand.'

'Well, the boys have fronted up to the principal. He thinks they're lying but they remain adamant they saw you. He's asking me what to do. Are you sure there was nothing to even suggest what they're claiming?'

'No, no! Ridiculous. Wasn't it supposed to have happened in the classroom? Where were these boys? Hiding under the desks?' Cardilini asked and waited as the phone went silent.

Then Robinson spoke. 'Exactly, but, Braun would like some reassurance. Do you mind going out there and showing where it took place? Just so we can discount this last trio?'

'Nothing took place. I walked out of the room they'd given us for the interviews and that little jackass followed. He basically told me it was a set-up and would stop when I stopped investigating Edmund's death.'

'When? You're suspended. You're not investigating anything are you?'

'No . . .'

'Bloody hell, what have you been doing?'

'Nothing, really.'

'When did this kid tell you he was "setting you up"?'

'At East Perth.'

'Where?'

Cardilini took a breath and shaking his head exhaled. 'In the toilet.'

Cardilini imagined Robinson jumping from his chair. 'What? Who else was there?'

'No one.'

A pause before, 'And he was in there?'

'No, he followed me in.'

'You should have left straight away.'

'I was taking a piss,' Cardilini said indignant.

'Bloody hell. That's all we need.'

'Nothing happened.'

'You piss with your dick in your hand, I suppose? How do you think that's going to sound?'

'I know who's at the bottom of this,' Cardilini said.

'You are, Cardilini. Right at the bottom.'

'I'll go to the school.'

'Remember, you're suspended. On Monday, drop by and see Braun and come in to the station on Tuesday. And don't go to a toilet at St Nicholas College for Christ's sake. That's an order.' A sharp click resounded in Cardilini's ear.

THIRTY-SIX

Day 17
East Perth Police Department
9.00 a.m. Tuesday, 10th November 1965

'So, how did it go?' Superintendent Robinson asked, standing over Cardilini at his desk.

The other detectives at their desks, eager for any interruption from paperwork, expectantly turned their eyes to Cardilini.

'I went to your bloody school and ate bloody humble pie. What else could I do?'

Robinson lowered his voice, 'Nothing has improved so far.' Raising his voice he turned to the other detectives, 'This is not a sideshow, get on with your work.'

'We're interested, boss. It could happen to any of us.'

'Bloody well better not, that's why you're supposed to work in pairs.'

Robinson indicated for Cardilini to follow him and turned to the corridor. Cardilini, with a shrug to his colleagues, followed him from the room.

Robinson was seated when Cardilini entered his office. 'It seems you weren't very convincing.'

'My bet is you'll get a call. They just want me to sweat a bit.'

'Let's hope so. Something else, the commissioner has been contacted by the coroner, Mark Hammer, have you met him?'

'No.'

'You sure about that?'

'Yes. Positive.'

'How would he know your name?'

'Why not? He's seen plenty of reports from me.'

'Yep. Okay. Have you spoken to him concerning anything at St Nicholas?'

'Never met him. Never spoke to him about anything. Check with Spry, he did the report on St Nicholas,' Cardilini said.

'Yes. Hammer agrees with Spry's finding.'

'That's good.'

Robinson, looking embarrassed, said, 'The commissioner doesn't want you talking to anyone, anytime, without running it past me first.'

'How's that going to work?'

'We'll find out, won't we?'

'How long for?'

'Until we're out of the woods with this St Nicholas business. Now go home, Cardilini, and stay home until you get a call from me.'

As Cardilini stood Robinson reluctantly said, 'And the commissioner mentioned he's getting flack regarding Paul's appointment to next year's cadet intake.'

'What are you saying?' Cardilini turned cold.

'The commissioner thought you should know. Just in case.'

'Paul could lose his position?'

'No one's saying that,' Robinson pointed towards the door, 'now get out of here.'

Cardilini walked away, shaken. He could manage with the loss of his career but he wasn't up for being responsible for another disappointment to Paul.

'Colleen, it's Cardilini. Could we meet up again? Not the office. Where we met the second time. Something you might be able to help me with. Okay. Thanks.'

* * *

Cardilini was early. The warmth of the day had filled the city. Two oscillating wall fans mounted just below the ceiling hammered air around the cafe. He sat stirring his tea. It was milky. His paper napkin flapped and danced each time the air hit it. He stopped it flying away five times before tucking it beneath his saucer. He had his back to a wall and could see the other tables, their occupants, and down London Court. Images of Paul's enthusiastic face filled his thoughts.

'Detective Cardilini.'

Cardilini rose from his seat. 'What would you like?'

'I've ordered,' Colleen said and sat. 'What did you need help with?'

'Your boss, the coroner, contacted the commissioner,' Cardilini said, 'and must have mentioned my name.'

'Yes.'

'At the moment it's very important I don't create any waves at the department.'

'The coroner is aware of the complaint against you.'

'It's not that. If there was any suggestion, even the slightest, that an investigation into the suicides was to involve me, it could really hurt me.'

'I don't understand.'

'What's to understand?'

'How could such an investigation hurt someone?' Colleen asked.

Cardilini put his spoon in his cup and then decisively took it out.

'If such an investigation was to impact on the reputation of a school and the old boy network, and the simplest way to stop it was to dismiss a detective, that's what would be done.'

'And you're the detective?'

'Yes.'

'And you want me to tell the coroner to forget about the investigation, or just you?'

'Both.'

'Isn't that asking too much?'

'He's done nothing for years,' Cardilini said frustrated, 'apart from pump his bleeding heart in front of you.'

Colleen's tea arrived. She immediately put the napkin between saucer and cup then placed it precisely midway in front of her. Once organised she said, 'He has difficulty getting answers.'

'How can he have difficulty? He's the bloody coroner.'

'He's an academic. Brilliant but not . . .' she searched for a word.

Cardilini smiled, '. . . abrasive, pig-headed?'

'Is that what you are?'

'I hope not. But I know how to get answers.'

'That's right, and you're not afraid to follow your instinct.'

'I am now. That's why I don't want to have an association with anything that he might do,' Cardilini said, keen to make his point.

'That's disappointing. He was hoping you would carry out an investigation into the country boys' deaths.'

'What's disappointing would be me losing my job and my son losing his place at the academy.'

'I see.'

'My name mustn't come up again in any discussion between him and the commissioner.'

Colleen turned her cup on the paper napkin.

'I'll tell him.'

'Will that be enough?'

'Yes.'

'I'm sorry,' Cardilini said and settled back in his chair.

'No. He'll appreciate your predicament.'

'Good. It's very important to me.'

'I understand. Particularly your boy, I imagine?'

'Yes.'

'Don't worry,' Colleen said reassuringly, 'he's a very intelligent man.'

'Wonderful.' Cardilini felt himself jealous of the coroner and smiled at the ridiculousness of it.

'Why are you smiling?'

'Being an intelligent man is not something I've been accused of,' Cardilini said.

'Intelligence isn't the answer to many situations.'

'Oh?'

'Yes,' Colleen said with a glance around the cafe, 'he didn't marry wisely.'

'Oh.' Cardilini had not anticipated that bit of information.

'She doesn't appreciate what she's got.'

'The coroner's wife?' Cardilini asked and wondered where this was going.

'That's right,' Colleen continued, 'she behaves as if his prominence and standing are simply there for her to shine.'

'Right.'

'Some women can be like that.'

'Right. I'm surprised he didn't see it when first they met,' Cardilini said thinking, *the coroner being such an intelligent man and all*.

'He has a guileless heart.'

Cardilini had heard enough of the coroner, 'Another cup of tea?'

'No. Thanks. I'd better go.'

At the door she turned briefly with a tight smile and caught his eye. Cardilini watched until passing pedestrians obscured her from his view.

THIRTY-SEVEN

Day 17
Kilkenny Road
1.00 p.m. Tuesday, 10th November 1965

Cardilini was sitting on the back step smoking.

Paul came to the back door. 'Dad, there's a Mrs Lockheed at the front door.'

'Did you invite her in?'

'She said she would wait there.'

Cardilini looked around for a place to grind out his cigarette. Seeing none he handed it to Paul.

'I don't want it.' Paul replied annoyed. 'Put an ashtray out here.'

'I will . . . can you just poke it in the garden, somewhere?'

'Bloody hell, Dad.'

Cardilini checked what he was wearing as he walked to the front of the house. *Shabby enough*, he concluded.

'Mrs Lockheed, would you like to come in?'

'No. Your son was very polite.'

'Paul. Yep, he takes after his mother.'

'I've come to invite you to the rectory. We're having a meeting at seven tonight and Father O'Reilly thought it was best to have it there.'

'Why am I invited?'

'Sheppard, the Doneys, Mrs Masters, myself and Father O'Reilly will be there,' Mrs Lockheed said ignoring his question.

'Same question, why am I invited?'

Mrs Lockheed looked straight at him. 'We don't want any other boys from St Nicholas doing harm to themselves.'

Cardilini shook his head. 'So, now you believe your son?'

'I always did,' her voice was definite.

'Why lie to me and Braun then?'

Mrs Lockheed indicated she wasn't going to answer.

'You know Edmund was murdered?' Cardilini asked.

'Murdered? I don't know that. If he was intentionally shot, it was an execution, like Cooke's, pure and simple.'

'Only the state can execute a person.'

'No, an individual executes a person, as directed by a judge, as directed by twelve members of a jury.'

'Is that what happened?'

'No. Don't be ridiculous. We're meeting at seven, this evening.'

'I can't come,' Cardilini said.

'It won't get back to the school, hence, not back to your police department.'

'How can you know that?'

'I don't. I've been told that will be the case. I was asked to invite you. It's not my idea. And I don't think it's a good idea.' She frowned.

'Who's asking me then?'

'Sheppard, probably.'

'I can't come.'

'I said you wouldn't,' she continued with a wry smile, 'they got you into line, didn't they? I knew you'd be no match for them.'

'Who?' Cardilini asked gruffly, knowing full well she was right.

'The old boys, the establishment.' Mrs Lockheed turned in disgust and walked to the pavement.

'Does Robinson know what really happened?' Cardilini called after her. She shrugged her shoulders without turning and continued walking.

Ashfield
7.10 p.m. Tuesday, 10th November 1965

Cardilini parked 200 yards past the church. He recognised Sheppard's Chevy Impala. He stood looking at the rectory. Without success, he'd repeatedly told himself that he couldn't attend the meeting because the risk was too great. He tapped on the door. O'Reilly opened it, nodded a greeting, and gestured him in.

'What did I say?' Sheppard announced. 'I said you'd come, a real bloodhound. That's your seat.' Sheppard pointed to a dining chair in front of the kitchen door.

Cardilini looked to the chair, then around the room. The Doneys sat on a sofa to the right of his chair. Neither met his gaze. Mrs Lockheed and Mrs Masters sat in single chairs next along. O'Reilly stood by the front door and Sheppard stood in the centre of the room. Mrs Sheppard wasn't there, Cardilini noted, and smiled at the fact.

'Mrs Lockheed,' Cardilini said as he went to his chair.

Sheppard and O'Reilly took the remaining chairs.

All eyes followed Cardilini as he sat and Sheppard immediately addressed him. 'Mrs Lockheed said you kept asking about how Edmund died? We don't care how he died.'

O'Reilly coughed.

'Apart from O'Reilly, none of us are complaining. Much more important is how do we make sure no one else dies because of that ratbag? Now you mentioned to me that revealing the truth about Edmund, and having the school recognise it, is the best way to support any other boys. Right?' Cardilini nodded. 'So that's what we intend to do. Any questions?'

Cardilini looked around to the group. 'Do any of the boys at St Nicholas know you're doing this?'

'You mean, Carmody? No. Word of mouth only to the people here. We know the spot you're in,' Sheppard assured Cardilini.

Cardilini turned to Father O'Reilly. 'Surely the father has divided loyalties?'

'Myself and Doney had a chat to him about our boys' deaths,' Sheppard said, 'and he agrees with us now.' Father O'Reilly nodded. 'But we still have a few people to convince,' Sheppard finished.

'Braun?'

'Yeah, Braun, but he's not the power house.'

'Who?'

'The school board, an ex-judge, your bosses and a cohort of old boys.'

Cardilini turned from face to face. 'Do they control Braun?' he asked.

'They employ him,' Sheppard answered.

'Robinson and I'm sure Deputy Commissioner Warren know the punishment of boys standing with a rifle above their heads,' Cardilini said.

'We all do. Edmund's additions are what we need to convince them of. Now,' Sheppard asked, 'you're the copper, what do we have to do to get your bosses sitting up and paying attention?'

'The coroner suspects your two boys' deaths to be suicide also,' Cardilini said.

'News to me. What about you, Doney?' Sheppard asked.

'News to me,' Doney stated.

'You could start with that, but leave my name out of it,' Cardilini said.

'Okay. We will. What else?' Sheppard asked.

'Get Braun to tell you the names of the boys who have complained about Edmund and speak to them,' Cardilini said.

'Thought of that. Braun wouldn't do that unless the board, the old boys, told him too. What else?'

'Can I get a cup of tea?'

'Not yet.'

'Get Robinson, Warren and whoever is in the power house to listen to John Lockheed. He convinced his mother,' Cardilini said with a look to Mrs Lockheed.

'Not his father,' Mrs Lockheed said.

'I know Robinson, he's no fool. He'll know the truth when he sees it,' Cardilini stated.

'Anything else?' Sheppard asked.

'Carmody would know the other boys who complained,' Cardilini said.

'We're not going to deal with him.'

'Why not?'

'We don't understand what he's trying to do,' Sheppard answered.

'Siding with Braun. If you ask me,' Doney said.

'He thinks he's protecting the identity of whoever shot Edmund. Isn't that so, Mrs Lockheed?' Cardilini asked.

She turned aside.

Sheppard asked. 'Have you got anything else to persuade Robinson and Warren?'

'Convince the officers who made the initial reports on your boys' deaths to tell Robinson and Warren what they really believe,' Cardilini said.

'What do they really believe?'

'I think you know.'

'Why didn't they write that then?'

Cardilini felt he knew the answer for himself: the overwhelming realisation of your boy taking his own life was too terrible to think about. If a constable could avoid plunging the parents into that hell by simply writing 'accidental' he might just do that. Cardilini wondered if he would. Speculating on suicide and consequently looking for physical evidence to support it wouldn't serve anyone. And if you discovered the boys staged their deaths to look like accidents, why betray that young man's last desperate attempt to save his parents from the agony he was suffering?

'No positive proof and they won't speculate when writing reports,' Cardilini answered. 'That's for the coroner to do.'

'Okay, we can do all that,' Sheppard concluded.

'That could take forever. We don't have that much time,' Mrs Lockheed said. Frightened faces turned to her.

'Cardilini,' Sheppard prompted when no one spoke.

'Bring Edmund's killer to justice,' Cardilini offered.

'Oh you stupid man,' Mrs Lockheed blurted.

Sheppard stood. 'Right, how about that cup of tea? We'll just smoke outside,' he said as he nodded sharply to Cardilini and Doney.

'Off you go, boys. Enjoy yourselves,' Mrs Lockheed called to them as they left.

The rectory had flowerbeds bordering the buildings. Six pencil pines standing as upright sentinels emitted a sharp, sappy scent. A solitary gum tree grew in the middle of a drying lawn. Its branches, free of decorum, twisted one way then another, centuries from the rigour of the pencil pines. At night the branches were dark silhouettes against the points of light gathering millions of miles away. Cardilini thought the gum tree's branches thrown high and awkward as if in horror reflected what the Sheppards, Doneys and Masters were going through. He wondered how they were coping.

Doney leant against the trunk of the gum and commenced rolling a cigarette. Sheppard took a cigarette from Cardilini's offered packet.

'I know Senior Constable Saunders had his suspicions,' Sheppard said.

'He played footy with Colin.'

Cardilini inhaled deeply, he wanted to be home with Paul, he wanted to put his arms around him and never let him go. But Paul was working.

'I know what Peter did,' Doney replied hollowly.

Sheppard looked to the ground and pushed some leaves aside with his shoe. Cardilini's eyes wandered to the rectory windows glowing gold, framed by shadow. He could see Father O'Reilly standing surrounded by the three women, Mrs Lockheed laying down the law and Father O'Reilly slowly nodding.

After a pause Cardilini said, 'Mrs Lockheed told me she was shut out from the St Nicholas community.'

'That was shameful. We didn't help, did we, Doney?'

Doney sighed.

'We just couldn't go there at the time. We didn't want to believe her or John. Then when the school said it was all part of a conspiracy to discredit Edmund for demanding high standards, we jumped at it like drowning men. I'm sure you would do the same, Cardilini.'

Cardilini turned his eyes from the window to the sky and wondered if Paul would be outside watching the movie at the drive-in or helping the girls in the cafe.

'Mrs Lockheed can say what she likes, when she likes, as far as I'm concerned,' Sheppard said watching her through the window.

'Yep,' Cardilini added after a pause.

The men watched the cigarette smoke push at the night then disperse as tiny tendrils.

'We had a hell of a dog problem a few years back,' Sheppard drawled. The others listened without looking. 'It was during lambing. Town dogs and a couple of strays would hunt in packs. Not for food. They would run down a mob of ewes and their lambs. Some of the lambs would run with their mothers, others stood bleating, too terrified or too young to know what to do. The dogs would latch on to the weakest ones first, crushing them in their jaws several times until blood filled their mouths, then they would rush to the next. Sometimes two dogs went at a lamb until it was decapitated or torn in two, then onto the next, leaving broken, squealing lambs in their wake. This would continue until no lambs were left or the dogs started on the ewes. The ewes, heavy with mothering, terrified out of their minds, would be latched upon by a mob. The head, the throat, the downy underbellies were torn at by as many as ten dogs until, blood-sated, the dogs would bound to the next.'

Cardilini wondered where Sheppard was going with this but felt content to stand, take in the night, and listen.

Sheppard continued, 'In one attack I lost twenty-two lambs and three ewes. That night, six dogs were spotted trotting along one of the roads. Not dingoes, town dogs: mongrels, a big shaggy black bastard leading them. A bunch of farmers had lost lambs. It was a killing spree and the dogs were expert. When we got to the paddock, lambs and ewes in all stages of dying were scattered bloody across the field under the most glorious night sky. Some ewes, dragging their intestines, staggered bleating through the carnage, others pushed and nosed at limp corpses. One lamb, missing a hind leg, stumbled and fell screaming as if it was still being torn at. I shot two ewes and twelve lambs that night.' He paused. 'We're not sentimental men, are we, Doney?'

Doney slid down the trunk and squatted, peering at the ground while Sheppard looked into the far distance. 'We do what has to be done, we accept it like drought or fire. But town dogs? Once the owners knew what had happened they would put the dogs down. Or that's what we thought. I stood in front of the owner of the shaggy black dog. He said it was some fancy German breed that were used as police dogs. We went around the back and that bastard dog sat as sweet as could be, a real pet. No, he said, it couldn't have been his dog. It turned out it couldn't have been any town dog. They were pets.

'We demanded a full council meeting. Senior Constable Saunders, farmers, owners, anyone who wanted a tyre to kick was there. Plenty of screaming, yelling and abuse, a real old free-for-all, even a couple of fights in the car park, one of them had nothing to do with the dogs.

'One skinny mongrel from the pound was offered up to be shot. Only trouble was, it was locked up the night the mob formed. That didn't seem to trouble anyone though, so the dog-catcher shot the poor mongrel later. Case closed. Stupid farmers don't know the difference between town dogs and dingoes. Shit, we thought. We *are* bloody stupid. So we decided to wise up. A dozen of us, all good shots, got together.'

The jury, twelve angry farmers, thought Cardilini.

'One farm next to mine hadn't been attacked. Smart old bugger kept his lambs in the house paddock. But that night he agreed to put them in a paddock adjoining the road from town. And to save any sweet dog the trouble of climbing through a fence, the gate facing the road was left open and a hundred yards from that, on top of a hill, he put his flock. It was a full moon, the first since the last attack, the sheep stood out like mushrooms on the darker ground: ready tucker.

'We waited in the scrub along the fence, upwind of the road. We didn't expect anything but we felt good, we were doing something. The old fella, whose sheep they were, said he would start the shooting and he didn't want any dogs getting within fifty yards of his sheep. The previous attacks were around midnight. We chatted until ten and then lay still, no smoking. You get a funny feeling, lying there, rifle out in front of you, knowing five yards either side, someone you know well, was doing the same thing. You get to looking at the sky, glorious and heartless. You smell the ground, feel the insects, hear the insects, hear a mopoke, hear it again. Then you hear a chatter, almost like school kids, a single smoky sound followed by others that were high pitched. Dogs. You get murderous, you get hungry to kill, kill the smug complacence that allows dogs to slaughter at will. The night became stiller. I'm sure we all felt it. I hardly breathed, so badly I wanted those dogs in my sights. I was nervous as hell, thinking they might just turn down the road to my place, or turn around or go somewhere else.

I prayed. I prayed to someone I don't believe in to deliver those bastards to me; maybe we all did.

'I couldn't see it but the bloke closest to the gate said later, probably while I was praying, that the big shaggy dog stopped and looked towards the open gate. The dog stood stock still, he said, sniffing and straining his eyes against the night. The other dogs became impatient. The black one gave a growl, deep and menacing, and the other dogs settled. Then a stupid-looking dog, that seemed to have his head on sideways, started running to the sheep. He was silent, so silent, no bark, nothing. Then they all took off, silent, dark streaks. They were thirty yards from me when the first shot rang out, then it was Guy Fawkes Night, but deafening, you couldn't aim, not like roos that just stand there, or rabbits in a spotlight, these were ghosts. I just fired like mad aiming a foot above the ground where their torso would be. The night became all sound. We were being battered by the sound of rifles, deafening, echoing, smacking our ears, then another sound, an almost human sound, a desolate howling that pulled at your insides. Did I stop at this? No, none of us did. We became the silent pack, full of bloodlust but we weren't going to be sated so easily.

'Then a voice broke the spell, the old farmer whose sheep they were, was walking our line yelling at us to stop, he wanted to get to his sheep without being shot. The gunshots ceased. The silence was deafening. Then we heard dogs screaming to the heavens, ten of them, as our lambs must have done. We walked across to the mongrels that were flipping around, letting out a hell of a racket, some biting at their wounds and thrashing about. It was hard work finishing them off, they knew what was happening and wanted no part of it. A few suddenly became house pets and crawled on shattered legs to the closest farmer's feet. We wandered the paddock whistling and calling, figuring a town dog would respond to that out of habit, one did. The bloke who shot him said that was nearly as hard as having to shoot his own sheep. When everything was silent again we closed the gate, leaving the corpses there. A couple must have got away. One even ended up at the vet days later because the owner said the dog had been crawling scratching his backside on the ground. He had a twenty-two calibre bullet up his backside, must have been at some distance when the dog was running away. I knew the farmer and his .22 Hornet. Next morning we piled the corpses up in a ute, drove into town and laid them out on the lawn in front of the council building.'

Sheppard lit a cigarette from the one he had been smoking and pushed the old butt into the ground below the leaf litter. 'There's a lot of bitterness still around after that day. But we have nowhere near the problem we had.'

Doney got up and walked to the house.

A couple of times during Sheppard's story, two of the women had come to the door and then retreated.

'Is that why Edmund had to die?' Cardilini asked.

'Edmund,' Sheppard muttered, 'Jesus, you go on.'

'Did you set a trap for Edmund, to get him to the window?'

Sheppard started to the house. 'I'm getting that cup of tea. Thanks for your advice. I think we'll speak to the constables.' As an afterthought he said over his shoulder, 'You're welcome to come in if you want.'

Cardilini felt anger rising in him. 'You're no better than a murdering dog.'

Sheppard stood still, made a decision then turned, and walked back to Cardilini. Cardilini tensed for a fight, but before Cardilini saw it coming Sheppard's fist hit him squarely on the side of his jaw. Light like a camera going off flashed before his eyes. He felt his knees hit the ground. He couldn't hear or see anything but the flashing light. When he did open his eyes, Sheppard was squatting beside him, prodding his shoulder saying, 'Come on man, come on man, I didn't hit you that hard.'

Cardilini pushed himself into a sitting position. His head spun, he tried to steady it by placing his hands to his face. It didn't help. Sheppard was pulling at his shoulder.

'Stand up man. You'll feel better.' With Sheppard's help, Cardilini got to his feet. He tried turning his head slightly to ease the throbbing. 'You went down like a sack of spuds. I thought you coppers were supposed to be tough,' Sheppard admonished. 'Come on inside we'll say you had a turn and get some ice on your face.' He was smiling, 'You can have a crack at me later when you're feeling better if you like. Can you walk?'

Cardilini pushed Sheppard away and stood alone swaying for a moment. 'It's against the law to hit a policeman.'

'I don't remember being told that.'

'Well, I'm telling you now.'

'Okay. Noted. Can you walk?'

'Of course, I can bloody walk. You got me off guard that's all.'

THIRTY-EIGHT

Day 17
Ashfield
9.40 p.m. Tuesday, 10th November 1965

Cardilini refused ice and sat with a cup of tea on his lap. Father O'Reilly sat talking on one side and Mrs Masters sat on the other.

'I now understand that other boys are at risk,' Father O'Reilly said. Cardilini squinted and moved his tongue along his teeth. They seemed in place. 'Dr Braun hasn't the power to act on his own,' the Father continued.

The scene before him played like a scratchy movie. Mrs Lockheed, flanked by Mrs Doney, prodded Sheppard with her finger. Doney watched on wide-eyed.

'We would only keep you another hour.' Mrs Masters said.

Cardilini gently fingered his jaw and nodded, agreeing to follow Father O'Reilly and Mrs Masters to the Masters' house.

As he followed the tail-lights he slowly opened his jaw a few times. It wasn't broken. He thanked a distant God.

Peppermint Grove
10.00 p.m. Tuesday, 10th November 1965

The Masters lived in the exclusive and expensive Peppermint Grove, a leafy western suburb. Cardilini parked on a verge while Father O'Reilly and Mrs Masters pulled into the tree-lined driveway of a two-storey stone home. Conical, slate-roofed turrets with slotted windows protruded from the two front corners of the house. *A man's home is his castle*, Cardilini thought. He ran his eyes over the grand edifice, acutely aware of the lush lawn with an extensive bordering of trim flowering rosebushes.

'Who does the gardening?' Cardilini asked when he caught up with Mrs Masters.

'Wilson,' Mrs Masters replied.

'Does a good job.'

'Thank you, I'll tell him.'

Mrs Masters opened one side of the double-front door. It was unlocked.

'Better to lock up at night.'

'My husband's home.'

'Still . . .'

Inside Cardilini was confronted with a corridor twice the width of his own, and which literally disappeared into darkness 20 yards away. Mrs Masters walked into a room on her right saying, 'Please take a seat. I'll see if my husband is available.'

Heavy drapes, linen sofas and expanses of floral-patterned carpet greeted them as they entered the room.

'Mrs Masters has beautiful taste,' Father O'Reilly whispered into Cardilini's ear. Cardilini chose a large, winged-back chair that dominated the setting. 'I think that's Mr Masters' chair,' Father O'Reilly said, still whispering.

Cardilini appeared not to hear. 'Who's Mr Masters?'

Father O'Reilly smiled benignly. 'An old family. A philan-thropist.'

'Donates to the church?' Cardilini quizzed.

Father O'Reilly sat straight in the plush, velvet sofa and straightened the pleat on his cassock with both hands but did not reply. He soon stood up as Mrs Masters entered followed by a very tall man in his fifties dressed in a suit and tie.

'Don't get up, Detective Sergeant,' Mr Masters waved at Cardilini who hadn't moved. Cardilini figured Masters was six-ten. He stood and they shook hands. He thought he could feel Masters' hand trembling, and took in the deep lines etched around his eyes. His handshake was mechani-cal, as if Cardilini's was the hundredth hand he had shaken that day. Masters released Cardilini's hand, moved away and folded awkwardly to sit on the sofa beside Father O'Reilly. Mrs Masters sat on a bridge chair beside the sofa. All three faced Cardilini. His head had ceased its throbbing and now felt as if a warm iron was pushing against it.

Father O'Reilly spoke first. 'Detective Sergeant Cardilini alerted me of the risk to more of our boys. A risk I didn't under-stand until Mr Sheppard and Mr Doney approached me.'

Masters moved his hand and patted the Father on the knee. 'We all missed the obvious, Father O'Reilly.' To Cardilini, 'It was my idea to have Geoffrey board at St Nicholas. I was a boarder there.'

Cardilini inwardly quaked at the pain on the man's face.

'I appreciate you coming over, Detective Sergeant. I believe you have brought trouble upon yourself by pursuing Edmund.'

Cardilini shrugged.

Masters turned to Father O'Reilly, 'I have to tell Cardilini something it's better you didn't hear.'

'I see,' O'Reilly said, nodding sagely.

'Would you come with me while I arrange some supper?' Mrs Masters stood and gestured to O'Reilly.

Masters smiled up to him, 'Thank you, Father.' He watched the two depart.

Masters stood and closed the door to the passage then turned to Cardilini. 'Edmund's killer left the .303 rifle, one he had previously taken from the school armoury, placed across two branches on the tree from which he fired.' Cardilini rose slightly from his chair in surprise. Masters continued, 'At the tree's base he placed a pair of army boots. The display was to draw attention to the punishment Edmund enjoyed delivering.'

Cardilini started forwards, Masters held his hand up to halt him. 'The killer wanted there to be no doubt why Edmund was killed. Have you found any mention of those objects?'

'No.' Cardilini shook his head, amazed.

'Someone removed them from the tree,' Masters said.

'Where did you get this information?'

'I had a phone call. I didn't recognise the voice. He just wanted me to know what really happened.'

'And you believed it?'

Masters cast his view around and looked back with sad eyes and gave a gentle smile.

'So, if it's true, who removed them and why?' Cardilini asked, 'To protect the killer?'

'No. The killer didn't believe them to be incriminating,' Masters stated.

Cardilini tried again. 'To protect the school?'

Masters nodded. 'It would appear so. Who was first on the scene?'

'Superintendent Robinson and Deputy Commissioner Warren attended first.'

Cardilini considered the corpse's arrival at the morgue. And the fact he was assigned to the case. Did Robinson and Warren believe he would sign it off as an accidental shooting just to get out of there? Case closed. And why didn't he? Because he reacted to what he saw as privileged arrogance. He was jealous, envious, had a chip on his shoulder. He had behaved the same way when arriving here this evening.

'So he was shot from the school?' Cardilini asked part in disbelief but with an overwhelming feeling of, *I was right*.

'That's what I was told.' Masters returned to the couch.

'For God's sake, come and sit here.' Cardilini stood smiling and chose another lounge chair and sat.

'Thanks. Getting old.' The chair seemed to shrink when Masters sat. 'I was hoping you might be able to tell me if it was true.'

Masters' eyes pulled at Cardilini. *He wants it to be true*, Cardilini thought and answered, 'No rifle or boots were found.'

Masters' nodded as if he expected that to be the answer.

Cardilini said, 'I believe a student *is* at the bottom of the accusations designed to stop me finding out what happened.'

'Mossop?' Masters asked distracted.

'No, a sixth form boy, Carmody.'

Masters looked at his watch. 'We will have to have that cup of tea.'

'You know Carmody?' Cardilini probed.

'Of course.'

Cardilini persisted. 'Well?'

'A very capable young man.'

'Why is he protecting the school like this?'

'Carmody supported the boys who spoke against Edmund,' Masters began, 'he wanted the school to act. I know this for a fact. He lost personal status because of it. He wouldn't be doing it to protect the school, of that you can be sure.'

'He convinced Mrs Lockheed to change her statement about believing her son,' Cardilini pointed out.

'But she did support her son,' Masters argued.

'Carmody told me he and his mate, Burnside, knew John Lockheed had lied. Mrs Lockheed supported this.'

'No,' Masters said in disbelief.

'Yes,' Cardilini insisted, 'and he and Burnside are Braun's new best buddies.'

Masters pushed two shaking fingers across his forehead, wrinkling the skin like the wake of a boat. He took a big breath, dropped his hand and said, 'We need to go.' Then pushed himself off the chair, stood and walked carefully to the door. Cardilini watched him leave before asking: 'Why did you tell me?'

Masters stopped and turned.

'I wanted it to be true.'

THIRTY-NINE

Day 18
Kilkenny Road
12.10 a.m. Wednesday, 11th November 1965

Later that night Cardilini sat smoking on his back verandah. The air was still. He exhaled, the smoke stayed suspended. He waved it away. Masters' harrowed features and ponderous words had left him unsettled. He asked himself again: What was he prepared to do to protect Paul? How would he be feeling about Edmund's death if Paul, like Masters' son, took his life because of Edmund's actions?

There had been times when he and other officers were required to overlook the actions of individuals. A minister in the current government crashed into parked cars when driving home drunk late at night. The investigating officer knew it; the vehicle accident officer verified it. A senior detective went to interview the minister and returned with a stolen car report. They all knew what had happened. It was seen as being loyal to those who supported the police, just like supporting a fellow officer. It was second nature, loyalty.

This led Cardilini to the real reasons he pursued Edmund's killer. Was it justice, the law, or grandstanding to make up for his twelve months ineptitude? Cardilini threw his cigarette into the garden, looked at it for a moment before retrieving it and pushing it into the ashtray he had brought out. He walked inside.

He stood at Paul's closed bedroom door. 'You awake, Paul?'

'No.'

'Can I come in?' Cardilini opened the door and turned the light on.

'I was asleep,' Paul answered, shading his eyes with his arm.

'You still keen to go to the academy?'

'Dad,' Paul turned to the wall, 'couldn't you have asked me that in the morning?'

'Would your answer be different?'

'Of course I'm keen.'

'Police work isn't all fun and games, you know.'

'What's the problem?' Paul turned squinting at his father.

'Nothing. Will you be changing your mind?'

'No.'

'You sure?'

'Yes.' Paul began to sit up.

'You're not just doing it for me are you?' Cardilini asked.

Paul shook his head. 'Mum really believed in what you were doing. She was very proud of you. She respected you, Dad.'

'She wouldn't be too proud now,' Cardilini suggested.

'You stopped drinking. You're coming back. Now, can I go to sleep?' Paul said.

'Everything's not black and white,' Cardilini said, avoiding Paul's strong gaze.

'I never thought it was.'

'The law, I mean . . .'

'I know all about the law, remember. I *didn't* steal that car,' Paul said.

'Yes. Okay.'

'Having the charge dropped means a lot. Now, can you turn the light off and close the bloody door?' Paul asked.

'Yeah. Sleep well.' Cardilini shuffled out.

Day 18
Bayswater Library
3.40 p.m. Wednesday, 11th November 1965

Carmody had agreed to meet him at the library. The library presented like an old book: noble binding, embossed title, politically endorsed, stolid, immutable, holding vast secrets and stories. Weathered limestone adorned its entrance and the towering windows. Broad, inviting steps led to immense wooden double doors, secured open despite the heat of the day. Cardilini approached, uneasy.

He checked his watch. He and Betty had gone to the Floreat library. Betty preferred fiction. Cardilini had picked up one of her books. Four pages in, a child had been abducted and suspicion had fallen on the mother for no reason that Cardilini could see. He'd put the book down; he preferred non-fiction, war history mainly.

He scanned the library. Carmody was sitting by himself at a table with a stack of books at his side. Cardilini thumbed through cards in the history catalogue and watched him for a while before approaching.

'Detective Sargent Cardilini. What a surprise,' Carmody smiled up at Cardilini.

'Can we talk outside?' Cardilini asked.

The park opposite the library offered several timber benches stationed along gravel paths. Cardilini chose one in the shade and sat. Carmody remained standing.

'How long will this take?' Carmody asked.

'Sit down.'

'I'd rather not.'

'I want you to put an end to the Mossop charade,' Cardilini stated.

'I thought you might.'

'Will you?'

'The question should be, can I?'

'We both know the answer to that.'

'Next question. Why would I, if I could?' Carmody asked.

'Because you know it's false.'

Carmody looked away.

'Okay, you win. I thought I was the tough guy and you beat me,' Cardilini said and took out a cigarette.

Carmody watched him light it before saying, 'It wasn't a competition.'

Cardilini decided on a gamble and said, 'You thought you were protecting someone by removing the rifle, boots and bullet. I get that, and you got what you wanted. A judgment of "accidental shooting".'

Carmody stared at Cardilini, mouth agape.

'Oh, didn't you know I knew?' Cardilini asked, smiling back at Carmody. 'How do I know? Is that what you would like to ask? Did your mate, Burnside, tell me? How could I know unless through you and your mates or . . .?' Cardilini left the sentence hanging; he was enjoying Carmody's lost composure. He felt he was seeing the child in the young man for the first time. Carmody sat, pulling at his lip. Cardilini warmed to him.

'A young boy told you this?' Carmody asked.

'Maybe,' Cardilini parried.

'A boy Mossop's age?'

'Maybe.'

'So like Mossop it could be a lie,' Carmody stated.

Cardilini smiled, satisfied. 'I don't think so, maybe this boy knew right from wrong,' he replied smugly.

'Did the boy tell you what was happening?'

'He told me what happened, yes.' Cardilini continued his bluff.

'If the boy told you what happened I don't understand why you want to pursue any of this?' Carmody asked, genuinely perplexed.

'A crime's been committed. I'm a policeman. And there are other boys who need protecting.' Cardilini wondered which of Carmody's scaly mates was now going to be accused of speaking to him. He didn't care.

'You think you're protecting that boy, exposing him like this? You have no idea. I don't even believe you're doing this because you're a policeman, you're just following your own self-interest, like everybody else. Well that's not good enough. Your self-interest fails to protect the ones that need protecting.'

'And you're protecting them, are you?' Cardilini demanded.

'I'm not harming them,' Carmody replied.

'I'm willing to forget the whole thing if you get Mossop to retract,' Cardilini said. 'Besides, Mossop's story is already suspect and the new witnesses are in trouble.'

'How?'

'Because they didn't see anything, because there was nothing to see. So things will get nasty for a while, the finger will be pointed at you eventually, the school will dump you real quick. You have an opportunity to withdraw your troops or suffer a loss.'

'What about the story of the boots and rifle? What's going to happen with that?'

'Why? Is it true?'

'I don't know anything about it.'

'Sensible boy. Now is Mossop going to retract his story?' Cardilini asked.

Carmody looked out to the park then turned to Cardilini. 'What Edmund was doing has possibly resulted in three boys taking their own lives. You understand that?' He demanded.

'Yes,' Cardilini shot back.

'Did you check with his previous school?' Carmody asked.

'They were glad to see the back of him. That's why his reference was glowing.'

'Was he ever going to be stopped?' Carmody was now looking directly at Cardilini. Gone was the smugness, gone the arrogance. Instead, Cardilini saw a strong, youthful demand for justice.

Rumours of abusive behaviour would occasionally jump up all over the place. Cardilini couldn't remember anything coming of them. And he didn't know why he would usually dismiss them as nonsense. He shook his head in answer to Carmody's earnestness.

'Don't you want Edmund's behaviour exposed?' Cardilini asked.

'For what purpose?'

'Justice.'

'Three boys I know ended their lives for fear of exposure. There could be any number of others. You want those boys to do the same?' Carmody asked.

Cardilini sat astonished staring at Carmody then asked.

'Isn't that what they want? To be recognised, to be apologised to?'

'Not the ones I've spoken to. That's why I'm staggered the boy said anything to you,' Carmody replied.

Cardilini turned his head aside and watched some children playing. Then turned to Carmody and said, 'Concealing evidence is a crime that receives jail time.'

'But protecting an abuser of children isn't a crime?' Carmody asked.

Cardilini thought about that and realised Carmody was right. Concealment of paedophiles hadn't been seen as a crime.

'What're you going to do?' Carmody asked.

'I'm not doing anything. You made sure of that,' Cardilini answered. Carmody stood and walked away.

'What are *you* going to do?' Cardilini called.

'I'm going to speak to the boy you spoke to,' Carmody said, without turning.

FORTY

Day 19
St Nicholas College
12.20 a.m. Thursday, 12th November 1965

A boy, Burnside, had told him to report to the sixth form common room after school the next day. He had hoped Carmody would want to see him again and decided he would get the bullet just in case Carmody wanted it.

He'd lain awake in bed for the two hours since lights out. He hadn't moved for an hour. He knew people were still when asleep. He had often stayed awake while all around him slept. Tonight he didn't have to wait so long. He heard the third formers getting ready for lights out, they were the noisiest; the fourth formers had deeper voices, there was a lot of volume but it wasn't noisy. The chooks were noisy, the cows had volume. The fifth formers were the quietest but they were the bossiest. Some of them slept in lower school dorms, one slept in their dorm. The fifth formers in their dorm picked on the weaker boys. The fifth former knew Carmody had spoken to the boy, the boy saw it in his eyes; they looked cagey like their mongrel dog's when it had done something wrong. He didn't care about the fifth former anymore, he wasn't frightened of him. He heard the fifth former come in, he heard him slide his locker door, he heard the coat hangers striking the back of the cupboard, he heard shoes drop to the floor. A sixth form boy would place his shoes, the fifth form boy dropped his. A sixth former didn't have to impress anyone, he was at the top. The boy wondered if he would ever get that old. He knew he would be a different fifth former to this one, he would help the weaker boys and he would protect them, like Carmody did. He felt the tears tickle as they ran from his eyes. Some plopped onto the pillow. Some stuck to his ears and gathered before more pushed them onto the pillow. It seemed very loud, but he couldn't move, he couldn't draw attention to himself. He knew he was good at that. Once he used to be noisy and run around like the other boys but now he could lie perfectly still for hours, like a stone. Stones don't sleep, they just sit there, eyes open. They don't blink either, they don't have eyelashes, they don't need them, their eyes, too, are stone. Like a stone he lay in his bed. Like a stone he sat at his classroom desk. Like a stone he ate his dinner. He remembered sitting like a stone in his father's car as he was driven home last holiday and more tears came. Stones must still be able to cry.

He could now move. The fifth former jerked like a busted rabbit when he first fell asleep. His stone eyes had seen the jerks, which were a long time ago now. His feet touched the floor, the boards were quiet beneath him, they liked him. His bed was the tenth from the door. There were four rows of twelve beds. The fifth former's bed was on the right side of the dorm. On the left side of the dorm was the sixth former's bed, he wasn't there, they had exams, and without Captain Edmund they did what they wanted to. Some fifth formers had tried the same, but the sixth formers told them off, he'd seen it. He smiled as he remembered. He wondered if the fifth formers would change into sixth formers, it didn't seem possible. If he pretended the fifth former wasn't there as he walked past his bed, he wouldn't wake up. It worked again. Now he just had to be silent and listen for sixth formers going to bed. He knew if he said 'toilet' timidly, the sixth former wouldn't say anything, not a fifth former though, they would carry on as if you were stealing their chickens.

He reached the end of the corridor. The bursar's office was on the right and to the left, double doors led to the bitumen paths. Outside those doors he could make it to the edge of the building and look into the quadrangle and then he could run across the gap to the administration building that held Captain Edmund's old room. No one was allowed to go up the stairs in that building anymore. Everyone was talking about what could have happened to Captain Edmund: some said they knew, and they knew who did it; some said they knew who had the bullet but it was a secret and they couldn't tell; and some said there wasn't a bullet because really Captain Edmund hung himself. The best was that Captain Edmund dropped dead trying to beat the record of holding the rifle above his head while his pants were down. Some said he had put his baton up his own bum, that was the fifth former that had told the second formers that and the second formers knew that to be a lie because no one would put anything up their own bum.

The boy had buried the bullet beside the last step going onto the hockey oval. Pieces of bitumen and blue-metal flakes clinging to his feet bit when his foot hit the stone of the step. He sat and scraped the blue metal from the soles of his feet. The stone was cold. He looked out across the hockey oval. The streetlight wasn't running, wasn't streaking. He decided he wouldn't cry again. He knew he could do that now. His older brother cried when the house lamb was slaughtered last holiday, his older brother cried and couldn't watch Dad cutting it up. The boy hadn't cried, he had learnt not to cry because of pain. His father had looked *at him and asked if he was okay. He had said, 'I don't have to cry anymore.' His father said, 'It's okay to cry son,' and he had answered, 'Not if it's pain.' His father looked shy at that, like a weak second form boy. The boy had hated that and walked away, he didn't turn even when his father called. Old men all smell the same.*

The soil was loose where he'd buried the bullet, it was deep but he found it easily. He would hand it to Carmody who would have a big smile on his face as he did it. He made a note to look down when he handed it over. He squeezed on the bullet; it burnt his palm as if he had caught a star. He looked up, stars smaller than his bullet winked at him, they were happy for him too. He wanted to sleep there, beside the steps, where the stars could see him and wink all through his sleep; he felt that way he might sleep without becoming frightened. He tried to sleep, but he couldn't close his eyes, he didn't want to miss the stars winking. More were doing it now, at first there were only a few but now they were all doing it. He inhaled and the joy caught in his throat. He knew he couldn't sleep here no matter how tired he became. He would be like his aunt's new baby who wouldn't sleep at their house. He was tired, his aunt kept saying, but he kept forcing his eyes open. Maybe the family were stars winking at him. The boy wasn't one, he knew that much, he could never be a star. He knew he couldn't smile at the baby because Captain Edmund had pushed his dick into his mouth and maybe the baby would see that. He stayed away, even though everyone wanted him to hold the baby, which made him angry. His father became shy at that too, he had asked the boy, 'What's the matter son? You're upsetting your aunt.' The boy didn't have an answer. At home he held that door shut tight. It was silly of his father to ask questions that couldn't be answered.

At home he would go outside the house, but the questions lined up like soldiers chasing him. He would call the dogs, the dogs didn't care what had happened to him, they were worse, they licked each other's bums. He wouldn't do that no matter what Captain Edmund said, he didn't think he could live if he did that. He had to stay alive for his parents but now he wondered if they even wanted him alive. He dreamt that one day, if he could keep the door shut tight and his parents didn't hate him, he would be able to take a dog, maybe Tina or Paddy, and wave goodbye. He knew what would be in his father's eyes, but he could go, and go, and go, and never, ever have to hurt them. That's what he prayed for even though he knew prayers didn't work. He'd prayed himself dry many times and it didn't change anything. Captain Edmund was more powerful than God. He'd told the boy that. But the boy was willing to try prayer again, maybe God was the next most powerful.

After midnight he had the school to himself. If he wanted to, he could go to the principal's office window and pull a face. He didn't because he imagined the face would still be there in the morning, even if the boy had gone to bed hours before. The principal would say to him, 'What's your face doing in my window?' And the boy knew he had to stay invisible long enough to get away with it. He wasn't sure exactly what he had done, but he knew it to be the worst of the worst. But Carmody had told him not to worry and that he was a good boy. He wished other people, his father, could see that too. He thought his mother was frightened of him; she pretended she wasn't but she was. His older brother didn't say anything to him now. He'd been proud of the boy when he first arrived and even boasted about him, but that had all changed.

Before entering the corridor that led to his dormitory he sat on the bursar's doorstep and cleaned his feet. The doormat was like doublegee. The corridor was linoleum, it was always cool, like under the house. He could live under his house at home, while everyone was looking for him. He could watch them from under the house. No one would ever go under the house because of red-back spiders, but he didn't care if they bit him. If they did, and he blew up like a pumpkin, they could have a funeral.

As he walked past the fifth former's bed, he wondered why he hated him so much. He never used to. He heard a hiss and turned. It was the sixth former calling to him. The sixth former was angry. The boy felt awful. He liked the sixth former, he'd told the fifth former to pull his head in once when the fifth former was picking on him.

'Where the bloody hell have you been?'

'Sorry. Toilet.'

'A long time at the toilet, Harper,' the sixth former whispered at him.

'Sorry.'

'Don't do that again. I do prep in twelve PG. If you can't sleep, you come there. Don't wander off. You frightened the life out of me. Promise,' the sixth former said.

The boy couldn't make out the sixth former's face, it was just a dark form sitting up in bed whispering at him. It made him fearful but he promised.

'Now, go to bed.' His feet started then his head followed. 'Good boy, Harper,' whispered past his ears.

FORTY-ONE

Day 19
East Perth Police Department
11.50 a.m. Thursday, 12th November 1965

Port Augusta to Perth was 1500 miles. Adelaide to Perth was 1800 miles. Between Ceduna and Eucla was 320 miles of dirt. Cardilini considered the possibility of driving it. Then he checked the time the train left Adelaide and arrived in Perth. It would have arrived in Perth the morning of the 26th, nearly 36 hours after leaving Adelaide. By car, either from Adelaide or Port Augusta, averaging 60 miles per hour, it was possible to arrive to Perth and make it to St Nicholas College with a few hours to spare.

Cardilini knew that Sheppard's Chevrolet Impala would have the big block 409 cubic inch motor. A car that no vehicle in the traffic branch could chase down. Sheppard and Doney could have attended the Elders sale, greeted old friends, then late at night been on the road to Port Augusta or Adelaide, arriving hours before the train. Williamson could have easily joined them and then they'd have taken turns driving non-stop to Perth.

* * *

'Why aren't you out playing golf?' Detective Spry asked Cardilini as he walked into the East Perth detective offices.

'I don't play golf.'

'You're suspended. You've got to have something to do.'

'Nup.' Cardilini proceeded to his desk.

'When you were meant to be working you were always at the pub. Now you've got an excuse to be at the pub, you come in? You need your head read, Cardilini.'

Cardilini had compiled a list of service stations from Eucla to Perth. Balladonia, Norseman, Kalgoorlie, Yellowdine, Southern Cross, Merredin and Northam were towns they would have passed through. The Impala would have needed at least four petrol stops and Doney, Sheppard and Williamson would have needed to eat.

On his first call to the Border Village station near Eucla, an attendant remembered a Chevrolet Impala. Two-tone, plum and cream. It came in on the evening of the 24th. Cardilini sat dumbfounded; this could be his first actual evidence.

They were running late, Cardilini thought. With 1200 miles to Perth still to go, taking roughly 24 hours. But they must have made it. The attendant's description of the driver: 'An old guy. I think.' He didn't note the number plate. 'Why would I?'

If they stopped in Norseman no one remembered them. At Kalgoorlie an attendant remembered the car, he didn't know what time it was or who was in it, 'But it was late.'

'Hi, I'm Detective Cardilini from East Perth station. I'm making enquiries about a two-tone Chevrolet Impala that might have got petrol mid-afternoon on the 25th.'

'Midday.'

'You remember it?'

'Yes. Don't see many. A cockie. Bloody farmers always com-plaining about how tough it is while they drive around in a Chevy Impala. I'd like things to be that tough.'

'Do you remember who was in it?'

'Three blokes. Two older and another, maybe a son of one of the farmers.'

I've got them, Cardilini thought. 'How do you know they were farmers?'

'Country plates.'

'Did you remember the numbers?'

'I'm not Sherlock bloody Holmes.'

Cardilini considered. They needed to average 70 miles per hour to arrive at Merredin at midday, so plenty of time to get to Perth. Now he needed a witness to say they saw the Impala parked near the school. He wanted to tell Williamson, Doney and Sheppard he knew how they managed to shoot Edmund.

'Cardilini, Robinson wants to see you,' Bishop called from the door to the detective's section.

'How did he know I was here?'

'He must be psychic. Get going.'

'Come in,' Robinson said when Cardilini reached his door. Cardilini sat. 'There's been a shift in the complaint against you.'

'Really?' Cardilini said and thought, *finally*. The claw that had hold of the back of his neck released.

'The Deputy Commissioner has had a call from Dr Braun.'

'Okay.'

'Yes. It seems a sixth form boy spoke to Mossop.'

'Good to hear.'

'I don't know about that. He returned to Braun with the story that Mossop had convinced him that he wasn't lying.'

'What?' Cardilini was forwards and squeezing the life out of the armrests of his chair. 'That can't be possible.'

'I'm afraid it is.'

'I warned the arrogant . . .'

'Warned who?'

'Carmody.'

'When you were with Braun? And Braun saw you do it?' A look of disbelief spread across Robinson's face.

'Yeah. No.'

'What did you say?'

'I told Carmody I knew his role in disposing of evidence to Edmund's murder.'

Robinson shouted, 'What?'

'I said he removed the rifle, boots and bullet.'

'What rifle and boots?'

'The ones that, I think now, were placed at the tree opposite Edmund's window.'

'Are you mad?' Robinson looked genuinely concerned.

'No.'

'Okay. And you know this because . . .?' Robinson asked.

'I was told.'

'Who told you?'

'I can't disclose that.'

'Don't talk rubbish, I'm your commanding officer, you tell me right now.'

Cardilini straightened his back. 'Mr Masters.'

'Masters, whose son hung himself?'

Robinson turned away from Cardilini and stood facing the window.

'What will happen now?' Cardilini asked.

'Shut up. Let me think.'

'Maybe if I go back to the school.'

Robinson turned. 'Great plan. And who will you threaten this time? Did you threaten that boy in the toilet?'

'No.'

'But you threatened Carmody in front of witnesses?'

'I warned him.'

'Oh, wonderful. That makes a world of difference. What did the others think you were doing?'

Cardilini shook his head.

'Were you alone with him?' Robinson asked in disbelief.

'Yep. I suppose.'

'Oh boy. What happened, Cardilini?' Robinson looked incredulous. 'You were such a smart cop.'

Cardilini wondered also. 'What should I do now?'

Robinson walked to his chair and sat. Cardilini watched his movements.

'What?' Cardilini asked as Robinson fingered a typed sheet of paper on his blotter. 'Nothing has really changed, has it?' Cardilini asked when Robinson failed to answer.

Robinson sat back and squarely addressed Cardilini. 'St Nicholas decided it was time to examine the claims about Edmund. Some Melbourne coppers are going to interview the principal of his previous school.'

'As if he'll say anything. He'll be covering his own arse. And his job.'

'You don't know that.'

Cardilini looked away and wiped his brow.

'That's happening right now. But . . .' Robinson was pushing the sheet of paper away with one finger and drawing it towards him with the other. '. . . this is not the deputy commissioner's idea, nor mine . . . but, the feeling is we can't ask

Braun to pursue one line of accusations while we're ignoring another.'

'What does that mean?'

'It means both sets of accusations will be dealt with without bias.'

'What sets?'

'As in the ones against Edmund and the ones against you,' Robinson finished and sighed.

Cardilini looked back confounded. 'What? I'm now ranked with Edmund?'

'The board didn't know about this until last night. Half my bloody night was spent on the phone. The deputy commissioner and I have appeared to sweep the complaint against you under the carpet, so we're told.'

'Who can tell you two that?'

'A number of people, a high justice for a start. The right powerful voice in the commissioner's ear and it all gets very sticky, very quickly.'

'"Sticky". Oh, I can cope with "sticky". And all this last night?' Cardilini asked.

'Yes. Something lit a bonfire under them yesterday. It wasn't your visit. We got through that amicably.'

'Great.' Cardilini said but kicked himself for thinking he could bully Carmody. 'So what does this mean for me?'

'Fortunately, you were already suspended. And you're not speaking to anyone without running it past me. Right?'

'Um . . .' Cardilini started sheepishly.

'Cardilini?' Robinson threatened.

'What if I could tell you how the shooting was done?' Cardilini asked.

'You have evidence? Evidence that will stand up in court?'

'I don't have a name. Just how it could be done by people capable and willing,' Cardilini said.

'You mean let's smear a bunch of possibly innocent people to take the heat off you. That would look just dandy. Don't you think?'

'Robinson, you can't hang me out to dry. Not now. What about Paul?'

'Oh Jesus.' Robinson sat up facing Cardilini. 'I don't know. There are people who could put this on the front page of the newspaper, the department has to be seen as —'

'Bullshit. Come on. We've been fudging for years to cover our stuff-ups.'

'Shut up, Cardilini. Don't think you can threaten me.'

'I'm not threatening you. I'm just saying how it is.'

'I would have to disagree with you. If the deputy commissioner or commissioner hears that, you'll be out of the force so fast your head will spin. Got it? This is me, not your super, me, telling you, don't even think of going there.'

'I'm not. Of course not. I'm not completely stupid. But what about Paul?'

'Can we just get over this first?'

'Robinson, give the kid a break!' Cardilini shouted.

'I know. Don't worry. I know what it means. But believe me, now is not the time to rock the boat.'

'Oh, Jesus. It's over, isn't it?'

'No. No, I'm not saying that. There are people who don't appreciate us raking over what Edmund got up to.'

'Do you believe Edmund was abusing those boys?' Cardilini asked and waited.

Robinson expelled a breath heavily and answered, 'I think I do now.'

'What changed your mind?'

'Senior Constable Saunders, from Williams, but you know that. He and I were at Kellerberrin together. He rang me. Want to know what he told me?'

'Yes.'

'The Sheppard boy gave up footy and going out with his mates shortly before propping a rifle under his chin.'

'Oh.'

'Then I got a call from Constable Young at Fremantle. You know him. You could strike a match on him. He thinks the Doney boy drove himself into a tree.'

'What're you going to do about Saunders and Young?'

'Nothing. Their reports were precise. They aren't paid to speculate. They rang me by the by. They trust me.'

'You told the board?'

'A lot of resistance. There's a group pursuing the coroner right now, and we both know he'll not specify suicide in his findings. Some bull ant nests you shouldn't poke at.'

'Salt told you that?' Cardilini asked.

Robinson nodded. 'Yes. But maybe we're all to blame for this mess. Don't think you're the only one in the firing line. As you pointed out, the deputy commissioner and I weren't as thorough as we could have been in the initial investigation. You produce a murderer right now and it will be our blood on the floor.'

'Surely, the minister could help. Christ, he owes us a favour,' Cardilini stated.

'And if we said anything about what we did to save his backside it would support the theory of police cover-ups. No thanks. Look, I just want you to know things could quickly move out of our control.'

'Meaning?'

Robinson paused before saying, 'There's a push within the school board to bring a prosecution against you.'

'Jesus.'

'Would you come out squeaky clean? Factually, evidence-based, squeaky clean? Or are there things that could be brought up, such as lone meetings in toilets or elsewhere that could sink you?' Robinson asked.

'Oh, no.' Cardilini hung his head.

'Don't tell me. Don't tell me. Jesus, Cardilini.'

'I could have been played from the beginning,' Cardilini said.

'Maybe, or maybe you went in as a disaster waiting to happen.'

'What?'

Robinson replied. 'You heard. Anyway, that's what the shrink said. Can't say I disagree.'

'Shrink? Bloody Pudsworth? He's a bloody idiot,' Cardilini shot back.

'Yeah, and I know you've told him on a number of occasions.'

'Only because he is,' Cardilini insisted.

'Well, the worm has turned, Cardilini. I wouldn't keep repeating that if I were you.'

'But he is.'

'Cardilini!' Robinson warned.

'Bloody hell.'

Robinson continued. 'You're going to go through the ropes on this one, as in by the book, so there's a good chance you'll have to front up to him sometime. Go home. If you're capable of not upsetting things further, do so. If you can't, don't look to the department to save your backside. And remember, even if

Edmund was doing what's suggested, it still doesn't mean he was murdered.'

'No. Okay. What if all further investigation to do with Edmund were to stop? And the whole thing was forgotten? What would happen then?'

'Is that what you're proposing?' Robinson asked.

'Just asking?'

'It would make a lot of people happy and get them off our backs.'

'What about my back?'

Robinson considered for a moment then said, 'I should think so.'

As he walked from Robinson's office he repeated to himself, *Save your arse, Cardilini*, for the length of the corridor.

He stopped at Bishop's door and asked, 'This is your fault, Bishop. Why did you give me the St Nicholas case?'

'Your mate Salt will be asking that too. He's just been bounced to the Wickham police station. He went from a rooster to a feather duster real quick.'

'Salt?'

Bishop nodded. 'Yep. And you wonder why no one wants to work with you.'

FORTY-TWO

Day 19
Kilkenny Road
2.45 p.m. Thursday, 12th November 1965

Cardilini was cutting back the geraniums growing wild along the back fence. They were much longer-stemmed and straggly than the last time he'd looked at them. The pungent smell was the same. He wondered for a moment at the fairness of geraniums and their scent outlasting the one who cared for them. To complete the task he needed to stop a number of times and tell himself it's what Betty would have wanted, but cutting the stalks felt like he was cutting Betty from the yard.

While tidying up he thought, if he left the police service, without a conviction, there were still jobs available for the 'right' copper. Some of those ex-coppers had been his serious drinking buddies the last twelve months. Coppers he, at one point, had no respect for: coppers who were more concerned about their comfort than any idea of justice. They were the ones he would need to turn to for employment. It was a good thing Betty wasn't here. Maybe he should try a bit of bum-kissing and ring up possible opportunities. He knew if he waited until he was fired he and Paul would suffer. Days ago he had scorned work at the coroner's office. Now, he could only wish the opportunity would come up again. He decided to make a call.

'Mrs Pass?'

'Yes.'

'It's Cardilini.'

'I know.'

'You know I could have been a bit hasty the other day.'

'In what way?'

'Making judgments about the coroner.' Cardilini frowned as he spoke.

'I think so.'

'Not knowing the circumstances, and all.' His frown deepened.

'I'm glad to hear. Now I'm very busy. Is that all?'

'Um. I suppose.'

'Goodbye, Mr Cardilini.' The receiver clicked in Cardilini's ear. *Maybe you needed to plan that conversation a little better,* Cardilini told himself.

He wondered how Paul would feel about selling the house. He was beginning to think he couldn't keep living in it anyway. Too many things – actions, smells, neighbours – reminded him of Betty.

He rang Colin McBride at the Royal Perth Hospital.

'McBride, it's Cardilini.'

'The answer is no.'

'I haven't asked for anything yet.'

'Saving you the trouble.'

'What's your problem?'

'I got a balling out for hiding that bloody corpse,' McBride said.

'Yeah, sorry about that. I got caught up.'

'So, no.'

'You told me you thought it was a .303 from two hundred yards that made the hole, right?'

'I can't remember.'

'Well you did, I based everything I did on what you said.'

'And?'

'Could you have been wrong?' Cardilini held his breath.

'Of course I could be wrong. But in Europe, forty-four to forty-five, I saw what a .303 could do too many times. And I knew the distance we were firing from,' McBride said.

'Forensics didn't support your theory of the distance the bullet had travelled prior to striking Edmund.'

'I read the report.'

'So?'

'So? Scientists have to go by the rules so naturally they didn't discount that it could have been three or four times that distance. They cover their arses. If it ends up in court and they stated a fixed distance, they could be made to look stupid real quick by another "expert".'

'But you could be wrong?'

'Yep.'

'I'm chasing ghosts,' Cardilini said, exasperated.

'Better than them chasing you.'

'Yeah, thanks.'

'Anytime.'

Cardilini considered Braun's reaction. Maybe he was just trying to cover up the complaints against Edmund. Maybe that was the only reason he was so bloody cagey. Maybe Carmody was just protecting kids who Edmund had got to, protecting them from exposure, and there were never any boots or rifle left. Maybe all that. But his gut still told him Edmund was murdered.

FORTY-THREE

Day 19
St Nicholas College
3.45 p.m. Thursday, 12th November 1965

The boy stood in the corridor outside the sixth form common room waiting for Carmody. One hand was in his pocket clutching the bullet, the pressure and sharpness of it bringing a smile to his face. Across the corridor, a third form boy they called Binder stood on a chair. Twine was his surname. The boy knew Binder well, Binder had hit him square in the middle of the back for no reason, and he'd had a sharp pain there for weeks. He didn't know how to explain it to the nurse, so he'd just hoped it would go away. Which it did.

Binder was standing on the chair as punishment. A prefect would be punishing him, or maybe just a sixth former. While standing on the chair anyone passing was at liberty to say what he thought of you. 'Dickhead', 'wanker' or 'durr', most of the lower school students would say. But if they were second formers that said anything, Binder would hunt them down and bash them later. The boy thought that worse than a bashing would be the sixth formers looking through him.

Binder didn't seem very happy. When the boy looked at him, he threatened him with a fist.

'Harper.'

The boy turned, a sixth former was standing in the doorway signalling to him. The boy walked to him, not taking his eyes off the floor.

'Your name Harper?'

The boy nodded.

'Stand inside the door.'

The boy stepped through the doorway. He pushed the heels of his shoes against the skirting. A few pairs of shoes left, then gradually the room quietened and the common room door was closed. The boy didn't dare look up, but he felt comfortable, he had heard Carmody's voice.

'Look at me.' The boy looked up. It wasn't Carmody speaking, it was 'Double' Daws. He was in the first fifteen rugby team and looked older than the boy's father. The boy felt a tremor go through his chest. 'You lack loyalty, Harper.' The boy's eyes involuntary darted to Carmody. Carmody had turned to ice. Now he was frightened.

'You've been talking to the police,' Double rasped at him. The boy looked back in horror, he felt the little world he had managed to build inside him melt away. A breath caught in his throat as his chest and stomach hollowed. He wondered if anyone would pick him up when he fell, or just move away.

'No,' trembled from his throat and eyes.

Double turned to Carmody. Carmody gave a brief nod. The door opened, someone said, 'Out.' The boy walked out and stood with his back to the corridor wall opposite Binder.

'I'm going to bash you,' Binder hissed at him. The boy looked up at Binder in wonder. Binder made several ugly grimaces and

clenched his fists at the boy as if at a mortal enemy. The boy felt his legs shaking and locked his eyes on the floor.

'You're dead,' was hissed. Some of Binder's third form friends slouched slowly along the corridor.

The boy could hear Binder hissing, 'Hit him.' A fist landed in his stomach. The boy groaned and fell to a crouch gasping for air. 'I'm going to kill him,' Binder was hissing at the passing feet.

It was 5.30 p.m. and the day boys had left. The boy sat by himself at the bottom of the steps and pushed his fingers between the bottom limestone block and soil, the depth of his hand, then released the bullet, it slipped past his fingers easily and rested. He pushed at a sharp edge to hide it deeply. Carmody's ice eyes told him to push himself into the earth. He shook at the image and walked away.

A hand grabbed the boy's hair.

'Edmund's not here to protect you anymore, creep,' Binder hissed in the boy's ear while forcing his head back. Four other third formers quickly stood around shielding Binder's actions. The boy had been caught at the back of the gym.

'We know what you are. Where I come from we would put you in a bag and drown you,' Binder hissed into the boy's ear.

'That's not his fault, Binder,' one of the third formers said. The boy couldn't turn his eyes to see the boy who spoke, but then he realised he didn't want to, he didn't want to recognise him, he didn't want to see any pain that might be in the other boy's eyes.

'Shut up, Slug, or you're next,' Binder jeered as he pulled the boy's head back further.

'We're going to come to your dorm at night, creep, and drown you in the pool,' he rasped into the boy's ear.

'Look, his legs are shaking,' another third former said with a laugh. The boy knew they were, he was having trouble keeping his feet on the ground.

'He's going to piss himself.'

'What're you boys doing?' It was Mr Abbott, a boarding master.

'Nothing, sir,' Binder said and released the boy's hair.

'What're you doing there, Harper?'

As Abbott approached the third form boys stepped aside.

'Nothing,' the boy managed, looking at the ground. The road was rough there; small shards of blue metal penetrated the black bitumen. The boy saw one shard, a pinprick; it would take years for it to work its way out unless the boy helped it.

'Stand up, Harper. What do you think you're doing?' The third formers laughed. 'That's enough from you lot,' Abbott barked.

'Yes, sir,' the third formers murmured.

'I don't want to see you lot hanging around here anymore. Why aren't you at sports training?'

'We're sick, sir,' Binder mocked. He locked eyes with Abbott defiantly.

'Go!' Abbott yelled.

'Come on, Harper,' Binder said.

'Harper, stay.'

'We'll catch you later, Harper, like we said.' Binder and the third formers walked away. The boy watched the heels of their shoes until he couldn't see them without raising his head.

'What did they want, Harper?'

'Nothing, sir.'

'Don't talk rubbish. What did they mean, "They'd catch you later"?'

'I don't know, sir.'

'No one can help you if you don't say anything, Harper.'

'Yes, sir.'

'Well?'

The boy looked for the pinprick of blue metal. He couldn't find it, and he shuffled his feet and moved his head quickly searching for it.

'Harper. Don't be stupid. Look at me. What's going on?'

The boy looked up to the side of Mr Abbott's head.

'Why were you outside the sixth form common room?'

'I was told to be there.'

'Who?'

'It was a day boy. I don't know his name,' the boy lied.

'A sixth former?'

'Yes, sir.'

'Had you told on Twine?'

'No, sir.'

'Are you sure?'

'Yes, sir.'

'So what do the third formers want with you?' Abbott asked.

'I don't know.'

'Was Twine threatening you?'

'No, sir.'

'You stay away from them. You understand?'

'Yes, sir.'

'If they cause you any trouble, you come straight to me. Understand?'

'Yes, sir.'

Abbott stood looking at the boy. The boy hadn't met his eyes.

'I want to help you, Harper.'

'Yes, sir.'

'Don't come back this way again.'

'Yes, sir.'

'Go.'

'Thank you, sir.'

The boy walked in the opposite direction the third formers had taken.

FORTY-FOUR

Day 19
Legget's
4.25 p.m. Thursday, 12th November

The Swan River snaked its way from the port of Fremantle to the limpid stretch that lay before St Nicholas. Cardilini pulled his car over to the river side of the road. One hundred yards of marshy land lay between his car and the riverbank. Thickets of 10-foot high bamboo penetrated the canopy of castor oil trees. The ground, black mud under the trees, was covered with sprouts of coarse grass that clumped in places suggesting more solid ground. Cardilini remembered when he was a constable he'd chased a criminal across such a riverbank. The mud sucked at his boots, sucked at his ankles, sucked the energy from his legs until he had only curses and threats that could keep up with his prey. Eventually they too failed and Cardilini spent considerable time extracting his legs so he could return to the road, only to find the sergeant he was with had taken the car in pursuit.

On the other side of the road there were blocks of land designated for housing. Three had buildings on them. The one closest to the school was the house Cardilini had observed when preparing his night-time visit a few days ago. In the evening it was shrouded by dark trees and looked deserted but in daylight the trees were alive with colour. Cardilini recognised jacaranda, grey myrtle and waratah trees, which all grew on Reabold Hill too. He wondered if someone like Betty lived there.

He locked his car and needlessly looked along the road before crossing. The conversation with Robinson had unsettled him. It had made him question his desire for a just and civil world as opposed to one based purely on self-interest. He hadn't quite figured the logic that had him walking towards this house.

The waist-high fence was made of heavy timber framing and cyclone mesh. Along its length, wild oats on the outside and roses inside battled for sunlight. The gate was of white pickets and the latch and hinges seemed outsized compared to the usual domestic variety. The gate had a welcoming creak, and a path of gravel wound around a silver princess mallee leading to the verandah. Everlastings and marigolds covered the spaces between the other trees. A solid timber balustrade, also white like the pickets, surrounded the timber verandah. Some loose and warping verandah boards had been returned to order by a steel barrel strap, now sheened with rust. An ornate green timber flyscreen door hung loosely. Beyond the door Cardilini could see a dark corridor travelling to sunlight at the rear. He tried rapping his knuckles on the timber door frame. The door rattled but little noise penetrated the depth of the corridor and he received no response. He tried again more firmly with the same result. Walking to the right side of the verandah, he saw that it extended to the rear of the house past three pairs of

French doors. The rear verandah was populated with chairs of all sorts: from cane lounge chairs to stiff, timber highbacks. He approached the rear entrance where another flyscreen door hung lazily. He knocked and called, 'Hello.'

'Over here,' a male voice answered from behind him.

Cardilini turned and looked out onto two squares of green lawn extending to the dense foliage of trees.

'In the lean-to.'

Cardilini started down the path. Off to his right was a bush shelter; four tree trunks sunk into the earth with cross-timbers supporting brush packed and tied to about a foot deep on the roof. He saw the rear of a man's head under the shelter. Cardilini walked towards him.

'Sit down,' a voice said, though the man didn't look up. Cardilini sat opposite and recognised the lean old man who had been talking to Carmody at the cricket match. Cardilini thought it might be the same man he'd seen exiting Braun's office the first day he went to the school. The man's long limbs were narrow and sinewy; his face, complementing the lack of flesh on his body, was almost skeletal with tight, raw skin drawn across his cheekbones. His downcast, hooded eyes were locked on a book.

'That's ginger beer there, help yourself,' the man said without looking up.

'No thanks,' Cardilini said.

'I make it myself.'

'Okay.' Cardilini grabbed a glass and filled it. 'I'm Detective Sergeant Cardilini.'

The man put his book down. Sharp, luminous blue eyes scrutinised Cardilini.

'I saw you at a St Nicholas cricket match,' Cardilini said.

'Oh, yes. I wander up sometimes. I make suggestions to the players who politely listen then walk away. What can I do for you?' The elderly man asked.

'We're trying to locate a car that was seen in this area.' Cardilini thought he would take a general approach rather than immediately discussing the shooting.

'Stolen?' The man asked. Cardilini nodded, uncommitted.

'Where?'

'Along the riverbank.'

'Go on,' The man said with a brief glance to his book.

'Parked under the paperbarks,' Cardilini said.

'Today?' The man looked up to confirm.

'No. October twenty-fifth around ten p.m.,' Cardilini said but doubted the old fellow would be aware of today's date let alone a date a few weeks back.

'At night?'

'Yes.'

'Who can see at night?' the old man asked.

'Someone saw it, it was reported,' Cardilini lied.

'A lot of trouble for a stolen car. Is it there now?'

'No. Did you see a car that evening?' Cardilini asked with the sinking feeling that he was wasting his time.

'Why are you asking where it was weeks ago?' The old man asked.

'You didn't say your name,' Cardilini said.

'Leggett.'

'Mr Leggett,' Cardilini said, the name sounded familiar.

'You got that right.'

'How long have you lived here?'

'Long before the twenthy-fifth.'

'How long?'

Leggett took his time observing Cardilini. 'Is that what you came to ask?'

'No. On the twenty-fifth of October the car was parked there for an hour, maybe less, and left before eleven.'

'Not stolen this time?' Leggett asked.

Cardilini shifted on his seat and assumed the voice of law and order. 'Listen, this is a police investigation, I suggest you answer the questions from now on with full disclosure of anything you saw.'

Leggett straightened his back and sharpened his glare. '*Listen,* I'm eighty-six, so I'll do whatever I damn well please.'

Older people usually fall over themselves to assist the police. And I get this old crock, thought Cardilini.

'Arthur, what are you doing to that man?' a female voice called from the house.

'It's not me, he's making up stories,' Leggett called.

The speaker was a woman in her fifties, blonde hair streaking to grey, fair skin. *A delicate face like Betty's,* Cardilini thought. She wore an artist's smock coloured by paint.

'How do you do, I'm Detective Sergeant Cardilini,' Cardilini said, standing.

'Detective Sergeant,' Leggett said mockingly.

'Jean Leggett.' She held out her hand. 'I won't break,' Jean Leggett said as Cardilini gently took it in his. 'Why are you here?'

'This will be interesting,' Leggett said to no one in particular.

'We're interested to know if a car was seen in this vicinity on the night of October the twenty-fifth.'

'Is that the stolen one or the other one?' Leggett queried.

'Two cars?' Jean asked.

Trying to ignore Leggett, Cardilini answered, 'No. A very distinctive car, an American car. Cream and plum.'

'Cream and plum sounds like a pudding,' Jean said, walking past Cardilini and sitting next to Leggett. 'What did Arthur say?'

'Miss Leggett, it would be better if you could encourage your father to just answer my questions honestly and frankly.'

'It's Mrs Leggett and Frank is my husband.'

Cardilini tried to conceal his surprise but knew his eyes flicked between the two several times. Leggett laughed, Jean Leggett reached for the ginger beer and a glass.

'You don't know who my husband is?' Jean asked Cardilini.

'Frank Leggett? No,' Cardilini replied, looking to the old man.

'Francis?'

Oh my God, thought Cardilini. Of course he knew who the man was.

And Jean Leggett confirmed. 'He was the crown prosecutor and then a justice of the High Court. He knows exactly what is required of him.'

Cardilini sat back down. He couldn't believe that this was possible.

'Was he an old boy of St Nicholas College?' Cardilini asked dumbly.

Leggett laughed out loud, Jean joined in. Cardilini was feeling sick.

'The school was built on what once was Leggett land. All this side of the river up to the town.' Jean smiled back. 'I should've answered the front door but I knew Frank was getting bored with his book.'

'I'm hoping you've never heard of me,' Cardilini said.

'Oh, yes we have. Mark Carmody is a frequent visitor,' Leggett replied.

'The boy Carmody at St Nicholas?' Cardilini asked, appalled.

'That's the one. Not a fan of yours,' Leggett said.

'The feeling's mutual,' Cardilini said, standing.

'What's your rush?'

'Knowing your lot, I'll get my marching orders in the morning. I better start looking for a job.'

'Please yourself, but given how long it took you to get down here, it seems a shame to rush off,' Leggett said.

Jean stood and said, 'I might leave you two. Drinks in half an hour.' She walked off. Cardilini watched her walking away while thinking that's what he should be doing. The light, loose fabric of her smock swished from side to side like a horse's tail.

'You find her attractive?'

'Sorry. No. Just thinking, I should go too.'

'You don't find her attractive?'

'No. Yes. Do you know what Carmody has been up to?'

'Maybe not. You tell me.'

'So you can tell him? I don't think so,' Cardilini replied.

'I don't need to tell tales to anyone,' Leggett said, laying aside his book.

Cardilini sat. There was nothing about this guy that was eighty-six.

'Put your policeman's head on for a moment,' Leggett said.

My policeman's head? What does this old geezer think this is? 'Okay.'

'Think of this from Carmody's point of view.'

'Are you kidding? He's an arrogant little brat.'

'For an arrogant little brat he seems to be managing you successfully.'

Cardilini poured himself a ginger beer and hoped the tremors of anger in his hand weren't too obvious.

'So you've never thought of things from his point of view?' Leggett asked.

'Never. He doesn't interest me.'

Leggett smiled at that. 'Then I can't help you,' he said and picked up his book. Cardilini had a rush of words but caught them all. He needed to calm down, leave the emotion out of it, and 'put his policeman's head on'. He was failing Paul, he was failing who he should be. He watched Leggett reading. He knew he had to sit this out, maybe he could book the ex-high court justice for withholding information. If he was still a policeman, he corrected himself.

'Okay. My policeman's head's on,' he finally said.

Leggett gave an expression of, 'It's about time,' and put the book down.

'What do you think Carmody is doing?' Leggett asked.

Cardilini sighed deeply. 'He's interfering with a police investigation.'

'The police investigation is completed and Edmund's death was found to be an accidental shooting by parties or party unknown and impossible to determine.'

'So what's Carmody doing?' Cardilini asked.

'He thinks other boys' lives could be at risk if the abuse they suffered was to become known.'

'I'd heard that,' Cardilini said.

Leggett nodded his head sagely before asking, 'Then why are you risking so much by continuing to poke around?'

'Did you see a car here on the evening of the twenty-fifth of October?' Cardilini heard himself demanding.

'You can't expect an old man to remember such details.'

'I'll speak to your wife then,' Cardilini said.

'No, you won't. You'll go straight out the way you came,' Leggett threatened.

'Or?'

'Do you really want to play games with me?'

'What can you do?' Cardilini asked.

'I'm the legal advisor to the St Nicholas board,' Leggett said with a challenge in his voice. Cardilini looked back stunned. Was this decrepit bag of bones behind the pressure on Robinson and Warren?

'Do we understand each other?' Leggett asked.

Cardilini stood staring at Leggett, he felt blood rush to his neck and head, he bit his mouth closed. Leggett looked back like a surgeon, cold and implacable. Cardilini turned and walked away.

FORTY-FIVE

Day 19
St Nicholas College
6.10 p.m. Thursday, 12th November 1965

After dinner the boy was told to report to the sixth form common room again. He stood in the corridor. Darnley, a fourth form student, wandered in and stood opposite the boy.

'What are you doing here, creep?' Darnley asked. Everyone knew Darnley would be expelled. He was the size of a sixth former and had wisps of dark hair on his upper lip like a moustache. He stole things. He had stolen money from boys' lockers. It was rumoured he had stolen gym equipment and stashed it down by the river.

The boy shrugged. Students were not allowed to speak while standing outside the common room.

'Creep,' Darnley said in a normal conversational voice and smiled.

The boy shrugged.

'You got any smokes?'

The boy shook his head.

'Creep.'

The boy shrugged.

'Is Carmody in there?'

The boy looked up, lifted his shoulders and let them drop.

'You glad Edmund got shot?'

The boy looked up. Darnley seemed to have no interest in his questions. Some of the second formers were proud that Darnley had stolen their property. They didn't dob on him. One time when money was stolen from a second former's locker twice in a week, the second former was boasting to all the boys gathered around his locker. He showed the open padlock, he showed where the money was, he told them how much was stolen the first time and how much was stolen the second time. The second formers were laughing with him, punching his arms and ruffling his hair. Darnley's name was whispered again and again. How did Darnley manage to get out of prep? That's when he must have done it. How did he manage to pick the lock? What locks had Darnley not managed to pick? One boy had a Lockwood lock and the group went to look at it. The boy had looked at his own lock when the group wandered away and wondered if he could buy one that Darnley could pick.

The boy shrugged at Darnley's question. But inwardly he seeped blood, he knew it to be blood because he felt it run from his face and neck. All the teachers hated Darnley. The sixth formers constantly punished him. The fifth formers were scared of him. The 'good kids' of every year avoided him, but the 'tough kids' looked up to him. More blood seeped. If Darnley knew about what Edmund had done to him, he felt it appropriate he seep to death while standing waiting for Carmody.

'Did you shoot him?' Darnley asked again with a smile but no real interest in his question.

The boy smiled, despite the seeping, and shook his head.

'Did you want to?'

The boy still looking at Darnley, nodded. Darnley casually nodded back and began picking his teeth with a match.

'Do you know who has smokes?' Darnley asked.

The boy nodded he did.

'Who?'

The boy whispered a name.

'Does he keep them in his locker?'

The boy shrugged.

'You find out his locker number and come back and tell me.'

'Now?' the boy whispered.

'Don't be stupid,' Darnley laughed.

The boy nodded back, smiling.

'You a bit nuts?' Darnley asked, spitting something from his tongue.

The boy shrugged.

'Why're you here?' Darnley asked.

The police brought Darnley from the city once when he had been caught stealing from David Jones men's department. Darnley had taken three pairs of black jeans into a booth to try them on and only returned two; he had a pair on under his suit trousers. Another student dobbed on him to the cashier. One cashier didn't care and smiled at Darnley, but the other made a fuss and called the police. Everyone knew the story, Darnley made sure they did. He wanted to find out who dobbed on him. Some boys who hated Darnley said he was damaging the school by his behaviour and should have been dobbed on, others said Darnley shouldn't have been dobbed on because it hurt the school's reputation.

'Carmody,' the boy answered with some pride.

'I hate him,' Darnley announced. The boy was shocked. He had never heard anyone, any student or teacher, ever say anything but praise for Carmody. The boy looked closely at Darnley.

'Why?' he asked.

'He's a prick. Thinks he's boss of everything.'

But he is, the boy wanted to say. He was puzzled. How could Darnley think like that? Darnley and Carmody were in the same stratosphere in the eyes of the second formers. He wanted to tell Darnley that, then he wouldn't hate Carmody.

'What did you do?' Darnley asked.

'I don't know.'

'Bullshit.'

'I don't mind being here.'

'You're mad,' Darnley said, smiling, as if he was saying, 'You're a good kid.'

The boy shrugged and smiled.

'You in love with Carmody?' Darnley asked.

The boy wondered if he was. He loved his father and mother, he wasn't sure about his brother. He knew he loved Dianne Mullick, the daughter of a neighbouring farmer. He knew that he worshipped God because he went to church. But he did worship Carmody more than God, he decided. He wondered if that was bad. He would find out when he was dead.

'I'm not,' the boy said but Darnley had lost interest; he was picking threads from the narrow end of his tie to make it look shredded. It was against school rules and only the absolute worst kids wore their ties like that. Darnley could be the worst boy in the school, the boy thought, and only being in Form Four that was quite something. Darnley showed no fear, even when the police brought him back to the school. He had smiled and talked about 'pigs', and some said his father was in prison though others said he wouldn't be allowed in the school if that were true.

'He thinks I spoke to the police,' the boy said.

'Who?'

'Carmody.'

'Did you?'

'No.'

'Why does he think you did?' Darnley asked.

'I don't know.'

'I'll ask him,' Darnley said with no interest.

'No. No. Please.'

'Don't you want to know?'

'I don't care.'

'You got a brother here, too, haven't you?'

'Yes.'

'Get him to sort it out,' Darnley said.

'Yes,' the boy said but knew he never would, he would confide in Darnley before he would confide in his brother. 'But he's busy.'

Darnley laughed. 'Too busy to look out for you?' he asked.

'Very busy.'

Darnley laughed again. 'You got any money?' he asked.

'No,' the boy said quickly.

Darnley laughed out loud, the boy smiled. He wanted to laugh like Darnley.

'Quiet,' was yelled through the door. Darnley made a wanking motion with his hand while staring at the door. The boy shuddered. He felt laughter rising in his throat. He had thought laughter had gone forever and began coughing and spluttering in confusion. Darnley looked at him and laughed out loud. The door opened.

'That you, Darnley?' a sixth former asked.

Darnley looked around as though to say, 'who else could it be?'

'Why are you here?' was snapped back at him.

'Carmody,' Darnley sneered.

'Your father out of prison yet?' the sixth former sneered back. Darnley took a quick glance at the boy. The boy saw Darnley was trapped.

'He's never been to prison,' Darnley bit back.

'Yeah. So what did you steal this time?'

'Ask Carmody?'

'He's not here.'

Darnley lowered his head and swung it from side to side like the boy had seen a bull do when teased.

The sixth former turned his attention to the boy.

'Why are you here?'

'Carmody.'

The sixth former closed the door, Darnley made a wanking gesture with both hands and arms as if he had a penis the size of a lamppost. Laughter broke in the boy's throat. The door swung open. Darnley quickly dropped his arms.

'We know who you are, Harper. You disgust us.' The door closed. The boy's insides twisted, his breathing stopped. Darnley looked at him in alarm.

'Hey. Hey. Harper.'

The boy saw Darnley crossing the corridor towards him before a black river caught him.

FORTY-SIX

Day 19
Taylor's Farm
6.10 p.m. Thursday, 12th November 1965

Cardilini experienced surges of emotion as he drove from Leggett's house. *I'll get these bastards*, kept running through his mind. The road took him to the town bridge crossing the river to farmland. He knew the shot hadn't come from there, then corrected himself – he suspected it hadn't.

The bridge had seen better days. Its triangular timber supports stretched to the meandering river some 60 feet below. The road base was made up of timber sleepers lying end to end from one side of the bridge to the other. Some sleepers were loose and bounced up to meet the tyres of Cardilini's car, slapping and thudding as he passed. The result was a very noisy crossing. The car bounced from the bridge onto a single-lane bitumen road. Cardilini cruised slowly, avoiding the steep gravel banks of the road while he searched through the bordering gum trees for sign of a homestead. He saw one sheltering in a grove of tall gum trees surrounded by sheds and rainwater tanks.

Cardilini turned left off the bitumen onto a gravel road. A cyclone gate blocked the way.

He got out of the car and opened the gate, noting the name 'Taylor' painted on a tin plate. He drove through and closed it before continuing.

Stubble from a recently harvested wheat crop stretched out on either side of the driveway. The car bumped over corrugations in the gravel before the road smoothed and snaked into the grove of gums. Cardilini pulled the car up in front of the house which was of the same vintage and design as the Leggett house. He lit a cigarette and considered the possibility that he was about to encounter another branch of the Leggett family.

He stepped onto the broad front verandah and rapped on the flyscreen door, which, like the Leggett's, also hung loosely in its doorframe.

'Come in,' was yelled from the depths of the house. Cardilini entered and pulled the flyscreen door to behind him. He walked the length of the corridor and stood at the entrance to the kitchen where a man and a woman sat at a scrubbed timber table with large mugs in front of them.

'Who the hell are you?' the man asked in surprise.

'Detective Sergeant Cardilini from the East Perth branch. I just wanted to confirm the information you provided regarding the use of firearms on the property.'

'Oh. For Christ's sake. Are you all bloody dense?' the man snapped. He was wizened and balding but had bright blue eyes and a lopsided, cheeky grin.

'It can appear that way,' Cardilini conceded.

A tall, austere and handsome woman with hair tied back in a tight bun said, 'Well, you better have a cup of tea. We were expecting someone else. Sit down. Sit down.' She went to a kitchenette for another large mug.

'Yeah, well, I'm Taylor. This is my wife, Mrs Taylor,' Taylor said and held out his hand.

'Cardilini. Thanks, sorry if this is a trouble.'

'No trouble.' Mrs Taylor poured from the teapot. 'Milk?'

'Thanks.'

'So, what do you want to know this time?' Taylor asked.

'The report stated that a stray .303 fired from this side killed the teacher.'

Taylor and his wife shared an irritated look.

'The fact of the matter is .303's aren't used over here. Too bloody dangerous.'

'The coroner believes the shot came from here.'

Taylor snapped back, 'Well he's a bloody idiot.'

Cardilini nodded. 'The school community believes it also. So what do you think's going on?'

'No idea. The roo-shooter is going to trap the roos further north, from now on. At one of the dams. Suits us, right Missus?'

'Suits us. Going to keep the roos from the feed along the river. Suits us,' Mrs Taylor agreed.

'Too right,' Taylor confirmed. 'Anything else?'

'The police didn't take your rifle?' Cardilini tried to ask casually as he sipped his strong tea.

'Why would they? It's not going anywhere. They did take my word though.'

'You told the police it would be impossible for the shot to come from this side of the bank?'

Taylor reacted affronted. 'No. I never said that. I said, and Digger the shooter confirmed, that a shot from this side of the river was not in any way connected to Digger shooting roos.'

'You had only one man, Digger, shooting that night?'

'You can speak to him. He butts and skins the roos. Sells the meat for pet food and the skin to a fella in the city. Occasionally he'll put a joey in the chook pen, if one's in the mother's pouch. Digger's a bit of a softy, isn't he, Missus?'

'He's a bit of a softy all right. We give them away as pets. Wouldn't be surprised if they end up in a stew, though,' Mrs Taylor said.

'Nothing wrong with kangaroo stew,' Taylor confirmed.

'Did Digger say he heard any other shots that night?'

'You can ask him. He's in the shed. He's also a bit of a mechanic.'

'A local?'

'Of course. Finish your tea and we'll go over,' Taylor said.

'And tell Digger afternoon tea doesn't last all day,' Mrs Taylor added.

Cardilini and Taylor smoked as they walked across the yard of hard-packed white sand towards one of the sheds. As Cardilini inhaled, the heat of the afternoon gave the cigarette an acrid taste. *Not like smoking on a winter's day*, Cardilini thought. The shed was timber-framed with walls of vertically placed planks. A weathered, corrugated iron roof, rusted red at the edges, seemed to hold the structure together. A tall, thin man in overalls was bent over the wheel arch of an old Humber, his head and arms buried within the engine bay.

'Digger. Another policeman. A detective sergeant, from the city this time.'

'Oh, yeah,' came from the engine bay.

'Can he fix carbies?'

'Can you fix carbies?' Taylor asked.

'No.'

'Seems he can't.'

The overalled legs firmed on the ground and Digger pulled his torso from the vehicle. He had dark hair, a tanned and lined face, dark eyes and was missing several top teeth. He observed

MAN AT THE WINDOW

Cardilini and gave a nod to Taylor. Then he pulled a rag from his pocket and wiped his hands slowly.

'The missus wanted to inform you that afternoon tea doesn't last all day.'

'Tell her I'm sorry. Got busy.'

'He drank your tea, anyway,' Taylor said indicating Cardilini.

'From the city?' Digger asked.

'Cardilini. East Perth.'

'An Itie,' Digger said.

'Itie and Scot. You got a problem with that?' Cardilini asked.

'The Scot part of it,' Digger said with a knowing look to Taylor.

'Hilarious,' Cardilini replied. 'Do you use hollow-point bullets?'

'I have, why?' Digger asked as he finished wiping his hands and looking sideways at Cardilini.

'What for?'

'Crocs. Why do you ask?'

'Where do you get them?'

'I make 'em,' Digger said throwing his rag onto the Humber running board.

'How?' Cardilini asked. Digger looked to Taylor who shrugged to indicate he had no idea what Cardilini was on about.

Digger turned and walked into the shed. Cardilini turned to Taylor quizzically. The farmer indicated for him to follow. Digger reached into the back of a ute and pulled out several rounds. At a manual drill press, he set the bullet head up in a timber frame and clamped it to the bench below the drill.

'That looks dangerous,' Cardilini said stopping several steps away.

Digger ignored the comment and lowered a narrow drill bit onto the tip of the bullet and slowly turned the drill. A thin thread of lead began to peel its way from the bit and bullet. Digger stopped after a number of turns, released the bullet and tossed it to Cardilini. The bullet had a neat hole down it's centre.

'That's it?' Cardilini asked.

'That's it.'

Cardilini tossed the bullet back. 'Thanks. You use them for roos?'

'No need, besides it a makes a bloody mess.'

'Okay. How many of you were shooting that night?'

'Just me.'

'I got the impression there's often more than one shooter.'

'There can be but not a lot of feed about for a few years so the roos don't give birth. They can put it off you know. No feed means fewer roos, means fewer skins, means less money if you're splitting it, which means I shoot by myself,' Digger finished and Taylor looked to Cardilini to see how impressed he was with Digger's logic.

'Did you hear any shots the night the teacher was killed?' Cardilini asked.

'Apart from my own, you mean?'

'Yes. Apart from them.'

'Why?'

'A man was shot. If not by you, by someone else,' Cardilini stated.

'Oh, now it's by me, is it? You can see how these boys work,' Digger said to Taylor.

Cardilini assured, 'That's not what I meant.'

'Yeah, well. Easy enough for you to say. But if people start thinking I shoot in all directions, I'll lose a lot of work. Won't I, Taylor?'

'Yep. That could happen,' Taylor confirmed.

'Did you hear a rifle shot other than your own?' Cardilini asked.

'I must've, mustn't I?'

'Why must you?'

'Because the fella got shot. Didn't he?' Digger said with a smile to Taylor.

'Were you asked about the sound of another rifle that night by the police?'

'Yes.'

'What did you tell them?'

'That sound can be funny,' Digger said with another look to Taylor who was obviously enjoying the banter.

Cardilini looked at the pair before asking, 'Would a shot have been obvious if it came from this side of the river?'

'Ah. He's not as silly as the other ones,' Digger said to Taylor.

'Well?' Cardilini prompted.

'You'd think it would be. And yes, it is when you hear your mate make the shot, because he's standing by you,' Digger spelt out.

'So it wasn't like that, the shot you heard?' Cardilini asked.

'The shot I think I might have heard – if it wasn't the funny sound the night can make – was not like that, no,' Digger said seriously.

'So, not this side of the river?' Cardilini asked.

'That's where it gets complicated. Doesn't it, Digger?' Taylor asked.

'Too right. It surely does,' Digger nodded, confirming Taylor's statement, then said, 'See, you take a few roos out by the river, then the rest are bouncing off in all directions, then you need to catch them in the light. So I drive across to the rise and catch them with the spotty.' Digger pointed west to the raised ground.

'You had someone holding the spotlight?' asked Cardilini.

'No.' Taylor shook his head. 'He's got it all rigged up.'

'All rigged up. That's right. I do it for money, you see,' Digger said.

'Okay. So you've driven across to the rise, what happens then?' Cardilini asked.

'And I shoot two roos, frozen in the spotlight staring at it. Then I hear what seems to be a late echo. Only trouble is, I know what a .243 echo sounds like. I've heard it plenty of times. And this didn't sound like a .243 echo.'

'What did it sound like?' Cardilini asked.

'.303, .308. Take your pick,' Digger replied.

'Coming from the direction of the school?' Cardilini asked.

'That's difficult to say because sound ca–'

'. . . can be funny.' Cardilini shook his head, exasperated, and asked, 'Is it possible it came from the school?'

Digger looked to Taylor, who gave a noncommittal shrug, then back to Cardilini. Cardilini, following their exchange, asked with some urgency, 'What?'

'I reckon that shot came from the school,' Digger said.

'You told the local coppers that?'

Digger shrugged, 'They didn't believe me. They reckon I'm covering me arse.'

Cardilini nodded smiling, 'Thanks.'

Back at the Humber, he held out his cigarette packet to Digger and Taylor while admiring the Humber's running boards and the elegant sweep of the bodywork.

'Nice old car,' he said.

'Piece of shit,' Digger replied taking a cigarette.

Cardilini drove to the front gate, feeling elated; he could finally close the trap on *the bastards*. The shot was definitely made from the school, just how he'd figured. McBride was right first up. Sheppard, Doney and Williamson were responsible – there was no doubt now.

He knew why the local police wrote the report they did. 'Sound can be funny,' wouldn't look very intelligent. He wanted to go to the local station but knew he could be risking too much already. He went home, satisfied, and decided to clean out the weeds along the side of the house. If there was enough light, he would prune that bloody tea tree.

FORTY-SEVEN

Day 19
St Nicholas College
8.00 p.m. Thursday, 12th November 1965

The boy felt the blanket before he saw it. It cut across his back like a scimitar. It was the slash of it that woke him up. It was evening; he was lying on a bed in sick bay. His body didn't want to move. His eyes and ears travelled to the door, he could hear voices, then Mr Abbott entered and called back through the door, 'His eyes are open.'

The nurse pushed past him. She didn't do it on purpose, she pushed everyone. She was round like a bowling ball and was known as Four Stars because she travelled to the four points of the compass as she walked. She'd been called that for generations, every boy's father could tell stories about Four Stars. When walking on the quadrangle paths the little kids stood to the side because you didn't know from which star of the compass she would attack as she walked past. For a while, the tough kids banged into her so she would swing a beefy arm at them and they would duck away laughing. Some boys she would chase for several steps swinging her arms. Everyone loved it when she clobbered another kid by mistake. It got so bad that a boy was suspended and a teacher had to walk with her. The boys, and even Four Stars it was said, missed the fun. It was whispered she had accidentally killed a boy.

Four Stars pushed her face at the boy. It filled his vision, bright blue eyes surrounded by florid, puffy cheeks, thick lips around a mouth that never closed. Never closed on a barely contained tongue that seemed to breathe for her. To tell a boy he'd been kissing Four Stars was enough to cause a fight. She was so close the boy thought she might kiss him.

'Where are you hurting?' Four Stars demanded, feeling the boy's head. My head, thought the boy as Four Stars bounced her knuckles off it as if sounding a watermelon.

'Nowhere,' he answered. He knew Four Stars' cures were more harmful than all the ailments the second formers could think of.

'Rubbish,' she splattered. Each spittle had been equipped with a pick and shovel and they started about their task on the boy's face.

'Where did he punch you, Harper?'

The boy looked back totally mystified.

'How stupid is this boy?' Four Stars asked as if vital to her diagnosis.

'Smart enough,' Abbott said.

'Concussion,' Four Stars announced and moved a finger back and forth across the boy's eyes. The boy followed it.

'Did he bang your head against the wall?' Abbott asked.

The boy stopped following the finger and looked back at Abbott and wondered if he should say they had the wrong student.

'Concussion. I'll undress him and put him into bed.' The boy tried to sit up. One of the stories told was you must never let Four Stars undress you, no matter how many limbs are missing.

'That won't be necessary, just leave him with me for a few minutes,' Mr Abbott said quickly.

'Don't let him go to sleep,' Four Stars said and started tacking from the room, the boy watched her negotiate the doorway perfectly. If he had anyone to tell, they would've been interested in that sighting.

'Can you sit up, Harper?'

'Yes, sir,' the boy replied before he knew if it was a fact. He managed to swing his legs over the side of the bed. The room moved for a little while before looking normal again.

'What happened?'

'I don't know,' the boy replied.

Abbott raised his voice, 'Harper, no one can help you if you don't tell us what's going on.'

'I had a pain and then . . .' the boy said and thought, a black river, so black it pushed at me like a big invisible pillow, pushed at me until nothing was left of me.

'"And then", what?' Abbott asked.

'I don't remember.'

'Where did he hit you?'

'I don't remember being hit.'

'Platmore said Darnley punched you in the stomach.'

Platmore was the sixth former who'd spoken to Darnley and the boy. The boy wondered why Darnley had hit him. But Darnley had been known to hit boys out of the blue and neither the boy nor Darnley would say why it happened. The boy thought Darnley had hit him for being . . . he started to cry.

'Why did he hit you, Harper?' Abbott asked.

'I don't know,' the boy sobbed. Fat tears dropped and spread dark patches on his trousers.

'Why are you crying?'

'The blanket hurt my back,' the boy lied, twisting. Tears fell with a plop on the blanket.

'Darnley will be expelled this time, you can be sure of that. Hitting a boy your size.' Abbott shook his head in disgust as he said the final sentence. This started a new flood of tears and the boy rubbed his back, pretending pain.

'Darnley's in detention. Don't you go anywhere near there. Can you walk?'

'Yes, sir.' And the boy was surprised he could. He took a step forward and backward to show Mr Abbott.

'You don't have to go back to the sixth form common room. I'll speak to Carmody. He told you to stand there, right?'

The boy nodded.

'Why did he want you to stand there?' Abbott asked.

'I don't know,' the boy replied. 'I don't mind standing there.'

FORTY-EIGHT

Day 20
Kilkenny Road
2.45 p.m. Friday, 13th November 1965

Cardilini had managed to garden all day. However, his mind travelled again and again over any possible hard evidence that could be presented in court. No identifiable gun, no identifiable shooter. The bullet. He knew he had to find it and that it had to match a St Nicholas' rifle. He needed the names of the boys Edmund was abusing, one of them must have picked up the bullet.

Standing, frustrated, sipping a cup of tea, he looked down one side of the house. The timber picket fence between his and the neighbour's block was about a yard from his wall. On the other side of his house, the car could be driven to the rear past wild orange and lemon trees. He'd glanced in their direction a few times that day but didn't feel any motivation to do anything about their lengthy, searching branches. Winter was the time for that, he reminded himself.

Along the front of the house, a low brick wall barely contained a variety of dishevelled shrubs. He placed his cup on the wall, then saw another cup sitting there. A tremor went through him. He tried frantically to remember when he had placed it there. He looked inside it. There was a layer of dried and crumbled leaves in its base. He felt sick, his legs folded and he collapsed on the wall. Betty could have left it there. His chest ached, his throat convulsed, he put his hands out to support himself. He stared at the cup, convulsions running through his body as tears dropped onto the brickwork.

He couldn't remember crying sober, even at the funeral service. But now he found himself apologising through the convulsions and tears. Apologising for being so weak, apologising for being so selfish. His hand went towards the cup, then stopped beside it. He whispered his love to his wife, he made promises he let the sorrow take its course, he didn't want to control it, and he didn't want to run from it. He wanted to be honest with himself, Betty and Paul. He felt any future happiness depended on it. The dreams Betty and he had had for Paul depended on it.

Twenty minutes later, spent of grief but still propping his torso on his outstretched hands, a ringing broke into his awareness. He let it ring out. He sat up and wiped his eyes and cheeks on his sleeve. The ringing started again. He left both cups side by side and walked into the house.

'Cardilini, it's Leggett,' the voice answered.

'What can I do for you?' Cardilini asked, spent, uncaring.

'I thought you might like to come by this evening.'

'No, thanks,' Cardilini replied flatly.

'A mutual friend is coming down briefly after the boarders' dinner. Shall we say eight fifteen?'

'No.'

'You know who I mean?'

'Carmody?'

'Yes. Wouldn't you like to talk to him?'

'No.'

'He would like to talk to you.'

'He knows where I live and my phone number, no doubt,' Cardilini said.

'It's not that easy for him to get away from the school.'

'Each time I speak to that boy, I end up in deeper trouble.'

'I know,' Leggett said.

'What do you know?'

'I know what he's doing. I want to make it stop.'

Cardilini paused. Could he believe the man?

'You know that the shot that killed Edmund came from your side of the river?' Cardilini asked.

'I can't answer that.'

'Then I can't come to meet Carmody.'

'Would you be amenable to Jean driving Carmody and me to your house tonight?'

'I don't think so.'

'If I gave you my word no damage to your career would come from the meeting?' Leggett asked.

'Give me your word that no charges will ever be brought against me by the school,' Cardilini bargained.

There was a pause. Cardilini expected to be angry at himself but he wasn't. He remained calm, looked at his watch. Paul should be back soon.

'You're asking us to surrender a great deal,' Leggett finally said.

'You came up with the idea of bringing charges against me, right?'

'Yes.'

'Then you can stop any charges. Either way, I'll prove that you and your bloody board protected Edmund and now you have Carmody protecting his killer.'

Cardilini wondered if he was getting his copper's head, back or if he just didn't care anymore. No, he knew deep down that he cared. He became nervous. 'I'm going out for an hour. You ring me with your answer,' Cardilini said and hung up. He didn't want to hear Leggett's voice any longer. He showered and changed back into his day clothes.

FORTY-NINE

Day 20
St Nicholas College
4.30 p.m. Friday, 13th November 1965

*It was 4.30 and the boy had been standing outside the sixth form
common room since 3.45. He wanted to be 'in trouble' so stood
there even though Abbott said he didn't have to. The story of
Darnley punching him in the stomach had spread like wildfire
but he didn't want to talk about it.*

*Students frequently walked by, occasionally one would pre-
tend to punch him in the stomach then pull his punch at the last
moment and the boy would buckle; this generally brought laughter from all who saw it. The boy, after the third time, became
confident that no one would actually punch him and stopped
buckling in anticipation. The laughter failed to come as different
boys tried to scare him in that way.*

*Darnley was in detention. His parents would be called that
evening, so the gossip went. For a while the boy was the centre
of attention.*

'Darnley is going to be expelled.'

'*Did you dob on him?*'

'*No.*'

'*Platmore saw Darnley punch him.*'

'*Did it hurt?*'

'*Don't know.*'

'*But you fainted.*'

'*Yes.*'

'*What did you say to Darnley?*'

'*Nothing.*'

'*You must have said something.*'

'*I don't remember.*'

'*Amnesia.*'

'*It can happen if you get punched.*'

'*Harper's got amnesia.*'

'*Darnley said he didn't punch you.*'

'*Oh.*'

'*Did he?*'

'*Platmore saw Darnley punch Harper.*'

'*Platmore dobbed on Darnley.*'

'*Platmore's a sixth former, it isn't dobbing when you tell on someone like Darnley.*'

'*Of course it is.*'

'*Harper should be allowed to fight his own battles.*'

The second formers turned their eyes to Harper.

'*Darnley shouldn't have punched Harper. Harper's a weed, and Darnley shouldn't have punched him. That's why it's not dobbing when you tell a teacher.*'

The second formers' attention shifted from the boy as they chased and punched each other in the stomach. He watched them disappear down the corridor.

After a while the boy saw movement at the other end of the corridor and turned quickly towards it. Carmody was standing *there looking at him. The boy felt a stirring in his stomach. Did he love Carmody? Carmody looked back like ice. No, he didn't love Carmody, he was just terrified of displeasing him. He looked down and waited. Shoes passed him. There was silence in the corridor, more shoes passed. The boy imagined the wearers watching their shoes flick out in front of them as they walked with their heads down, but then there were other boys who wouldn't be looking at their shoes, the boys Captain Edmund couldn't touch. He screwed his face up, he wanted to be one of those boys, boys who didn't fear everything. He would give the bullet to Carmody and then he would be better dead. He thought about the speeding car; or on the farm he could use a rifle. But he would have to wait until the holidays.*

'Do you still have it?' Carmody asked.

The boy looked up, puzzled, and nodded. 'Yes'.

Carmody thawed a little. 'Do you have it with you?'

The boy shook his head. He had it but he'd buried it again. The boy felt a tremor around his neck.

'Can you bring it to me?' Carmody asked.

The boy nodded.

'You didn't give it to the policeman?' Carmody asked.

'No,' the boy said frowning.

'Where is it?'

'Near the hockey field steps,' he told his shoes.

'When the bell for dinner goes, wait for everyone to go, then you run down there, and come straight here after dinner.' The boy nodded. 'Who supervises your prep class?'

'Lower,' the boy said. Fifth form boys supervised Second Form prep classes.

'You'll bring it to me?' Carmody confirmed.

The boy looked up, surprised, and nodded vaguely. 'Yes.'

'Did you speak to a policeman, a detective?' Carmody asked.

The boy shook his head.

Carmody smiled. 'I believe in you, Harper. Don't disappoint me.' The boy shook his head. 'You get that for me and you'll never have to hang your head again. I promise you that.'

The boy felt the heat of tears as they ran from his eyes. Carmody reached across and ruffled his hair firmly so the boy's bobbing head scattered tears to each side. The boy smiled to himself and breathed fully. The shaking of his head stopped. He heard Carmody walking away. He looked up to see if anyone saw but no one did.

The bell for dinner sounded, the boy watched the sixth formers leave and pull the common room door closed behind them. A few, in curiosity, looked in the boy's direction. The boy wasn't sure if he was grimacing or grinning in response.

'What are you still doing here?' a fifth former asked as a group of fifth formers passed him. The boy shrugged. 'Idiot. Get going. Run.' The boy took off and laughter echoed in the corridor. He knew if he was quick enough he could get to the end of the building before they entered the quadrangle and there he'd be able to hide in the bushes until it was clear to run down beside the administration building and onto the hockey oval.

The bushes, a hedge of tea trees, pushed at him as if saying, 'You should be lining up for dinner.' Some scratched at his arms, but soon they stopped pushing and scratching and concealed him, protected him in their world of sharp smells and tiny leaves on long, scratching fingers. Voices passed him, then all was silent. He crept forwards, the bushes whispered around his ears. He watched the last line of boys enter the dining room. He ran from the bush to the oval and dropped down by the steps. Some day boys stood near the front gate. He quickly pushed his fingers into the dirt – it was wet this time – and wiggled his fingertips, searching. Then he felt it, still sharp, still snagging. He pushed and closed his hand around it. He didn't need to look, he knew what he had. He thrust it into his pocket and ran to the dining hall, slapping the sand and dirt from his hands.

'Where have you been, Harper?' the sixth former demanded.

'I was at your common room and had to go to the toilet,' he replied.

The sixth former looked back, angry. 'You should be on dinner duty, not going to the toilet. Lock is standing in line for you,' the sixth former said.

The boy ran to the line. Lock, another second former, was towards the front.

'What are you doing?' a fifth former asked.

'Swapping with Lock.'

Lock punched someone behind him and ran laughing from the line. The boy grabbed two plates and beat Lock back to the table.

'Go, Harper,' someone called from his table. The boy ducked and weaved to the line, he'd made up three places. He dodged fake punches and faked punches back, he was told off for mucking around. He was the fastest boy, he thought he might be the fastest boy ever seen, he made up two more places. He was being cheered at his table. He smiled as he ducked in and out, he'd made up two more places. The supervising sixth former sent him to the back of the line, to the cheering and jostling from the rest of the boys. It was a distinction, being sent to the back of the line for being too fast. He was smiling and pushing back. A fifth former from his table came and took him back to the front of the line, then another fifth former did the same

to his second former, until a teacher stood up and supervised the line.

'Slow down,' he snapped at Harper. The boy was pushed backwards and forwards and a couple of boys ruffled his hair. He couldn't remember being so happy.

At the table while they ate their dinner, the sixth former asked why Darnley had hit him.

'I don't remember him hitting me,' the boy said. The boys stopped eating and turned to him.

'You didn't see him hit you?'

'No.'

'But he knocked you out,' a fourth former said.

The boy shook his head. 'I don't remember him hitting me.'

'But you had to go sick bay.'

'Did Four Stars take your clothes off for you?'

The boy replied sharply, 'No way.' Everybody laughed, the boy smiled.

'Platmore said he saw Darnley hit you,' the sixth former said. There was silence.

'Yes,' the boy answered.

'Was Platmore in the corridor before you fainted?'

'No,' the boy said.

The boys turned their attention to the sixth former.

'Did you tell any teachers you don't remember Darnley hitting you?'

'Yes.'

'Who?'

'Mr Abbott.'

The sixth former talked quietly to the fifth former, who left the table. The third formers, the boy's enemies, had said nothing to him the whole meal. Lock pretended to punch him in the stomach, the boy turned and did the same thing to Lock and the sixth former told him off, giving him another week's table duty. This was greeted with a cheer. They had been the first table with all their meals.

After dinner the boy ran to the sixth form common room, one hand in his pocket holding the bullet. A few boys attempted to chase him but he outran them. He pushed his back to the wall, in his spot, panting. He watched boys file through, a few faked a punch to his stomach to which he made exaggerated ducking moves which were greeted with pushing and laughing. Binder came through with his gang.

'Show me how Darnley hit you,' Binder ordered.

'No.'

'You know what you'll get if you don't?'

'I can't, I don't remember, I'd fainted.'

'You fainted, you little girl,' Binder said and turned looking for applause from his mates. He didn't see the first four punches that landed on the back of his head. When he pushed back from the boy, the boy ran at him, kicking and flailing his arms. Binder staggered among his mates who were also ducking. Binder was sitting on the floor with his arms up protecting his face when the boy was plucked from him. His arms and legs still struck out while Double Daws held him three feet from the ground. Yelling and laughter filled the corridor. A group of second formers were cheering and running at the other third formers as if to bash them too. Binder scrambled backwards and was pulled to his feet. A few sixth formers shouted commands. Double Daws threw the boy to the floor where the second formers picked him up and crowded around him, jeering at the third formers.

Carmody arrived. The second formers ran, the boy was dropped on his backside, but quickly scrambled to his feet. The *third formers also tried to run but a sixth former caught Binder by the collar. His legs flew out in front of him, he dropped to the floor, jumped up and was pushed against the wall by Double Daws' massive hand pushing on his chest. Binder had a lump on the back of his head and reddening on his forehead and cheek. The boy ran at him again swinging his arms. Binder cringed and tried to slide away from the pressure Double Daws had on his chest.*

Another sixth former caught the boy mid-flight around the waist and threw him against the opposite wall where he held him. The sixth formers were laughing, some folding double in merriment. The sixth former who held the boy nearly lost grip of him due to his laughter. Double Daws said 'boo' to Binder in a massive voice and Binder ducked. The boy saw this, he saw Binder as he had never seen him before. Binder, the threat and fear of all second formers, squirmed like a pinned insect, tears squirted from his eyes, reddening patches on his face. The boy realised he had done that, he looked at his fists, bunched like steel, he felt his arms as branches that could swing any weight. He pushed against the arm and elbow that pinned him to the wall, it pushed harder and the elbow dug deeper. He tried to look past the head of the boy who held him. When he saw Binder staring at him, the boy's arms and legs began flailing again. A noise was coming from his mouth, he didn't know what it was saying or even if it was saying words, he just felt the noise strain and tear at his throat. Another boy grabbed him and between the two of them they pushed and carried him to the other end of the corridor. He saw them release Binder and threw all his strength and strained every sinew in his throat to grab at him again. Binder was helped from the corridor by a swinging leg and laughter from the sixth formers. When Binder disappeared the boy collapsed to the floor. The sixth formers who had held him dropped back exclaiming at the boy's ferocity as they laughed to each other. Eventually the boy looked up; smiling faces looked down on him.

FIFTY

Day 20
Kilkenny Road
6.30 p.m. Friday, 13th November 1965

The phone rang.

'Don't get it,' Cardilini said.

'Dad?' Paul questioned.

'Let it ring.'

'It might be work.'

'It won't be.'

'*My* work,' Paul said.

'You don't work tonight.'

'Doesn't matter. I'm getting it,' Paul replied shaking his head.

'Okay. But I think I know who it is.'

Paul left the kitchen. Cardilini heard him talking on the phone. He heard Paul replying 'yes' and 'that's right' several times before Paul called for him. They crossed each other in the passageway. Cardilini gave him a quizzical look, and Paul shrugged.

'Hello.'

'Cardilini,' the caller said.

'Leggett, what were you talking to my son about?' Cardilini asked.

'I wanted to know how keen he was for the academy, and to wish him luck.'

'Did you say who you were?'

'Of course. And I asked him if he would accompany you here tonight.'

'What are you playing at, Leggett?'

'I'm trying not to *play* at anything. Why not come and hear what we have to say? Believe me, I want this finished for the sake of the boys, for you and the school,' Leggett answered.

He wanted to tell Leggett to go to hell. 'I'll come, but Paul's not coming.'

'You come with Paul and I'll tell you exactly what you want hear. So will Carmody.'

'Why Paul?'

'I need him to witness your response.'

'What're you up to?' Cardilini asked after a pause.

'Trust me, I'm a judge of the high court after all.'

'Ex-judge,' Cardilini said and took the phone from his ear before turning to Paul who stood in the kitchen doorway. 'He wants you to come.'

'I know, good.'

'It's about the abuse of those boys.'

'I know.'

'It mightn't be pleasant.'

'Christ, Dad, I'm going to be a bloody policeman, aren't I?' Paul answered.

'We'll be there at seven,' Cardilini said and hung up. He swore to himself then turned and said, 'He's a real old fox.'

'Justice Leggett?'

'Yes. I wouldn't believe a word he says.'

FIFTY-ONE

Day 20
St Nicholas College
7.50 p.m. Friday, 13th November 1965

*The boy arrived at the sixth form common room just before the
end of prep, as requested. Carmody and the other sixth formers
were having a meeting. He wondered when he would be getting into trouble, when a teacher would come. The punishment
would start with the cane across his backside. Who the teacher
was would decide how many 'cuts' he would get. He'd listened
ardently to the stories from those who'd had the 'cuts'. Don't put
your hands or arms back, if the cane touches bare skin it will
open it up like a bursting pomegranate, keep your arms forward,
don't tighten your bum, stay as relaxed as you can, a tight bum
is more painful, don't make any sounds unless it's Mills. Mills
is the weakest, he doesn't hit hard and he makes so much noise
grunting you'd think he was the one being hit. If you have to
fight, fight when Mills is on duty after school, the other teachers
know Mills is weak and will step in and belt you if it's near the
change of their shift. The worst is Abbott, he deals it out like it's
the hand of God, he thinks it's good for you so he really puts*

*his heart into it. You can't make any noise for him, if you don't
make noise he says 'good boy' while he belts you and goes easier.
If you make a noise he thinks you're complaining and belts you
harder. Abbott would have belted Darnley. The boy wanted to
be belted by Abbott, and he wouldn't make a noise, not because
Abbott might go easy, but because Darnley wouldn't have made
a noise.*

The bell for prep sounded and the sixth formers left their
common room. Carmody and Mohr stopped in front of him.

'Harper, have you got it?' Carmody asked.

'Yes.'

'Good boy,' Carmody looked relieved.

'Did Binder hit you?' Mohr asked.

'Not tonight.'

'Before?'

'Yes.'

'Why?'

The boy shook his head. Carmody smiled and shared a knowing look with Mohr.

'You're going to go out of bounds, Harper, does that worry
you?' Carmody asked.

'What about the cuts?'

Both boys laughed. 'You want to get the cuts?' Carmody asked.

'For fighting.'

'Maybe later.'

'Show us what you have,' Mohr said.

The boy put his hand in his pocket and closed his hand on
sharpness. He pulled his fingers out and opened his palm.

'Shit,' Mohr said. The two older boys stood staring at what
was in the boy's hand.

'How did you find it?' Carmody asked.

'I trod on it.'

'Are you glad Captain Edmund's gone?' Mohr asked.

'Yes. He wasn't a good teacher,' the boy said.

Mohr laughed at that.

'Will you promise us you'll never try to hurt yourself because Edmund hurt you?' Carmody asked.

The boy tried to understand what Carmody meant.

'You heard about Masters?' Mohr asked.

'Yes,' the boy answered. Masters hung himself from a verandah roof. What sort of rope was keenly debated. Being all country boys the second formers knew about rope. Some rope would cut. Some rope would break. There wasn't a mention of a chair, so other options were discussed. It was decided you would need plenty of time and that there wouldn't be much height for the 'drop'. You needed a good drop.

'Do you know he killed himself?' Mohr asked.

The boy felt guilty. That's what he thought he should do, but he hadn't told anyone. 'Yes.'

'Will you promise you'll never do that?' Carmody asked. The boy looked at the frozen splash of metal in his palm. He couldn't promise that. The three boys stood in silence.

'Edmund was hurting four other boys – that we know of – this year. They all made that promise. The pain that Edmund caused is over, you mustn't hurt yourself because of it, otherwise he's still controlling you,' Carmody said.

The boy looked up sharply and frowned at Carmody.

'Do you want him still controlling you?' Mohr asked.

'No,' the boy answered.

'Then you should promise,' Mohr said.

'I promise,' the boy said to Carmody. Carmody and Mohr nodded and gave each other a quick glance. They were happy, the boy thought.

'Do you know anyone who had a road accident?' Mohr asked.

'No,' the boy replied, shaking his head.

'If you were in a road accident would you punish yourself?'

The boy frowned, confused because he had been planning a road accident to stop the images. 'No', he replied slowly after a pause.

'Same with Edmund. Not your fault. Wrong place, wrong time. Just put it behind you,' Mohr said.

The boy looked back to Carmody. The boy's frown was giving him trouble with his eyes. They kept closing and he had to keep opening them. 'Are you going out of bounds with me?' the boy asked.

This brought more laughter to the sixth formers. Their laughter wasn't as dignified as he imagined it would be, they were more like second formers.

'Yes. We are. We're going to Justice Leggett's house. Have you been there?' Carmody asked.

'No. But I know where it is,' the boy said.

'Good boy. We're expected,' Carmody said.

The boy's mouth dropped at this, fear of humiliation dripped from his eyes.

'Harper,' Carmody snapped. 'I've told you, no one is going to hurt you, I won't let that happen no matter what, no matter what,' he said and laid his hands firmly on the boy's shoulders.

The boy nodded. Carmody gave the boy's hair a ruffle. The boy wasn't sure which way he had to walk when it finished. Carmody and Mohr laughed. He followed them down the corridor and into the night.

The boy watched them walk ahead of him through the dark. He realised that the other boy with Carmody the night he found the bullet must have been Mohr.

They left the school by a gate between the front fence and the limestone wall. The moon hadn't come out, the boys had to feel for the latch.

'Careful, there's a gully,' Carmody said. The boys stepped over a black shadow that snaked by the side of the road, gravel crunched under their shoes. Then they were walking on the bitumen of the road. Through the trees the Leggett house glowed gold.

'We have a question to ask you, Harper,' Carmody's voice floated in the darkness. The boy looked in Carmody's direction but he couldn't make out any features. They walked, angling away from the Leggett house, to avoid the gully at that side of the road.

'It's an important question, you must be honest with us.' Again Carmody's voice without a face.

The boy continued sliding his feet down the gradient of the road. He was rarely in this degree of darkness unless he was on the farm. He felt comfortable in the dark.

'Do you want to catch the person who shot Captain Edmund?' Carmody asked.

'Catch him and send him to jail?' Mohr added.

The boy hadn't thought of that, it was the bullet that killed Captain Edmund. He thought of his father shooting roos.

'No,' the boy said.

'We were very sad when Masters killed himself, we didn't do enough, we knew and didn't do anything, we didn't really under-stand what was happening, but Lockheed told us. Have you heard about Lockheed?' Mohr asked.

'He was expelled last year,' the boy said.

'Do you know why?' Mohr asked.

The boy thought about that. It had to be bad, he'd heard lots of things, but they were second former things that even third formers thought stupid.

'No.'

'He tried to tell on Edmund,' Mohr said.

The boy felt a chill in his stomach. He couldn't even conceive what words would be used to tell on Edmund. The tears he felt now were for Lockheed, he was glad it was dark and they were walking slowly.

Mohr continued, 'He told the school and the school did nothing about it, so he was able to continue hurting other boys. We're glad Edmund is dead, we think the person who shot him did a good thing.'

'What do you think?' Carmody asked after a while.

The boy shrugged then said he didn't know.

They were opposite the front verandah of Leggett's house. The surrounding air was damp and had a muddy smell. The front gate creaked when the boy pushed it closed behind them, he jumped at some leaves that brushed his face. The verandah steps were in shadow and he stumbled on them.

'You okay?'

'Yes.' But he could feel a scratch from the timber boards on his knee.

Carmody knocked on the door and called. A woman replied to them. The boy saw a figure walking towards them, she was in light, smiling, then the light was behind her. She opened the door and said Carmody and Mohr's names then let them walk past her down the corridor.

'And who are you, sir?' she asked.

'Harper,' the boy said. He saw Carmody looking back at him. He'd forgotten to ask Carmody why he was there.

'You call me Mrs Leggett,' Jean said, smiling. The boy felt her hand on his shoulder as he walked beside her. 'Would you like some ginger beer, Harper?'

'Yes please, Mrs Leggett.'

'You follow me then.' She walked ahead and pointed to a room on the right for the older boys. The boy glanced in the room as he passed. He could see an old man standing, all spindly, and on the couch was a big man with a very sad face sitting next to an older boy.

FIFTY-TWO

Day 20
Legget's
8.10 p.m. Friday, 13th November 1965

Cardilini parked his car where he had that afternoon. Now blackness surrounded him. Light coming from Leggett's house made it seem even darker.

'Is the school up there?' Paul asked, pointing beyond the house.

'Yes.'

Cardilini and Paul walked to the house.

Jean Leggett let them in and showed them to the lounge where Leggett was waiting.

They had just sat when Cardilini heard the voice of Carmody call from the front door. Jean Leggett jumped from her seat. She called a greeting as she left the lounge. Leggett and Paul chatted like old friends while Cardilini sat moodily. Carmody and another boy entered and stood just inside the doorway. Jean walked past, followed by a very slight, younger boy who looked into the room. Cardilini made eye contact with him. The boy looked lost.

'Who's that?' Cardilini asked before acknowledging Carmody and the other boy.

'That's Harper,' Carmody said and gave a nod to Mohr, realising that it hadn't been Harper who Cardilini had spoken to.

'Why's he here?' Cardilini asked.

'He has something you want, I think,' Leggett said and received a nod from Carmody and Mohr.

Cardilini screwed up his face with questioning impatience.

Carmody turned to Cardilini and said tightly, 'Captain Edmund had summoned him for some buggery. He must have gone in after Edmund was shot. He trod on the bullet and picked it up.'

'Are you saying, that boy . . . he looks like a ten-year-old.' Cardilini said incredulous.

Paul, white faced, looked at his father.

Leggett said, 'This is Mohr. Mohr, this is Detective Cardilini and his son, Paul.'

Cardilini and Carmody eyed each other. Paul and Mohr shook hands.

Before Cardilini saw Harper, he felt on sure footing. He was going to hear them out and work towards them dropping the false accusations against him. He wanted Paul to hear that, but now he felt he'd walked into a closing trap.

'Paul isn't aware of all the details and there is no need for him to know . . . so Paul . . .' Cardilini nodded for Paul to go.

'I think he should hear what we're about to discuss,' Leggett said.

'I'd like to, Dad. I know what you said that man did, but . . .' he nodded to the door, '. . . I don't understand.'

'None of us do, Paul. That's why he was able to do what he did for so long. And all of us here are guilty of aiding him,' Leggett said.

'Dad?'

Leggett interrupted with, 'A child's word against an adult's word without any supporting evidence, there isn't a lot that could be done. Isn't that right, Cardilini?'

Cardilini nodded.

'I know the shot came from the school,' Leggett said as he crossed and closed the door to the passage.

Cardilini mockingly asked, 'Do you know who's responsible?'

'I said you'd hear what you wanted to hear. Didn't you believe me?'

Cardilini slowly shook his head.

Carmody and Mohr looked at each other, concerned.

Leggett walked back to the chair, sat and ran his gaze from one to the other before repeating, 'I know the shot came from the school. I know, because I made that shot.' The four sat staring at him in stunned surprise.

'It's a confession. I wanted you all here to witness it.'

The air seemed to be sucked from the room. Cardilini and the three young men looked dumbfounded at Leggett.

Leggett started, 'On two previous occasions as the presiding judge, I have declared the death penalty . . . and I would come home and pray for the executioner, a man, to my shame, I could never look in the eye . . .'

'I don't believe you,' Cardilini interrupted.

'Which part?'

'That you pulled the trigger to kill Edmund.'

'Well, as we both know, what you believe is irrelevant when all the evidence points to me. I had motive. I know how it was done. I know where the weapon I used is and how I obtained it. And how I disposed of it. And now, it's possible to prove that the actual bullet I placed in the chamber is the one young Harper has arrived with. You will find, Detective Cardilini, when it comes to providing *bullet proof* evidence, I know exactly what I'm doing.'

'But your age – you're frail, no one would believe you could climb the wall, let alone make that shot.'

'What wall? There's a gate you know.'

'What did you do with the murder weapon?'

Leggett smiled. 'The rifle? I returned it to the armoury.'

'Which rifle did you use?'

'I couldn't tell. But then there's no need for me to tell, you'll have a bullet to find the matching rifle.'

'How did you get into the armoury?'

'Idle tongues unintentionally told me where the keys were kept,' Leggett glanced at Carmody and Mohr.

'But you still couldn't make the shot,' Cardilini insisted.

'I think when put to the test I'll be accurate enough, but some practice wouldn't go astray.'

Cardilini sat back in his chair. Carmody and Mohr had sat speechless throughout.

'But, sir . . .' Carmody started.

Leggett held up his hand. 'Don't say anything, please, Carmody.'

'I still don't believe you,' Cardilini said.

Leggett looked steadily at Cardilini. 'Knowing what that man was doing any given night of the week. I had to act.'

'But you didn't know. You and the board didn't believe it to be true,' Cardilini stated.

Leggett looked sheepishly at Carmody and Mohr. 'That's true. Carmody convinced me otherwise.'

Mohr shot a puzzled look at Carmody, who gave a brief shrug.

'Right. Without further ado, let's get that brave little man in here.' Leggett walked to the door then turned. 'He's got the bullet that will take me to trial. My lawyers will call on him and the other abused to tell their sordid stories in court to reduce my sentence. I obviously haven't many years left so they'll go as hard as they can. Difficult to say how the public display will harm them or their families.'

Carmody stood aghast. 'You can't. We promised, no one would know.'

'I'm afraid I'll have to,' Leggett replied, opening the door.

'Dad,' Paul said in alarm.

'You're bluffing,' Cardilini stated.

'No,' Leggett replied and looked each of them squarely in the eye. 'At the moment the boys Carmody has spoken to feel some relief, feel they have another chance, feel that a type of justice has been done. Is that right Carmody?'

A confused Carmody turned to Cardilini. 'We've spoken to six boys including Harper and Lockheed. Yes, that's still the case.'

Leggett smiled at Cardilini. 'Here's your chance; you've got a confession, everything's in your hands now, Cardilini.' Leggett paused, then added. 'Carmody and Mohr will deal with the Mossop matter as we agreed.'

'Yes, sir,' Carmody and Mohr replied.

'Tell Detective Cardilini,' Leggett instructed.

Carmody turned to Cardilini, 'Mossop will withdraw his allegation.' He turned to Paul, 'Sorry, we just wanted to protect the other boys. We were never going to let your father lose his job.'

Leggett motioned to Paul and asked, 'Can we have a chat?' Paul stood and looked to his father, who nodded. 'I'll send Harper in.' He left and Paul followed.

'The old bastard. You know he's lying,' Cardilini said and stood to pace the room.

'Would he really go ahead with it?' Mohr asked.

'Do you believe Leggett did it?' Cardilini asked, turning on the boys.

Carmody and Mohr looked at each other. 'No,' Carmody said.

'I don't either.'

Mohr asked. 'But is he correct? Would the boys have to testify about Edmund?'

'Yep. That could happen,' Cardilini replied.

'I know he wouldn't do it,' Carmody said. Cardilini and Mohr looked doubtfully at him.

'Tell me about Harper,' Cardilini instructed.

Carmody and Mohr sat and stared back gloomily.

'Carmody?' Cardilini prompted sitting.

Carmody took a deep breath then started to speak slowly, outlining in detail what Mrs Lockheed had already explained to Cardilini. He described how Edmund would put the boys' penises in his mouth while they stood holding their rifle, then threaten to reveal to their parents what they allowed him to do. The boys at this stage, he said, were completely under Edmund's power, fearful of the pain it would cause their families. Cardilini listened to the sound of Carmody's steady words, sinking further back in his chair as if trying to distance himself from them. At several points Mohr swore and vigorously wiped tears from his eyes. Camody told him about the boy having the bullet and of the fight he'd had with a third form boy. When he finished and looked imploringly at Cardilini.

'What are you going to do, sir?' Mohr asked earnestly, just as the boy stood in the doorway.

FIFTY-THREE

Day 20
Legget's
8.15 p.m. Friday, 13th November 1965

After he'd walked past the room Carmody and Mohr had entered, the boy followed Mrs Leggett into the kitchen. He sat at the kitchen table.

She had curly hair and tiny lines that all grouped up when she smiled and the boy couldn't help smiling back. She placed a glass in front of him, it held a cloudy liquid.

'Leggett makes it. Do you make ginger beer?' she asked. He didn't, but he had wanted to, other second formers did and they always talked about it and swapped it between themselves. He breathed a smile, he might be able to do that now.

'I'm going to,' the boy said and Mrs Leggett smiled again.

'Leggett did when he was at school, when he was your age.' The boy wondered if she meant the spindly man. 'Drink up.'

The boy put the glass to his lips, the bubbles on the surface tickled his top lip. He sipped, and it was cold and sharp and sweet.

'How does it compare?' Mrs Leggett asked him.

He wasn't sure, he'd never tasted any of the other boys' brews, he'd been a 'creep'. Even if they didn't know, he knew, and a 'creep' couldn't do things that other boys did. A frown travelled across his face. He couldn't be a creep anymore because . . .

'Does it taste funny?' Mrs Leggett said and poured herself a small glass to taste. The boy shook his head, smiling.

'You looked worried,' she said.

The boy nodded and took another sip; it was less sharp and sweeter this time, and he took another sip and looked around the kitchen. The sideboard was huge, big plates were stacked on it like at his mother's. He could see out into the backyard through the window over the sink, there were gold light globes on a long cord hanging like bunches of grapes. He shifted to the side to see more out the window.

'Do you want to have a look outside?' The boy nodded. 'Bring your glass.'

The boy slid from the chair holding his glass out in front of him like a precious jewel. Mrs Leggett walked before him to the passageway and held the flyscreen door open. He walked through onto the verandah. The lights started on one end of the verandah, went out into the yard to a post, made a line across the back of the lawn to another post and then back to the other side of the verandah. There had to be twenty or more; he would count them if he got a chance. They were lights like the sideshows use but he'd never seen them in a backyard before. He wondered if they had shows out here.

After the Royal Show had come to his country town, he and his brother put one of his father's tow ropes between two pear trees in their backyard. They tried to walk it like they saw in the show, but close to the lawn. One time they had put chairs up and their mother and father watched them. Only trouble was, neither he nor his brother were able to stay on, even though they *had nearly walked to the middle another time. Not ready to leave home yet, his father had said. He hadn't left home and didn't want to. That was years ago. There were thirty-one lights and some big trees where you could put a tightrope.*

'Have a look at this,' Mrs Leggett said, and the boy followed her to another shelter that had a Tilley lamp glowing. Moths were circling around the lamp, some were lying still at the its base, others were flipping and flapping. They had got too close, they would still be there in the morning, dead. A shiver went through him.

'Are you cold?' the woman asked.

The boy shook his head and he went into the shelter and looked up at the branches all packed and tied. He wondered if the spindly man did it, he knew his father could make this if he told him. He would tell him about the lights, too. He imagined what their backyard would be like with gold lights hanging like grapes.

'Take a seat,' the lady said to him and he pushed himself onto a chair. 'Would you like some more ginger beer?' He nodded, yes. She smiled at him and walked back to the house.

He felt very homesick. He hadn't wanted to go home last holiday, he was frightened his mother and father would see in his eyes what had happened to him. Terrible images jumped at him, he shook his head.

One time, at the pool, he'd punched a town boy who had said the boy's parents 'do it'. The town boy punched him back and then there were six of them fighting. They were wet and slippery from the pool and slipping on the lawn. Wally, the pool man, was yelling at them and the girls were laughing. They stopped fighting, and a town boy said he had cigarettes. So they all went behind the toilet block where buffalo grass grew up against the cyclone fence and made a hiding place. The town boy had three *cigarettes, he'd pinched them from his mum. The boy coughed and coughed. They all laughed except the boy. Then a town boy coughed and coughed and the boy laughed at him. They all began pushing each other against the dunny wall, saying the boys they pushed smelt like dunny paper until some older girls yelled at them to get away from there and stop behaving like babies. They left and the town boy said it was because the girls were wetting their pants and couldn't go if we could hear them. For some reason this was very funny and they rolled about on the lawn, laughing.*

The lady poured some more ginger beer into his glass. She was smiling. She asked where he came from, he said Wongan Hills and saw the road leading to the farm house, it made him happy. She asked if he had brothers and sisters? He nodded. If he liked school? He lied that he did. She asked what he was going to do when he grew up. He said he would work on the farm. She said he might like to do something different. He'd never thought of that.

He watched the spindly man and the young man stand on the verandah. At one point the spindly man had his hand on the young man's shoulder while he spoke, like the boy's father did when he wanted to tell the boy something the boy didn't want to hear.

'Jean,' The spindly man called. The spindly man and the young one were now turned, looking at the boy, smiling.

'You go in and see Carmody and Mohr if you like,' Mrs Leggett said to him. 'Here, I'll hold your glass.'

The boy reluctantly surrendered his glass and started towards the verandah. He didn't think Carmody had brought him here to see the lights. Maybe his brother would like to see them. As he walked past the spindly man, he felt the bones of the man's fingers ruffle his hair. He looked up at the spindly man who gave

*a nod and another ruffle with his nobbles. The boy walked to the
kitchen but nobody was there. He walked to the door Carmody
and Mohr had entered and stood. The big, sad man was standing
up and signalled him in. The boy looked behind him, perhaps,
Mrs Leggett was there and that's why the sad man was standing
but she wasn't.*

'This is Mr Cardilini, Harper,' Carmody explained.

'Harper,' the big man said.

'How do you do, Mr Cardilini?'

*Carmody and Mohr were sitting in chairs on the boy's left.
Carmody signalled him to a chair between them. The boy went
over and sat. He thought Carmody would want to go back to
school and he wouldn't get to finish his ginger beer.*

*'Mr Cardilini has a few questions . . .' Carmody hadn't
finished but the boy turned his head sharply in Carmody's
direction. 'It's all right. Mr Cardilini is like me and Mohr, he
wants what's best for you, he would be very angry, like me and
Mohr, if anyone . . .'*

*'That's okay, Carmody,' the big man said. 'You have noth-
ing to fear from me, Harper.' The boy looked at the big man's
eyes. They were like two lost streetlights way out in nowhere, each
didn't know the other existed. He trusted the big man.*

'Carmody said you found something, can you show me?'

*The boy looked to Carmody who nodded back at him so he
reached into his pocket and held it lightly before extending his
arm and opening his hand. The big man bent over and looked at
it, he was seeing the spreading eucalyptus flower side.*

*'Do you mind?' he asked and gestured to the bullet. The boy
indicated he didn't and the big man's big fingers picked it up
and turned it over. He measured it against his little fingernail,
turned it over a few more times, then shook his head. He eventually sighed like a bull sighs when it's sick of waiting for the boy*

to open the gate. He placed the bullet back in the boy's hand, the boy closed his fingers on it and looked to Carmody. Carmody nodded, he had done well.

'Carmody said only he and Mohr know you have it.' The boy looked to Carmody and shrugged. 'Have you told anyone else?' the big man asked.

The boy shook his head. The big man sat back in his chair and asked, 'Do you want to keep it?'

Again the boy shook his head.

'Would you give it to me?' The boy looked at Carmody who said it was up to him. The boy opened his palm and held it out for the big man, who now didn't seem to want it. He just looked at it and the boy's arm was getting sore, but no one said anything. Finally the big man sighed like a bull again and reached for it but paused, holding his fingers over the boy's palm without touching the bullet. The boy turned to Carmody and then Mohr, both were looking intently at the big man's fingers. The boy shifted his other hand to hold up his outstretched arm at the elbow. He wondered if they had poured his ginger beer out because he was taking so long. The big man sat back and said.

'I hear you had a fight this afternoon?'

'Yes,' the boy said looking at his outstretched arm.

'Why do you think I want the bullet?'

The boy shook his head.

'What if I told you I was a policeman?'

The boy pulled his hand back and put it on his lap in alarm, he imagined a policeman was asking for his father's bullet.

The big man stood up and walked to the doorway then turned around and faced Carmody. Carmody and Mohr stood up. The boy stood up. The big man was shaking his head again. Finally, he stepped forward with an outstretched hand. Carmody and then Mohr stepped forward and shook it. The big man held his *hand out to the boy. The boy dropped the frozen splash in his pocket and reached his hand out and watched it disappear as the big man shook it and let it go so the boy saw it again. He felt the big man's big flat hand on his head and heard, 'You're a good man, Harper.'*

The boy looked up into the lost streetlights, small lines gathered at the side of them, the lines knew each other, maybe they can help the eyes. The boy thought they would.

The big man walked to the passageway and called, 'Paul.'

Mr Leggett and Mrs Leggett shook hands with the big man and then the young man. The big man said to the boy. 'This young fella is Harper. Harper, this is my son, Paul.' Harper smiled and shook hands with Paul. Paul smiled back. Paul was a big open doorway shining out into the night like Carmody.

'You listen to Carmody. You promise me that,' the big man said. The big man had eyes now that could stop a train.

'Yes, sir.'

The boy had to say yes, but he wanted to.

FIFTY-FOUR

Day 20
To Kilkenny Road
10.10 p.m. Friday, 13th November 1965

The car lights picked out the edges of the over-hanging branches. It appeared as if Cardilini and Paul were driving through a tunnel of foliage. Neither had spoken.

'I don't quite understand what happened, Dad.'

'I'm not sure I do, either.'

'You didn't arrest Leggett.'

'I didn't believe him for an instant.'

'But he confessed.'

The pool of light before them weaved effortlessly with the curves of the road. They could have been alone on the planet, or on another planet, following a pool of moving light.

'Did you believe him?' Cardilini asked.

'Have we missed the main road turn off?' Paul asked.

'Don't think so. Did you believe him?' Cardilini repeated.

'No. And I don't think he cared if he was believed or not,' Paul eventually said.

'I think you're right.'

'So, you're not going to find Edmund's killer?'

Cardilini felt they had been released from the real world, left to meander through a tunnel of trees until the end of time, or until Betty joined them.

'Did you take the bullet Harper found?' Paul asked hesitantly.

'No.'

Insects, struck by the car lights, glittered.

'Do you think I've done the wrong thing?' Cardilini asked Paul, and Betty.

'Why didn't you take it?'

'Leggett was correct in everything he said about what would happen.'

'You can't know that. Things have surely changed since he was practising law.'

'You'd like to think so but people's attitudes haven't changed. No, I believe the conclusions the school reached would just be reinforced.'

'That's terrible.'

'Yesterday I went to the farm where the shot is thought to have come from.'

'And?'

'One hundred per cent possible that the shot came from there,' Cardilini said and received a nod of approval from Betty.

'The bullet would have proved it, you should've taken it.'

'If it was the actual bullet? We don't know that, and never really will. Maybe Harper just wanted to boost his popularity. He's a cadet, maybe he picked it up from a rifle range after target shooting.' He felt like he was lying to Paul even though what he was saying was plausible.

Paul considered this as they watched the tunnel disappear over their heads.

'We haven't done this in a while. Maybe we should do a trip away,' Cardilini said.

'Aunty Roslyn might like that.'

'Yes, she would. Let's do it around Christmas.'

'We're having a staff party at the drive-in on the twenty-third.'

'After Christmas then?'

'They're going to give me more work.'

'As long as it doesn't interfere with the academy.'

'So, I'm definitely going to the academy?' Paul asked.

'I think Leggett is as mad as a cut snake but I believe him. So, yes,' Cardilini said with some relief.

'What about the boy, Mossop?'

'I believe that's all over now, too.'

The car rose and fell over the depressions in the road's surface, and then the road veered to the right, away from the river. Up ahead on the main road into the city they could see street-lights.

'Why did you say you didn't believe Leggett did it?' Paul asked.

The car bounced up onto the main road. No other traffic was in sight and they travelled from streetlight to streetlight, the glow of each filling the interior of the car for a flash. Cardilini became conscious of Paul watching him and he worked his lips wanting to say something so as to appear more human than the granite rock he felt himself to be. As a passing street lamp cast a yellow hue across his face he turned to Paul with a question in his eyes.

'What is it, Dad?'

'Do you think, as a policeman, I am obliged to follow the law regardless of the consequences?'

'I think I would, or how would you know when to stop?'

Cardilini concentrated on the road. He didn't have an answer.

FIFTY-FIVE

Mid-morning a few days later.

The boy stood in the alcove opposite Darnley outside the principal's offices.

'*You got any smokes?*' *Darnley asked with a smile.*

'*No.*'

'*I hear you took the skin off Binder?*'

The boy smiled and shrugged his shoulders.

'*Mention my name to Binder, I don't think he'll mess with you.*'

The boy nodded his gratitude.

'*Talkative little prick, aren't you?*'

The boy shrugged.

'*Okay, in you come,*' *the head boy, Burnside, said. The boy and Darnley followed behind. Miss Reynolds rolled her eyes and shook her head at Darnley who smiled in return.*

Braun was standing behind his chair. Carmody and the sixth form boy, Platmore, who'd said Darnley hit the boy, were standing to his right. Mr Abbott was standing to the left. Burnside joined Carmody and Platmore and pointed to a spot in front of Braun's desk. The two younger boys stepped up to it and stood.

Darnley had a defiant look on his face, the boy looked to the sixth formers, then to Principal Braun.

'You're skating on thin ice, Darnley,' Braun said.

'Yes, sir.'

'You know I was about to start proceedings to have you expelled?'

'Yes, sir.'

'But it appears we have been too hasty this time.'

Darnley gave a slight shrug.

Braun continued, 'Mr Abbott said he has already caned you for striking Harper.'

Darnley nodded.

'Well, you can count that as one towards the things we haven't caught you for,' Braun said dismissively.

Darnley shrugged.

'So, Harper, did Darnley hit you?' Braun asked.

'He hadn't hit me before it all went black.'

'That's not much good,' Braun announced.

'Platmore, did you see Darnley hit Harper?'

'I saw him beside Harper who was on the floor. I naturally assumed Darnley hit him.'

'Quite so. You see the reputation you have created for yourself, Darnley?' Braun asked.

'Yes, sir,' Darnley hid a smile.

'Think yourself lucky. If Carmody hadn't put it all together you'd be getting your marching orders,' Braun said.

'Yes, sir. Thank you, sir.'

'You're a bad influence, Darnley. I will expel you if I get half an opportunity. I think you're a thug. I think no good will come of you,' Braun said.

'Yes, sir. Thank you, sir,' Darnley replied.

'Ridiculous. Out you go, both of you,' Braun commanded.

Darnley and the boy walked from the principal's office.

When they were outside, Darnley asked. 'Hey, how come you didn't get into trouble for belting Binder?'

The boy shrugged.

'Ridiculous,' Darnley said, imitating Braun and walked off.

The boy smiled. He'd started a brew of ginger beer with Brain-Box yesterday and knew where the ginger beer gang would be hanging out. He ran from the principal's alcove.

'Stop running, boy!' was yelled. He stopped then did his fast walking; he knew he was really fast at walking.

FIFTY-SIX

It was 11 p.m. several days after he and Paul had driven back from Leggett's house. Cardilini had heard nothing from the department. He drove his car into the airport car park. He knew he was taking a risk but wanted to speak to Williamson before he left for Sydney and Vietnam.

An easterly had blown all day, the hot air swept along the bitumen whipping at his trouser legs and fanning the heat onto his face. His cigarette glowed brightly with each gust of wind. Taxi drivers and passengers moved with lassitude as if the heat had a weight of its own.

Cardilini pushed through the doors and was immediately hit by cool air, he marvelled at it. Inside, the people moved normally. Passengers and well-wishers were surrounded by a sense of the surreal. Interstate travel by air was an adventure. He remembered the flight to Sydney he, Betty and Paul had taken – the anticipation, the wonder, the anxiety. The hostesses appeared as Hollywood actresses, beautifully made up, gracious and unreasonably generous. They said they would go again the following year. He couldn't remember why they hadn't.

He looked for the black swans as he walked to the stairs up to the bar. They were huddled to the left of their enclosure and he wondered if they also had the benefits of the air conditioning.

Most drinkers sat in an orderly and composed manner. The soldiers and their visitors were rowdily gathered towards the glass overlooking the runways. He saw Williamson in the thick of the gathering, smiling, yelling, and backslapping. He walked in his direction.

Williamson caught sight of Cardilini and shook his head in disbelief. Cardilini gestured with his head towards the bar, where he went and ordered a lemon lime and bitters.

Williamson clapped his pint glass onto the counter beside Cardilini and asked, 'You come to wish me well?'

'Yep. I do wish you well and was hoping you would tell me what happened the night Edmund was shot.'

Williamson shook his head from side to side again in disbelief. 'We had this conversation.'

'You didn't tell me.'

'I told you I was on a train,' Williamson said.

Cardilini caught and held Williamson's eyes as he said, 'I think Doney and Sheppard picked you up in South Australia, drove through to Perth. All in plenty of time for you to make the shot that killed Edmund on the night of the twenty-fifth of October.'

Williamson sighed and asked, 'What're you drinking?'

'Bitters.'

'Let me buy you a real drink.'

'No, you'd be doing me a favour not to offer. I have a drinking problem,' Cardilini said.

'Don't we all? Can't get enough of the stuff.'

'I'm right, aren't I? That's how you did it. I'm sure I could find a witness to say they didn't see you after Adelaide.'

'I'm sure you could find plenty. I was asleep in my cabin with the door locked,' Williamson said.

Cardilini shook his head.

'You've got a one-track mind, Cardilini. However, I'm happy to be your target.' Williamson smiled as he looked over Cardilini's shoulder. 'Hey, lads, what the hell are you doing here?' Williamson walked away from Cardilini.

Cardilini turned and saw Carmody and Burnside being pushed and punched playfully by Williamson. Cardilini finished his drink and started to the door.

'Cardilini,' Williamson flung his arm over his shoulder. 'You protect your family, you protect your mates, you protect those who can't protect themselves. Isn't that what you did in the war?'

Cardilini looked back past Williamson to Carmody and Burnside. 'Don't visit your war on those boys.'

'I won't need to, the dates for conscription are about to be announced, either one or both could be in Vietnam in twelve months. What about your boy?'

'He missed out.'

Williamson nodded and walked back to Carmody and Burnside.

In the car Cardilini confirmed to himself the Royal Corp Australian Infantry badge he'd seen on Doney's sideboard was identical to the one on Williamson's hat.

FIFTY-SEVEN

Midday Cardilini was at home when he received a phone call from Robinson.

'Braun has been in touch with the deputy commissioner and it seems Mossop has had a change of heart,' Robinson said.

'Fancy that.'

'Yes, he'd got some wild notion in his head to save the school. Obviously, seriously misguided and very harmful.'

'What's going to happen to him?' Cardilini asked.

'Yet to be decided. Thought I might have a chat to you about it.'

'He's come clean. No harm done.'

'The deputy commissioner is severely embarrassed,' Robinson said.

'Poor chap.'

'He should have stuck by you. He's quite apologetic.'

'Okay.'

'You could kick up a fuss.'

'Am I off suspension? Is Paul's spot still happening?' Cardilini asked.

'Paul's spot was never in jeopardy and you're off suspension.'

'Good to hear. Is that it?' Cardilini sighed deeply.

'Deputy Commissioner Warren wants some feedback on Mossop. We could get the parents and the school in for a formal apology,' Robinson said.

'What about the other boys?'

'Led astray by Mossop.'

'Let it rest, that's my request,' Cardilini said, suddenly feeling tired.

'Warren will appreciate that.'

'I'm not doing it for him.'

'I didn't think for a moment you were.'

'Anything else?' Cardilini asked.

'You tell me. Is this going to blow up in our faces at some point in the future?'

'How?'

'When you were in the toilet, did you put pressure on him to change his story?'

'No,' Cardilini said emphatically.

'You sure?' Robinson asked.

'Yes. But what will it matter if he changes his story again?'

'Exactly. Stay clear of anything to do with St Nicholas.'

'Shall do.'

'So you've accepted the coroner's verdict?'

Cardilini looked down the passageway to the front yard. Paul was standing idly watering the lawn. He had his finger on the end of the hose causing the water to fan, just as Betty used to do, just as he'd be able to do for the rest of the summer without a care in the world and with a future to look forward to.

'Yes.'

'Don't take it hard. You behaved like the real thing, Cardilini, not many coppers would do that.'

Cardilini laughed out loud. Paul turned around with a quizzical look, Cardilini nodded and smiled to him.

'I'm serious, keep doing that and you can have Bishop's job. Don't say anything but he's talking about retirement.'

Cardilini laughed again.

'What's so funny?'

'Nothing. Is the school going to address any of the complaints about Edmund?'

'Oh, yeah. Braun has been instructed to offer Lockheed reinstatement and give a proper hearing to any boys who feel unjustly treated. But the school still won't accept any accusations against Edmund, naturally enough, without Edmund being able to defend them. We're all learning from this, Cardilini, so don't get on your high horse about it.'

'If you ever see me on a high horse, give me a kick up the backside.'

'With pleasure. Drop by the station today to sign this off so the deputy commissioner can sleep peacefully.'

Cardilini hung up and walked to the front flyscreen door. Paul had moved to the right side of the lawn. Cardilini pushed through the flyscreen door and let it clatter shut behind him.

'How's it going?' Cardilini asked.

'Nearly finished.'

'There's a sprinkler, you know.'

'I know. You laughed, can't remember the last time you laughed,' Paul said turning to his father.

'Yep, me either, you working tonight?'

'I told you I was.'

'That's right, and I'm cooking bangers and mash.'

'And some greens, Dad.'

'And some greens. I'm back at work tomorrow.'

'Fantastic. Finally, Dad, we're both on track. Mum would be proud.'

Cardilini nodded and picked up the two cups from the boundary wall.

Approaching the East Perth police station Cardilini saw Salt standing on the steps watching him.

'Salt,' Cardilini said as he went up the steps.

'Sir, I know everything that happened and... .'

'That doesn't surprise me.'

'. . . everyone, Leggett, Carmody, everyone owes you and have told me so.'

Cardilini stopped walking and, looking doubtful, turned to Salt. He started to speak then changed his mind, sighed and shook his head before walking on. 'The police work could have been better on that one, Salt,' he said.

'If you say, sir. And I should have told you from the beginning I was reporting to Superintendent Robinson.'

'Didn't Robinson order you not to?'

'Yes, sir.'

'You couldn't go against that,' Cardilini said continuing walking.

'But I feel I let you down. Sir, I don't want to be the copper others don't trust . . .' Salt said earnestly, Cardilini turned to him, Salt continued, '. . . but I'm not sure how to go about it now, maybe, I should just . . .'

'Going to university next year, aren't you?' Cardilini interrupting asked.

'Yes, if . . .'

'Make a good job of it. And come by to have a chat occasionally. That's an order,' Cardilini said firmly.

'Yes, sir. Thank you, sir.'

Cardilini nodded and walked through the entrance.

FIFTY-EIGHT

'Son.'

'Dad.'

'Tell me?'

Mr and Mrs Harper stood in the lounge of their farmhouse in Wongan Hills. They held the phone receiver between them. It was eight o'clock of the same evening Cardilini received his call from Robinson. Sundays, the boarders were allowed to ring home.

'He was a third former,' their elder son said.

'A third former!' The father looked to his wife.

'What will happen?' the mother asked her son.

'The sixth formers broke it up. Carmody and Mohr were there. They didn't even tell him off.'

'But they told Abbott?' the father asked.

'No.'

'They didn't tell the boarding master,' Mr Harper said to his wife.

'What does that mean?' she asked.

'It means he won't get into trouble,' her husband replied.

'Was he hurt?' she asked into the mouthpiece.

'No. Binder didn't land a punch.'

'Who's Binder?' she asked looking to her husband.

'The third former, Binder's a real ratbag,' the son answered.

'The boy he fought is a real ratbag,' the husband repeated to his wife.

'I don't like him fighting, he's too little,' the mother said. A tear caught in her eyelash and she pushed at it impatiently. Another took its place.

'It's all right, isn't it, son? He had to fight the boy. Isn't that right, son?'

'Everyone's happy he did and Binder won't do anything back, he got a big scare,' their son said.

'A big scare,' the father repeated.

'And how is he now?' the mother asked.

'He's good. He got into trouble for going too fast in the dining room. He was on table duty,' the son said.

'He was getting the meals for his table. That's good. That's really good,' the father said to his wife.

'But how is he?'

'He's much better, like the little tiger moth again, Dad.'

'The "little tiger moth",' his father repeated. 'So he's back with his friends?'

'Yes. He's brewing ginger beer.'

'That's good.' the father told his son. He put the phone aside with his other hand over the mouthpiece. 'It's good, darling, it's what we hoped.'

She nodded, pushed her husband's hand from the mouthpiece and said to her son, 'I don't want him fighting.'

'I'll tell him. But you are proud of him for sticking up for himself?' the boy asked.

'As proud as punch,' the father said.

'As proud as punch, we'll always be proud of you both, but I don't want either of you fighting,' the mother said.

'There go the beeps,' the son said.

'Ring next weekend and have young tiger with you.'

'Yes, Dad. Carmody is looking out for him now.'

'I don't like Carmody,' the mother said.

'Don't you get involved with Carmody, son.'

'As if, Dad. Bye.'

'Give our love to Tiger. Thank you son. You be a good boy.'

'Yes, Mum.'

The father hung up the receiver. His wife stepped away quickly, her back to him as she wiped her eyes.

'It can only get better, darling. It can only get better.'

The wife turned accusingly. 'I don't want them fighting. I don't care. I don't want them to think that's how they solve their problems.'

'They're not like that, really. But he stood up for himself against a bigger boy. That's really important, that means the fog has lifted on our little tiger.'

'I love you and my heart breaks for the Sheppards and Doneys and their boys. But the world can't be like that, tiger's not like that, he shouldn't have to fight, you shouldn't have had to . . . and the boys must never find out . . .'

'Shh . . . shh . . . shh. That's all over now. It's all over.'

Midnight and Cardilini was asleep. Paul had returned from the drive-in and he, too, slept. The boy slept, his small frame even smaller under the sheet. He would wake on occasion with a start, sweating, believing he was late, and then he would sink back into his mattress thankful he would never be required again. Sheppard sat on the back verandah, his eyes blurred by tears. Masters sat alone in his study, his features distorted, his hands aimlessly shifting as he stared at a photo of himself, his wife and their son. Mrs Doney sat in her lounge in the darkness looking out to the night sky, a pain in her chest as if a heavy rock had been implanted there. Mrs Lockheed, tea towel and dish in hand, stood at her son's bedroom door and listened to his whispering breath. Mr and Mrs Harper slept side by side. Mrs Harper would wake alarmed, thinking her youngest son was staring at her with unseeing eyes, then she would breathe deeply and whisper, 'Thank you,' to her sleeping husband.

ACKNOWLEDGEMENTS

Without my wife Rosalba's encouragement, editing, and endless support I wouldn't have had the opportunity to put in the hours required to write a novel. I am very thankful to Helen Budge, a fellow writer and poet, who worked with me on the initial drafts and spoke so positively of them, and to the readers Debbie Hedley, Margaret Pass, Tim Pass, Nadia Verrucci, and Imogen Woodward, whose encouraging comments gave me the belief in the novel to submit it to publishers.

I will be forever grateful to Angela Meyer of Echo Publishing for reading the unsolicited pages from an unknown writer and providing such positive feedback.

Want to read
NEW BOOKS
before anyone else?

Like getting
FREE BOOKS?

Enjoy sharing your
OPINIONS?

Discover

READERS FIRST

Read. Love. Share.

Sign up today to win your first free book:
readersfirst.co.uk